Praise for *O*

'A fast-paced and frenzied thr[...] guessing right up until the end . . . [...] great job at making seemingly random events come together in a way that does not feel last-minute or hastily put together . . . In short, Nikki Griffin is one spectacular heroine . . . and Lelchuk's *One Got Away* is one seriously entertaining read' *USA Today*

'There will be kidnappings, blackmail and twists . . . Lelchuk delights in showing just how shady everyone turns out to be' *New York Times Book Review*

'Rollicking . . . This breakneck-paced thriller . . . is unapologetically bloody fun' *Publishers Weekly*

'Bookseller/private detective Nikki Griffin lands in hot water when she takes on a wealthy new client . . . The nearly fearless and deeply empathetic Nikki is ridiculously easy to root for, and the pace is fast and furious all the way to a deeply satisfying finale. A smashing sequel. More please' *Kirkus Reviews*

'*One Got Away* is a delightfully complicated mystery, one that constantly keeps readers – much like Nikki herself – on their toes' *Bookreporter.com*

'Fans of the first book or of hard-boiled women detectives in general will relish this heroine's latest outing, especially given that Lelchuk's writing is more nuanced and atmospheric than that found in hard-boiled mysteries of old. Those who followed . . . TV's *Dexter* are another audience . . . A fine choice for mystery collections' *Booklist*

Also by S. A. Lelchuk
Save Me from Dangerous Men

S.A. Lelchuk

ONE GOT AWAY

SIMON &
SCHUSTER

London · New York · Sydney · Toronto · New Delhi

First published in Great Britain by Simon & Schuster UK Ltd, 2021
This paperback edition published in 2022.

Copyright © S.A. Lelchuk, 2021

The right of S.A. Lelchuk to be identified as author
of this work has been asserted in accordance with the
Copyright, Designs and Patents Act, 1988.

1 3 5 7 9 10 8 6 4 2

Simon & Schuster UK Ltd
1st Floor
222 Gray's Inn Road
London WC1X 8HB

Simon & Schuster Australia, Sydney
Simon & Schuster India, New Delhi

www.simonandschuster.co.uk
www.simonandschuster.com.au
www.simonandschuster.co.in

A CIP catalogue record for this book is available from the British Library

Paperback ISBN: 978-1-4711-8321-8
eBook ISBN: 978-1-4711-8320-1
Audio ISBN: 978-1-3985-0052-5

Printed and bound in Great Britain by CPI Group (UK) Ltd, Croydon, CR0 4YY

MIX
Paper from
responsible sources
FSC® C171272

This one's for my brother, Daniel—friend, mentor, and cellist extraordinaire

A good man can be stupid and still be good. But a bad man must have brains.

—*Maxim Gorky*

PROLOGUE

The U-Haul truck was parked alone at the back corner of the big lot.

A pair of California Highway Patrol officers regarded the confident, blocky lettering and energetic orange paint. A vehicle suggestive of all kinds of new starts and exciting futures, good things to come, uncharted horizons, reset lives, the limitless possibilities of a move from one place to a better place.

There was no sign of any driver. The engine was off, the cab locked and empty, a brass padlock fastening the rear roll-up door. Early morning, sky the color of dishwater, cars already trickling into the Walmart parking lot, employees readying the huge store for the coming swarm, customers eager for the best deals, the lowest prices, ready to get started on their weekend shopping.

The two men watching the truck exchanged a questioning glance.

Something was off. Something was wrong.

The younger CHP guy had a buzz cut and round blue eyes that gave him an earnest Boy Scout look. He got a pair of bolt cutters from their cruiser while his partner, twenty years older and forty pounds heavier, walked a careful circle around the truck.

By that point they had both smelled death inside.

The Boy Scout worked the bolt cutters and the cheap padlock fell away. He slid the door up. The carrion smell rushed out, putrid and overwhelming.

They climbed into the open truck, flashlights lancing into the depths, each with one hand pressed over his nose and mouth. The two beams of light probed, glancing off walls, bodies, still limbs, scattered possessions.

Six bodies. All women. All of them young.

Without hope, they checked the bodies for vital signs. A terrible odor, vomit and perspiration and decay, mixed with a cloying sweetness that was explained by a shattered perfume bottle near one outstretched hand. Dying sailors, frantic, try to drink the very ocean that is killing them. In the desperation of the final hours, gripped by heat stroke, the body's temperature rising lethally, any liquid would have been irresistible. Abruptly, the Boy Scout jumped down and retched onto the pavement. His partner followed, speaking into a radio, mouth grim, set, eyes tired. The younger one stood with his back to the U-Haul, clenching and unclenching his hands.

As the day brightened, the two men were joined by a small army of cars and trucks and vans bearing a galaxy of official seals. Yellow plastic tape was unspooled into a perimeter. A two-man team began taking pictures as another group of techs emerged from a panel van. A pair of ambulances sat idle. There would be no hospitals. Early morning shoppers gaped at the intense hive of activity.

The bodies were zipped into plastic bags. Six of them, lined up on the asphalt, sad white cocoons split lengthwise by a zipper's seam. The sun rose higher. Barely nine o'clock and almost eighty degrees, the whole of California seized by a ferocious September heat streak.

Along with the bodies were six small suitcases. Clothes, shoes, toothbrushes and hairbrushes, magazines and cosmetics. A one-way trip: somewhere to somewhere else. No identification. No cell phones.

Several news crews arrived in white vans bristling with satellites and sprouting telescoping poles twined with thick cables. Cameramen and production teams swarmed out, unpacked equipment, ran wires, opened laptops. Reporters did hasty makeup, gulping coffee before assuming somber expressions and placing themselves to ensure background shots of yellow tape and stretchers.

The sun rose higher. As soon as the reporters were off camera, they wiped away sweat and gulped bottled water in the shade.

By noon the activity had diminished. The bodies had been taken away by the medical examiner and a big municipal tow truck came for the U-Haul. The news vans were off in search of new material. A last, local sheriff bundled up the yellow crime scene tape, taking his time in the midday heat. Now the shoppers didn't give the scene a second look. There was nothing to see. No candles or wreaths or crosses. No plaques or pictures. Nothing marking the fact that the world contained six fewer lives.

A passerby would never have known that anything at all had taken place.

MONDAY

1

When about to hand over the keys to something important, seeing doubt is never reassuring.

I raised my helmet visor. "You don't park motorcycles, do you?"

The young valet eyed my red Aprilia like it might rear back and kick him. "I can try," he offered. "I have a bicycle. Two wheels. That's kind of the same."

"I think I'll pass."

"There's street parking down the block," he suggested. In answer I pulled up next to the row of polished brass luggage carts, the motorcycle's big engine echoing under the confines of the covered entrance. I cut the engine, used my bootheel to flip the kickstand down, swung a leg over, and pulled my helmet off.

"I'm not sure if you're allowed to leave it there," the valet said, watching me with mild interest.

I headed for the revolving door. "Call me an optimist."

It was my first time at the Grand Peninsula in Nob Hill. A storied San Francisco hotel, white stone, colonnaded like a palace, partially rebuilt after catching fire in the 1906 quake. Presidents and movie stars had stayed here; weighty matters discussed by important people in tomb-silent suites. My motorcycle boots clicked through a marble lobby of soft peaches and grays, chandeliers spilling golden light. Whoever handled decorations had a healthy flower budget. Vases of careful arrangements spurted like bright fountains. The clientele seemed to be largely what someone had once described to me as WORMs: white, old, rich men. If there were other five-foot-eight women in leather bomber jackets and motorcycle boots, I wasn't seeing them.

A bony manager type in a funeral-black suit approached. "Can I help you find something?"

"I could use an elevator. Got one?"

He didn't smile. "Are you a guest?"

"In the next life, I hope."

"In that case, who are you here to see?" he prodded.

"I thought that was my concern," I said.

"If you're sticking to the lobby. But the hotel's concern—if you're going up."

I smoothed hair that had been mussed by my helmet. "Martin Johannessen asked me to meet him here. He should be expecting me."

The manager took a deferential step back, as though a scowling, ten-foot-tall Johannessen might pop up in front of him. "My apologies."

Apparently, the person I was about to meet could open doors. About five seconds later, I was in a very nice elevator, headed up to the penthouse level. The gilded door and ornamental bars made me feel like a bird in the world's most expensive cage.

"Nikki Griffin. Thank you for coming on short notice."

Martin Johannessen was in his mid-fifties, clean-shaven and fastidious, dressed in a navy suit. I didn't know much about men's fashion, but he didn't seem to shop in the clearance bins. I followed him into a spacious living area scattered with plush couches and polished furniture. Floor-to-ceiling windows showed off the San Francisco Bay. It was a mirror-clear day and I could see Alcatraz Island and, beyond that, the Golden Gate.

"Coffee? Tea?" he offered.

"Coffee, please."

Martin pressed a button on the wall. "They'll bring some. Come, sit."

We sat. I crossed my legs and got comfortable. "What's the problem?" I asked him.

He frowned. "How do you know there's a problem?"

"People don't hire me for wedding planning."

"True enough, I suppose." He seemed to be thinking about where to start. A distracted man who, even in the midst of his distraction, meant to be careful about what any speech might cost him. "There is, as you surmise, a problem," he finally admitted. "Rather a substantial one, in fact. It has to do with Mother."

He fell silent as a waiter rang and entered, pushing a linen-covered service cart. The waiter poured coffee for us out of a silver urn, then set the urn down and left. Johannessen fiddled with the creamer as he continued. "Mother is quite elderly, at eighty-one, but still insists on staying in the same Russian Hill duplex she's occupied for the past twenty-five years, since my father passed. She can be quite fixed in her ways. It was only after she backed into a gas station attendant last year that we got her to finally agree to a chauffeur."

"Better late than never," I observed, since he seemed to expect me to say something.

"That's quintessential Mother," he went on. "As her son, I feel I can use the word 'stubborn' with both affection and accuracy. And Mother insists on maintaining a rather high degree of control over her affairs."

"I like her already."

Johannessen gave me a thin smile. "Many people like Mother. She is undeniably vivacious. She is also undeniably wealthy." He offered a meaningful look. "Some people like that, too."

I didn't say anything. He wasn't done.

"After my father passed, she never remarried, but she continued to see a series of . . . well, *gentleman friends*, for lack of a better term. Dalliances, affairs of the heart, whatever you want to call it. Which is fine, of course. She should be free to see whomever she likes." He added sugar to his coffee, sipped, then added more.

I had already lapped him. I helped myself to another cup. Seeing he had fallen quiet, I prompted, "Except."

As I had hoped, the word seemed to wind the music box back up. "Recently, this past year, she began seeing a younger man," Martin resumed. "A much younger man. An Englishman, an Oxford-educated psychologist in town for a lecture series. Mother became quite . . . enamored of this fellow. Not that she shared a great deal of this with us, God forbid. She plays her cards close, Mother does."

"Us?"

He looked surprised at the question. "Myself and my three siblings. William and Ron—my two older brothers—and Susan, my younger sister."

I took advantage of the moment to ask, "Are you close with them?"

Martin stirred his coffee. "Maybe *close* is the wrong word. My sister maintains a certain remove from our family. As for my brother William, he was in a rather awful accident almost a month ago. It left him in a less than communicative state."

"And Ron?"

"Ron?" He seemed to be thinking how to phrase something. "At no time in my life would I have called us especially close." Family was not a topic that Martin seemed to relish discussing.

"So, Dr. Oxford, on the lecture circuit," I said.

Martin nodded. "Except it turns out that the fellow is neither a doctor nor an Oxford man."

As the saying went, a stitch in time saved nine. "How much?"

He stared. "How much?"

"How much has he taken? Isn't that why I'm here?"

"You certainly have a way of cutting to the chase, Nikki." He sipped his coffee, different emotions playing over his narrow face. "Mother, as I said, demands a high degree of autonomy over her affairs, but I've managed to get my hands on a few of her financial statements. As best we can tell, over the last year she has transferred at least one point five million dollars to Dr. Geoffrey Tyler Coombs. Needless to say, the man does his banking offshore."

"One and a half million. No wonder you want to get it back."

"Yes, indeed," Martin agreed. "A lot of money. And that's not counting several hundred thousand dollars' worth of luxury watches, hotel stays, and some extraordinarily sizable department store bills. And a Porsche."

I tried to think of something cheerful to say. "Boxster?"

"No such luck. A 911." His face drooped. "Fully loaded."

I poured myself a third cup of coffee. "How bad a dent did that leave?"

"Well, the money is obviously significant, but truth be told, Mother will be fine."

"Just to be clear, he's not actually *stealing* this?"

Martin shook his head. "I wish he was, believe me. Things would be a lot less complicated. But no, Mother has been duped into giving all this freely enough, from a legal standpoint."

"Then what's bugging you, the morality?"

He didn't answer directly. "May I ask, Nikki, what you know about our family?"

I shrugged. "Same as most people, probably. You oversee a pharmaceutical fortune over a century old, you give money to every worthy cause between here and Pluto, and you pop up on the *Forbes* lists as fast as they can print them."

"True enough." He nodded in assent. "But there's a reason you don't read much about our family in the papers. Despite our considerable holdings and fairly prominent place in San Francisco society, we have always prized discretion. No messy tabloid fodder, no melodramatic suicides or scandals. There's the well-known saying that all press is good press. Members of our family are taught from a young age to believe the reverse. With the exception of our charitable works and foundation, we try to avoid publicity."

There didn't seem to be anything for me to say, so I kept quiet.

Johannessen poured more coffee for himself. "My mother is elderly. She hasn't been in perfect health. I loathe the idea of her being taken advantage of—conned, to call a spade a spade."

"Does she feel that way?" I wondered.

"Does anyone who's being conned?" he returned. "By the time they understand the truth, it's too late. In the meantime, for all I know, maybe it feels like the most exciting thing in the world. As her son, I want to intervene before things reach a point of real harm. The man is a thief and deserves consequences, but I am also motivated by a more practical concern. If word gets out that our family is an easy target, every swindler in the world will show up with a bouquet of roses and sweet words for Mother."

"Why not go to the police?"

"He's done nothing illegal. Not yet, anyway."

"So what do you want me to do?" There were a few reasons people liked to avoid police. My prospective client had named only one of them.

As if confirming my thought, Martin steepled his hands and stared at his intertwined fingers. "I overheard a conversation between them. Very recently, this was, last week. I have reason to believe that my mother is being blackmailed by this man."

"What makes you think that?" I asked.

"They were talking quite frankly about money—but a much larger amount, in the millions. I heard him tell her that she needed to decide soon— something to that effect. Or *the genie would be out of the bottle*—that was the phrase he used."

"Do you know what it's about? The blackmail?"

He shook his head. "I have no idea. That's what I need you to learn."

"Did you try asking your mother? That seems easiest."

Martin's face soured. "My mother can be quite private. My whole life, she has always made it clear that *she* will come to us if seeking our advice. I tried to talk to her and got nowhere."

"What do you want me to do after I find out? *If* I can find out."

Martin had clearly thought about this. "Then we offer Coombs a choice. Either lay off and buy a one-way ticket out of town, or face immediate arrest." He turned the cup in his hands. "Can I count on you, Nikki? Will you help?"

"I can try." I poured myself more coffee. I'd gone through three cups already, and had every intention of continuing right through to the end of the pot or the end of the meeting, whichever came first. I drank my coffee black. Cream and sugar were distractions. The Grand Peninsula did a good job with their coffee. Fancy hotels didn't always guarantee good coffee. Kind of like family money didn't always guarantee good sense.

"You'll be working on an expense account, naturally," added Martin. "Spare no cost whatsoever."

I nodded, hoping he wouldn't add that I should leave *no stone unturned*. It was astounding how many new clients felt the need to drop that in.

He pulled a wallet-size photograph from his pocket. "Take this. You can keep it."

I put my cup down and took the picture, seeing a broad-shouldered, good-looking man in a tailored pearl-gray suit, sitting at an outdoor café. Gold flashed from a cuff link, and his eyes were piercing blue. I looked closely. There was something about his face. Even here, through the small photograph. As though his eyes seemed to promise interesting things.

"Anything else you need?" Martin wondered.

"What are your siblings' addresses? And your mother's?" I asked.

His face tightened. "Why?"

"To go talk to them." I had been going to add *of course* but decided that wasn't polite.

He seemed suspicious. "My siblings, sure, I suppose, if you can be discreet, but why is Mother necessary? As I told you, she hasn't been in perfect health. She's frail, and she's not quite as keen as she once was. Besides which, she values her privacy."

"I understand, but this whole thing is about her. I have to speak to her."

Martin thought this over. He nodded reluctantly. "Very well. She's in Scottsdale until next week, I believe—we have property there. When she's back, I'll set up a meeting."

He gave me a card with his number and wrote me a check for a retainer, signing his name with a meticulous swirl.

I took the check and started toward the door. "I'll be in touch soon."

"Oh, and Nikki?"

I looked back. "Yes?"

"This is very important, this job. I'm counting on you to leave no stone unturned."

"Right." I left the suite and stepped back into the elevator.

As the polished door slid shut, I was thinking again about a cage door closing.

2

I rode down Telegraph Avenue and parked in my usual spot just outside the BRIMSTONE MAGPIE bookstore. Telegraph was the usual jumble, dirty curbs and creeping buses, students in blue and yellow Cal gear, street vendors selling handmade jewelry, scruffy panhandlers lounging in clouds of marijuana smoke with dogs and guitars.

The bookstore was busy. We were holding a monthly book drive and a steady stream of people and books had been coming in all day. Books piled everywhere, overflowing the counters, rising in crooked stacks from the floor like stalagmites across a cave. Bartleby, the bookstore's normally social resident cat, had retreated behind the front counter. I could just make out a gray paw. A potted plant craned toward the daylight coming in from the door. It was a croton, green leaves threaded with sunset veins. I'd bought the plant after being assured it would flourish without demanding a lot of care. Many things in my life required a lot of attention. I didn't want my houseplants to be one of them.

"Quite a crowd," I said to Jess. I had hired Jess as a manager soon after opening the store, almost a decade ago. She had become not just a business partner but a close friend.

She glanced up from sorting through a box of books, cobalt glasses and raven bangs framing her fair skin. "Hey, Nikki."

I joined her in the sorting, smelling dry pages and cardboard. "How are the wedding plans?"

"Have I told you I hate weddings?"

I laughed. "Don't tell Linda that."

"We spent over two hours on the phone this week discussing flower arrangements. Two hours. Flowers."

"Remind me not to get married."

It was her turn to laugh. "Don't tell Ethan that. It would break his heart."

I slid a pile of books out of a box. "I think I have enough stress in my life without flower arrangements."

"You know we've been together five years and our parents haven't met?"

Still stacking, I gave her a look. "That bad?"

She nodded. "My parents own a holistic medicine shop in Oregon. They go off on spiritual trips to Joshua Tree every Christmas, where I strongly suspect they take psychedelics. Her parents live in Newport Beach in an eight-bedroom house, and every few years they ask her if she's absolutely, completely sure that her lesbianism isn't a phase."

"I say lock 'em all in a room together and see who comes out."

Jess didn't look amused. "Forget *Lord of the Flies*. I'm praying we make it through the rehearsal dinner."

I unpacked another stack of books. The bookstore had begun with unintentional good timing. A lump sum of inheritance money; a building purchased just before the East Bay became unaffordable; a tenant breaking a lease in the midst of the Great Recession. And me owning too many books. Everything else—sales, shelves, more books, eventually employees and insurance and distribution and all the million details involved in running a bookstore—had happened in sporadic succession. To my continued surprise, the bookstore even turned a profit. Despite Silicon Valley's best efforts, Berkeley remained a city that loved to read.

A freckled blond girl of ten or eleven came over. "Excuse me, do you work here?"

I smiled, still sorting. "I do. Are you looking for a job?"

"I can't," she answered with the special gravitas of small children. "I have to go to school. Do you have *A Wrinkle in Time*?"

"Sure," I said, standing. "Let me show you." Spotting a paperback in the stack I was sorting, I handed it to her. "Have you read this one?"

She took the paperback. "*A Wizard of Earthsea*?"

"Ursula Le Guin. I loved her when I was your age. It's yours. If you like it, you can give it to a friend after you finish." My favorite part about used books was the idea of their unpredictable motion. Maybe ten, twenty years in a basement, forgotten, then suddenly halfway around the world, passed, hand to hand.

A middle-aged man in khakis joined us. "Julie, are you bothering the lady?"

"Not at all," I said, noticing how his daughter held the paperback in both hands. At her age, I had held books like that. Marvelous objects, full of life, things that could shatter or leap away if not held tight. The age when there was nothing more compelling than a story on a page. When staying up with a flashlight under the bedcovers felt more thrilling than any emotion daylight might bring.

Fifth grade. My life in fifth grade had been normal. I had been normal.

Then two men had knocked at my family's door.

My life had stopped being normal.

I worked into the early afternoon and then walked north on Telegraph in the direction of campus. I stopped at Café Strada, a coffee shop always crowded with Cal students, and waited in line to buy two iced coffees. I put cream and sugar in one, crossed Bancroft, and walked over to Wheeler Hall, a stately white building housing the English Department. Afternoon classes were getting out and the campus was full of students.

I waited, the twin coffees dripping chilly condensation, until I saw the person I was looking for walk out of Wheeler in animated conversation with two undergrads. As they finished, I sneaked up behind him, pressing one of the coffee cups against the back of his neck. "Been looking for you."

He spun around. "Jesus, that's cold!"

My boyfriend, Ethan, wore a fraying sports coat over a chambray shirt, a leather messenger bag slung across his body. I patted down a stray curl of brown hair and handed him the coffee with cream and sugar. "Looked like an exciting conversation."

Ice cubes rattled as he sucked coffee through the straw. "Can you believe they hadn't read *A Dance to the Music of Time*? These poor kids. I don't know what they do in high school. Analyze 'Little Bo Peep'?"

"I think that's a nursery rhyme."

"Whatever. The point is—"

I laughed as we started walking. "Twelve books, what, three thousand pages? Such slackers."

"What've you been up to?" Ethan asked.

"Bookstore, plus another thing."

"I think you hit on the title of your memoir."

"Know any ghostwriters?"

It was his turn to laugh. "I'll write up an ad. *Candidates should be able to deal with mulish stubbornness, constant obfuscation, and CIA-level secrecy.*"

"Perfect," I agreed. "Just add, *Candidate should also be prepared to deal with an incredibly charming, witty, and beautiful*—OWW!" I rubbed my cheek where an ice cube had just bounced off it.

"Sorry, I don't know anyone who fits that description," Ethan said, readying another ice cube.

I laughed, ducked, and threw one back at him. "You're welcome for the coffee."

We passed under the green oxidized copper of Sather Gate to Sproul Plaza. Tables were lined up on either side, student groups advocating for a kaleidoscope of issues. The system the two of us had developed was rough and unwritten, but it seemed to work. Me sharing small pieces of what I did. Up to a point. Certain things I couldn't share. I didn't want my boyfriend traumatized. I also didn't want him subpoenaed on a witness stand.

"How was class?" I asked. After getting his Ph.D. in English from Berkeley the year before, Ethan had been hired by Cal as an assistant professor on tenure track.

"I think I'm getting the hang of this whole teaching thing." His pride was evident.

"Lucky students," I said, meaning it. Ethan was one of the very few people I had ever met who loved books as much as I did. "You have to be anywhere?" I asked. "There's a new Thai place on Shattuck I've been wanting to try."

He made an elaborate show of checking his watch. "I've always wanted to be the couple that finishes dinner by five-thirty. Maybe afterwards we could do something really crazy. Shuffleboard, or even Boggle?"

"Whatever. I have to be up early to go into the city."

"What for?"

"There's someone I have to see."

TUESDAY

3

I woke up wanting to do two things: to learn more about the man I had been hired to follow, and about the client who had hired me to follow him. Martin Johannessen had told me where Coombs was residing. I didn't mind work being easy once in a while. He was at the InterContinental on Howard Street, a blue glass rectangle that speared the sky just south of Union Square. I took BART from North Berkeley to Powell Street and walked from there. Finding any guest was easy enough with a name and a face. Coombs wasn't a celebrity or some visiting head of state; he wouldn't be rushed into the parking garage in a tinted SUV and ushered up in some back elevator. He was just a guy staying in a room. And everyone left their room sooner or later.

The InterContinental had a stack of newspapers in the lobby. Even better, free coffee. No one seemed to mind when I helped myself to a cup and a copy of the *Chronicle*. Sufficiently armed, I settled in to wait.

I made it through three cups of coffee and most of the newspaper. The lead story was ghoulish; police had found a padlocked U-Haul full of dead women in a Walmart parking lot south of Monterey. Heatstroke. No suspects, no leads, no motives. I read the long piece, feeling anger burn its way through my stomach. How could people do things like that? And yet they did, every day. I had learned that in sixth grade. I finished the article and moved on. A record heat wave, San Francisco's homeless crisis, a new ferry route planned. I drank coffee and flipped pages.

It was easy to tell when Coombs appeared. The lobby lit up.

I kept my face buried in the paper, every sense screaming that the man I was watching wasn't the sort to ignore details. I glimpsed a confident walk, a crisp checked suit, cuffed pants, dress shoes that clicked against the floor. I saw him throw a cheerful wave to the front desk clerks and get a row of smiles in return. He passed a bellhop, slipped the kid a whispered joke and a folded bill, nodded to a manager with a pleasant word that drew an appreciative chuckle. A popular guest. Affable, witty, courteous, charming. And affluent.

The kind of guest every hotel dreamed of having.

Coombs's first stop of the morning was the shoeshine stand. He sat on the high seat with his own newspaper in front of him, his feet resting on the little pedals. The shoeshine guy rolled up Coombs's cuffs and went to work on a beautiful pair of brown leather brogues that gleamed like a pricey bourbon, even before the shine began. When it was over, Coombs stood and handed the guy a bill that made him nod in vigorous thanks. He crossed the lobby to the restaurant, newspaper under his arm, full of purpose and energy and goodwill. Everything had the feel of well-established routine.

I watched a hostess seat him at a choice corner table. A handsome and confident man with the look of someone happy with his place in life. I watched him eat a bowl of fruit, and eggs over easy with toast. He dined slowly, reading his newspaper with apparent interest, twice accepting more coffee from an attentive waitress. A man who had all the time in the world, but none of its cares.

I watched him say something to the waitress, watched her face break into a laugh. Not a polite waiting-to-be-tipped laugh, but a real one. His good humor seemed infectious. He finished his coffee, signed for his bill, rose. I saw the waitress's admiring eyes on him as he walked toward the front doors.

A bellhop sprang to open them.

Graceful as a magician, Coombs slipped another bill into another hand.

He stepped outside.

He was gone.

My meeting with William Johannessen was neither long nor fruitful. A muscular nurse with a big body and round face led me into a Potrero Hill apartment that made me think of words like *cavernous* and *cadaverous* all at once. The windows were curtained with heavy drapes that allowed in almost no light. Our feet were soundless on sponge-like carpet. Glancing back, I could see our footsteps disappearing from the carpet, like snow melting in reverse.

William sat in a wheelchair in the parlor. A television showed scrolling stock prices, a talking head shouting soundlessly on mute. William didn't seem to be watching much of anything. If I hadn't known he was in his fifties, I might have guessed him to be ten years older. I was looking down at a face that might have been classically handsome at one point in the past. Now, in a red cashmere sweater and wide-wale corduroys, his skin was blotchy and he was too thin. His eyes seemed empty of interest, and of most other things as well.

"He hit his head in the accident," the nurse whispered. "The poor guy used to be a real lion, had the energy of a guy half his age. Now it's a good day if he can eat his oatmeal."

I perched on a neighboring ottoman and tried to make eye contact. "Hi, William. My name's Nikki."

He gave no indication that he'd heard or understood. His head tilted slightly to the side, but whether that had anything to do with my words was a mere guess.

I tried again. "Can I ask you a couple of questions, William?"

When William finally answered, he did so with his head bent toward his lap like something defective. "Questions," he repeated. His voice was hoarse and low, a lawnmower engine being primed after spending a winter in a garden shed.

"Do you remember Dr. Coombs? You met him, right?"

William's head stayed bent at the same odd angle, as though the bones in his neck had softened. "Questions," he said again. "Questions."

I looked up at the nurse. "Is this normal?"

"Define normal." The nurse shrugged. "Normal enough, I suppose."

"How long has he been like this?"

The nurse thought. "The accident was, let's see, about three weeks ago."

"You've been caring for him since then?"

The nurse nodded. "Since the day he left the hospital."

"Just you?"

"We work as a team. Three of us, eight-hour shifts. Twenty-four-seven care." The nurse grinned for the first time, allowing himself to step out of his somber caretaker's role for just a moment. "If you got money, you can get most other things, too."

"Except a working brain," I said. "What happened, exactly? With the accident?"

The nurse's smile was gone, as if he'd been chastised. "A hit-and-run, right outside. From what they told me, the poor guy was crossing the street for coffee and a croissant, same as every morning."

"Did they catch the driver?"

The nurse shook his head. "Never did. They say they're still looking, but in this city, who knows?"

I was mildly surprised. "No cameras?"

"None pointing the right way."

I nodded at William, lolling in the wheelchair, a splotchy island rising out of a pristine white sea. "What were the injuries, exactly?"

"Banged up, cuts and bruises, cracked a rib—that's the less important part. He also suffered a traumatic brain injury. Bleeding and swelling of the brain. The doctors say he could be like this in ten years, or he could be back to his old self next week."

"Who are his doctors?"

"UCSF Neurology. The best in the city."

The injury explained the darkened apartment—a heightened sensitivity to light was not uncommon with brain injuries. I tried one more time, kneeling in front of the wheelchair. "William. Can you hear me?"

This time, his neck raised a few inches. He looked at me, or through me, his expression vague as pudding. "Questions, pensions, mentions, tensions," he mumbled, and then his head lowered again.

I looked up at the nurse. "What do you think that means?"

"I think it means it's time for his nap."

The nurse walked me to the door, our footsteps tracking and fading behind us like a wake.

Outside, I walked up and down the block. A leafy, pleasant, residential street. Mostly tall, fancy doorman buildings that surely had cameras pointing street-ward. Up maybe fifty feet I could see a small bakery at the end of the block. The coffee and croissants. Not much else. A dry cleaner and, down at the other end, a little grocer. Basic needs. Opposite the bakery was a construction site, torn-up earth and temporary fencing, creating a camera-free pocket in the street. Abreast of the bakery, I crossed as I imagined William would have crossed. Familiar, routine, maybe a cursory glance in each direction.

I pictured a car ripping down the quiet street, too fast, distracted, the driver maybe texting or late for work, looking up too late. And just like that—life different forever.

I knew that feeling.

William wouldn't be giving me much.

I decided to talk to his sister next.

4

Susan Johannessen's gallery was in Hayes Valley, on Grove Street, a neighborhood that was the heart of the city for music and performing arts. The gallery took up the bottom half of a two-story building, a condo or apartment above it. It was in between a sleek wine bar and a Ritual coffee shop marked by the distinctive white star against a red background. I went inside. The displayed work seemed mostly contemporary painting with a bit of sculpture thrown in. I tried to make sense of a vivid, three-dimensional orange spiral popping out against a six-by-eight-foot sea of brilliant turquoise. The work was priced at about my annual income. A model-thin guy in black, skintight jeans and wavy bleached hair smiled automatically, sized me up as unlikely to be a serious buyer, and went back to his laptop.

The only other person in the gallery was a woman sitting at a desk in the back. She was clicking away on a laptop, too, and hadn't looked up. I recognized her at once. Despite their professed distaste for publicity, photographs of the Johannessen family were easy enough to find online.

"Susan?"

She looked over for the first time, then stood. Susan Johannessen was a slight woman with the same sharp cheekbones and narrow, anxious face as her brothers. Gold Cartier bangles jingled on a thin wrist as she took in my scuffed motorcycle boots.

"Who are you?" In spite of the question's directness there was something diffident in her manner.

"My name is Nikki. I was hired by your brother Martin. Do you have a few minutes?"

At the mention of her brother she gave me a closer look. Her brown eyes weren't unfriendly, but they contained no warmth. "*Hired . . .*" she repeated. "Such a specific word, and yet so vague. I'm guessing you're not his new personal assistant?"

It was a good guess. I told her as much.

"Then what do you do for him?"

"You deal with art. I deal with people."

Her voice still gave nothing away. "And does someone need dealing with?"

"That's what I was hoping to talk to you about."

She frowned and shook her head. "Right now isn't good at all. It's a very busy time for me; we have a major show coming up next month." She named an artist I had never heard of. "A wonderful British painter, if you're unfamiliar. I've been practically living here, trying to prepare."

"Just five minutes?"

She dusted invisible dirt from a corner of a frame. "Nikki, did my brother happen to mention anything to you about *my* relationship to my family?"

"I understand that you don't call each other up asking what you had for breakfast."

"That's one way to put it." She smiled in spite of herself.

"What's another?"

Susan regarded a blue metal sculpture of a huge bird, rising almost to my height. The beak was ferocious and its talons were wrapped around what I realized was a prostrate man, frozen in his wiggling. A placard identified the piece as *EARLY BIRD*. "Do you know, Nikki, much about the metaphor of an albatross?"

In answer I quoted Coleridge: "'Instead of the cross, the Albatross across my neck was hung.'"

Susan nodded. "My personal albatross has always been my family—my surname, my siblings, the expectations placed on us since birth. Laugh if you will—the bratty whining of a trust-fund kid—but I mean that as honestly as anything you'll ever hear from me."

I didn't say anything.

"Long ago," she continued, "I determined that the only realistic way for me to lead a life of my own was to distance myself from them. And so that's what I did."

"You didn't seem to get all that far," I felt compelled to point out. "Your mother lives pretty much right up the street. Your brothers, too. And you're across the Bay in Tiburon."

If being contradicted annoyed her, she did a good job of hiding it. "Distance can be many things besides literal feet and inches. It's true that I live in Marin and work in this city. But I mean that I make my own money. I have a career, my own life, my own friends. I do my best to remain out of the fray, you might say."

"I just visited William. He didn't seem to be in much of a fray. That was a hit-and-run, right?"

Her face grew somber. "Poor William. He was the golden boy, you know, growing up. That was so terrible, what happened to him."

"They never caught the person?"

"Not yet, anyway. The police are searching for whoever it was." She thought of something. "That's why you're here—my brother hired you to help them?" Her brown eyes showed irritation, but maybe a bit of amusement, too. "You have a way of getting your five minutes without it being given. Are you always like that?"

"I saw there's a coffee shop next door," I answered.

"Your point being?"

"Let me buy you a cup. Espresso, if you want. That way you can drink it fast."

Once she made the decision to step outside, Susan seemed to relax. It was a nice day and we took our coffee to go, strolling along Hayes Street in the direction of Alamo Square. Back in the '80s no sane person would have walked Hayes Street by herself, day or night. It had been an unforgiving neighborhood, people bolting in and out for the symphony or opera. Now Hayes Valley was one of the trendiest in San Francisco, full of upscale clothing boutiques and tempting brasseries. Where San Francisco would stop was anyone's guess. They were even developing the badlands of Hunter's Point. Soon there wouldn't be anywhere to go but up.

"So, William," I prompted Susan. "The golden boy?"

She nodded assent. "When we were kids he was always the most charming, the handsomest, the one who could get away with anything. Star tennis

player, good grades . . ." She smiled, remembering. "I mean, he was a choirboy. Literally—he was in a choir. A tenor. Not a bad one, either."

"Better than your brother Ron?"

She laughed. "Ron was the literal opposite of a choirboy. In *every* way."

"What do you mean?"

Susan smoothed a strand of hair and considered. "Ron was a little
devil. He was handsome and clever, like William, and that doubtless helped
him to extricate himself out of most situations, as a boy. It caught up to him
eventually—I think he was nearly suspended from Princeton—but he managed to make it through unscathed."

"Suspended for what?" I asked.

Her face clouded. "I don't really know. Not exactly. I overheard our father
talking about it—I was still in high school."

"You don't sound that enamored with your brother."

Her face shifted and I felt I could almost glimpse the nervous girl she
must have been, growing up, forever a middle sister, timorous in the shadows of her elder brothers. "Ron could be quite cruel to me when we were
children," she said matter-of-factly. "He's not the nicest fellow, even now. If
you need me to tell you that, you're not much of a detective."

"And how about your relationship with William?"

Her voice softened. "William was different. He could be very
judgmental—I was his younger sister, I was desperate for his approval—but
he was never *mean*. He protected me from Ron when we were children—he
was the only one Ron would back down from."

"Is William married?" I asked.

"He was. He married young—right out of college."

"Was? What happened?"

Susan sipped her coffee. "I liked his wife. Later—after the cancer—well,
that changed my brother. He developed a sadness, a kind of gloom. I've noticed
that, from certain people. The golden ones, so to speak. Things go so well,
so easily; then, when they don't, they don't have the same armor, the same
protective calluses."

"And Martin? Tell me about him."

She glanced at me. "Your *client*, you mean? Doesn't that make him off
limits?"

"I'm not asking for skeletons," I replied. "I'm trying to understand your
family."

We had reached Alamo Square and the Painted Ladies, a cheerful hilltop row of ornate Victorians painted in bright colors. We found a bench and sat. I watched a leashed dog stare at a gray squirrel as though astonished at its audacity. Braced on its hind legs, the squirrel looked back, bright eyes gleaming, tail quivering. Then the squirrel leapt up a tree trunk, breaking the standoff.

"My younger brother," explained Susan, "was more of an introvert. He never fit in quite as well. Our father was rather old-fashioned—he prized activity, energy, athleticism, maybe just raw competitiveness—what was popularly known as *manhood*. Martin never excelled in any of the areas our father felt mattered most."

"Was he close to your mother?"

She shrugged. "As close as anyone could get to my mother."

"What does that mean?"

"Our mother kept everyone at a certain distance—my father included. That was her nature. That *is* her nature."

I used the opportunity to shift the conversation. "What about Dr. Coombs? Did she keep him at a distance?"

Susan looked startled at this. "I'm just trying to get a sense of things," I repeated.

"From what I understand, my mother has a certain . . . faith in Dr. Coombs."

"Did you ever meet him?"

She nodded. "Several times, all brief. Although I strive to keep distance from my family, there are certain events, fundraisers and benefits, where my presence is required."

"What did you think of him?"

She drank coffee. "He seems a perfect gentleman. Charming, witty, urbane, educated, handsome. Everything. The whole package, as that dreadful saying goes. The subject of art came up and I could have mistaken him for a collector, he was so knowledgeable. The kind of man that everyone probably wishes she could go around town with."

"Were you upset seeing him going around town with your own mother?"

The warm afternoon light made the Painted Ladies, with their pastel tones of green and yellow and blue, look even more stately and beautiful. Susan finished her coffee and watched a sparrow forage in the grass. "I wasn't upset. Why would I be?"

"Isn't it obvious? Martin certainly was."

She laughed. "Of course, poor Martin was! He spent his whole life trying to be close to our mother. Then some strange man waltzes along and does it effortlessly. I can't imagine how that made him feel."

"But not you?"

Susan paused, as though marshaling her words. "Like I said, I've spent my whole life trying to put distance between us—my family, and most certainly my mother. Besides, I've developed a certain laissez-faire when it comes to my attitude toward what people should or should not be doing—my family included. Let people try to be happy. It's easy enough not to be, God knows. If it made my mother happy to run around with Coombs, who am I to get in the way? Besides," she added, "Martin is a man. They're always bound to be more jealous of that sort of thing."

"Jealous, or protective? You must have known she was being awfully generous—and that Coombs wasn't exactly saying *No thanks*."

She shrugged. "Mother has sufficient money." Her face showed no sign that she was probably making the understatement of the year. "And our family has a million-man army of financial advisors and bankers looking after our interests. If there was anything truly outrageous, anything that could really hurt, I'm confident that they would alert us." Susan seemed to be finished, then added, "She's in her eighties, Mother. Let her spend her money the way she wants. Assuming I reach that age, the last thing I want is nosy people looking over my shoulder telling me what I can and cannot buy."

"Can I ask you something personal?"

Her eyes grew distrustful. "Maybe?"

"When your mother dies . . . how does the inheritance work?"

"That *is* personal. A bit too much for my liking."

"Sorry." I didn't withdraw the question.

She thought about it, then shrugged. "I suppose I don't see the harm in answering. The bulk of the estate will be split evenly between myself and my brothers. Nothing very exciting." Susan turned to face me square. "Now *I* have a question. What exactly did my brother hire you to do?"

I had been trying to decide how to answer this. I settled for a degree of honesty. "He has a few concerns. One of them is that Coombs might try to blackmail your mother."

The word seemed to frighten her. "Blackmail? What could he possibly know?"

"You tell me. Is there anything in your family he could use?"

She considered this for quite a long time before she spoke. "As is probably the case with any family like ours, I can't claim the origin of our wealth is perfectly pristine. I know, for example, that during the Second World War, our family firm manufactured pharmaceuticals used by the German army and, probably, the SS—but that's hardly revelatory, and some journalist dug it up years ago."

"I see. Nothing else?"

She thought some more. "Nothing comes to mind. I'm sorry I can't be more helpful."

The conversation seemed to have ended naturally. Susan consulted a delicate rose gold watch, not bothering to hide the action, and stood. "It was nice to meet you, Nikki. Please do keep me informed if you learn anything. I would appreciate that."

I said I would, and said goodbye.

My meeting with Ron Johannessen turned out to be both the shortest and least pleasant. I caught up to him in his driveway on Lombard Street. Behind a high row of hedges, I glimpsed an enormous Spanish Revival home, all stucco walls and marmalade roof tiles. Ron seemed to be just leaving. He was in a two-seater Aston Martin convertible. A good-looking man in the prime of his life, his looks were marred by an arrogance that dripped off him like syrup. There was a woman in the passenger seat of the sculpted silver car. To calculate her age, a mathematical formula might have divided Ron's age by two, and then subtracted five. Even seated, she looked as thin and sleek as a gazelle. Her hair shone, and gold glinted against her skin.

Ron looked up as I called his name, my voice raised over the noise of the V12 engine. He wore a leather jacket and designer sunglasses that he didn't bother to remove as he stared up at me. "Who are you and what are you doing in my driveway?"

"My name's Nikki. Your brother wanted me to help him with—"

That was as far as I got. "Do me a favor, Nikki, okay?"

"Yeah?"

"Fuck off," he said, with no change in his expression. "Now, immediately, and forever. And don't try to talk to me again. I don't want to buy whatever crap you're selling, and you can tell my brother I said so."

Before I could respond, he threw the car into reverse and was gone.

If I learned anything from the meeting, it was that Aston Martin exhaust fumes smelled just as bad as those put out by any other, cheaper engine.

There was one last stop before I headed back to East Bay. A fancy doorman building in Russian Hill. "Delivery," I said. "For Mrs. Johannessen." I held a bouquet of flowers that I had picked up from a florist down the street.

The uniformed doorman crossed the lobby toward me. "I can take them for her."

"Can't I just run them up? That's what I usually do."

The doorman shook his head and held his hand out. "I'll make sure she gets them."

"Today? They need to get to a vase, you know."

He snatched the bouquet, shaking his head in exasperation. "Of course, today. I've been doing this job close to twenty years, lady. You think our tenants like wilted flowers?"

I left the apartment building, wondering why Martin had told me his mother was in Arizona. Something that only made me more curious about my new client.

WEDNESDAY

5

Wednesday morning, I stopped for breakfast at the Golden Eagle Diner in Emeryville. Several freeways connected almost within sight of a billboard sign that towered over the diner, and thanks to a shrewd owner who'd built out a huge, tempting swath of parking lot, the Golden Eagle drew a lot of the trucker traffic that churned up and down the coast. Guys with ten, twelve hours of driving in front of them, wanting to tuck into a big plate of potatoes and eggs and plenty of coffee before hitting the road. The sky was parchment pale when I pulled in, the early morning filled with sounds of groaning semi transmissions and idling motors and passing traffic. Inside, the diner was bustling with a mix of truckers and off-to-workers.

I found one of the few free stools and a waitress splashed steaming coffee in my mug without bothering to ask. Ignoring the proffered menu, I ordered eggs over easy, crispy bacon, and home fries as the waitress scribbled on her pad. The short-order cook's back was to me, so I raised my voice to make sure he'd hear. "If that goddamn bacon isn't crispy, I'm going to jump over this counter and—"

"And what, give me a hug?"

My brother Brandon turned, laughing, handsome even in his white apron and grease-stained T-shirt. In the past year he had put on much-needed weight, and his green eyes were alive and vital under mussed hair. He threatened me with a battered spatula. "Don't forget, I'm armed."

I looked at him fondly. "If I was a potato, I'd be running for the woods."

"You're not supposed to taunt the chef if you want your breakfast on time." He turned back to the grill as he spoke, cracking eggs one-handed onto the sizzling metal and flipping a couple of sausage patties before turning back to me. Most of our morning conversations at the Golden Eagle went this way. Him cooking, me eating, a few words here and there. A year ago, my brother had been a different person. A thin, malnourished wreck, days and nights filled by heroin, bad company, and not much else. More at home holding a syringe than a spatula. Bad days, many of them. Bad years. Wondering when my phone would ring with the worst news in the world.

He had been sober for almost a year, now. I was proud of him. After what he had witnessed as a boy, what he had been through, him standing here—healthy, employed, smiling—was, if not a miracle, at least somewhere on the spectrum of highly improbable events.

"Whatcha up to?" he said, stirring a pile of home fries and scooping an omelet onto a plate for a waiting server.

"Same as you—work." I watched him crack more eggs, again one-handed and flashy. "Show-off," I muttered.

Brandon cracked another egg and deposited it onto the grill with an elaborate swoop of his arm. "I've never believed in hiding talent. You at the bookstore later? I'm off at two. Want to get lunch? Your treat?"

I shook my head, trying not to smile. "As much as I love buying you lunch, I can't today. I have to be in the city."

He half-turned from the grill, raising an eyebrow. "*Work* work."

"Yeah. *Work* work."

"Who's the lucky guy?"

I laughed. "It's nothing exciting."

He handed me a hot plate, two eggs over easy, a pile of fragrant home fries, and perfectly crisped bacon. "Not sure if he'll agree with that. Whoever *he* is."

Like Ethan, my brother didn't know the exact details of what I did when not at the bookstore, but he had a better sense by far. That was my fault. A year ago, men with guns had visited him in his apartment, intending to use him as a bargaining chip to get to me. It had been the worst night of my life, and very nearly the last. But we were here, and they weren't.

That night, after everything happened, I'd sent my brother away and then dragged their bodies—three of them, one by one—down the stairs with the help of a very strong friend who had been born without the squeamish gene. A friend who also happened to know a thing or two about where to put a body. Or three of them. As far as I knew, the three men had been last seen in a landfill outside of Sacramento.

And here we were, eating breakfast. Life could be funny.

I picked up a piece of perfectly crisped bacon and bit into it, feeling a satisfying crunch. "What's new with you?"

"Things are good." The spatula flashed like a wand, seemingly everywhere at once. "Got a hot date tomorrow night."

"Oh, yeah?"

Brandon grinned mischievously over his shoulder. "Well, now that you're boring and settled down, at least one of us has to have some fun."

"I'm not boring. I'm just not single," I protested.

"Nik, please. I love you both—but you guys are the most incredibly boring couple in the world. Like, nursing home boring. The two of you spend Friday nights sitting in your living room watching old movies on TCM. When was the last time you were up past midnight?"

"I'm up past twelve all the time!"

"I called your place last week and literally woke you. It was eleven thirty."

"I was tired! That was one time!" I changed the subject back. "So, who is she? Let's hear some details."

His grin grew. "A doctor. And *hot*. A hot doctor."

I chewed a potato. "How the hell did you convince her to give you a shot? And stop sounding so damn satisfied with yourself," I added.

Brandon's voice tottered with a gleeful excess of dignity. "You know, many women find me extremely charming, although tragically, my big sister isn't one of them."

"Charming. You. Right."

"And in fact, I've been told more than a few times that I'm not so bad on the eyes, either." He shook his spatula at me. "What do you think about that revelatory information?"

"How many drinks do you have to buy these poor girls before they say that?"

"I'm telling you, Nik, online dating has opened up a whole exciting world. If you had a cell phone you'd know what I'm talking about."

"I think I'll let you enjoy the pleasures of Tinder all on your own."

We bantered on while I finished breakfast. It made me happy being around my brother, getting to see him like this. Dating, working, laughing. Happy. He'd been talking recently about wanting to one day have his own restaurant. Regardless of my teasing, Brandon had become an undeniably skilled cook in the last year. And responsible. No unexplained disappearances or shady friends. In the last few months I had been checking leases near my bookstore, and had recently learned that the noodle place next door was closing down and would be on the market. I'd talked to Jess to ask if the idea was totally crazy, but to my relief, she hadn't shot me down. I was considering it. It would be good to have my brother in the neighborhood.

I pushed my empty plate away and put a twenty-dollar bill under my mug. "Gotta run. I owe you lunch."

He leaned across the counter and gave me a quick hug. "Knock 'em dead." He winked. "Or at least, out."

I gave my brother a wave of assent, already headed for the door.

The Bay Bridge was clogged with cars doing the morning commute into San Francisco, but I lane-split my way across the five-mile span at a steady twenty-five, drivers throwing me jealous looks. The sky had cleared into blue, and the Bay sparkled in the morning sun. I fought through more downtown traffic and finally parked my motorcycle across the street from the Inter-Continental.

Following a pro was tricky. Someone naturally inclined to suspicion, habitually alert. But Coombs had seemed comfortable. I remembered his lobby entrance: the shoeshine stand, the cheerful nods and waves, the coffee and newspapers and leisurely breakfast. Easy, unhurried routine.

This morning I chose a different spot in the lobby. Hair in a bun instead of down, jacket off instead of on. Little details changed.

I waited. Just like last time.

Only this morning was different.

Today there was no Coombs.

Nothing said he had to get up at the same time. Maybe it had been a late night, or he could have spent the night somewhere else entirely. He seemed like a man who would have many opportunities for company.

I waited half an hour, wondering whether I should come back later in the day, or the next morning. But something was telling me that this should be sorted out now. I waited a few more minutes, then decided to take a chance. I walked over to the front desk and asked for him.

The clerk shook her head. "There's no guest staying here under that name."

Nothing said Coombs had to be using his real name. I described him, and the clerk shook her head again, her face turning from neutral to un-friendly. "I'm afraid I can't answer these questions."

I didn't want to press it. I thanked her and walked away.

A dead end.

As I was crossing the lobby, I slowed, my eyes on the shoeshine stand.

"When was the last time you had these shined, miss?"

"Possibly never," I admitted.

"You're lucky I like a challenge." The shoeshine guy shot up a smile. He was getting a workout on my motorcycle boots, whipping an inky rag back and forth across the many scuffs. I wasn't sure if I'd ever had a shoeshine. A very gender-specific activity, reinforced by the magazines he kept near at hand, *Esquire* and *GQ* and *Sports Illustrated*. Like a male version of a pedicure.

I thought over the tangle of convoluted and murky relationships I was glimpsing. Martin, my client. William, who was incapable of speaking to me, and Ron, who refused to. Susan, so determined to leave her family in the rearview mirror. And the elderly matriarch, Mrs. Johannessen, a woman crumbling and secluded as some fog-swept Scottish castle.

Was she being kept away from me, or from the world?

What had she done? What did Coombs have on her?

This was a powerful, proud, and secretive family. The whole Gary Coo-per attitude, strong and silent to the end. What had made Martin worried enough to involve me—an outsider?

"There you go, miss. That's as good as I'm gonna get 'em."

The shine guy was looking at my boots with satisfaction. A job well done. The leather gleamed, most of the scuffs gone. The boots looked inky-black and brand new. He blew out his breath with exaggerated effect. "Come back and see me before another ten years go by, okay? Quality leather is the same as people. Gotta be treated right to stay healthy."

"Deal." I climbed down from the chair and gave him a bill, watching his face change as he saw the *100* and keeping my voice casual. "I was supposed to meet a friend for breakfast, a tall, good-looking British guy who stays here. You haven't seen him this morning, have you?"

He didn't hesitate. "Oh, you must mean the doctor? You just missed him."

"Missed him?"

"Sure did, just barely. He checked out this morning."

I kept my voice casual. "Checked out? How do you know?"

"He had his bags with him—besides, he told me. He was in too much of a rush to even get a shine. He usually comes every morning, like clockwork. That's a fellow who knows how to dress," he added with approval. "Never even saw him in sneakers, not once."

"What time did you see him?"

The shoeshine guy checked his watch. "Oh, I dunno, musta been an hour or two ago. You didn't miss him by much, if that makes you feel better." He smiled, as if remembering something pleasant. "I'll miss him. He'd been everywhere, seen everything, and oh, boy, could he tell a story. You could have given him a stage and a mic and sold tickets all night long."

"Where was he going? Did he happen to say?"

He didn't hesitate. His words slammed into me. "Back home, to London. Seemed like something unexpected had come along. Like I said, he was in a rush. Sort of like there was a fire and he was running to put it out." The shoeshine guy pointed across the wide lobby. "I think it was JD who helped him with his bags. You should talk to him."

JD the bellhop was young and skinny and puppy-eager to please. "Sure, I remember your friend," he said. "Hopped in a Yellow Cab."

"Any chance you remember the license plate or cab number?"

The bellhop shook his head. "Sorry. I must call a hundred cabs a day."

"Did he happen to say where he was going?"

JD nodded readily. "Sure, I called the cab for him. He was going to SFO."

6

Traffic lightened as I hit the city outskirts on 101 South. I reached SFO in under twenty-five minutes, glad I habitually traveled with my passport. I pulled into short-term parking and discreetly emptied my handbag of several possessions that didn't belong anywhere near a security line. My motorcycle sported a pair of secure metal lockboxes. My things would be fine.

In the International Terminal, I checked the Departures monitor, picking through the usual blur of letters and times until I found what I was looking for. A British Airways flight. SFO-LHR, San Francisco to Heathrow, departing in less than an hour. I had maybe half that time to board. If Coombs had been rushing to the airport, he wouldn't want to wait around all day for a flight. He'd want to be thirty thousand feet up as soon as possible.

I scanned the monitor once more. No other London-bound flights were showing.

At the British Airways counter, they were sold out of Economy-class fares. I swallowed and put a $3,400 first-class ticket on my credit card, reminding myself that I was on the expense account of a very wealthy man who had instructed me to spare no expense. I asked the woman at the counter if any other London-bound flights had left recently and she consulted her computer, then shook her head. "Most of the trans-Atlantics leave later in the day. You'll have to hurry," she warned. "They're about to start boarding."

I didn't need to be told twice. I ran through the terminal to security. They'd close the cabin doors ten minutes before departure, which left me twenty minutes. Maybe five or ten minutes to get through security and then I could sprint to the gate.

I'd make it. Barely.

The TSA guy studied my passport in what felt like slow motion, then scrawled his initials on my ticket as I headed for the X-ray. Two minutes later I was through.

"Hold on a second." A blue-shirted TSA agent was standing in front of me. "Would you step aside for a minute, miss?"

"I'm going to miss my flight!" I protested, holding my ticket up as evidence.

Another TSA officer, this one a woman, had appeared next to the first. "Just a few questions."

They must have flagged me at the counter. Maybe the last-minute ticket, or absence of luggage. More probably both, combined into a giant red flag screaming *Not normal*.

The two of them were watching me with unfriendly expressions.

I followed them.

I spent an endless fifteen minutes in a small room, dutifully answering a series of plodding, uninspired questions while they practically took apart my handbag.

Finally, the female agent nodded and said, "You're free to go." No hint of apology in her voice for making me quite possibly miss my flight.

I checked the time. Eight minutes until the gate closed.

I ran.

I reached the gate maybe a minute too late.

The Jetway door was closed, but through the floor-to-ceiling windows I could see the plane, agonizingly close, its tail painted with ribboning red and blue flags. There was a lone gate agent at the boarding counter, remaining after the flood of passengers like some abandoned sentry, busy with some kind of final paperwork for the departing flight. I ran up to the desk, ticket outstretched, my desire plain enough that I didn't bother to speak.

"I'm sorry," the gate agent said, looking actually regretful as she checked my ticket. "They closed the cabin doors."

"Please. I have to be on that plane."

She spread her hands helplessly. "I wish I could do something. But when they seal the doors . . ." She trailed off.

"Could you make an exception? Please, just this once?"

Her eyes were sympathetic. "I'm sorry. If you talk to our main desk, I'm sure they'll be able to rebook you on the next available flight."

"Could you check with the pilot?" I knew I sounded like I was begging, but didn't care.

The sympathy in her eyes waned and the corners of her mouth firmed up. "This isn't a rom-com. I'm sorry, but you can't just go running onto the tarmac."

I started to say something else, then gave up as I saw the Jetway swing away from the plane like a decapitated snake. The plane, freed, inched forward, the nose ponderously angling out toward the expanse of runways. No other flights were leaving for hours. By the time I could get to London there would be no way I'd catch up to Coombs. No way I could find him in his home city. Not with a man so clearly practiced at fleeing and evading. He had gotten away.

I walked back through the terminal, thinking, frustrated with the closeness of the miss. Around me were the usual airport scenes: people slumped in chairs, stretched out on the floor, on barstools staring up at televisions playing news shows and sports recaps, flipping through magazines in kiosks. Bored travelers killing time in a dozen different ways.

People, everywhere. Just not the person I wanted. Had Coombs been scared by something? *Like running to put out a fire*, the shoeshine guy had said.

Then I stopped and exclaimed, *"Damnit, Nikki!"* loud enough for a mother pushing a stroller to give me a dirty look.

I was annoyed at myself. I had to start thinking smart instead of quick. Coombs, by all accounts, was a pro. If something had spooked him, he wasn't going to walk around blabbing the name of his destination to every shoeshine guy and bellhop he ran into. If he was blackmailing anyone, he might have assumed the Johannessen family would have him followed. Walking around broadcasting his next stop to anyone with a pair of ears would be akin to a fleeing hare dropping a trail of biscuits for the dogs to follow.

Coombs had been in a rush. Yet he had bothered to tell the shoeshine guy that he was going back to London. He made sure that the bellhop knew he was going to the airport. Had the airport itself been a bait and switch? He could have gotten in the cab and changed the destination by the time they pulled away from the hotel. Maybe he had dropped false crumbs all over San Francisco, for anyone chasing him to pick up and follow. Distractions, obfuscations. Buying time to flee.

Like a squid squirting ink.

One thing seemed certain, the more I thought about it. If he had told anyone who would listen that he was going back to London, I could be sure that London would be the one city in the world where I would not find Dr. Geoffrey Coombs. A small part of me wondered whether the $3,400 British Airways ticket in my hand was refundable. A bigger part wondered what to do next. The longer I delayed, the more ground he could cover. The less chance I had of finding him.

I had to start over.

I had an idea.

7

Coombs had left the hotel in a Yellow Cab. That gave me something. I exited the terminal, went up to the Information booth by the baggage claim, and asked the man working the desk for the Yellow Cab phone number. I called the number and reached a dispatcher. "I left something in one of your cabs," I told him. "This morning, going from the InterContinental to SFO."

There was loud conversation in the background and his voice was hard to hear. "We keep a lost and found at our office, 2060 Newcomb. If you forgot an item, they clean out the cabs at the end of the day and you can pick it up there."

"Can I ask the driver directly? It's important. Time-sensitive."

"Hang on a second," he said. "Let me look up the trip."

I spent a few minutes listening to scratchy elevator music and wishing they offered a Silent option. Then the dispatcher was back. "Lorenzo did the trip. He didn't find anything, but he's at lunch now if you want to ask him yourself. The Egg Up Diner on Turk, off Van Ness. You can meet him if you can get over there quick."

"Great. What's he look like?"

The dispatcher said, "Forties, swarthy, bald, fat."

That seemed clear. "Got it. Thanks."

He wasn't done. "But if he asks, I told you like Marcello Mastroianni, only taller."

"Marcello Mastroianni, only taller. Got it," I said again.

Fifteen minutes later I was headed north on the 101. Back to San Francisco.

I found Lorenzo at the lunch counter of the Egg Up Diner, wolfing down a triple-decker pastrami sandwich with a heaping side of fries and a deli pickle the size of a water bottle. There was a slice of apple pie next to him on a smaller plate, waiting its turn. He was clean-shaven but had a yellow-brown mustard mustache under his nose. The small diner was mostly empty, but I would have found the cab driver easily even if it had been packed. The dispatcher's description had been accurate.

There was an open stool next to him. I sat and ordered coffee, then turned to him. "Lorenzo?"

He looked up, startled, and used his napkin for what looked like the first time. The yellow mustache disappeared. "Yeah, that's me. Who're you?" His voice was a baritone, hoarsened by food.

"You picked up a friend of mine this morning. From the InterContinental. Tall, good-looking British guy."

"Oh, yeah, sure, you're the one Syd called me about." He sipped a Pepsi. "Clever-sounding fellow in a blue jacket, looked sharp. So, he forgot something in the cab? What was it? I didn't see nothing in the back, but maybe I missed it. Been a busy morning."

"Actually, I was hoping to talk to you for a minute."

He took a tremendous bite of his pastrami sandwich and followed it up with an equal chomp off the pickle. "Me? Why? You think he's cheating on you or something?"

"What makes you say that?" I asked, surprised.

"I dunno, I get the question here and there." He laughed. "Sometimes a fare means *affair*, y'know? That's what we say, anyway. And the two of you . . . well, y'know. You look like a good pair, that's all I mean. No offense."

His question got less surprising the more I thought about it. Cab drivers must get asked that kind of thing all the time. Did so-and-so get out at this address, was so-and-so with him or her . . . I couldn't be the only one looking to learn about someone who had taken a cab ride. Cabs were useful ways to learn about people. Especially in this age of Uber and ride-sharing, everyone's route permanently traceable for anyone who could access a smartphone. Which spouses and partners often could. Compared to that, cabs were like disappearing ink. Climb into a taxi, pay with cash, and you could still be anonymous. Not so easy, anonymity, anymore.

Lorenzo had asked the question with a degree of sympathy in his eyes. Maybe being cheated on wasn't a terrible way to play it. "I don't know," I said. "I'm just trying to figure out what he's been up to. He's been acting strange. It's been a confusing day."

"Sorry to hear that," he said, but volunteered nothing more as another substantial section of the pickle disappeared.

"I was hoping you could tell me where you dropped him off," I prompted. Something said not to push too hard. Lorenzo seemed like the kind of man who would help if he wanted to, and would otherwise clam up. He wore a wedding ring and had an old-school, stolid air about him. The kind of guy who could have been driving cabs a half-century back, same style, same manner of speech, same values. The kind of guy who, if pushed too far, would lock up like a shopping cart's wheels.

Lorenzo ate some fries. "Not really supposed to do that."

I tucked a hundred-dollar bill under his pie plate. "It's important to me."

His eyes moved from the bill to his plate. "It was an airport run. Do a million a day."

"An airport run?"

He nodded. "Yeah."

"Which airport?"

"Don't you know that already?"

"I know what they told the dispatcher."

"You mean Syd," he said.

"Right," I agreed. "Syd said SFO." Another bill joined the first. I was going off guesses and nothing more. Letting the conversation wander like he wanted, yet tighten in like I wanted. "That's not the only airport around," I hinted. "Maybe he said one airport and went somewhere else?"

Lorenzo pushed aside his plate. "Look, you seem like a nice lady. I want to help."

"You can help," I urged.

"Did he not treat you well? Is that it?"

"Let's just say that he owes me an explanation for walking out without a word."

Why did so many men need to feel like they were saving someone? Did all men fantasize about problems befalling women, just so they could be the one to fix things?

I saw his face reach a decision ahead of his words. "It was funny. As soon as we left he said he'd gotten mixed up and given them the wrong airport. He's British, he said, still getting used to this whole California thing."

"Where'd you take him, Oakland?" I guessed.

"No, that's what was funny about it. He wanted to go north."

"North?" I was puzzled. "What's up north?"

"Sonoma."

"Sonoma?" I repeated, my mind running through possibilities. There weren't many. Just one that I could think of. "You mean Charles Schulz Airport? The tiny one?"

Now that the cab driver had opened up, he seemed more willing to talk. "Seemed strange to me, too. I double-checked, said, 'Sir, you really want to go up there?' Not too many flights, more expensive, all that jazz. But he did, so I took him. Not my job to argue myself out of a fare, now, is it?"

"No," I agreed. "I guess it's not." Why would someone like Coombs want to fly out of an airport so small that tracking flights would be a cakewalk for anyone looking?

A third bill joined the first two. For the second time that morning, I felt happy to be on an expense account. "Thanks for your time, Lorenzo," I said. "I appreciate it. I think I'll hit the road now."

He knew where I was going, so he didn't bother to ask. As I walked out, he called after me, "I hope it's not what you think. Like I said, you two seem like a good match. I got an eye for those things, always have."

Sonoma Airport was about sixty miles north of San Francisco, barely north of Santa Rosa. I followed the 101 over the Golden Gate into Marin County. It was a clear day and the last of the city's fog vanished as I crossed the bridge, the temperature growing noticeably warmer from one end to the other. The water of the Bay was a beautiful turquoise. A cargo ship, stacked high with containers, seemed frozen on the surface as it crawled into the Bay from the open ocean to my left. Tiny flecks of white sailboats cut this way and that, almost indistinguishable from the smaller white pinpoints of wheeling gulls above them. I passed the exit for Sausalito and toed the Aprilia up into fifth gear, the motorcycle thrumming with satisfaction at the increased speed. It was a motorcycle that was happiest going fast.

Coombs. Who was he?

I was getting more curious about the man I was chasing. Maybe because I was becoming more impressed with him by the hour. He seemed far smarter than a run-of-the-mill, sweet-talking swindler out to hustle a few bucks. How many moves ahead was he seeing? Had he anticipated this, too? I hadn't ruled out Sonoma being an intentional dead end, just the way SFO had been. He could have been dropped in Sonoma, waited for the cab to pull away, and then gone anywhere else.

I remembered his effortless charisma. The way he seemed to light up the hotel lobby. A quality that went far deeper than physical good looks or mere charm. No wonder the Johannessen mother had fallen for him. I was starting to wonder something else: How many others had?

Coombs.

His face was in my mind. I wondered where he was. I wondered what he wanted. *Who* he really was. I could be dealing with someone who was very, very good at what he did. I rode on. Trying to ignore the tingle of excitement brought on by this thought.

Off the freeway, a long, straight, wide road led to Sonoma Airport. It was tiny. The kind of regional place probably struggling to attract carriers and stay in business in this age of long-haul flights connecting to big hubs. This was a small, single terminal, an air traffic control tower rising up in the background. One of the perks of tiny airports was ease of parking. Within a couple of minutes, I was inside, looking around. There couldn't be that many departing flights each day. Maybe a couple of dozen, compared to a thousand daily at SFO. I looked at the Departures board. Only four airlines were listed, flying direct to about a dozen cities, mostly on the West Coast.

I walked over to the single TSA security checkpoint, where a bored-looking guy in a blue shirt slouched on a stool. He barely looked up as I approached.

"I was supposed to meet my friend here," I said. "Tall British guy in a blue jacket. He would have been through here a few hours ago, if you were working this morning?"

The guy listened without interest. "Drawing a blank."

I had the photograph that Martin Johannessen had given me. "Here's what he looks like."

The TSA guy gave the picture a cursory look. "Haven't seen him," he said with even less interest.

I stepped back, out of line. Coombs could have passed through and been missed. The TSA guy could have been on a coffee break. Or forgetful. Or Coombs hadn't gone through the security line at all. Meaning he hadn't gotten on a plane and was somewhere else entirely.

Putting me back to square one.

This time I was out of ideas.

I walked back outside. Another dead end and this time no lead. Maybe someone else at the InterContinental had seen something. I could check there once again. The roar of a low plane filled my ears and I looked up, seeing a white body sweeping into the sky, tail unmarked by anything except a number. The airport was probably popular with the private jet crowd—an easy way to avoid the bigger commercial airports down south. There was plenty of wealth in Sonoma and Napa. Plenty of people who could look at flying private as a realistic and even pragmatic expense. I watched the white plane disappear into the blue sky, considering something. Then I went to find a payphone.

"Charles," I said.

"Nikki?"

"Yup. Got a question."

"Don't you always?"

He was right. Charles Miller was a former investigative journalist and, as such, the best person I knew for tracking down any information that wasn't easily accessible. "Flight logs for private planes," I asked him. "Are they publicly available?"

"Generally, yes. FAA figures taxpayers pay for airports, aircraft control, all that. That entitles us to a bit of public sphere knowledge. Unless it's a big-money person using corporations and shells to stay quiet, flight paths are usually gettable."

"I need private flights departing from Charles Schulz Airport this morning."

"Charles Schulz, the *Peanuts* guy?"

"Apparently they named the Sonoma Airport after him."

"Great cartoon. Used to read it to my kids." His voice contained a whiff of regret. I could guess why. After running a hard-hitting investigative piece against a Texas billionaire, my friend had been sued, bankrupted, and subsequently divorced. Texas courts weren't friendly to broke, disgraced fathers seeking joint custody. His move to California had been a fresh start. It had also meant leaving his children behind.

"Do you know the destination?" he asked.

"That's what I need."

"Any guess?"

"Not really. But it would have to be a plane taking off this morning, possibly with the name Coombs on the log. Is that hard to find?"

"Shouldn't be. It's a small airport. Where are you?"

"I'm there. At the airport. It's urgent."

"Give me thirty minutes and call me back."

While I was at the phone I made another call. This one was to the cell phone number my client had given me. I reached a voicemail, one of the anonymous, computerized voices instructing to leave a message. "Martin," I said, "it's Nikki. Coombs is running. I'm trying to find out where. I'll try you later."

I bought a coffee, drank it, waited for time to pass. After twenty minutes, I returned to the pay phone. Charles worked fast.

"Six private flights took off this morning," he said after he picked up. "According to the logs, the destinations were Los Angeles, Monterey, Palm Springs, Vegas, St. Louis, and Austin."

"Okay. And the people on them? Could you find anything?"

"You're in luck," he said. "There was a Coombs on one of the rosters. In a Cessna 172 Skyhawk. Going to Monterey."

"Who else was on the plane?"

"Nobody."

"He was the only passenger?"

"No—he was the only *person*."

I took that in.

Apparently, I was chasing a man who knew how to fly.

8

My Aprilia had a range of about one hundred and fifty miles on the free-way. I filled up at a gas station near the airport. A big, new Chevron station, perfectly positioned for everyone to gas up before returning rental cars. Monterey was 175 miles south of the Sonoma Airport. I could get most of the way down before refueling. Three hours plus change. I got back on the freeway, southbound once again, feeling like a yo-yo, bounced up and down, north and south. Almost as though the person I was following had an impish sense of humor. Like setting up a scavenger hunt for a kid's birthday party. Wanting anyone following to feel like a kite in a gusty wind.

South of San Francisco, I followed the 101 through Palo Alto, passing the NASA Moffett airfield hangars, looming, vast, looking like they had been built to house some kind of secretive rocket ship. South of San Jose, the freeway stretched into a comfortable two-lane road, winding through brown hills. I refueled in Gilroy and got back on the freeway, doing a steady seventy-five, leaning into the wall of wind and wishing I could go faster. Never a fun feeling racing an airplane. Especially when the airplane had gotten a head start.

Just north of Castroville, I cut west to the coast, linking up with Highway 1. Suddenly the views went from plain agriculture, all neat rows and endless fields, to the kind of stuff they put on the covers of guidebooks. The Pacific surged into visibility, bold and blue and sudden, bordered by tawny sand dunes.

Monterey Regional Airport was several miles southeast of Monterey Bay. Like Santa Rosa, it was a tiny airport, scattering smaller planes out to the larger hubs, designed to allow people to move around the West Coast

without having to resort to the sprawling big-city airports. I parked ille-
gally on an empty stretch of curb. My chances of ticket avoidance seemed
pretty good. There was only one empty police car parked at the airport
entrance. The same principle of deterrent presented by a scarecrow, with
hopefully the same chance of punishment. I walked into the single terminal, looking around, already knowing I was off course by the time I took in
the sparse handful of check-in counters. I was chasing someone who had
flown on a private plane. He wouldn't have come through the public terminal. If Coombs had really been at this airport, he hadn't stood where I was
now standing.

I walked back outside, eyes lifting to follow a little plane as it lunged
upward into the blue sky. There were probably only one or two runways
here. There would be a record of arriving flights, carefully recorded landing
times, passenger information—somewhere. I felt reasonably optimistic that
I could find that. The question was how long it would take, and how far
Coombs might get in the meantime.

I needed someone who had actually been on the ground. A mechanic or
maintenance guy—whoever was responsible for handling an airplane after it
landed and taxied and got parked wherever airplanes were parked. Someone
must have seen Coombs. The question was finding them. I thought again of
the scavenger hunt.

"What are you looking for?"

I looked over, surprised. The speaker was a chubby boy of about eleven
or twelve in a Monterey Bay Aquarium T-shirt. He sat on a curbside bench
and had a little green spiral notebook in his lap.

"How do you know I'm looking for anything?" I asked.

"Everyone at airports is always in a rush. You're not."

I smiled. "I could say the same about you." The boy had a yellow #2 pencil to go along with his notebook. Under round, plastic-frame glasses, his
brown eyes were intent and sensitive, his skin smooth and clear, too young
to be troubled by teenage acne. I saw there was a pair of binoculars next to
him on the bench and had a bizarre thought of bird-watching.

"So, what are you looking for?" he repeated.

"Just someone I was hoping to meet." I gestured at the notebook, my
mind still on Coombs. "What are you writing in there? Homework?"

He shook his head. "I'm not writing. I'm taking notes."

I appreciated the distinction. The boy had an almost scholarly manner.

Brown hair fluffed around his ears, as though there were more important things to do in life than brush.

"Notes? On what?"

He looked up into the sky as another plane came into view. This one bore Alaska Airlines markings. I could see the trademark blue face on the tail and heard the engine roar with increased volume as the plane floated downward. Then it was skimming the air before vanishing from view behind the terminal. The boy wrote a careful line in his notebook, then looked up to me. "That was an Embraer 175. It carries 64 passengers, 4 crew, has an 1,800-mile range, and the biggest windows of any Alaska plane."

I was impressed. "How do you know all that?"

"They're pretty much the only model Alaska uses here. The airport is too small for 737s."

I nodded toward the bench. "Mind if I sit?"

The boy moved a backpack and a beat-up paperback out of the way for me as I sat.

"You want to be a pilot when you grow up?" I asked.

"No."

"Then why do you like planes so much?" I prompted.

He shrugged. "I just do."

His eyes told a different story, but I didn't press him. Instead I said, "I'm Nikki."

"Nice to meet you, Nikki. I'm Mason." He held out his small hand and we shook.

"Do you come here a lot?" I asked.

He nodded. "Almost every day. Besides the library, it's one of my favorite places."

I nodded at his paperback, seeing the title. "*Boy*—good book."

"You read it?" He sounded dubious.

"I love Roald Dahl."

"It's one of my favorites," he said, with an affectionate look at the wrinkled cover. His voice was right on the edge of adolescence, deepening but with flashes of unsteadiness, like a foal on new legs. "This is my third time reading it."

Another plane surged into view, taking off, nose angling up, engine whining. This one was smaller than the Alaska plane, white with jaunty red stripes and propellers. Mason grabbed his binoculars, tracking the plane as it lifted. Satisfied, he nodded, traded binoculars for pencil, and wrote in his notebook. Then, as I watched with surprise, he lay down in the grass and did ten sit-ups followed by ten modified push-ups.

Then he sat down back on the bench.

"What were those for?"

"The kids at school all say I'm fat. I'm trying to get in shape so I can make the soccer team. My goal is to do fifty sit-ups and fifty push-ups every day."

"I think you look good," I said. He blushed and wiped his glasses and didn't say anything.

"So, which plane was that?" I asked. "The one that just took off?"

"A Beechcraft Bonanza. Six-seater, single-engine. It's been in production longer than any airplane, ever."

"That was a private flight?"

The boy nodded.

"Mason, were you here earlier today? Watching the planes?"

"I've been here since the morning," he said. "It's a teacher development day, I biked over right after breakfast."

"And you've been taking notes on every plane?"

"I always do. Why?"

"Did you happen to see any Cessnas landing?"

Mason nodded. "Sure. I see a lot of them."

"Did you see a Cessna 172 this morning?"

He consulted his notebook, flipping back a page, his face intent. "Only one so far. Usually there are more. They're really popular. Did you know that more Cessna 172s have been manufactured than any airplane in history?"

"I didn't know that," I said. "Can you tell me about the one that landed, Mason? What time it was?"

He glanced again at his notebook. "It landed at 11:54 this morning."

"Did you happen to see anything? After it landed?"

"See anything? Like what?"

"Any of the passengers?"

"No, I can't see them after they actually land. I used to sit closer to the runways, but someone yelled at me."

"That's okay. Thank you." I was already on my feet. "It was nice to meet you, Mason."

"Where are you going?" He sounded disappointed.

"I have to find the person I'm looking for."

I was three steps away when his voice stopped me. "A tall man with shiny brown shoes and a blue jacket?"

I stopped and turned. "I thought you didn't see anyone get off the plane."

"So that's him?" The boy looked delighted. "Why do you want to find him? Are you with the police? Is he a criminal you're chasing?"

"No," I said. "Nothing that exciting, I promise."

"I can help, you know."

I smiled. "You don't know what I need help with."

"Yes, I do!" he retorted. "You need to find that man."

I sat back down on the bench. "And you can help me do that?"

"Yes," Mason said with great confidence.

"I'm not a policewoman. I'm just doing boring, grown-up things. It's not what anyone would call exciting."

"You're patronizing me," he said matter-of-factly. "You weren't before, but now you are. Because I'm younger than you. Teachers do it to me all the time."

I had to smile. "You're right. I'm sorry. I shouldn't have."

"Let me help."

"Don't you have friends to play with?" I regretted the question immediately.

"No," he said simply. "I don't. That's why I'm alone. You can trust me, I'm reliable and I can keep my mouth shut. If you promise to let me help, I'll tell you everything I know about the man you want to find."

"I can't make that promise. But you would be helping me a lot by telling me. Was this the man in the blue jacket?" I was holding out my photograph of Coombs.

The boy took the small picture, looked closely, and nodded. "That's him."

"How did you know what he looked like?"

"I watch planes, but I like watching people, too," he answered. "I try to guess which people match up with which planes. I like to make up stories about who they are and where they're going. A few minutes after the Cessna landed, a tall man in a blue jacket walked out. There were no other planes for at least ten minutes before or after, and not many people around."

"What made you remember him?"

"Because he noticed me," the boy said.

Now I was intrigued. "What do you mean, noticed?"

"He *saw* me. Most people walk past like I'm invisible, or they're on their phones or talking to someone. But the man in the blue jacket . . ." The boy paused, trying to frame his words. "He *noticed* me. The same way you did, actually. Like I mattered. The way I notice the planes."

"Did he say anything to you?"

"No. He just waved and gave me a little wink—like the two of us were in on some secret and no one else in the whole world got to know what it was."

"Did he have a car?"

"Someone was waiting for him."

"Who?"

"A chauffeur driving a white Range Rover."

"You didn't happen to see the license plate, did you?"

"No," the boy said, sounding ashamed. "I didn't think it was important or I would have written it down."

One problem was leading into another. A white Range Rover. This was Monterey, not rural Mississippi. The vehicles were everywhere. Like trying to find a specific white sheep in New Zealand.

"But there *was* something," he added. "The driver had a polo shirt with a logo."

"A logo? Can you draw it for me?"

"Sure." The boy flipped his notebook to a clean page and sketched with an assurance that spoke of art lessons somewhere in his past or present. He tore the page from his notebook. I took it, seeing a trio of trees with a matching trio of stylized waves behind them, bordered by a circle.

"Thanks, Mason," I said. "This is really helpful."

"Can I come with you?" he asked. "Please? I can help more."

"I'm sorry," I said, standing. "Not this time. But you've helped me a lot. I owe you one." As I walked away, I glanced back. He was still watching me, eager and inquisitive, notebook forgotten on his lap.

I rode into downtown Monterey and found a tourist booth by Cannery Row. The pier jutted out into the Bay, the famous Monterey Bay Aquarium adjoining. In the water I could see sleek otters bobbing, buoyant and serene in their hammocks of kelp. The tourist booth had a stack of brochures. I took one. One of the ubiquitous pamphlets printed by tourism bureaus in every city, colorful with print and pictures, creased into a trifold. Unfolded, one side was a map of Monterey, little red stars showing the different attractions.

The other side was devoted to small ads listing hotels and fishing rentals and restaurants. I didn't know for sure if Coombs had been picked up by a hotel shuttle, but it seemed a good bet.

The man working the booth looked like a retiree, tan and bald and cheerfully wrinkled, the kind of guy who liked chit-chatting, got stir-crazy inside all day, someone wanting something to do more than needing a paycheck. When I caught his eye, he gave me a big smile and said, "Welcome to beautiful Monterey."

"Thanks." I returned the smile. "I was hoping you could help me. My friend is staying somewhere in town but I didn't get the name of the place."

"Can't you call him?"

"He doesn't have a phone yet—he's visiting from Europe."

"That's a tough pickle," the info guy said. He scratched his nose as if to indicate that he was still ruminating on the problem and how it might be solved. "A very tough pickle indeed," he said again.

"I bet you've been in town a while," I observed.

"Me? I've been here longer than the darn pier," the man said with cheery pride. "Surprised I don't have barnacles on me."

I held out Mason's sketch. "That's the logo of the place he's staying. Does it ring a bell?"

The info guy raised his glasses and squinted down his nose at the logo. "I'd say it was the Lone Pine—you know, they own Pebble Beach and all—but there's three of them." He studied the drawing critically. "Not exactly a lone pine when there's three of the suckers, now, is it? So that's out." He scratched his nose again, this time with more conviction. "Oh, I know the place all right. It's only about ten minutes from here."

I tried not to sound too eager. "What's the name?"

"The Cypress Grove Inn."

"The Cypress Grove," I repeated. "That's very helpful."

"You should stay on his good side."

I was startled by the sudden warning. "What?"

"Your friend," he clarified. "Whoever he is. He's staying at the nicest place in town. World-class. You should stay on good terms with him, is all I meant. Sounds like a good guy to know."

"He has good taste, that's for sure," I said. "Just about everyone seems to agree on that." Walking away, I slowed at a stylish little boutique, seeing colorful sundresses and handmade jewelry displayed in a window. The kind of place that charged three times the value of whatever they sold, but made the buyer feel good knowing that it was all local artisans and sustainable fabrics.

I stopped at the display window.

Coombs. The Cypress Grove Inn. Good taste. The nicest place in town.

An idea was forming.

9

Immediately south of Monterey Bay, the coastline bulged out like a burl on a tree trunk before retreating inward to form the smaller Carmel Bay and then continuing south toward Big Sur. The Cypress Grove Inn was located on the southern side of the burl, the entrance marked by a hand-cut redwood sign with an arrow pointing the way in. Titular cypress trees bristled on either side of the drive, stern as uniformed sentries.

I followed the arrow's direction up a private drive that climbed sharply toward a tollbooth. The paving here was newer than the main road, black and fresh and immaculate. A guard emerged as I pulled up. He was handsome, maybe twenty or twenty-one, wearing creased khakis and a tucked-in white polo shirt that showed an athletic build. The shirt bore a distinctive circular logo. A trio of trees in the foreground, a trio of waves in the background.

I flipped up my visor and gave him my name. "Checking in."

He glanced at a clipboard, then took a longer look after not finding what he expected. "Sorry, I don't see your name here."

"Maybe the booking didn't go through? I'll figure it out at reception."

He looked doubtful but I looked confident. Sometimes that was enough. He hesitated, then nodded. "Follow the driveway."

"Thanks."

"I like your motorcycle," he blurted.

"You ride?"

"Not yet. I want to."

"What's stopping you?"

"My mom. She hates motorcycles." He reddened a bit under his tan, as though he realized how that sounded only after saying it. "I'm at Cal State Monterey. I'm not like a live-in-the-basement type. I'm just staying at home to save up some money while I'm in school."

"Smart move," I said.

He smiled as though relieved I hadn't laughed at him. "My friends give me crap for it. But it's only for another year."

"Well, I won't," I said. "I'm Nikki, by the way." It never hurt having a friend in a new place. The thought gave me a flash of guilt. Sometimes I wished I could meet people without wondering if they'd be useful in an emergency.

"I'm Ben. It's a really nice place here," he said. "People come from all over the world." He smiled tentatively, as if worried about being too forward. "If you're checking in here, you've done something right."

"Today's been one of those days when I don't feel like I've done anything right at all."

"I have those days." Ben shifted, uncomfortable, as though he had overstepped a line. "Anyway, I'm sure you want to head up and relax."

I gave him a smile. "Nice to meet you, Ben. I'll see you around."

In my handlebar mirrors, the tollgate chopped downward behind me like a descending sword.

The reception building was understated redwood and granite that oozed seductively out of the sculpted grounds. A spotless pair of white Range Rovers were parked in front, looking like they spent half their lives at a car wash. Unlike the imposing Art Deco hotel where I had met Martin Johannessen in San Francisco, the Cypress Grove seemed desirous of blending into the landscape, rather than dominating.

I could see why. The landscape was magnificent. Stunning. To each side of the reception building, manicured green lawns slanted down, giving way to rockier ground dotted with freestanding bungalows that were half-hidden behind cypress trees and low palms. Then the terrain changed dramatically as it dropped steeply off, racing downward to the edge of a high bluff overlooking blue water joined to a seamless horizon line. I stood for a moment, taking in the view that swept out and down with such dizzying pleasure.

Inside, the sole reception desk seemed carved from a single, massive piece of redwood. Ben must have called up because the receptionist was expecting me. She shook her head apologetically as I approached. "I'm sorry, but I don't believe we have you listed as a check-in. There must have been some mistake. You said you had a reservation? Could it be a different name?"

"It was sort of last-minute," I said. "But this is a special occasion. I was hoping there might be room?"

She clicked into her keyboard with a mournful air, like a doctor looking at an unpromising X-ray. "We usually fill up quite a few weeks in advance. Months, actually, during our high season."

"I was hoping to get lucky."

She clicked some more. "What's the special occasion?"

"Kind of a reunion."

"That sounds fun." The receptionist looked up again. She was a pretty, freckled girl, Ben's age, sporting the same white polo and the same tan, healthy skin. The two of them could have been in an Abercrombie ad together. "The best I can do is a one-night stay. Tomorrow we're completely booked."

I was already handing her my license and credit card. "I'll take it."

She typed and talked. "I have you in a king bungalow with fireplace and ocean views, for $1,400 nightly, plus tax. Number 4, down the path to your right."

"Jesus. You said $1,400?" I almost choked as I did some quick math to make sure my credit card wouldn't max out. Between the morning's plane ticket and this, it was getting close. I'd never paid more than two hundred for a hotel room in my life, as far as I could remember. "I don't suppose you take Triple A?"

"We do not." She smiled to take the sting off. "Do you need assistance with your luggage?"

I had the usual backpack I wore when riding long distance, plus a paper shopping bag from the boutique. "I'll manage." I took the key she handed me. It was an actual physical key, weighty brass attached to a solid lump of redwood. It vaguely reminded me of an elementary school bathroom pass. I thanked the receptionist and headed to Number 4.

I followed a sloping path down behind the reception building and discovered a sumptuous oasis that had been blocked from view. The scene looked almost too perfect, as though a film crew was going to rip away a painted backdrop any second. Low palm trees and high green ferns lined a sunken, emerald-green hot tub, the water appearing to bubble from the very rock. It gave the impression of a pool that had been hidden away since the Cenozoic Era, secret and pristine. Adjacent was a small swimming pool, the water tinted perfect aquamarine. Below, the ocean crashed into the cliffs with a low rumble; above, blue sky swept out to the horizon to meet equally blue sea.

The only imperfection in the picture was a small group of pasty-chested men lounging in the hot tub. They didn't look perfect or pristine. One of them saw me and called out, "Wanna join the party?"

"No thanks." There were two magnums of Dom Perignon and a bottle of tequila arranged at the rim of the hot tub, along with flutes and shot glasses.

"You're making a mistake. We're way more fun than anyone else here," chipped in another.

A third voice added, "Including your husband." There were schoolkid snickers from the group of them.

I couldn't resist. "Whoever said that is obviously single."

Three of them laughed. The fourth, the one who had made the husband crack, didn't. He looked pissed. The classic I-can-dish-it-but-not-take-it type. He was well on his way to losing his hair, maybe four or five years remaining before the final exit date, and like he'd been making up for it by lifting exactly two muscle groups, biceps and pectorals, for all he was worth.

He tossed back champagne, flushing. "Being single is fun. Means I get to talk to girls like you."

"Yeah? How's that working out for you?"

He made an elaborate pantomime of checking the nonexistent watch on his wrist. "Ask me in about two hours." In case I didn't get the point, he added, "After you decide you're ready for the best time of your life."

"*That's* supposed to be a pickup line? Do they even let you near schools or parks?"

His friends were laughing louder, and his face grew correspondingly darker. "You know what we've been up to this week? We got bought by Facebook, bitches. I just booked a month in Phuket. How about you? What have you been up to this week?"

"This is the part where I get really impressed, right?"

He angrily refilled his glass. "If you were smart enough, yeah. Clearly you're not."

"Don't stay in the tub too long or your skin will prune," I advised. I gave the group a wave and continued down the hill, wondering for the millionth time whether something would come along, some badly needed bubble or dot-com crash, and wipe away this generation of tech bros the way the dinosaurs had been banished by an asteroid. Dominance could only continue for so long.

Or so one hoped.

Behind me, the tech bros laughed and hooted like jackals in their tub.

I wanted to take a look around. I passed my bungalow and followed a crumbly dirt path through landscaped gardens planted with native shrubs and flowers. I smelled primrose and sage and the sweet vanilla of Jeffrey pines. It was a garden that made me want to take a glass of wine and a book and not get up for the rest of the day.

Instead, I followed the path to the edge of the cliffs. I looked down, careful not to get too close to the crumbling edge. Not a place to swim. The ocean wasn't friendly and there was nothing resembling a beach. Beauty and menace went hand in hand. Waves beat and frothed, surging and swirling against the vertical, sea-flecked stone. Sharp, algae-slick rocks showed like knives between the pounding surf. Today the ocean was azure, white-capped, and dangerous as it rushed against the slate-colored cliffs. Millennia from now, maybe the water's force would carve straight through the gray stone; in a million years, these cliffs might not be anything more than bits of sediment within the waves. Watching the ocean, from above, was like standing on the roof of a high building, the mind filled with hypnotic Siren thoughts of the penalties of a fall or leap.

I turned away, still seeing the sharp rocks daggering out of the froth.

I wasn't sure if any room in the world was worth $1,400 a night, but Bungalow 4 was making a good argument. I stepped into a redwood cathedral curved in a vaulted ceiling, broad windows showing huge swaths of sparkling blue sea. Sunlight splashed and leapt along the walls, beams floating dust motes that spun in lazy disdain for gravity. A California king bed, dressed in the purest papal white, proved to hold the most comfortable mattress I had ever felt. A redwood soaking tub stood under a picture window, and the bathroom offered an alternate choice of a steam shower, tiled with mosaic that glinted like mother-of-pearl. I was pleased to note that there was no television. Just a turntable and an ornate brass-and-cherry bar cart crammed with every possible option of high-end spirits. A fireplace was preloaded with logs, and curtained French doors led to a patio deck.

The phone started ringing.

I picked up. "Hello?"

It was the receptionist. "I wanted to make sure everything is to your liking?"

"Except for the boys in the hot tub, absolutely."

Her voice was understanding, even though her words were neutral. "Yes, I think I know who you mean. They seemed quite friendly when they checked in."

"I don't suppose you were lucky enough to get offered a month in Phuket?"

She giggled. "I think that might have been on the table." Her voice returned to its professional distance. "Is there anything you need? We can book you a massage in the spa if you'd like? Or a restaurant reservation for this evening?"

"A dinner reservation would be great. Maybe seven o'clock?"

"For how many?"

"One," I said, and then added, "or maybe two."

"Your reunion."

"Exactly."

"Call me for anything you need," she said.

I thanked her and hung up, then called my client to fill him in. Martin Johannessen was a busy man. For the second time that day, I couldn't get through. I left another brief message, placed a quick call to Jess to let her know how to reach me, and then dialed a third number.

He answered on the second ring. "Don't tell me this mysterious number could possibly be my girlfriend? Calling me from wherever in the world she might be?"

"I'm not Carmen Sandiego," I laughed. "I'm two hours south, in Monterey."

"Why do I always get left behind for the fun stuff?" Ethan complained. "You had no problem dragging me to the mall last weekend."

"I needed new curtains," I laughed, kicking my boots off and sitting cross-legged on the bed. "You have a good eye for those things. Don't sell yourself short."

"Curtains. That's not at all emasculating. My girlfriend doesn't want me anywhere within a hundred miles when she's chasing down a mysterious stranger . . . but as soon as she has some interior decorating to handle, I'm the first one to get the call."

"Which should flatter you," I said sweetly. "See how much I depend on you? If I had been alone I might have gone with teal instead of lavender. You save me from my worst impulses."

"Yeah, well somehow I remain un-flattered. Speaking of interior decorating," he added. "Have you thought anymore about what we talked about?"

I twisted a finger through my hair. "A little."

"And?"

"I'm not sure."

"I guess that's an answer."

"Come on," I said. "Give me a little time. I'm thinking about it."

"I'm not saying we need to get married or, like, sign lifetime vows of commitment. It's just moving in together. It's practical, a natural step. People do these things, you know. It's not some weird sexual kink."

I leaned back against the headboard. "Can we do one of those instead?"

"Nik, come on. I'm serious."

"I know. But still. It's a big step."

"I'm not nearly as sinister as Gilbert Osmond," he exclaimed. "This doesn't mean the permanent end of your freedom and independence. I'm not secretly plotting to trap you."

I felt myself growing defensive. "And I'm not nearly as rich or witty as Isabel Archer. I just like my space."

"Easy for you to say. You don't have two grad school roommates whose average Friday night is splitting a twelve-pack and seeing who can be louder on Guitar Hero. And I'm not even *in* grad school anymore."

"Funny. I seem to remember you staying over at my place most Fridays."

"Look, think about it, okay? I'd be a great roommate. I'm clean but not creepy clean, I won't take up more than fifteen percent of available closet space, I find washing dishes to be therapeutic, I always put the seat down, and I can build Ikea furniture like an absolute champ. You should be *begging* me to live with you."

"Because my closet feels so empty without a big, broad-shouldered man's suits dangling off the racks."

Ethan laughed. "That's more like it. How much longer are you down there for?"

"Hopefully a day or two."

"And you're doing *what*, exactly?"

"Find a man. Ask him a couple of questions. Easy."

"And it won't get . . ."

"Of course not." I issued the trio of words smoothly, quickly, before his ellipses could take shape and solidify into any specific question. Any specific worry. Denying the unspoken was always easier.

I checked the time. "Speaking of which, I should probably get going."

"Okay," Ethan said. "I'm off to eat leftover pizza and grade Tennyson papers. The thrilling life of an assistant professor."

"Love you," I said. Suddenly missing him with a sharp pang. Still not something I was used to feeling about anyone except my brother. Missing someone. Not an unpleasant feeling, exactly. Maybe even *unpleasant*'s opposite. But unfamiliar enough to be disconcerting.

"Love you too, Nik. Be safe."

We hung up.

Unspoken words, unspoken fears, hanging between us in the air.

10

I was used to a daily workout and felt uncomfortably restless if I went without. I also figured I should take advantage of the amenities. I probably wouldn't stay at a place like this again. Not without the proverbial long-lost uncle leaving me a forgotten gold mine. The gym and spa were on the lower floor of the reception building. Although technically basement level, the ground dropped off steeply enough that the spa reception area boasted another level of sweeping Pacific views. Tranquil piano music played—a Bach piano suite, I guessed despite my limited knowledge of classical music. A receptionist offered me chilled coconut water and a warm smile.

I spent an hour in a fitness center full of gleaming, brand-new machines but devoid of people. Best of both worlds. Mostly free weights, then two fast miles on a treadmill, and finishing with five minutes of crunches and planks. Feeling better for having broken a good sweat, in the dressing room I undressed and wrapped myself in a plush white towel and a pair of slippers so comfortable that I knew I was going to steal them. I found the steam room in an adjoining coed section of the spa. In keeping with everything else, it was luxurious and understated and vaguely eco-friendly, teak benches and eucalyptus scents and lighting so subdued it barely registered as illumination. No one was in the steam room, either. Aside from a sole attendant cleaning the locker room showers, I hadn't seen a single person in the entire spa. It was midafternoon. Maybe the guests were out doing ocean-side yoga or golfing or shopping. Whatever people did for fun when they could drop $1,400 a night on a hotel room.

As if sensing my presence, the vents in the steam room turned on as I entered. I sat on an upper bench and leaned against the warm wood. Clouds of steam billowed out of unseen grates, swirling voluptuously around me, thick as a wool cloak. The scent of eucalyptus filled my nostrils. I breathed deeply, relaxing into the hot, fragrant steam, letting the heat work its way into my muscles. Eyes closed, body limp. The vents stayed on. The steam hissed into the room until I could barely make out my own legs stretched in front of me. I drifted into a languorous semi-doze, mind adrift. From what seemed like far away, the glass door was opened with a sound that was barely audible. I cat-slitted my eyes open but could see nothing more than a few inches in front of me, as though caught by a white-out in some mountain blizzard. There were rustling noises. Someone sitting, adjusting a towel, getting comfortable. The noises stopped. I closed my eyes again, drifting back into semi-consciousness, inhaling teak and eucalyptus, muscles supple with sweat and steam and heat, breathing in slow, deep breaths.

He was in the room with me.

I didn't know exactly how or when I knew this.

But I knew.

An animal sensation. Vivid and immediate. A feeling that *eyes were on me*. The feeling of being seen. Watched. Even through the opaque curtains of steam. My languor was joined by a prickle of watchfulness. A tingle that *something* had changed.

I opened my eyes again but could see only the dimmest shape on a bench across from me. I pulled my towel tighter around myself and tried unsuccessfully to make out any details. Now the billows of steam felt claustrophobic, pressing around me, sealing me in like plaster. Blocking important, maybe crucial things, from my vision.

For the first time I heard his voice.

It was deep and soothing and knowing, clipped with a perfect British accent. Although the words were throwaway, it was a voice that snagged in the mind like an important memory.

"I always feel like a lobster in one of these tanks. And yet so remarkably pleasant. I suppose being cooked always feels good—until it doesn't."

He was talking to me. He had to be. There was no one else.

We were alone.

"Always that fine line," I agreed.

Talking. The two of us. Here.

I hadn't planned this. And yet it was happening. Had he? He couldn't have. Could he have? That first intense prickle I had felt was back, even stronger. Watchfulness, only—or some kind of budding excitement?

"I'm delighted to find at least some trace of human presence," he went on. "I was starting to feel like I was in one of your Western ghost towns, down here all alone. I don't suppose you have a mining pan to spare?"

"I'm not sure if I want to help you with your prospecting."

"But you don't know what I'm looking for."

"If you need a mining pan, wouldn't that be gold?"

"Gold comes in many forms," he observed.

"You strike me as the type to want the yellow kind."

"How very superficial of you."

"Or, if I'm right, of you."

"Enough about me," he laughed. Like his voice, his laugh was rich and melodious. "And what could you be prospecting for, down here, I wonder? What brings you to town, besides wanting a good *schvitz*?"

"Why don't you guess?" I challenged.

He didn't hesitate, his voice playful, easy, untroubled. "An anniversary. A special treat from your beloved husband, to celebrate another milestone in your blessed union."

"I'm not married."

"Wait—of course—some sort of high-powered corporate retreat. Your team just finished coding the world's Next Big Thing and now you're down here, bonding, celebrating, enjoying the fruits of your labor."

"Me, coding? I don't even own a cell phone."

He laughed again. A clear, convincing laugh, rich and whole-hearted. "I can keep guessing, you know. I'm an absolute fountain of speculation, when I care to be."

"You haven't guessed right yet."

"A bridal party. Something fancy, yet tasteful. Four or five of you, best friends since the uni days. You're here because the wild one, the one everyone said would never settle down, is tying the knot. A weekend to laugh at past shenanigans while secretly sizing each other up to see who's done well and—the delicious part, of course—who has not."

"I'm here alone."

His words were laconic, vaguely self-deprecating. As though he didn't really believe anything he was saying but was merely lobbing words like a boxer probing with his jab. Nothing forceful. Maybe not even real curiosity. Just to learn how I might reply, what I might say.

Idle study. Habitual. Reflexive as drawing breath.

"I'm afraid I give up," he said. "I'm oh for three, struck out, as you baseball-loving Yanks would say. You've stumped this poor, panless prospector with your mystery. Why you're down here at this swanky place is beyond me."

"Maybe I was curious to see if the real thing lives up to the hype."

"And the verdict?"

"I think the jury's out."

"When will the jury be in?"

"Possibly by dinner?"

"Dinner's superb here," he returned. "I recommend the rockfish. My guess is you'll be quite content. Sometimes the hype, as you put it, is real."

"You seem to like guessing," I observed. Trying to stay with him. Keep up with his easy, fluid shifts from metaphor to literalism and back, twisting, turning, until it was hard to know which was which. Like seeing what was real, and what was apparition, in this steam-choked room.

"Is that so?" He laughed again, that same clear, rich, easy sound. Warm, nourishing. Like drinking hot broth on a cold night. "We're in a bloody steam room, my dear. What else would I be doing? I don't see a billiards table or chessboard anywhere."

"You're a chess player?"

"I've been known to move a piece or two, on occasion."

"Do you win when you play?" I asked.

"Almost always," he replied. "I suppose one of the things I've learned from life is that I prefer taking others' pieces to giving mine away."

"You don't seem like you'd lose," I acknowledged. "But I guess nobody does, until they run into someone who plays better."

"Now who's guessing?"

"We're in a bloody steam room," I said. "What else am I supposed to do?"

He chuckled, appreciative. "And when did you arrive at this sun-kissed Shangri-la?"

"Guess," I challenged.

"Today."

"How'd you know?" My surprise was real.

"Guesses are like magic tricks. Once you explain them, they stop mattering."

"I'll file that away."

"How very . . . clerical of you." I saw a shape shift in the clouds of steam. Heard feet against the floor.

"You're leaving?" I asked. Wondering why I felt surprised.

"The trick with being cooked," he answered, "is to know when it's happening, and to depart just before it does." I could glimpse his form, vague, shadowy, indistinct. Shrouded by the steam that still hissed out of unseen vents. "I'll be seeing you around, I'm sure," he said. His voice farther away.

Fading. Leaving.

I felt an involuntary pang. I didn't want him to go. As though, despite everything, I had been enjoying myself in his company. Enjoying our conversation, rife as it had been with such probing, guessing, concealing.

The two of us.

"Seeing me?" I repeated. "You don't even know what I look like."

He sounded like he was smiling. "I have your voice. That's all I need."

I heard the door shift open. Another footstep. The smallest sounds.

Then nothing.

Once again, Coombs was gone.

Beyond the most muted, steam-shrouded glimpses, I had never really seen him.

11

It was nearing dusk when I returned to my room. The tech bros were gone, the bubbling emerald water no longer besmirched by pale flesh, the stillness of the air equally free from their hooting voices. If anything, the property looked even more beautiful in the early evening, the sun beginning to pinken the waves, shadows lengthening across the ground. I passed a bench, secluded in a grove of trees, glimpsed a man in a linen shirt whispering something to a woman wearing flowing white pants. A bottle of wine perched on a rock between them and they seemed as happy as a Mastercard commercial. My eyes were drawn to sudden movement off the path: a jackrabbit, speeding from one clump of bushes to the next. I wondered how far the property stretched, and what else moved within its boundaries.

Back in my room, I stripped off the luxuriant bathrobe I had worn out of the spa. I took a long, hot shower, scrubbing my skin with fragrant bath products that seemed on a different plane of existence than the Target supplies I stocked my own shower with. Wrapping a towel around myself, I poured a straight scotch from the bar cart. It was a smoky single malt, so velvety and smooth that ice cubes would have been a distraction. There were sheaves of records next to the turntable. I flipped through them and put on Janis Joplin, hearing the haunted, beautiful voice drift through the room. She had been one of my mother's favorites. I knew many of her songs almost by heart, from childhood.

Coombs. Here. The two of us.

We had finally spoken. And yet I knew as little about the man as ever.

Who was he? Why was he here? What was he running from? He didn't seem like a man on the run—but the more I saw of him, the less he seemed like any man I'd met. Maybe these herky-jerky movements, leaps from one point to the next like the jackrabbit leaping bushes, was his normal style. A man used to being chased, habitually cautious. I'd known hardcore military guys who took evasive action when driving to the grocery store.

I had felt *something* in the steam room. Not menace, exactly. But not just excitement.

Risk.

That's what it was. There was risk attached to him. Clinging like tendrils of steam.

I took another sip of scotch and noticed that the red message light on my phone was blinking. I spent a minute playing around with the phone, trying to figure out how to access my messages. The voicemail was from Jess, asking me to call her as soon as I could.

I dialed the bookstore. "Hey," I said when she picked up. "What's going on?"

"A woman called about two hours ago," she said. "She left the name *Johannessen*. It sounded urgent, whatever it was. She really wants you to call her."

I was confused. Could she have mistaken Martin's voice? "A woman? You're sure?"

"Pretty sure . . . She left a number."

I took down the number she dictated, hung up, and dialed it. Sure enough, a female voice picked up on the second ring. A familiar voice.

"Susan?"

The voice sounded cautious. "Who is this?"

"It's Nikki. I got your message."

"Where are you?" she said immediately. "I need to see you."

"I can't. Not now. I'm out of town."

"Why?" She sounded puzzled. "I thought you were looking into my brother's accident. Where are you?"

"Something else," I corrected. "An unexpected development. Everything okay?"

She was quiet for a long moment. When she spoke again, her voice was strained. "I've learned that Martin didn't tell you everything about what's going on between Coombs and my family."

I put my glass down on the nightstand. "What did he leave out?"

"The most important parts."

"Which are?" I prodded.

There was another pause. "It's my brother—Ron."

"What did he do?"

"Not over the phone," Susan said. "I need to talk to you in person."

"Tonight? Sorry, but that's impossible."

"I'll come to you," she said.

"I can't. Not tonight." Coombs might vanish by morning. I had been lucky to find him once. Next time I might not be able to.

"Then tomorrow," she insisted. "Where are you?"

"Monterey," I told her, trying not to sound irritated by the sudden flurry of requests.

"Where are you staying? I can meet you there."

I didn't need a panicked Susan Johannessen doing a midnight Paul Revere to the Cypress Inn. "Cannery Row," I told her after a moment's thought. "Meet me there at noon tomorrow. On the pier."

She didn't hesitate. "I'll be there." Then she added with a rush, "You need to be careful, Nikki. I've glimpsed this—this rot—this web." As if reading my mind, she added, "Don't think I'm being hyperbolic. You'll see. Be careful. There are frightening things you don't know."

"See you tomorrow." I hung up. Through the picture windows the sky was darker, tainted with orange, the ocean more restless, stirred by the last bit of evening breeze. I tried to brush the phone call out of my mind. That could wait. I had to focus on what was right in front of me.

Dinner.

"Here you are."

The waiter set a bottle of champagne in an ice bucket on my table. I had changed for dinner. Scuffed motorcycle boots and road-dirtied jeans would have made me stick out at the Cypress Grove as though walking around naked. Besides, I was going for a different look tonight. I wore an elegant black dress that fell above my knees, showing my long legs to good effect. A silver and jade necklace hung from my neck, and heels stretched my feet past the point of comfort. I had spent a half hour getting my makeup just right and my hair was down, a trace of perfume hanging like invisible flowers off my neck. The Monterey boutique had been a good choice. The Johannessens' expense account was taking a beating, but they could handle it.

I looked good.

More than good. I looked wealthy.

A sexy, successful, glamorous woman.

I sipped from the champagne flute my waiter had filled and looked around the dining terrace. It was a beautiful evening, the ocean chill held at bay by propane warmers placed strategically between the tables. The sun was headed downward into the Pacific in a fiery splash, scarlet and orange ricocheting around the sky, filling the clouds with vibrant slashes of color. Torches burned quivering amber cones into the dusk and tea lights shimmered in glass jars on each table. The majority of the tables were filled by middle-aged couples, a larger group here and there. I was the only one who sat alone.

Men shot looks my way. More attention than I usually got, but then usually I was walking around in a T-shirt and bomber jacket. Fashion had never been a big thing of mine.

A man stood and walked toward me.

The wrong man.

The tech bro from the hot tub. Next stop, Phuket. Now he wore a too-tight black T-shirt and ripped selvage jeans that doubtless cost ten times what a normal pair should go for. From far away he could have been handsome, but as he approached, his face was too arrogant, lips curling in a smile, cheeks flushed with alcohol from the day-drinking. Not just day-drinking; behind him I could see the tableful of his pasty friends, leering at us over a fresh bottle of tequila.

He grinned down at me. "I feel like we got off to a bad start."

I didn't return his smile. "Agreed."

"Hey, I came over to apologize. I was rude."

"Apology accepted. Have a nice night."

He wasn't done. "Don't tell me you're gonna drink that all by yourself?"

I answered without meeting his eyes. "I didn't really tell you anything."

Most guys heard a cold tone, saw an averted gaze, and took a hint. Basic, unmissable social cues that had probably been around for the last ten thousand years. Not this guy. He reacted as though I had pulled out a chair. He picked up an empty water glass from the table and reached for the champagne, giving me a kind of bargain-basement James Dean grin that had probably worked on all too many girls in his college days. "I'm thirsty. You mind? I'll get the next bottle, don't worry. In fact, your dinner is on me."

There was a place setting in front of me. Convenient. I gave his knuckles a hard rap with my butter knife. An audible *thunk*. Like ringing a very dull, solid chime.

He yelped, and his hand shot back in retreat.

"No one ever taught you to keep your hands to yourself?"

"I was being friendly," he said. "You were sitting here all alone."

"Ever think that's because I want to be alone?"

"What is *with* you? I said I was sorry."

"You're missing the point."

"Whatever," he sulked. "Have fun being by yourself all night. Pathetic." His face was a couple of shades redder than it had been as he stalked off toward his buddies, shaking his head in disgust. As though, as magnanimous as he was, even he didn't have the ability to help such a sad-sack basket case.

I poured myself more champagne and watched the sun inching down toward the water. It really was a beautiful evening. Maybe Ethan and I could come back here someday. If the place ever ran off-season discounts. Say, about 80 or 90 percent off. For the hundredth time, I wondered about his request. Moving in together. I owned my apartment, but it was a one-bedroom. Would there be enough room for two? It had been a long time since I had lived with anyone. I valued my space. And I didn't want to move too fast and risk ruining what we had. That made sense.

Right?

Or was that me being my natural, walled-up, hermetic self?

"I told you I'd find you."

A familiar voice. A rich baritone, polished with an immaculate British accent.

My attention snapped back to the moment. I looked up, seeing the sharp eyes, the aquiline nose, the forelock of jet-black hair falling perfectly over a high forehead. He smiled, showing strong white teeth, and his eyes seemed to glow with understated confidence and good humor. Unlike the tech bro I had sent packing, this man looked like if I told him to leave he'd be about as bothered as a duck getting wet.

"The prospector. From the steam room," I said.

He ignored the obvious. "I admired the grace with which you dispatched that poor brute," he went on. "Admirable efficiency, estimable panache. Good show all around."

"You were eavesdropping?"

His laugh was as warm as cognac, his eyes were deep blue, and pleasant crinkles spread around their corners as he smiled. A trustworthy, assertive face. Someone who would know what to do in any situation: which soupspoon to use at a state banquet, or how to rub flint and get sparks if caught in the Yukon.

And movie-star handsome.

"Eavesdropping? Hardly. More like by-standing." His eyes twinkled. "But at least now I know better than to dare reach for the champagne."

He was tall, maybe six foot two, and well built. Broad shoulders and a flat stomach under a blue-and-white striped cotton shirt with a cutaway collar. A royal blue, knit tie crowned with a perfect, asymmetric four-in-hand knot. He wore gray slacks and a sharp, silver-buttoned navy blazer, the soft gold dial of a wristwatch peeking from under his left cuff. Framed by candlelight, the ocean behind him, he could have posed for a Most Eligible Bachelor photo shoot without moving a step.

"Please don't tell me you sold a software company."

"Ah, I see." He nodded with a glance back at the tech bro table. "San Francisco's finest computer scientists are out to play."

Why did charm always go so well with a British accent? Like cold gin and a touch of vermouth. A perfect fit, and the why didn't really matter.

"They can play all they want—just not with me."

"A reasonable stance." He straightened. "Anyhow, I don't wish to intrude, and for what it's worth, I say that not only out of fear of your butter knife. Good manners, I've found, are an endangered species, although I like to imagine they haven't gone the way of the dodo quite yet." He gave me a last smile, rueful regret at what might have been, mingled with impeccable courtesy and something more molten underneath. As though refusing to consider, even within the privacy of his own mind, the very possibilities that he was walking away from. "Enjoy your evening, and keep the ruffians at bay."

He was good. Really good.

He started to turn away.

I couldn't help but feel a sting as he turned to leave, as though the best part of my night had chipped away like a snapped ice floe. I couldn't miss a step. Underneath the charm, I had felt him probing, guessing, studying.

This man reminded me of someone.

He reminded me of myself.

He was setting a scene. Just like I was. And at this game he was maybe even better than me. He had the experience, the talent, and that unteachable mental ability to reach into someone's mind and figure out what they wanted. I had seen his eyes moving fractionally, all his senses firing, a constant intake of information, like a hedge-funder trying to get in that 0.001 hairsplitter advantage on a trade. Noticing everything. Trying to find the one throwaway scrap that might make the crucial difference. The only way I could tell was because I knew what to look for.

Tonight, being my usual state of competent wouldn't be nearly enough. I had to be perfect.

"I won't get through this whole bottle on my own," I admitted. "Pull up a chair and have a drink with me if you want."

He turned back but made no move to sit. He looked into my eyes. Not flirting anymore. Challenging, now, under the politeness. "Forget about me. Is that what *you* want?"

He was better than good. He was great.

I said, "I generally speak my mind."

As he lowered himself into a chair, his eyes never leaving mine, I was struck again by his presence, the gleaming obsidian courtliness that seemed to cover a deep, unspoken core of something fiery within. I wondered how many of these scenes he had gone through. More than I had? He was older by at least a decade. More than a decade of extra experience.

"My name is Dr. Geoffrey Tyler Coombs," he said as he sat. His nails were manicured, I noticed, the edges too neatly trimmed for a clipper. "And forgive me for saying so, but I can't help but think that this is the beginning of something very exciting."

As it turned out, he was right.

Exciting.

Because that was how things really started.

12

"You're a bit of a devil under the polish, aren't you?" I teased.

My new companion had just finished a ribald story involving a dueling piano bar in Singapore known for all the wrong kinds of entertainment.

"I venture you're a bit of a devil yourself," he replied, refilling our glasses from the second bottle of champagne.

"And how would you know such a thing?"

"I am, after all, a psychologist. Although these days, I confess, I'm mostly on the lecture circuit. The private practice seems to trot along without me." He grinned easily. "They say being wanted is the best feeling in life—but as far as I'm concerned, not being needed is twice as good." He touched his glass to mine. "Enough about me. I fear I've been prattling on without giving any proper consideration to the origins of the beautiful and mysterious woman I'm sharing a table with."

I smiled. "You seem like a man who gives proper consideration to *everything*."

"My question stands."

I toyed with my glass. "I'm just a California girl trying to find all the right things."

"And what things would those be?"

"Now you do sound like a psychologist," I said.

"And you dodged my question," he returned.

"Maybe I'm trying to find the right guy."

His eyes were skeptical. "You strike me as rather self-sufficient. A woman like you? Really? Just looking for a man?"

"The *right* man. There's a world of difference. Call me a romantic."

"You don't believe that sometimes we have to settle for the best we can get?"

"I never settle," I said. "Not when it comes to anything important."

He blinked less often than average and his facial muscles had a way of barely moving when he listened. As though he was utterly focused on every word, hearing me more closely than anyone ever had. His concentration felt hypnotic.

"And what's important to you?" he asked.

"Right now? I just want to get to know you better."

He took that in, watching me. Radiance from the tea light on the table lightly touched his face. His hands were perfectly still. He didn't toy with his fork or crumple his napkin or scratch his nose—none of the mannerisms that accompanied most conversation.

I finally broke the silence. "Did I say something wrong?"

Coombs shook his head, eyes still on mine. "I feel like I've known you far longer than only a few minutes. I'm trying to decide why I feel such a connection."

I couldn't tell whether he was being truthful. No idea—nothing. No verbal cues or physical tics to point me one way or the other. I wasn't used to feeling that level of blank uncertainty. Like trying to climb a vertical rock wall that had been stripped smooth of all the natural crannies and ledges in which to put one's hands and feet. I couldn't remember the last time I'd felt such uncertainty. Maybe never.

It was exciting.

I lightened my tone. "Two bottles of good champagne could be the answer."

He caught the shift. "Dodging, again."

"And maybe you say everything a little too perfectly," I challenged. "Connection, knowing me . . . are you being honest? Or is this your standard opener?"

For the first time he looked disappointed. I felt a flash of the same disappointment echo through me, as though I had let us both down with my flippancy.

"Maybe I'm being more honest than you're comfortable with," he suggested.

"Says the psychologist."

"Forget labels, for a moment," he returned. "You Americans always want to label everything, put a perfect little sticker on all of us that shows the world exactly who we are. The whole human race walking around with a price tag and a bar code hanging off their necks, so anyone can scan away and take their full measure without bothering to work for it. But we are who we are. Whatever the name—whatever the profession or degree—whatever you want to call it. *I* am who I am. Aren't you? And I daresay I'm being more honest with you than you even know." He paused. "And yet I would have hoped *you* would understand that—of all people."

"Why me? Out of everyone?"

He held my gaze, his hands clasped in front of him. "Take it as a compliment. I am forming an opinion of you, as you surely are of me. That's what I do." He leaned forward. "You want to know what I do? I look into people. That's what I do for a living. That's what I'm good at."

"Look into people?"

"Until I understand what they want. Their fears, their desires, their foibles, the things that make them proud or ashamed or delighted. I help them learn things about themselves. Sometimes obvious things, and sometimes the deep-down, unadmitted stuff, the stones at the murky bottom that we know are there—whether we admit it or not. I try to learn the things that make people who they are."

I smiled. "Doesn't sound like the robots will be taking your job any time soon."

He didn't return the smile. "I'm serious, you know. That, in a nutshell, is what I do. And I'll never have to worry about robots."

"So, what are my fears? And a free hint to a new friend—I've never been scared of the monsters under the bed."

"No, I don't imagine you are." His eyes bored into mine as he studied me without bothering to hide it. "I don't think the monsters particularly scare you. No—you fear yourself."

"Myself?" I repeated. "I don't understand. What do you mean?" For the first time all evening, my voice sounded fake.

"I get the impression that you're a woman who is not especially frightened of anything—except perhaps yourself."

My face showed skepticism. "Isn't that a pretty universal prediction that anyone could say about anyone? Like a fortune-teller promising I'll experience great joy and sadness somewhere in life?"

"No," he said. "I don't believe that's the case. Not at all. Not in my experience. Everyone is different and everyone fears different things. I've met people frightened of relationships, solitude, poverty, physical appearance, intelligence, lack of purpose, being forgotten, being remembered for the wrong reasons—I could go on and on. Lately, I've been speaking to an impressive woman, someone who wouldn't appear to have any reason to worry about anything. But I realized that her greatest fear was her own family, her children—the crippling of a legacy she spent a lifetime building. No, most people are far more afraid of what's under the bed than of what they see in the mirror."

I was struggling not to get lost in the conversation, lost in the man in front of me. "Okay, so I fear myself. What does that even mean?"

"You fear your reactions," he replied. "Like when I watched you rap that idiot's knuckles—for a moment, you looked as though you wanted to stick that butter knife straight through his hand. *Did you*? I wonder. *Could you have*? A big, strong clod like that? I was watching you—and I know where my money would have been. You fear losing control. You fear your impulses. That's what keeps you up at night."

Prepared as I was, his words had pushed me off balance. "So how about you?" I returned. "What keeps you up at night?"

He relaxed into his seat. "Nothing a good brandy can't fix."

"Now you're dodging."

He laughed. "Fair."

With a little electric rush, I felt his leg brush mine under the table. As though in approval. As though I had scored a point.

I didn't move my leg. Even as I kept talking. "And that's what scares *you*."

He raised an eyebrow. "Pardon?"

"You're good at dodging—but maybe that's because you have a lot to dodge? A handsome, exciting man like yourself? I'm sure you find plenty of adventure. And maybe one day something will come along that you can't dodge. And all the brandy in the world couldn't fix that, and all the brandy in the world couldn't get you to sleep if that's what you're worrying about as your head hits the pillow. You don't seem to mind flirting with trouble."

"Interesting." He fell quiet and regarded the candle flame that flickered between us. "I'm flirting with you," he finally said, raising his eyes to mine. "Are you trouble, then?"

"You don't know what I am. And you like that. Just like I do."

His hands unfolded and he smiled as if I had passed a test. "I believe," he said, "that I've never met anyone precisely like you before."

"So now what?"

His leg pressed harder against mine. "Now we keep getting to know each other."

Guiltily, I was aware I wasn't moving my own leg. I tried to ignore the undeniable thrill the contact sent up my skin. Tried to ignore the excitement of the moment. It had been a long time since I'd felt totally locked in with another person. Connected. Not only his charm or looks, or the setting, or the wine, or the physical brush of contact. Those things were nice, but nothing more than the frame around a picture. What mattered was that I was sitting across a table from someone who *knew* me—somehow, instinctively, and deeply.

A man who wasn't a civilian. A man who was like me. A man whose words made me feel alert and alive in a terribly exciting way.

I had told my boyfriend I was meeting a man for dinner. I hadn't known that the man in question would turn out to have a more intuitive sense of who I was than perhaps anyone I had ever met. And I wasn't sure exactly what that meant.

"So, you have no problem sucking face with this dude all night?"

We both looked up, the mood snapping. The tech bro was back, drunker and more obnoxious than ever. He wavered on his feet, the endless drinking taking hold.

"I own suits ten times more expensive than that boat jacket," he sneered. "I just don't pack them to the beach."

Coombs's eyes were cold but his voice stayed perfectly measured. "I don't recall anyone inviting you over here."

"What are you going to do?" the guy challenged. "You don't own the place."

I was running through scenarios in my mind. A fight would be a disaster. Even this might have ruined things. The mood, so carefully attained, had been broken into pieces. I felt a burst of fury and tried to tamp the anger down, knowing it was useless. I was in character. I couldn't do anything even if I wanted to.

"Perhaps we all need to take a breath," Coombs said.

He pushed his chair back from the table.

I tensed. My companion didn't seem like the violent type, but that didn't mean anything.

After all, neither did I.

The tech bro clenched his fists.

Coombs snapped his fingers.

Within seconds, the maître d' materialized. Coombs didn't bother to raise his voice or stand as he said, "I fear our young friend has overdone it on the sauce. He's become quite the bother."

The tech bro glared. "You're the bother, dude."

"Is there a problem?" The maître d' had been joined by a large man in a black polo with the Cypress logo.

Coombs said, "This fellow intruded and insulted us without cause. In fact, he's doing his best to muck up quite a nice evening for no good reason."

The maître d' didn't hesitate as he turned to the tech bro. "Please come with us."

The tech bro swayed and glared. "I'm a guest. I'm not going anywhere."

Two of his friends had joined our group. They looked more sober, and more nervous. "Come on, man," one of them said. "Let's go back to the room and party there."

"You go back to the room, asshole!" he said, loudly enough that every nearby table turned to him. "I do what I want!" His eyes swiveled around. "Do you people even understand how much Facebook paid us?"

The other guy pulled his arm. "You're gonna get us booted, man. Come on."

The big guy put his hand on the tech bro's shoulder. "This way, sir."

Gradually, the small group exited. There were scattered claps from watching diners as peace descended once again. As the waiter came back to check on us, Coombs said, "All that excitement gave me an appetite. Shall we order dinner?"

To hear him talk, nothing had ever happened.

I nodded, feeling the mood recalibrating to its former place. The energy between us returning. His skin glowed warm in the candlelight. The conversation came easily and the food, when it arrived, was predictably delicious. As we finished a shared chocolate lava cake and the last of the champagne, he rested his hand against mine.

The first time I felt his skin against my own. My skin prickled at the touch.

"I always like a short stroll after dinner," Coombs said. "Care to join me?"

"I can't think of any good reason to say no."

He insisted on paying the bill. Signing it to his room with an onyx and silver Montblanc pen that he slid from his jacket pocket. He pulled back the table slightly so I could stand, then rose in a smooth motion.

"Shall we?"

Together, we left the terrace and walked into the night.

13

The two of us walked side by side. His body brushing against mine. Down the sloping ground, away from the lights of the restaurant. Voices faded behind us. We passed the deserted, glowing pools in their manmade oasis, the surrounding trees now black curtains. The emerald and sapphire water shone with unearthly light. Above, a sliver of moon looked plastered onto a black sky tattooed by stars. A cold breeze rushed in from the ocean and I shivered, wishing I had brought a jacket.

Coombs must have noticed the shiver. The way he noticed everything. Without a word, he removed his jacket and draped it around my bare shoulders. It was strange to feel his jacket cloaking me. A more personal feeling than I would have thought. As though he had covered me with something beyond inanimate cloth. Cologne, rich and spicy with masculinity, drifted from soft fabric that was weightier than it had looked against his broad frame.

We left the last of the guest bungalows behind. The terrain falling away more steeply, our feet sending pebbles and little clods of soil rolling down the dirt path. The night was completely quiet. The stars overhead shone with intensity, no longer leashed by urban smog. Neither of us talked. Walking together, yet alone with our thoughts.

I wondered what the man next to me was thinking. I wondered if he wondered the same of me.

There was no one else in sight as we neared the cliffs.

My foot snagged painfully on a root and I lurched, feet skidding on the pebbly dirt as I flung out an arm for balance. Coombs's hand was on my arm, steadying me, holding me for a moment longer than necessary. His body very close to mine.

"Careful," he said. "It appears we've reached hazardous terrain."

I knelt and pulled off my heels. I wasn't used to heels. I hated wearing them and avoided doing so whenever possible. I regretted choosing them. Being off balance was the last thing I needed tonight. I stood, holding the shoes by their straps in one hand, welcoming the feeling of the cool dirt against my bare toes.

"Isn't hazardous terrain the most exciting kind?" I replied.

"For a certain type. Others prefer simply being able to stand on solid ground."

"What kind of terrain do *you* prefer?" I asked.

"The kind that allows me to spot the cliffs before I step over the edge."

"I think we're at the edge right now," I said.

We were. We slowed as we reached the sudden drop. It was the same place I had stood earlier in the day. Then, the sunshine and blue sky had endowed the ocean with a fierce postcard beauty. Now, at night, the landscape had a different power. With eyesight so limited, the rest of my senses sharpened. The noises of the ocean filled the air, the waves rushing and crashing into stone. I smelled brine, sea salt, the fecundity of moldering algae or rotting kelp that had washed up on the rocks. The easterly breeze whipped against us. The dagger-sharp rocks beneath us were invisible in the moonlight, but I could hear the ocean plunging and bucking around them. It was hard to tell how far below the water was. The sheer drop was at least a hundred feet straight down.

The two of us stood still, in silence. Taking in the night, the ocean. The breeze had strengthened and chilled. The wind scattered my hair and flattened my dress against my body as I crossed my arms against its strength. Tufts of pale clouds fled against the sky.

"How many ships, do you suppose, have met their ends upon these rocks?" Coombs mused. "How many sailors, hoping only for a safe harbor and a warm bed, have been flung into these icy currents?"

"That's hardly a romantic line of thought."

He turned from the water to regard me as if for the first time. His face looked different under the frail moon. Something colder in his eyes, or the way the shadows fell about his face. He looked older, more distant. At that moment he could have been an utter stranger.

"I never claimed to be a romantic," he reminded me. "Only you did."

"Should I feel deceived?"

He stepped closer to me. "I thought you enjoyed standing on hazardous terrain."

"Everyone has a limit."

Another step toward me. "Why do I feel we haven't yet reached yours?"

I couldn't help but be aware that the man in front of me was considerably bigger than I was. The six-inch height discrepancy was enhanced by my bare feet and his dress shoes. He must have outweighed me by sixty pounds if not more. The affable smile that had danced along his face and in his eyes all evening had disappeared.

Gone as cleanly as if he had removed a mask.

Our dinner, the restaurant, all felt very far away. Removed not by minutes and feet, but separated by endless years and infinite miles. We could have been the only two people in the world.

Who was I looking at? Who was I seeing?

This after-dinner stroll had become something else.

Or had it?

Nothing seemed clear. Was I standing here at the edge of this lonely cliff with a handsome, harmless con man? Or with someone of a more dangerous caliber?

And was my heart hammering with fear—or with excitement?

We both started as we heard a rustle from nearby bushes.

"Is someone there?" I whispered.

"Something," he answered. He was watching the bushes intently. "I'm not sure what."

Our question was answered as a dark, low form emerged and took shape. Its ears and paws and eyes had the lithe felinity of a cat, but the body and head were much larger. I saw a triangular head, tufted ears, and green eyes, watching us. A thick tail stirred lazily.

I took an involuntary step back. "What is it?"

"A mountain lion," Coombs answered in a low voice. "Stay still. Don't back away."

The mountain lion watched us for another moment. It was big—bigger than I would have thought. It had to be close to 150 pounds.

Its mouth opened in a yawn or silent growl. I saw fangs gleam under the strange, green light of its eyes.

Then it was gone.

My voice was quiet. "I've never seen one before."

"An omen?" Coombs wondered.

"Good or bad?"

"We'll have to wait and see what happens." He put his hand on my shoulder, the fingers resting comfortably on the fabric of his own jacket.

The other hand slipped against my hip.

I looked up at him. Acutely aware that the edge of the cliff was no more than a step from where I stood. I could hear the waves beating and crashing against the rocks, steady and vital as a heartbeat.

"What do you want from me?" I asked him.

He was very close to me. "I could ask you the same question."

"I told you. I want to know you better."

"Maybe I feel the same way."

I swallowed. It sounded loud in the still night. "So how does that happen?"

Without a word he stepped forward and kissed me.

I felt his lips against mine and filled with all kinds of contradictory wants and urges. Almost to my surprise, I realized I was returning his kiss, our lips interlocked, tongues probing, hard against each other as though in combat. Now he was pressed against me, one hand still on my hip, the other against the small of my back, his grip light but powerful. I didn't know this man at all—I knew him so well—I didn't know which was true. Dizzy, dangerous excitement pounded in my head.

Still in the kiss, bodies against each other, I felt his weight shift. Our feet rotated slightly, as though without intention. Then my back was to the black water behind me. My bare toes curled into the rocky ground. I could feel the wind, cold against my neck, stirring my hair like an unseen hand.

He stepped back. The kiss ended.

I pushed thoughts of Ethan away. Not now. I couldn't dare lose focus.

We watched each other.

"You're too close to the edge," Coombs warned.

I took a step toward him. Away from the water. "You're right. I was."

He looked at me searchingly. "If you had fallen, do you think I'd dive in after you?"

"I don't know what you'd do," I admitted.

"And that excites you? Not knowing?"

I answered almost reluctantly. "Maybe."

His eyes were still on mine. Probing, searching. "If I fell, do you know what I think?"

"What?"

"I think you'd try to save me without even thinking about it."

"Why do you think that?" I asked.

"I'm not sure," he said. "But I don't believe I'm wrong."

"So, what does that mean?"

His voice was light, flirtatious, but with something serious within, like a plain rubber cord hiding electric currents pulsing through copper innards. "It means I know something about you that you don't know about me. Which is an advantage."

"If that's true, lucky we seem to be so friendly."

"Lucky indeed," he agreed. "But they say it's easier to make friends than to keep them. Do you think we'll stay friends?"

I smiled and ran a finger down his cheek. His skin was warm and smooth, the faintest hint of stubble sandpapering my fingertips. "As long as we don't kill each other first."

He took my hand and brushed his lips to my skin as he returned my smile. "I've never minded a gamble if the stakes are worth the risk."

"Are you saying I'm worth a lot? Or risky?"

"Those two things go hand in hand. But you knew that already."

A spike of cold wind rushed in off the water, blowing my hair in a tangle around my face. I shivered even through the jacket that was still draped over me.

He took my hand. His fingers strong against mine. "Let's go."

"Where?"

"I think you should come to my room for a nightcap."

"Isn't it a bit late?"

"Some nights are meant to end early. Others aren't."

"What if I say no?"

"Then I'd wish you good night and thank you for a pleasant evening, of course." His congenial smile was back. As though the coldness in his eyes had never been there. The light had shifted, and his face, no longer shadowed and obscure, was open and affable.

"*Are* you saying no?" he asked.

I took his hand. "Lead the way."

We walked slowly up the path. I tried to place my bare feet carefully, wishing to avoid another stumble on terrain that seemed all too eager to trip me up.

I thought my room was nice. Coombs's put it to shame. His bungalow was easily double the size, with a separate suite-like living area away from the enormous, plush bed. My eyes took in the large Louis Vuitton suitcase, a row of suits and bright, perfectly pressed shirts hung neatly in the spacious closet. He accepted the jacket I handed back to him and placed it on a hanger.

"Do you always travel in such style?" I asked.

A smile lingered on his lips. "At the risk of sounding aged, I'm well past the days of roughing it."

"That must be nice."

"If you care about those things. Do you?"

I shrugged. "Not so much."

"Then you're staying at the wrong place."

"I never said I'm not enjoying myself." I placed my heels by the door. "Mind if I use your bathroom?"

"Of course."

In the bathroom, I squinted in the brightness of the vanity lights. The shower was lined with nacreous tiles the size of playing cards. All the toiletries I would have expected: European, high-end designer stuff. Several small bottles of cologne, an expensive shaving kit with a badger-hair brush set upright in a silver stand. There was a pearl-handled straight razor on the counter next to the sink. I opened it, brushing my finger sideways against the open blade and feeling the lethal keenness of the honed edge.

I closed the razor and put it back on the counter.

I took a brief look around the bathroom, unsurprised to see nothing out of the ordinary. It was just a very nice bathroom full of expensive toiletries. If I had been expecting to find a stack of incriminating documents taped to the showerhead, I'd have been disappointed. I flushed the toilet, put the seat down, ran the tap, and stepped out of the bathroom. Wondering if men did the same thing: pretending to use the bathroom when all they really wanted was a moment alone to look around and think.

Coombs stood by the bar cart, watching me cross the room toward him. He had rolled up his shirtsleeves, exposing blond-haired forearms corded with muscle, and he had put a record on the turntable. Fuzzy jazz filled the room, a trumpet cutting high above the swinging big band. Watching him as he reached for the bottles on the bar cart, I could have been looking at a liquor ad in some vintage *Esquire*.

"I didn't know you bartended," I said.

"And I don't know your poison."

"You haven't yet led me astray."

"No," he agreed. "Not yet."

I watched him muddle sugar cubes into two glasses. Ice cubes rattled and bottles clinked as he poured and stirred. He took an orange from a large welcome basket spilling over with fruit and chocolate and used the small blade of a wine opener to slice two curling twists from its skin.

"Old-fashioned?" I asked.

He nodded and extended a glass. "Cheers."

I raised my glass. "What are we drinking to, universal prosperity or world peace?"

He shook his head. "I'm a pragmatist. I prefer toasting to events that might actually happen."

"And what would those be?"

His eyes locked into mine. "To new friendships, exciting possibilities, and many more surprises."

We clinked our glasses.

Drank.

Watching each other.

He stepped over to me and ran his hand through my hair, fingers grazing the back of my neck. When he kissed me for the second time it was a softer kiss than the first had been. Searching, lingering, restrained. I felt his nails drift down the small of my back as my free hand ran along his side, feeling the muted strength of his body. Feeling his hands on me. As though without a single word he understood me.

I broke away after a moment, feeling guiltier than after the first kiss. His hand left my skin. I put the guilt somewhere far away in my mind. I'd find it later. Not now.

He picked up his glass and took a sip. "Everything okay?"

"Maybe we could just talk for a bit."

"Of course. Anything in particular?" Behind him, through the unshaded window, night hung like a blackout curtain. He smiled, teasing. "I could ask all sorts of brilliant questions: How many siblings you have, or where you grew up, or perhaps your favorite color, or what you do for work."

"Brother. Bolinas. Blue. Bookstore."

"You work in a bookstore," he said. "Now there's a surprise."

I sat on the edge of the bed. "Why does that surprise you?"

"You strike me more as the action type."

I crossed my legs. "I could tell you I'm a Navy SEAL. Would that be more enticing?"

"Anyone can tell a dime store lie. To me, the truth is always most exciting."

"If that's the case, you must associate with very interesting people."

"Not really." He tossed the orange into the air and caught it. "I'm more of a loner."

"You?" It was my turn to be skeptical. "You seem like the opposite of a loner."

"One can't always trust appearances. I'm sure you know that by now?" Ice in the bucket rattled as he added several cubes to his glass.

"I agree," I said. "One can't. Not always."

"One also can't always trust new friends who pop up in unexpected places."

I smiled. "What's that supposed to mean?"

"It means," Coombs said, "that I daresay we know each other well enough to be perhaps a touch franker. Wouldn't you agree?"

"I'm always honest. I haven't told you a single untrue word the entire day."

The smile was still on his face, his tone still light and teasing. Like when he had asked me my favorite color. "And yet I get the distinct feeling that you aren't exactly pouring your heart out to me. Why is that, I wonder?"

I tried to keep my tone light as well. "Wouldn't that bore you just about to death?"

"Nothing about you bores me."

My handbag lay on the bed next to me. I inched an arm closer to it.

"I'm flattered to hear that."

"In fact," he continued, "I find myself intrigued by you."

"You know just what to say to a girl."

My hand inched closer.

Almost there.

"And you seemed so . . . familiar," he added. His teeth showed white, the smile flickering on his face like flame. "I couldn't for the life of me think why. I never forget a face."

"Neither do I. And we've never met before today."

"No," he agreed. "We haven't. And yet I realized I knew you just the same."

I recrossed my legs, my fingers barely a handspan from my bag.

So close.

"How could that be?" I asked.

"A mystery, I suppose. Perhaps one day we'll solve it." Coombs was reaching back in the bucket for more ice. "And also, kindly stop fidgeting about so much. No need to reach into that bag just this minute."

His hand emerged from the ice bucket holding a nickel-plated revolver.

He clicked the hammer back with his thumb.

"And I really do insist."

14

He put his drink down on the counter and scooped my handbag up from the bed, taking care to keep several feet between us. His gun never wavered. He looked comfortable holding it. Like a man who had held one many times before. He ran a hand through my handbag, never taking his eyes off me, and fished out my subcompact Beretta. His thumb found the release. The magazine fell away and Coombs worked the slide, careful to keep his revolver on me while he did. The remaining round ejected from the chamber and landed on the floor with a forlorn little click.

He put the empty Beretta down and kept searching. He didn't seem surprised to have found the gun, but let out a low whistle when he came up with my stun gun and roll of electrical tape. The stun gun was small, not much bigger than a box of staples, one end curving inward. Two metal barbs set an inch apart protruded from the curved end like stingers on a scorpion's tail.

"What kind of party were you planning?" Coombs asked, arching an eyebrow.

I didn't say anything.

"Don't sulk," he advised, pocketing the stun gun. "It's nothing personal."

"What are you going to do to me?"

"Hopefully nothing bad. Hopefully we just continue our pleasant conversation."

"You never told me your favorite color," I pointed out.

He didn't laugh. "I need to know why you were following me and who sent you. To start off, that will do nicely."

"What if I don't want to talk about those things?"

He sighed. "Then, I'm afraid, it's going to be a long night for you." For the first time he stepped closer. The roll of black tape in one hand and the revolver in the other.

"Lie down on your stomach," he instructed.

"No."

His eyes were almost sympathetic. "For whatever it's worth, and whether you believe it or not, I'm a man who has always held violence to be the option of last recourse."

I said nothing.

"But," he continued, "I'm afraid that based on the contents of your purse, I'm not going to feel comfortable until we get your hands taped."

I said, "If you don't feel comfortable, that's your problem."

Coombs sighed in annoyance. "I can't imagine what it must be like dating you. The poor sops. Are you always so mulish? Now turn over and lie down," he said again.

I made no effort to move.

"Well, we can't stand here all night," he said, "so I'm going to give you a choice. Either you allow me to tape your hands, or"—he pulled the stun gun out of his pocket with the hand holding the tape—"I'm going to have to use this as a means of encouragement." His eyes flicked down to the device, taking in a number stenciled in bright yellow on the side. "I've never felt seventy-five thousand volts of electricity myself, thank heavens, so you'll have to tell me all about it. Once you can talk again, of course. The choice is yours. I hope you can be reasonable."

We both knew what was going to happen, so I didn't argue further.

"Fine."

I lay on my stomach. I didn't like the feeling. A helpless feeling. The plushness of the mattress and the clean, laundered smell of the sheets pressed against my face seemed to worsen my plight. Like house arrest in a mansion, the comfort just mockery disguised. Pressing against a cold concrete floor would have been more physically uncomfortable. It also would have felt more honest.

"Put your hands behind your back and cross your wrists," Coombs instructed.

I complied without argument. I had already known he was going to tell me to do that. It was the obvious demand. I would have made it myself. I had already run through every possible scenario I could think of. None of them looked good for me.

"Now I'm aware," Coombs said, "that in the next few seconds you might take my proximity as an invitation to the tempting possibilities of physical rebellion. If that's the case, please do remind your more tempestuous side that there is a loaded, cocked revolver several inches from the back of your head, and any sudden movement on your part might prove sufficient to trigger an outcome that neither of us—but especially you—desires."

"Do you always talk this much?" I asked him.

"Does my loquaciousness bother you?" He laughed as he knelt, a leg on either side of me. I felt a claustrophobic rush as his weight pinned me down. "Those fortunate enough to have a natural talent should not stifle it, I've always felt. I was never going to get paid to kick a football or play the saxophone, but early on in life I found that I could talk a bear out of a tree by promising honey when it reached the ground. One should cultivate their talents."

As he talked he was wrapping the electrical tape around my wrists in short, precise motions. The tape made sticky, tearing sounds as he jerkily unspooled the roll. He hadn't been exaggerating about the revolver. I could feel the barrel pressing into the back of my neck. Right where his fingers had caressed me earlier that night. Shivery-cold at first from the ice bucket, then less so, as my body heat warmed the metal.

"Do you plan on hurting me?" I could feel the tape tightening around my wrists in relentless figure-eights, back and forth. It was already impossible for me to wriggle my wrists even the slightest bit.

"That's up to you," he said. "It's not my wish—but I need some questions answered."

"How about after we talk? What then? Do you let me go?"

"I'm afraid that depends on how satisfied I am with your answers. Particularly whether you can keep up the admirable candor that you've displayed all evening." I felt a sharp tug as Coombs severed the tape behind me. "Despite your mulish tendencies, please don't try to kick me," he added, "while I do your ankles. That little stun gun of yours is very close at hand."

I felt his hands, strong and sure on my bare legs as he wrapped layers of tape around my ankles. My dress had ridden up my thighs but there wasn't much I could do about that. He used plenty of tape. A cautious man. By the time he finished, my ankles felt like they were conjoined by cement.

"Much better," Coombs said, satisfied. "I apologize for that intrusion, my dear, but in the circumstances such drastic action really did seem necessary to ensure continued peace between us." I felt his hands on my shoulders, helping to roll me into a seated position against the headboard, my hands tied behind me and my legs stretched in front. I hated being tied up. Bad memories pushed against me. I didn't show it. I didn't want to give any hint of fear.

This man knew too much about me as it was.

Now that I was immobilized, Coombs seemed to relax. He stood, found his drink, and brought my glass over to me, holding it to my lips. "No reason to let a good drink go to waste."

I didn't see any reason why I should refuse. I took a big sip of the cold, sweet bourbon. The record had clicked off. He flipped it, placed the needle back on the vinyl, added bourbon to his glass, and pulled an armchair over to the edge of the bed next to me as music once again filled the room. He still held the revolver, but the barrel was no longer pointed at my head. Except for the gun and the tape, anyone walking in would have assumed two lovers were enjoying a pleasant, romantic evening together. All the scene needed was for him to light the fireplace.

As if reading my mind, he smiled down at me. "Aside from a few trivial details, we look the very picture of domestic bliss, don't we? We could pose for a catalog shoot if I put my gun down and we put on matching bathrobes."

"I'm not feeling a lot of domestic bliss right now," I said. "Just to keep being candid. Not a lot at all."

He shrugged. "It was a thought. But you do look quite gorgeous in that dress. I've been wanting to tell you that all night."

"We can skip the compliments. You've already got me in bed."

He laughed. "As you wish. Let's talk."

"Fine," I agreed. "Let's talk, then. Why did you run from San Francisco? What spooked you?"

He laughed again, showing strong, white teeth. "I must admit you have a certain temerity. I've barely finished tying you hand and foot, I'm sitting here with a loaded pistol—and somehow you're the one interrogating me."

"I might as well get something out of this," I retorted.

"Nothing *spooked* me, if you must know. Given my line of work, and who I was dealing with, I knew I was quite possibly being followed. I wanted to get a better sense of the quality of the opposition. Any fool could have followed a cab to the airport. Not everyone would have picked up the trail I left. Whispering to hotel employees, cab drivers, my name on a plane charter . . ."

I remembered my thought at SFO. Like a hare leaving biscuits for the dogs.

"Not to sound immodest, but if I was *really* trying to disappear," Coombs continued, "it would take the resources of a decent-size law enforcement agency to even have a hope of tracking me. I'm sure you're good enough at following people—but I'm *very* good at running. And I daresay I've been running since you were practically in the cradle. I chose to leave a light trail. I could have equally chosen to leave a heavier one—or none at all."

"Why would you want anyone to be able to follow you?" I wondered.

He paused for a few seconds, thinking. "I might as well tell you that I have an extraordinarily important meeting tomorrow—something planned for a long time, that must go off perfectly, without a hitch. If someone *was* watching me, I wanted my sudden departure to flush them out. Force them to chase me so fast they wouldn't have time to think. It doesn't do any good trying to go about important business with unseen adversaries watching—or interfering. Much better to be able to see them move."

"How did you know it was me?"

His eyes, unless I was mistaken, expressed real fondness. "I hope you know that tonight I was being as honest with you as you were being with me."

"Honest?"

"Our connection," he answered at once. "That wasn't idle dinner-table blather. I meant that. You know it—you feel it too, just as I do." He spoke his next sentence with great deliberateness. "*The two of us are different from every single other person here.*"

I didn't say anything.

"Besides," he continued, "a beautiful, solitary woman showing up the same day I checked in? Unlike some, I *do* stare a gift horse in the mouth, every time—close enough to count the teeth. I knew I'd seen you somewhere. I just couldn't place you from the InterContinental until it came to me later, over dinner."

I was thinking about whatever meeting he had mentioned. "Why Monterey? What's down here?"

Coombs grinned. "People come from far and wide to stay at the Cypress. Who am I, to turn down the delights of ocean-side golf and a fried abalone sandwich? Don't I seem like a fellow who appreciates a good vacation?"

I ignored his answer. "Why here, though? What's here?"

The Cheshire grin stayed on his face even as he shook his head. "I'm afraid this is where your questions end and mine begin."

"I'm not done asking."

His voice held tolerant exasperation. "Then I'm afraid that *you* should have been the one to tie *me* up."

I said, "There's still time for that."

"First off, an easy one. Who hired you?"

"No comment."

He nodded toward the stun gun on the counter next to him. "I was forth-coming with you. I expect you to return the courtesy."

"And my clients expect privacy."

He shrugged. "I know it was one of the Johannessen brats, anyway. I'm just not sure which one. Maybe all of them. They're a real pack of silver-spoon hyenas, the whole bunch. As a self-made man, perhaps I'm biased, but I per-sonally feel they're a walking billboard for the dangers of inherited money. If they ever stopped chewing each other's tails they'd be dumb enough and rich enough to be genuinely dangerous." His eyes were serious. "And I assure you that whatever they're paying you, it won't be worth a fraction of the trou-ble it brings."

I said nothing.

"What did they want you to do to me?" Coombs asked. His voice was sharper.

I kept quiet.

He picked up the stun gun, turning it over in his hand, inspecting it like some dug-up artifact or broken coin from a long-past era. The small device fit easily into his big hand.

He pressed the switch.

Instantly an evil blue arc crackled between the two scorpion-stinger points. He let the stun gun drift closer to me. The arc of electricity only a few inches away.

"You need to answer me," he said. The charm had left his voice as com-pletely as a train departed from a station. "I really don't want to hurt you, but I'm dealing with matters that are more extreme and urgent than you realize. Some rather large events are moving rather quickly, and despite my chipper mien, these circumstances have placed me under a certain stress. I can't afford to let you off the hook. I wish I could, but I can't. I need to know every-thing you know."

The blue arc had drifted very close to my face. "I'll use this in three seconds if you don't start talking, and I'm afraid right now I don't give two pence for those long legs or that winsome smile. *Three.*"

I tried to flinch away from the electricity but there was nowhere to go.

"*Two.*"

I said nothing.

"*One.*"

The jagged arc was almost touching my chin.

"Okay," I said. "You win."

He took his finger off the switch and the crackling electricity disappeared. "I'm listening."

"You've been stealing from a powerful, wealthy family. What did you think they were going to do? Nothing?"

Coombs frowned. "I don't *steal*. Please don't treat what I do as though I'm some common thief. You might as well compare the fellows who pulled off the Great Train Robbery to a pimply urchin shoplifting razor blades from a pharmacy."

"You asked. I'm answering."

"Very well," he acknowledged. "Go ahead, please. I won't interrupt."

"You were running around with the family matriarch, embarrassing the family. That was bad enough—but then you tried to blackmail her."

Surprise that he didn't bother to hide flickered in his eyes. "I was black-mailing her? *That's* what they told you?"

"Weren't you?"

He was watching me with a thoughtful expression. As though trying to decide whether to say something, or how much of it to say. He reached a de-cision. "You have no idea what you're mixed up with. If you think all of this is me trying to coerce a couple extra Swiss watches out of an old lady's pocket-book, you're not even in the right universe. There are deeper elements that go far beyond whatever flimflam they fed you."

"So tell me."

He frowned. "I'm afraid not."

"Maybe I can help you."

He laughed. "Says the woman trussed up like a chicken."

"Then untie me."

He shook his head. "I'm afraid that's impossible. I work alone."

"So do I."

"Then you understand."

I said, "I understand there are exceptions to every rule."

The slight trace of regret on his face could have been real. I couldn't tell. "In a different life, perhaps. The fact is that you were hired to be my adversary. Now you say you want to be my friend. How should I know who you really are? And since you're my captive at the moment, any reassurances you offer can't be believed, due to obvious self-interest."

"Okay. I can't help you and you can't trust me. Now what?"

Coombs looked uncertain for the first time all night. "I've been wondering that. We're at something of an impasse. I need to be able to go about my business unimpeded. I'm on an urgent time line. Which means that you cannot be free to go about *your* business, since your business seems to be following and obstructing me." He thought some more. "The pragmatic thing would be to suffocate you with a pillow, drag you down to that cliff, and toss your body off the edge. By the time they found you, there's not a cop in a hundred miles who wouldn't assume it to be accident or suicide. Or sharks, of course. From a purely logical standpoint, that's the best way to work this out."

I pictured the waves crashing into the jagged rocks. There wouldn't even be much of a body to recover. The coroner's office might never even get to offer an opinion.

"You'd get caught," I said.

"No," he replied with great seriousness. "At the risk of morbidity, I've thought it over quite a bit this evening, and I truly don't think I would."

"People know I'm down here."

"I doubt that. You work alone—as you said." He paused, then continued. "But I really prefer not to have to do that. I meant what I said about violence being the last resort."

"Then let me go."

"Also impossible, I'm afraid. There's a lack of trust between us at the present moment. I can't let you free." He frowned. "It's a conundrum, it really is."

I'd never liked debates where I couldn't weigh in. Especially when my health was at stake. I took advantage of his indecision to buck my hips, sweep my legs up, and kick the gun out of his hand. He didn't have time to be surprised. There was a tinkle of broken glass as his drink fell to the floor.

I wasn't done. Legs still in the air, I angled my knees out in a diamond shape and got my legs around his neck in a crude triangle choke. For all his caution, he hadn't taped higher than my ankles. A mistake. I squeezed my thighs together and watched his face redden as he tried unsuccessfully to pry my legs apart. The hem of my dress slid up as I squeezed with all my strength, feeling the delicate fabric tear as he thrashed and clawed at my legs, growing increasingly desperate for air.

I didn't know exactly where I wanted to end up, but I had decided that Coombs being momentarily unconscious was a good start. Then I could free my hands and deal with him.

I squeezed harder.

Although he was gasping for oxygen, he was strong and clever. He jerked sideways, allowing his weight to carry him off the side of the bed. With my hands taped behind me and my legs locked around his neck I had no choice but to follow.

I slid onto the floor, taking out the night table with a painful *thump*, but I kept my legs around his neck, squeezing for all I was worth. His face was scarlet, but he was still far from unconscious. He thrashed and flung his weight about.

Then I saw why Coombs had thrown himself off the bed.

The revolver had landed on the floor. It lay just out of his arm's reach. I watched his hand stretching toward the gun. I squeezed harder and tried to jerk him away, but he was strong and desperate. A bad combination. He had enough energy to continue reaching, even as I felt him weakening for lack of air.

His fingers grazed the revolver.

It seemed an open question of what would happen first: Coombs losing consciousness or shooting me.

We never found out.

The door opened and four men walked in.

15

My first thought was that our struggle had triggered a noise complaint from another guest. Two of the men were obviously security. Big, hardened, watchful. One was taller and one was shorter but both looked like they spent more time in the gym than in church. Each of them had a tattoo across the back of the right hand. A fanged snake coiled around a five-pointed star. The third man looked very different. He had a slender, reedy build, glasses, a sparse mustache, and thinning hair combed in a severe side part. He wore a gray suit two decades out of fashion, all padded shoulders and wide, pleated pants, and a lavender paisley tie as broad as a cutting board.

The three of them could have been a night manager and a couple of security goons. Not perfect. It didn't explain how fast they'd arrived after the noise began. Or why a place this nice would have security that looked like they'd be more at home guarding a back-alley poker game. But enough mental shoehorning could make it work.

The fourth man was different.

The fourth man was hugely fat. He must have weighed more than three hundred pounds. Black cowboy boots made out of what looked to be glinting, pebbled stingray added several inches to his height. A mop of tightly curled black hair frothed above swarthy skin and a pair of raucous black eyebrows seemed, like Pyramus and Thisbe at their wall, to be separated by only the tiniest of margins, and equally eager to rejoin. A giant diamond stud sparkled in his left ear. His broad, jowly face grinned at nothing in particular and his right hand bore the same snake and star tattoo as the other pair. He looked like a cross between an out-of-shape pirate and some kind of crypto-currency billionaire.

Coombs and I had stopped fighting as the door opened. My legs fell away and he rubbed his neck, gulping in fresh oxygen, the revolver on the floor, forgotten. Both of us sat up, startled and watchful.

I eyed the con man. Had he somehow gotten word to friends of his? His expression told me a lot. There was a new emotion on his face. Not happiness or relief. Not the delighted look of a man seeing his buddies coming to help at exactly the right moment. Something else.

Fear.

I wasn't sure if I liked that.

The fat man laughed as he saw how I was taped up. He spoke with a heavy accent. "So kinky, Dr. Coombs. I had no idea of your elaborate taste." He bent to take a closer look at me. He was so fat that bending seemed its own challenge. "And she's a pretty one, too, very pretty. Does she charge extra for you to tie her up?"

He saw the silver-plated revolver and picked it up with an appreciative whistle. Coombs's face tightened as the barrel drifted toward him. "So kinky," the fat man said again. "Bondage, gunplay . . . I'm impressed. I thought you would be more vanilla in your tastes. A man full of surprises." He looked down at me. "I'm curious. What do you charge for this kind of fun?"

I considered my reply. There might be worse things than him thinking I was an escort. "Depends on the work," I answered. "Sliding scale."

"Who do you work for? I know them all."

"I freelance."

His eyes were all over me, taking in my torn dress and unshielded legs. "Well, come find us if you ever need a job. You're old, but still pretty enough."

"What are you doing here?" Coombs muttered.

The fat man turned to Coombs like he had already forgotten my existence. "You see, I got tired of all the talk. So much talk, with you, endless, so frustrating. I had an idea—didn't I, Albert?"

The reedy man in the boxy suit nodded. "A very good idea."

"Dr. Coombs—do you know what my idea was?"

"No," said Coombs in a strained voice.

"I thought, too much talk—enough! Why not go pay a visit to our doctor? So we can finally meet. What do you think of my idea?"

Coombs looked like he was struggling to keep a measured tone. "How did you find me here?"

The fat man grinned. "This is *my* town, Dr. Coombs. We have eyes and ears all over, everywhere, all eager to talk, to be helpful. Besides—we were expecting you."

"*Tomorrow*. I had thought we had agreed to choose a meeting place tomorrow."

The fat man laughed. "But I wanted to see you *now*. I'm not a perfect man, I admit. After all, I'm only human. I have flaws, shortcomings, as do we all. And one of these flaws is impatience. I am afflicted with great impatience."

Coombs started to climb to his feet but the fat man shook his head. "Stay, for a moment. You're so comfortable." The revolver drifted down the length of Coombs's body. "Another failing of mine is my temper. I've always suffered from a bad temper. Why, I don't know. Genetics, perhaps." The revolver continued to drift as he spoke. Coombs watched the barrel move. "Even as a young child, my mother was always begging me, please, calm down, such rage, you can't live with such anger in you. She called me her *little thunderstorm*. But try as I might, I couldn't get rid of this temper of mine. It's here to stay, I'm afraid." He held up a hand with a thespian's flourish. "Like my hand, my fingers. Part of me."

Coombs said, "We had agreed to meet tomorrow. That was the plan."

"*Fuck* your plan," the fat man exclaimed, then seemed to catch himself. He smiled down. "You see? There I go again. My doctor tells me I must control it, this terrible temper of mine. He uses such fancy words, anger management, impulse control . . . I'm a simple man, I never graduated high school. What do I know about such things? He says all this anger is not good for my heart, unhealthy, he even suggests pills, medication. Modern medicine—it can do anything, yes? Anything except save us from the grave, I suppose." The fat man grinned at his own words, eyes shrewd and wicked. "But who knows what these tiny little pills do? Maybe they turn my brain to mush, make me sleepy and stupid . . . who can tell? So, I told my doctor, the pills, no thank you, I'll have to live with this ferocious temper of mine, this lava, bubbling away in my heart. I'll take my chances, we must all live with the consequences of the decisions we make. Isn't that right, Albert?"

"Absolutely, Mr. Z," said the reedy man from behind him. A real yes-man.

As if following my thought, the fat man explained, "Albert is my accountant." His voice contained pride, as though he was telling us about a fancy new car. "When there's money at stake, I like him close to me. He knows so much about money, figures, finance. Like a human calculator. He attended the MIT Sloan School of Management—the very best."

"You're too kind," Albert said. He tugged at his tie modestly. "Far too kind."

"And I didn't tell my doctor this," Mr. Z continued, "but I even thought to myself—well, perhaps, every gray cloud has a silver lining, yes? Perhaps this rotten, nasty temper of mine, this impulsiveness, can be a virtue, in its own way? Like tonight. For me to think, why wait, why go on, with this endless talking, this endless negotiating, this bellyache? Why? Why not pay a visit to our new friend and see what we can accomplish in person?"

He tapped the barrel of the revolver against his hand. "Cutting to the chase, I believe you call it. Is that right, Albert? This expression?"

Albert's voice sounded, dependable as an echo. "Absolutely correct, Mr. Z. Cutting to the chase it is."

Coombs's eyes reminded me of something. An elementary-school field trip to a science museum, watching as a mouse was placed in a python's tank. The mouse's glistening eyes, its quivering whiskers.

Coombs's face was like the mouse.

"You know that this was not entirely in my hands," he said. "Banks, wire transfers—these things take time. We're almost there."

The fat man ambled over to the welcome basket of fruit. He put down the revolver and rummaged around, coming up with a packet of salted almonds and a tin of bonbons. He tore open the almonds and ate them in two handfuls, licked salty crumbs from his lips, and turned to the bonbons, prying up the lid with a fat thumb. "You don't mind, Dr. Coombs, that I'm eating your pretty little chocolates?"

"Please," Coombs managed. "Be my guest."

The fat man gave a big booming laugh. "Your guest! Exactly! A play on words! Because here, in this fancy, beautiful hotel, we *are* your guests! And later, perhaps I can return the hospitality. Perhaps you can be *my* guest." Already halfway through the chocolates, Mr. Z stooped to the bar cart and rooted up a bottle of Belvedere. He poured vodka into a glass, scooped into the ice bucket, and looked up, disappointed. "It's melted."

"Happy to step out and get more," Coombs suggested.

The fat man liked that. He laughed. "I bet you would be. So happy, maybe you'd fly all the way to London for more ice, wouldn't you?" He sipped the warm vodka, shaking his head as though conducting an unpleasant chore. "Vodka without ice is like . . ." He stopped. "I'm stuck! What is it like, Dr. Coombs? Tell your guest what it's like. You're such a talker, so smooth, so slick—I'm sure you have the perfect analogy for my warm vodka."

Coombs stared at him as though stuck in a bad dream. "I—I'm afraid . . ."

"Your tongue, Dr. Coombs! If you don't use it, I will take it for myself. Vodka without ice is like . . ."

Coombs lipped his lips. "I don't know, perhaps . . . like a fox hunt without foxes?"

Mr. Z broke into uproarious laughter. "Exactly! Vodka without ice is like a fox hunt without the little fucking orange foxes!" He tilted the vodka into his mouth, set the empty glass down, licked his lips. "Yet sometimes we must accept that things cannot be perfect. Like warm vodka. Not perfect, but still, I drink it, because it is better than no vodka."

He walked back over to Coombs. "A speechwriter," he said, still chuckling. "You missed your calling, my friend. Such a way with words. Like Albert with numbers. Such talent. You could have worked for a senator or mayor, maybe even a president? Writing their bullshit for them, making it sound so pretty. Such a waste."

"I'm telling you, all this can be easily resolved! We all want the same thing. There's no need for these theatrics." Coombs started to get to his feet.

Mr. Z gave an almost imperceptible nod, and one of the bodyguards stepped forward and punched Coombs full in the face.

The blow made an unpleasant smacking sound. Coombs sprawled onto the ground with a cry of pain. The bodyguard kicked him once in the ribs, then again, curling him into a ball, the impact sounding dense and dull. The bodyguard didn't look angry or excited or happy. His face held the same level of dispassion and mild exertion as someone doing assisted chin-ups at a YMCA.

The bodyguard caught another look from Mr. Z and stepped back.

Coombs sat up slowly and spat red onto the floor. He rubbed his mouth and breathed heavily. "Christ," he said again, his voice thick with pain. "You split my lip open, you goddamn brownshirt."

The jolly mirth had disappeared from the fat man's eyes. There was an apple in the welcome basket and he munched it with noisy horse bites. "Is that too much *theatrics* for you, my friend?"

Coombs rubbed his lip. There was more blood. "I'll need stitches. What the hell was that about?" He touched his fingertips to his torso and winced in pain.

"That was a stamp on your passport, Dr. Coombs."

The con man stared up. "Have you gone batty? Passport? Stamp?"

Mr. Z looked down at Coombs, a child watching a bug. "You've left your world, my friend. Your fancy fucking world of pleasant conversations and tuxedo dinners and fruit baskets. Now you're in our world. Someone like you shouldn't be down here, with us. You should have stayed where you were comfortable. But you found your way here, and now you're here, and I want you to understand this."

"What do you want?" Coombs asked. His lip had already begun to swell and there was a slur to his words.

"You know what we want. We want what we've wanted all along."

"And you'll get it! Good God, man, do you not understand that? That's why I'm here! That's why they sent me! To facilitate—to hurry everything along. You know this!"

"No, not anymore." The fat man chomped away at the vanishing apple, turning it in his hand for fresh new angles. "You see, I've decided to fire you—as a *facilitator*." He held up a hand, silencing Coombs. "But not to worry. You see, there's a new job for you, a new role. Admittedly, it's a different one, slightly different, but I promise that you will not go to waste." He bit too deep into the core, wrinkled his nose, and spat a black seed onto the floor.

"A new role? What are you—"

"Now you'll be a hostage, my good doctor. Consider it a promotion. You're even more important. Tonight is Wednesday. Tomorrow morning, we'll give you a telephone, and you'll start making calls and explaining to your friends that the deadline has changed. I'll give you one day. Until tomorrow. And if we don't have what we're asking for, I'll watch while these two"—he gestured to the stone-faced pair of bodyguards flanking him—"chain a fifty-pound cement block around your ankles and toss you into Monterey Bay."

"That's not enough time!" Coombs exploded. "You know that! It's out of my hands! Everything was going to be settled by next week!"

The fat man watched him, unmoved. "Two months ago it was next week. A month ago it was next week. A week ago it was next week." His voice took on a mocking singsong. "Always *next week, next week, next week*." He leaned down and wiped his hands against Coombs's white-and-blue shirt. The chocolate left dark smears against the elegant cotton.

Coombs didn't move. Didn't even bother to look at his ruined shirt.

"Sometimes," Mr. Z continued, "when something is stuck, it needs—what's the expression—a kick in the pants. To move along. Maybe you and your fancy San Francisco friends took me seriously, maybe you didn't. Maybe you thought I was a foolish high school dropout, someone who could be played with and intimidated by shiny talk and big numbers. Now you'll take me seriously."

"I took you seriously," Coombs said. "All along. You know that. I know who you are." His voice was strained and anxious. "I need more time. You know how these people bank. The money's all over the globe and it gets flagged by the banks if they don't break it into pieces. We've started the process but it takes time. You'll kill me, fine—but you won't get what you want if I'm gone."

The fat man tossed his apple core to the ground. "Are you playing me, Dr. Coombs?"

Coombs's hair was disheveled and blood trickled from his lip, but he held the fat man's eyes. "Give me until Monday. Just until then."

Mr. Z considered, then said, "Two days. Friday. If I don't have my money by Friday night, my cobblers will fit you for concrete shoes." His small, piggish eyes wandered the room. "Such a fancy place. So expensive, everything, such beautiful taste, such luxury. You're a gentleman, my friend." His small eyes took in the closet, the row of colorful shirts and suits gleaming with the dull shine of expensive fabric. "I don't dress as nice as you, Dr. Coombs. I don't stay at this kind of fancy place. I don't think places like this are made for people like me. But that's okay. I have my own places, my own preferences. A simple man, like I said." He gestured to Coombs's suitcase, a brown hardshell stamped with golden, interlocked letters. "Louis Vuitton, correct?"

Coombs said, "Yes."

The fat man looked satisfied. "See, I know a little about these things. Not as much as you, but a little. A beautiful suitcase, so elegant. Go!" he abruptly instructed Coombs. "We will talk more later."

Coombs stared. "Go where?"

"Inside." A thick finger jabbed at the suitcase. "We will pack you, now."

"You've got to be kidding."

"I like to sometimes joke, it's true, but now I'm not joking. Go into that suitcase."

Coombs didn't budge. "No. Absolutely not. This is insane."

Mr. Z's eyes flashed. "You don't get it!" he shouted. "You still don't understand! In *your* world, your fancy fucking world with cocktail parties and nice polite manners, yes, maybe it's insane for men to be put into suitcases like old stinking laundry. In my world, these things make perfect sense. A man can be packed just as easily as the clothes he wears. No one thinks that's so crazy."

"I refuse," Coombs said.

"I see. You refuse." The fat man jerked his head toward the bodyguard who had hit Coombs. "Show him what we do to people who refuse us."

Without a word the bodyguard unbuckled something that had been strapped to his thigh. He straightened, holding the object casually in one hand. I saw the menacing star and snake on his skin, a lurid scar across his brow, the knuckles on his right hand red and raw from having been driven into Coombs's face.

He held the object up. We all took in what he held.

A hatchet.

Small, light, maybe three or four pounds, with a black rubberized grip. The kind of all-purpose tool that someone would take camping. Versatile, practical. Perfect for chopping firewood or trimming marshmallow sticks or slamming a tent peg into the dirt. The stainless-steel edge was honed to a barely visible line.

We all watched the hatchet.

"You'll go into the suitcase or he will chop pieces off you until you fit." Mr. Z shook his head, suddenly bored. "I'm hungry. Pack up and we'll go eat. We can get seafood. A place I like is nearby, it stays open late. If it was earlier, we could sit with cold beers and almost watch the boats bring our fish right up. Very fresh, very tasty." He nodded to the two big men. "Help our new guest. If he resists, chop his toes first, then his fingers."

Putting a grown man into a suitcase turned out to be easier than I would have thought. Maybe because, with the hatchet out, Coombs remained as limp and docile as a drugged animal. I got a last glimpse of his figure, curled into an awkward seahorse shape, breaths coming quick and frightened. Then the suitcase closed over him. One of the bodyguards latched the clasps and heaved it upright with a grunt.

Closed and upright, it looked like any other piece of expensive designer luggage. Impossible to tell there was a terrified man contained within.

"Where are you taking him?" I asked.

Mr. Z looked at me as though he had forgotten I was in the room. "It's better for your health that you don't ask questions like that." He paused, as though remembering something. "Ah, he did not pay you yet. I see." A doughy hand pulled a gold money clip out of his pocket. Several hundred-dollar bills flicked down at me. "There. Now you're paid, and you didn't even have to take your clothes off. But because you ask such nosy questions, I will let you decide how to untie yourself." He started to the door, one of the bodyguards rolling the suitcase behind him.

They left as abruptly as they had appeared. I watched the door swing shut. I was already moving as it closed.

To my relief, I managed to open the straight razor in the bathroom without slicing my hands open. Soon enough, I had managed to cut away the black tape binding my wrists. My feet were free a few seconds later. I took a hurried look around the room as I repacked my handbag. I had to move fast if I wanted to catch up to them.

It wasn't only about the Johannessen family anymore. No longer about a job I had been hired to do. My sense of fairness had been poked. Whatever his past sins might have been, I hadn't seen anything to make me believe Coombs deserved to be tortured and dropped to the bottom of Monterey Bay. I hadn't liked seeing Coombs being beaten. Hurting him had been gratuitous. Disproportionate. I thought of the hatchet. The expression on Coombs's face. The fear in his eyes.

Another reason, half-admitted, circled. Our dinner together. The way he had understood me, intuitively, at once, like no one I'd ever met. The feeling of his fingertips tracing down the back of my neck. The knowingness in his eyes. I wanted to learn what was going on. I also wanted to learn more about who he was. How he knew me so well.

I wasn't exactly sure how guilty I was supposed to feel for wanting that.
I think you'd try to save me without even thinking about it.

Well, he had gone off a cliff, now. No question about that. The terrain hazardous in a way that neither of us had understood. A fall perhaps even more dangerous than against those wave-lashed rocks and swirling currents.
I think you'd try to save me without even thinking about it.

Despite the urgency of the moment, I hastened to my own room first. I had no desire to get on a motorcycle in high heels and a torn dress. It took me under two minutes to change back into my jeans and boots. I was probably fifteen minutes behind them. Not great. But not impossible. Monterey wasn't Los Angeles. I had a chance.

I was halfway out the door when the phone in my room started ringing.

I looked at the phone. No one should be calling. No one except Jess knew I was here. Not even Ethan. Not even my brother. I had been told to follow Coombs. Had someone been told to follow me? The thought was unsettling.

The phone kept ringing. I took a step toward it.

The ringing stopped.

I turned back to the door.

The ringing started again.

I crossed the room, picked up the phone, and got the biggest surprise yet, in a night that was proving to be full of them.

"Ms. Griffin? It's the front desk. Someone has been waiting to see you."

I didn't bother to hide my surprise. "Tonight? Who?"

"Your son."

16

There were plenty of things that I didn't know anything about, but a few facts I was sure of. Martinis should be made with gin—always. Thomas Hardy should never have quit writing novels. I liked cats because they usually didn't do what people wanted.

And I didn't have any children.

None. That was a definite.

So, despite my hurry, I approached the main building with caution. Wondering who wanted to lure me into the open by providing an identity I couldn't possibly believe to be true. A trap so obvious there had to be a second layer. Somewhere. And yet a trap laid by someone who had managed to figure out where I was and who I was. So as I opened the lobby door, one hand rested in my handbag, feeling the comforting grip of my Beretta.

The girl who had checked me in was gone, replaced by a bleary-eyed guy a decade older. The night clerk, I assumed. He was sleepy, and doing his unsuccessful best to hide it. Or was he doing his best to act it? That was the problem with being held at gunpoint, tied up, and watching hatchet-wielding gangsters stuff a man into a suitcase. Twitchy flashes of paranoia started to pop up like carbonation bubbles.

I looked around the empty lobby. Nothing out of the ordinary.

I took another look at the clerk. Generally, bleary-eyed, sleepy men who sat at registration desks late at night wearing emblazoned uniforms were night clerks.

But nothing said they had to be.

Who had convinced the clerk to call my room? And where were they?

Years ago, somewhere in my early twenties, I had gone to three different Berkeley thrift stores and cleaned them all out of the cheapest handbags I could find. Then I had gone to an outdoor range and spent a weekend shooting through them until each was tattered with so many holes it was more air than fabric. A useful weekend, despite some very odd looks. Money well spent. Sixty bucks in used handbags had helped me conclude that although this method was far from optimal—not being able to raise and sight a gun took away ninety percent of what a gun could do—the handbag method could work. In a pinch. From close range, say ten feet, I could hit what I wanted. From twenty feet, sort of, if my target wasn't moving too much. After that, all bets, as they said, were off.

I walked up to the registration desk. "I got a call from you."

The clerk hid a yawn with his hand. His other hand had fallen onto his lap, behind the desk. Out of view.

"Name?"

"You just called me. Five minutes ago."

He yawned again. His other hand still out of sight. "He's been waiting almost an hour, but we couldn't reach you." Through the sleepiness, his voice contained a layer of reproach. As though I had been nightclub-hopping while my starving baby cried in a stroller on the sidewalk.

"*Who's* been waiting?" I tried to keep the impatience out of my voice. Trying not to think of Coombs, drawing farther away every minute.

"He's over there. *Waiting*," the night clerk added pointedly. He gestured across the wide lobby. My view was blocked by a bookcase. A diversion? But the four men hadn't seen me as even the slightest threat. To them I was just a kinky escort with the bad luck to be called by the wrong guy on the wrong night.

Another yawn. The clerk's expression clearly wondering why I was lingering.

I crossed the lobby. Someone was there. I could see the edge of a couch and, just barely, the tip of a sneaker.

Another step.

I stared in disbelief.

"Mason?"

The boy from the airport sat reading a battered mass-market paperback with a purple cover. I saw a picture of a spaceship, the title *Childhood's*

End. He looked sleepy, too. There was a huge mug of hot chocolate next to him. White marshmallows floated like miniature buoys in a muddy lake. He put his book aside, brown eyes worried behind his glasses. "Hi, Nikki."

I stared. "Since when are you my son?"

He blushed. "Sorry. It was the only way I could think of to get them to let me in."

"What are you doing here? How did you find me?"

He sipped his cocoa. "I thought maybe you could use some help."

"Help? How did you find me?" I repeated. Adrenaline from the last hour leaked away, leaving only confusion in its place. *What was this little boy doing here?* He seemed almost a hallucination, as though I was talking to an unusually polite and literate potted plant.

He put his mug down, took off his glasses, and used the hem of his T-shirt to carefully wipe condensation off the lenses. His hair, once again, cried out for a wet comb. "I figured you were going wherever that man had gone. And I knew the logo with the trees had to be important."

"But how did you find this place?"

He shrugged, as though that was obvious. "Google image search."

"How did you know to look in Monterey?"

"I figured he'd be here—otherwise he would have flown to a different airport, right?"

"True." I reluctantly admitted to myself that there were benefits to smartphones. I could have asked the boy for help in the first place, instead of running around town asking strangers.

I thought of something obvious and important. "Do your parents know you're here?"

He answered quickly, his eyes on his cocoa. "My father does."

"Honest?"

"Yeah." His eyes still hadn't found mine.

I tried to decide what to do. Coombs was moving farther away every second. But could I just leave a small boy alone at night? Mr. Z's group was already far enough that I wasn't going to catch them with speed. Too many roads. Even two or three turns could lead to almost infinite combinations, like the opening moves of a chess game. If I wanted to catch up I'd have to think my way after them.

I sat down next to him. "Mason. It's past eleven. You're seriously telling me your father knows that you're at a strange hotel waiting for a strange woman you met at the airport?"

"He doesn't care!" the boy exclaimed, finally meeting my eyes.

"Of course, he cares. He's your father."

"You don't know him." His voice was defiant. "He's probably asleep by now, anyway. He's not going to call the police or run around looking for me, if that's what you're worried about. Honest."

"Of course he will! That's exactly what he'll do!"

The boy didn't back down. "He barely notices me even when I am home. It would take him two weeks to realize I wasn't there."

I considered this. The last thing I needed was to get arrested for kidnapping a small child. Were there laws pertaining to this exact situation?

And why was I suddenly caring about laws?

"I have to take you back home," I said. "But I don't have time now. You'll have to wait here." On the verge of telling him he could wait in my room, I stopped again. Would inviting a twelve-year-old boy to wait in my room all night look more, or less, weird than the current optics? And would my room be safer, or less safe, than here in the lobby?

Seeing my indecisiveness, he pressed his advantage. "Let me help," he said again.

"You don't even know what I'm looking for."

"I think you're still looking for that man. What happened? He wasn't here?"

"He was here," I replied absently. "But he left."

"And you have to find him again?"

"Maybe."

"See? You need my help."

There was more in the boy's eyes. Distracted as I was, I wondered why he was so eager to help. Why he was out of his house so much. First the airport, now here.

I made up my mind. I couldn't leave him alone without knowing he'd be fine. I handed over my room key, deciding to hell with the optics. "You can wait in my room, okay? I'm in a hurry, Mason, I'm sorry. I'll be back later. You can order room service."

"I don't want room service. I want to come with you," he insisted.

"Why?"

"To help you!"

"Why are you so concerned with helping me?"

The defiance was back in his voice. "My whole life is boring! Nothing good or exciting ever happens except in books. My dad ignores me and the kids at school make fun of me and I've never had an adventure in my whole life. This is different. You're exciting. I *know* I can help—I know you need my help. I'm not just some stupid little kid."

I'd read somewhere that kids should be talked to like adults. Plus, I felt like his candor deserved my own. "I can't let you. It's dangerous, what I'm doing."

Apparently I hadn't spent enough time around young boys. I was out of practice. At the mention of *dangerous* his eyes lit up like a pair of thousand-watt candelabras. "I knew it!" he said, excited. "I knew it was dangerous. How dangerous? How many bad guys are there? Do they have weapons? You have to let me help you."

I had to smile. "Sorry. This one is nonnegotiable. Next time."

He folded his arms across his chest. "Fine. But then I'll have to keep my information to myself."

"What information?"

"You're not the only one with secrets." He uncrossed his arms just long enough to take a sip of cocoa. "Maybe I know more than you think."

"Mason, please. I don't have time to bargain. This is important. I'm in a hurry. What do you know about this?"

"Maybe I know who you're looking for. *All* of them," he said pointedly.

I stared at the little boy, bewildered. "How could you possibly know that?"

"Because I pay attention." He pulled his little notebook out of a pocket. "Everyone ignores me. And I write everything down."

"What did you write down this time?"

His voice was proud. "Maybe I wrote that I saw four men drive away a few minutes before you walked in, and maybe I noticed them because it looked suspicious that people would be checking out so late at night. I couldn't tell if the man from the airport was one of them," he admitted. "It was too dark. I was watching them through the window."

"What made you think they were checking out?"

He didn't hesitate. "Because they had a suitcase. A big rolling one. Who checks out in the middle of the night?"

I took a longer look at the boy in front of me. His eyes were bright and excited but his mouth was set in a resolved line. "Did you see what car they were in?"

"I knew it," he said. "It *is* them you're following, isn't it?" His hand clenched tight around his notebook. "How dangerous are they? Do they have guns? Do *you* have a gun?" He rummaged in a backpack next to him and came out with a strange-looking object. Bemused, I glimpsed a tubular band of beige rubber, a black wrist brace. "I brought my slingshot," he explained. "It's accurate and quite powerful."

"This isn't a game, Mason. People can get hurt. Sometimes they stay hurt."

His face clouded. "I know that. I bet I know a lot more about that than you think."

"What do you mean?"

"I don't want to talk about it."

I realized we were at an impasse that had to be broken. "Look—what do you want?"

"We make a deal. I tell you everything I know, and you take me with you tonight."

I tried to ignore visions of Amber Alerts and squadrons of police cars and buzzing helicopters on a manhunt for the heartless, wanted-dead-or-alive kidnapper of a small boy. I didn't relish becoming Public Enemy Number One in Monterey County.

On the other hand, I needed to know what he knew.

And I wasn't *actually* kidnapping him. I assumed that part must matter.

I made up my mind. "Fine. Deal."

He held out his hand and we shook. "Deal," he agreed.

"Tell me about the car."

He didn't hesitate. "We're looking for a black Mercedes G-Class, like a big jeep. That's the car the men got into." He looked anxious. "You're not going to welsh, are you? Kids at school do all the time. With me, anyway."

"Well, I don't. Let's go." I got up. He stuffed his book and slingshot back into his bag and scrambled after me, putting on a black windbreaker that he had pulled out.

"Want one?" he offered. I looked and saw he was offering me a granola bar. "They're low-fat," he added, as if that was stopping me. "Blueberry. We need to keep up our energy. I packed some trail mix, too."

"Maybe later. Two rules tonight," I added. "Seriously."

"Of course." He nodded with vigor as the granola bars vanished back into the bag. "Anything you say. I'm just the sidekick."

"One. You have to do exactly what I say. I mean it. Anything I tell you to do—you do it."

He kept nodding, his eyes shining. "Okay. You're in charge. And the second rule?"

"You're going to wear a helmet."

"I've never been on a real motorcycle!" Mason ran his hand along the curve of the Aprilia's cherry red body as though touching a wild stallion.

"The important thing is to hold on," I said. "If you feel me lean, you don't have to do anything. Just keep holding on." I helped him up first, while the kickstand was still down and the bike's weight rested solidly against the ground. His toes barely grazed the rear passenger pegs. "Careful," I warned. "The engine gets hot." I wriggled my helmet onto his head and adjusted the strap under his jaw. It looked a little loose, but it would do. "When we're riding I won't be able to hear you. If it's important, tap my right shoulder twice and I'll pull over." I worked my hair into a ponytail as I talked.

"Oh, don't worry," Mason said. "I brought a pair of walkie-talkies with earpieces." He was already rummaging through his backpack once more.

I stared at the small boy sitting on the red motorcycle. "Walkie-talkies. Earpieces. Of course you did."

"Benjamin Franklin said that by failing to prepare, you're preparing to fail." Mason handed me a clip-on walkie-talkie and an earpiece. "I figured that we might get separated and need to communicate. These should have an effective range of at least two miles."

I clipped the walkie-talkie onto the waistband of my jeans and fitted the earpiece around my ear, then swung my leg over the seat. "I'm not even going to ask what else you have in that backpack."

He had already fastened his receiver to his belt. He slid the earpiece through his open visor. "What are we waiting for?" As he shut his visor, he added, "We don't have all day."

I started the bike and the headlight speared out, causing the overhanging trees to cast stark, grim shadows onto the asphalt. I could feel the boy's arms tight around my waist.

"You okay?" I asked.

His voice crackled in my ear. "Roger. Doing fine."

The dark road unspooled before us. It was steep enough that I barely throttled, letting the downhill provide momentum. The tollbooth came into sight and, a moment later, so did the body in the road.

17

I braked hard, feeling Mason's weight press into me, and pulled over. "Wait here."

His voice was frightened in my ear. "Is that a . . . ?"

"Sshhh."

I cut the engine, conscious of Mason's presence. A headlight could make for a tempting target. I didn't want any attention drawn to the boy. I left him and walked toward the body. Had the fat man changed his mind about Coombs's value?

The tollbooth was empty. A single bulb lit it from within. The narrow line of the gate was raised. It shouldn't have been. I remembered passing under it. The way it had cut a sword stroke down after me. The body in the road lay completely still. Facedown, no indication of life. The shape could have been a fallen scarecrow, nothing more vital than straw-stuffed burlap.

Mason's voice sounded through my earpiece, anxious. "Is he—"

"Sshhh." I said again, my eyes on the shoes. Coombs had worn expensive leather oxfords. This person wore tennis sneakers. The body's proportions didn't fit Coombs's, either. This person had a more slender build. And a white polo shirt.

Ben. The friendly kid who had chatted with me earlier. Community college classes, saving up money, living at his mother's. That bashful look on his face, almost a blush, after he admitted that he lived at home. I knelt and cradled his head, feeling stickiness against my fingers.

He didn't move.

I rested my hands against his neck, feeling a pulse, and shook him slightly. "Ben?"

He groaned and muttered something unintelligible while I felt around his head, tracing the source of the stickiness. He had a swelling bump and a cut on the back of his head. They must have hit him with something. He groaned again. I went into the tollbooth and picked up the handset. The night clerk from the registration desk answered. "Call an ambulance," I told him. "Someone gave your security guard a concussion."

I dragged Ben closer to the booth, propping him up under the pool of light to ensure that a rushing ambulance wouldn't run him over. Police would come and want witness reports, but that couldn't be helped. If they wanted to talk to me, they could find me.

I walked back to the boy. "Was he . . . ?" Mason asked.

"He'll be fine," I said, helping Mason back onto the motorcycle. "Someone hit him."

His voice was fearful and fascinated. "The men you're following?"

I started the bike up. "Probably."

"Why would they hurt him?"

I answered as we accelerated down the hill, leaving the tollbooth behind, the pavement roughening as we reached the public roads. "Because he was in the way, and they're the type of people who would rather knock something down than bother to go around."

"Bullies." His voice was knowing.

I sped up and leaned into a curve, pushing the right handlebar down toward the ground. "That's one word for them."

"Now what do we do?"

"We find a good place for some late-night seafood."

My first thought was downtown Monterey. The touristy part. Places most likely to be open late, the best selection of restaurants. We rode up what was formerly Ocean View Avenue and was now Cannery Row, in Steinbeck's honor, even though the last sardine canning factories had shut down almost a half-century ago. These days, the economy was all about packing in people, not fish. I could see the black water of Monterey Bay on my left. Santa Cruz lay to the north, Carmel-by-the-Sea to the south, and to the west, beyond the bay, only the open, wild waters of the Pacific.

As we reached downtown, we were surrounded by cars full of late-night diners and drinkers. Most of the restaurants were already closed, but the night still had a bit of life left. I braked to avoid a couple jaywalking across the multi-lane road, haphazard as a pair of deer. The girl nibbled at a cone of cotton candy, her boyfriend's hand comfortable in the back pocket of her jeans. They didn't bother to see if I planned to stop.

Mason's voice was in my ear. "How do you know the men are here?"

"I don't. I'm guessing."

"They said they were going for seafood?"

"Yeah. Somewhere close."

I could hear his skepticism even through the walkie-talkie. "Here? My dad's always talking about how Cannery Row is a huge tourist trap."

I had been thinking the same thing. We passed one of the few open bars, blaring Jimmy Buffett. On the patio I could see a group of overweight guys clinking shot glasses. Next to us, an open-top Jeep Wrangler full of men shouted something at a group of girls on the sidewalk.

It didn't feel right.

The men I was looking for wouldn't want to brake for jaywalkers or trade tequila shots with drunk twentysomethings.

We can get seafood. A place I like is nearby, it stays open late. If it was earlier, we could sit with cold beers and almost watch the boats bring our fish right up.

Seafood. Close by, near the water, and still open.

Where?

I pulled over, seeing the Information booth that I had stopped at earlier in the afternoon. The booth was now unmanned and closed, a steel shutter drawn down around its center like a snail withdrawn into shell. But the pamphlets and brochures were still on the counter, advertising windsailing and whale watching and deep-sea fishing. No point in locking them up; they were advertisements. The drunk guy grabbing a random brochure at night might be the hungover guy looking for brunch the next morning.

I took a pamphlet and unfolded it, once more seeing the ads on one side, the crude map on the other. I could see the two-dimensional pier of Fisherman's Wharf jutting into two-dimensional water. The land where I now stood jutted out into a spur. I was on the northern edge of the spur. Under us, to the south, was Pebble Beach, with its famous golf course and 17-Mile Drive, the magnificent oceanfront homes lining the coast. Nothing would be open late down there, and if Mr. Z disliked elitism, that would be the last place he'd go. There was a toll just to enter 17-Mile Drive. So it had to be north. North of us was Sand City and then Seaside, just a few miles up the coast. A quieter, less touristy area, probably ignored by the luxe types wanting chauffeured Range Rovers and private chefs after eighteen holes of golf. *Such beautiful taste, such luxury . . . I don't stay at this kind of fancy place. I don't think places like this are made for people like me. I have my own places, my own preferences.*

We got back on the motorcycle. "Where are we going?" Mason wondered.

"Up the coast a bit."

Lighthouse Avenue became Del Monte Boulevard as it followed the water, tracing the edge of the spur north. We left Monterey behind, and with it much of the late-night commotion. No more gaudy neon displays or loud music or screaming Jeep-loads. Which made me feel better. I wasn't looking for a place with the best Yelp reviews or the most draft beer options. I wanted a place where a few locals might show up to sip cocktails and smell sea air late into the night. No crowds or shot glasses or Jimmy Buffett cover bands.

We were on Sand Dunes Drive, now, the closest I could get to the ocean. Mason's voice was in my ear. "How do you know where we're going?"

"I don't," I said. "I just have an idea of what I'm looking for."

We passed a sign for Del Monte Beach. Up ahead would be Seaside Beach, then Monterey, one by one. Different names attached to the same pristine line of sand and dunes. But state beaches were governed by the strictest conservation laws in the country. They wouldn't have oil-dripping marinas or noisy restaurants or developments.

Could they have gone all the way up to Santa Cruz? I didn't think so. Mr. Z had sounded hungry, and we weren't in Manhattan. Restaurants wouldn't stay open forever, and Santa Cruz was almost an hour north. We had to be in the right area—the only area that fit. But what if he had been speaking metaphorically? Not a place literally on the water, but close, within sight. Fishing boats not literally bringing in the fish, but close enough to feel that way. I got back on the main avenue, Del Monte. There were some restaurants open here, taquerias and sports bars. Casual. A definite maritime feel, signs advertising engine repair and fishing tours and water sports. I turned off Del Monte, combing the streets near the water, staying away from the darkened residential blocks. We passed a strip of chain businesses, all closed, a Subway and Jamba Juice and Starbucks.

I almost passed the Mercedes before I saw it.

A gleaming black G-Class, brand new, paint shiny, parked in a small lot marked by a red neon sign with a blinking crab. Johnny's Crab Shack. The Mercedes stood out. The few other vehicles sprinkled in the lot were older models, American pickups and Japanese sedans. Mason saw it, too. He tapped my shoulder urgently. "There it is!"

Slowing down, I saw water. The restaurant wasn't on the beach but rather on Laguna Del Ray, a small lake just off the coast. I could see the sign for a budget motel a few blocks up. The Seagull Inn. I pulled fast into the motel lot. "Stay here," I told Mason.

The boy's voice was tense with fear and excitement. "Where are you going?"

"I'm going to take a look around."

I walked casually down the shoulder of the road to Johnny's Crab Shack, hearing my footsteps crunch against gravel. The lot was empty of people. Maybe a dozen cars. From where I stood, I could glimpse inside through the glass door and a side window. A handful of tables visible. Mr. Z and his entourage, if they were indeed there, weren't anywhere in sight. I heard faint voices, carrying over the air. The back of the restaurant faced the water. A patio.

I cautiously approached the Mercedes and let my hand graze the hood, where the engine block would be. The hood was warmer than air temperature but not hot. An engine that had had some time to cool. I noted the blank dealer plates, Mercedes-Benz of Monterey, and the impenetrable tint over the windows. A red antitheft light blinked from within.

Mason's voice in my ear voiced the question in my mind. "Is it the right one?"

"I'm not sure."

There was a noise as the door of the restaurant opened.

I stepped away from the Mercedes fast.

I heard a woman's laugh and relaxed. Just a young, happy couple enjoying a night out. They climbed into a pickup, still laughing, and pulled out of the lot fast enough that the tires kicked up gravel. I walked back to the Mercedes and shined a penlight around the cargo area. Impossible to see anything through the opaque tint. I walked around to the driver's side and angled my light at the high windshield, where a white strip on the dashboard showed a minuscule set of numbers and letters, facing out. I quickly wrote down the seventeen-digit chain. A VIN could tell me all kinds of things.

No way to tell if Coombs was in the Mercedes.

No way to tell if it was the right Mercedes.

And no way I could chance going into the restaurant. If Mr. Z was there, being recognized would be disastrous. I scooped up a handful of gravel from the parking lot, then walked back up the street to the Seagull. Mason sprang to his feet when he saw me. "Was he there? What's the plan?"

"I'm going to be a really bad example," I told the boy.

He was confused. "What do you mean?"

"I need to borrow your slingshot."

I stopped about twenty yards from the Mercedes. The slingshot felt well-crafted, the brace fitting snug against the top of my left wrist, my left hand on the solid, pistol-grip handle, the leather pouch fit around one of the pieces of gravel I'd pocketed. I stretched the elastic tube back, feeling the tensile strength as it tightened. I could probably launch this stone the better part of a football field. Not the most accurate weapon, but I had a big, motionless target sitting right in front of me.

I stretched the elastic back as far as I could, aimed, steadied the sling-shot, and released my grip.

Two sounds, so close together as to be almost indistinguishable. The sharp metallic *ping* of the stone slamming into metal. Then a strident cacoph-ony of beeps and blinks as the wounded vehicle exploded in distress, de-stroying the quiet of the night.

Reactions happened quickly.

First, a waiter, sticking his head outside to see what had happened. Then he was thrust aside by a big man, who rushed out the door toward the noise. I recognized him. The bodyguard with the hatchet. If Coombs was in the Mer-cedes, the obvious conclusion would be that he had either escaped or set off the alarm while trying to. The bodyguard would immediately check the interior.

He didn't. He studied the SUV and then pressed a key fob.

The noise stopped and the headlights ceased flashing.

Two more men emerged from the restaurant. Mr. Z and his accountant, Albert.

They watched the bodyguard as he used a flashlight to check the Mercedes from all angles, kneeling to peer up at the chassis as though worried someone had attached an explosive. Mr. Z and the accountant maintained a wary distance, as though they had the same thought. I heard angry exclamations as he saw and pointed out the brand-new dent in the door panel. I was already walking back to the Seagull.

Four men had left the Cypress Inn, carrying a suitcase with a fifth man inside.

Now there were three men and no suitcase.

The second bodyguard must have been tasked to bring Coombs somewhere else. I walked faster. The Mercedes was my only link to Coombs. I couldn't let it out of my sight. That thought was in my mind when the police car pulled up alongside me, its searchlight pinning me like a moth.

18

I threw an arm up to block my eyes from the cone of dazzling light. A marked SUV idled next to me, striped like a tiger, two cops inside. Blue lights off. The female officer sitting in the passenger side gave me a long look and asked, "How's it going tonight?"

I squinted into the searchlight. "Did I do something wrong?"

"Nothing wrong. Saw you walking around, heard a car alarm, just thought we'd check in." She had the kind of excessively nonchalant tone that cops employed so frequently to insinuate that wrong-doing had been done and it was okay to tell them all about it. *Hey, we're all friends here . . .*

They wanted an explanation. That was clear. I nodded up the road. "I'm staying at the Seagull. I was taking a walk."

"Mind if we take a look at your ID?" she asked.

"Is that a request or an order?"

They exchanged a look and the cop nearer to me said, "We're just asking."

I hadn't been driving. I wasn't required to show ID. I also knew that cops could make any process shorter, or much longer, depending solely on their own preferences. The Mercedes wouldn't stay parked all night. Cooperating was the better bet.

"Sure. I'm reaching into my bag for my ID," I added. I was a woman alone and it was a nice area, but cops could be jumpy, especially late at night. I took out my wallet and handed over my license, seething with impatience. I saw headlights turn on in the parking lot of the restaurant.

The female cop typed unhurriedly into her laptop. Taking her time.

Making a point. The headlights were moving. A vehicle leaving the restaurant, headed in our direction. The Mercedes.

The female cop kept clicking away. Her partner said something to her and she laughed and nodded just as the Mercedes passed us, the driver maintaining what looked like a perfect twenty-five, dipping courteously over the center line to give our little group a respectful distance. Neither of the cops seemed to even notice it.

I watched my only link to Coombs drive leisurely away.

The cop finished what she'd been doing and handed my ID back. "Thank you, Ms. Griffin. Enjoy your evening in Seaside and stay safe."

"Thanks."

The cops headed in the opposite direction of the Mercedes. Toward the restaurant. Maybe looking to hang out and bust a few late-night drinkers. I kept walking. As soon as the SUV was out of sight I broke into a run. By the time I reached my motorcycle I was breathing hard and knowing it didn't matter.

The Mercedes had vanished.

"Why did you do that?" Mason wondered. He sounded more than a little jealous. To a boy his age, turning a slingshot on a luxury vehicle in the thick of night was probably like handing a baby boomer front-row tickets to a Stones concert.

I upshifted as the speed limit increased. "Setting off a car alarm can sometimes tell you a lot about what's inside, and how much people care about it."

"Did you learn anything about the man from the airport?"

"Just that he's somewhere else."

It had been a long night. My dinner with Coombs felt weeks distant. I stopped at a twenty-four-hour McDonald's on Del Monte. Only the drive-through was open, but that was all we needed. We parked the motorcycle and walked over to the window to order. I'd never figured out how to get drive-through on a motorcycle.

"I usually stay away from fast food," I said, feeling guilty. Late-night vandalism and fast food. I wasn't exactly hitting the gold standard of parenting. "But there's a time and place for everything."

We each ordered a chocolate milkshake along with our food, then carried bags of burgers and fries over to a bench at the edge of the parking lot. I was hungry, and the salted, crispy fries tasted delicious. Which was, of course, the problem with fast food. They were too good at making it too good.

"I'm supposed to be on my diet," Mason said, taking a huge bite of his burger. "But this is my first adventure, so it's different."

"I think you look good," I said. "Seriously. What's with the diet?"

He blushed. "I know I'm overweight. Everyone says so."

"Who cares about a couple of pounds?" I asked. "Trust me, you'll grow up and spend your whole life worrying about empty calories and utility bills and cholesterol and too many e-mails and a hundred other things. Now you should be enjoying yourself."

"That's easy for you to say. I bet you were never bullied when you were my age."

I shook a fry at him. "Wrong. Definitely wrong."

His voice was openly skeptical. "You're just telling me that to make me feel better."

"Nope—I mean it. Seriously. I moved twice growing up. To a foster family when I was about your age, and then two years later to a second one, in a different city, when I started high school. You wouldn't believe how much crap I got. Doesn't matter if you're skinny or anything else. Bullies will always find a way in—if you let them."

He was listening closely. "What did they say about you?"

I slurped at my milkshake and smiled ruefully. "Just about everything there is to say—minus anything good." DYKE *and* LESBO *written in black Sharpie across my locker after I turned down the upperclassmen boys.* FREAK. NUTJOB. *The cafeteria stares. Whispers twisting strands of gossip like hot wire. She murdered her whole family. She escaped from a psych ward. A secret sex addict.* NYMPHO. PSYCHO. DRUGGIE. SLUT. *Unrelenting.*

Mason stared at me, both hands wrapped tight around his milkshake. "What did you do about it? About the bullying?"

"I didn't handle things the right way," I admitted. "I hurt one or two of the kids who were doing the worst of it. I shouldn't have. They left me alone eventually, but it made me a pariah for pretty much the rest of high school. It wasn't worth it."

He nodded. "Like *The Old Man and the Sea*."

I was startled by the reference. "What?"

"You got what you wanted, but still lost."

"Exactly," I said, impressed again by the boy's literary knowledge.

"I've never been in a fight," Mason confessed. "The kids who tease me are mostly bigger than I am, so I don't think that would work too well. Plus, our school is zero tolerance on fighting. If I get expelled I won't be able to go away to college, and then I'll be stuck here forever."

"It'll get better," I promised. Along with the fast food and vandalism, fist-fights had somehow joined the list. Did this fall under the category of being an official bad influence? "I should get you home pretty soon," I said. "I don't want you to get in trouble."

He took a bite of his Big Mac. "Maybe you still need my help?" he suggested hopefully. "I could meet you tomorrow. I have more equipment and supplies I could bring."

"What's wrong with your home?" I asked. "Why don't you want to be there?"

He regarded the half-eaten burger he held. "My dad and I don't get along too well."

"Sorry to hear that."

He shrugged. "It's okay. I'm used to it by now."

"How about your mom? You get along with her?"

He fell silent. "She's not in the picture."

"Divorce?" I asked sympathetically. "That's hard."

There was a moment of quiet before he answered. "She died."

I put my food down and put my hand on his shoulder. "Mason, I'm so sorry."

His voice was softer. "It's okay."

"We don't have to talk about it. I didn't mean to pry."

"It's okay," he repeated. "No one—no one ever talks with me about her anyway, except the psychologist they make me see, who doesn't get anything about me. I don't mind talking about her with you. She was amazing. I write about her in my journal each night so I don't forget what she was like."

"What happened?"

"It was three years ago. A car crash. She—she and my sister. Someone ran a red light while we were going through an intersection."

"Your sister, too?" I hugged him without thinking about it. "Oh, God, I'm so sorry, Mason." Because of the enormity of his statement it took me an extra second to catch the word he had used. "We?"

"I was in the back seat. My sister was older, so she always got the front."

I released my arms from around him but took his hand. "Were you hurt?"

His eyes glistened, but his voice was even. "No. Just a few bruises and a bloody nose. The doctors said it was a miracle. I think that was what made it hardest for my dad."

"What do you mean?"

"I think it sort of bothers him to see me. Like I remind him of what happened. He's usually out, or at work. When he comes home he likes to be alone. I think I always end up annoying him—when we talk it's usually him asking me why I didn't make the soccer team or why my nose is always in a book. I really wanted him to let me go away to boarding school, but he won't." He looked up at me hopefully. "Do you think I could come with you? To San Francisco?"

"Sorry," I said, feeling much worse than sorry as I saw my words deflate the hope in his eyes like a nail in a tire. "I don't think that would work."

"Why not?"

"You're a minor, Mason. Your dad controls you until you turn eighteen."

His eyes flashed. "I can't wait to be eighteen! I'll leave so fast his head will spin!"

I asked the question without even thinking about it. "Would you like me to try to talk to your father for you?"

The boy shook his head quickly, the anger leaving his eyes as fast as the hope had. "He wouldn't like that. He gets pretty angry at me sometimes. If he thought I had tattled on him it'd be a lot worse."

"Tattled? What do you mean—what did he do?"

"Nothing. I mean, nothing that matters."

My voice was quieter. "Sometimes when I talk to people it's less about what they want to hear, and more about what they need to hear."

"It's okay," the boy said. "It wouldn't help, but thanks anyway."

"Has he ever put his hands on you?"

Mason shrugged and inspected a stray fry from his bag. "Can we talk about something else?"

"Sure," I said. "We can change the subject. Tell me more about some of your favorite books, why don't you?"

He started talking. I listened. Half-listened, anyway. Sometimes changing a subject was easier said than done. There was a thought bouncing around in my head.

I had told the boy that hurting people wasn't worth it.

I hadn't added the second part of the sentence.

That sometimes it was.

Mason's neighborhood was set in the hills above Monterey Bay. It was sickly-sweet with wealth. Hedged, floodlit driveways full of European cars leading to gated homes done up in extravagant European styles, Spanish Colonial and French Chateau. Mansions bulged out of sweeping, manicured lawns that probably needed sprinkler systems going 365 days a year. Enough water and resources to supply whole cities. I wondered if the people in the homes thought about those things. I wondered if they cared. Floodlights set into lawns painted Caravaggio swaths of light and shadow across the homes. The paving on the street was as immaculate as if the blacktop had been poured the day before. No debris or signs of life anywhere. So different than my East Bay neighborhood. No stray newspapers floating along the sidewalks, no graffiti or trash. The curbs were uncluttered by garbage bins. No flyers advertising community yoga or Italian classes stuck haphazardly on bus-stop glass—no bus stops, either. No need for them, I supposed. The people in these homes wouldn't ride the bus.

The whole beautiful, tasteful neighborhood was as soulless as a vacuum cleaner.

I didn't know what it meant. Whether any of it made people happier. Whether they still wanted things, and if so, what those things were. Like my clients. The Johannessen family with their secrets. I wondered what Susan would reveal, less than twelve hours from now. *This rot—this web.* What dirty laundry would be brandished in my face, tossed into my lap with an expectation of a nice wash and a neat fold? Were they happy—any of them? Wasn't that the point of all these things—all of this? Or did having so much just instill a twisting, earthworm-blind desire to hold, and gain, and hold, and gain, all the way to the very end?

I felt a stab of desire to be back home in Berkeley. Back in my bookshop. Graffiti and clutter and dirty streets and all.

When I dropped Mason at his house I understood more about why it was easy for him and his dad not to run into each other. The house was an enormous brick Tudor, the steep pitch of the roof stern and forbidding. It seemed a huge, sentient being, windows darkened, slumberous and still, but watchful, too, the gabled roof set in a suspicious squint.

Mason took off his helmet and accepted the walkie-talkie that I unclipped and handed back to him. He gazed wistfully at my motorcycle. "You can go pretty much anywhere on that, can't you?"

"As long as I have gas."

I thought of something that should have been obvious. "That's why you're always watching the airplanes, isn't it?"

"What do you mean?"

"You tell me. Why do you like them so much? Airplanes?"

He knew I had guessed the truth. "Because they can go anywhere they want."

"You'll be able to," I told him. "Soon."

He scuffed the ground with a sneaker. "I wish I could now. I wish I could go with you."

I looked at the house again. Again, I thought of some huge beast, slumberous yet watchful. I turned from the big house in front of me to the small boy next to me. "You really don't want to go home?"

"It's not my home," he said simply. "It used to be, but it's not. I wouldn't care if I never went back again."

I thought for a moment. "Do you have anyone you could stay with around here? If you had to?"

He considered this. "My mom's sister lives in Carmel. I like them, and her kids are my favorite cousins. Why?"

I made up my mind. "I'm going to talk to your dad for you. Wait here, okay?"

"No!" In his urgency he was clutching my arm with both hands, and for the first time I saw the bruises formerly hidden by his T-shirt sleeve. "It'll just make everything worse after you leave me!" he pleaded. "He'll blame me. Just forget it, okay?"

The intensity in his voice reaffirmed my suspicions. Usually people came to me for help. Needing help. But Mason was a child. It was different. It wasn't healthy for him to stay in this house. The house was bad for him. Somewhere tonight I had realized that fact. Which meant I had to make sure he could be somewhere else. Somewhere safe.

"It's okay," I said. Feeling that strange, familiar calm. That sensation of building, anticipation. "Stay outside, okay?" I said. "Just a few minutes. I'll be out soon."

There was a little nameplate by the door. DUNN. The front door was unlocked. I didn't ring the bell or knock. There were some nights when I asked for permission. Others when I didn't bother.

I stepped inside.

19

I found myself in a cheerless foyer lit by a pair of dim wall sconces. The first thing I saw facing me was an oil painting. A big one. About four feet by six. A delicate, raven-haired woman stood next to a tall, stern man with cropped hair. There was a little girl in a yellow dress next to the woman, her smile showing a slight gap between her front teeth that braces would have one day erased. One of the man's hands rested on the girl's shoulder, and the other was around the woman's waist, pulling her close. There was a lilac bush painted next to the little girl, its leaves nearly brushing her dress. Almost where a fourth person, say, a small boy, could have gone. But it was just the three of them.

Bemused, I walked further into the home.

The house was cavernous and somber. A house so full of the past that the present could barely find oxygen and the future had died stillborn. Too much past here, I felt with unease. The past was dangerous when it thrived uncontrolled. Like hedgerows pressed against window glass, the past had to be contained, trimmed, actively subdued. Else it would develop wildly, overrun.

The way my past once had done to me.

The knife on the kitchen floor. The two bodies. The pair of eyes peering at me from under the couch—eyes as familiar as my own.

My parents. My brother.

After the entranceway came a parlor, lit from above by a chandelier oozing yellow light. Mahogany walls were covered with framed photographs. The three figures from the oil painting. A family. Ice-skating in Union Square, festive holiday lights strung up in the background. High up on the Statue of Liberty. The little girl on a soccer field, a beach, a playground. Three happy people doing happy family things.

Mason was nowhere to be seen.

I felt the back of my neck prickle.

He had been edited out of his own family. Erased so completely that I had to wonder if I was in the right place; if I hadn't accidentally entered some other house, some other set of lives. There was no proof of his existence.

My pulse was starting to beat a lazy rhythm in my temple. Blood moving a bit faster, heart speeding up. A feeling of wakening, unfurling.

A familiar feeling.

A feeling that I had been trying to contain since the sixth grade. A feeling so specific and intense it was like some drug had been injected into my veins.

"Mr. Dunn?" I called out into the gloom.

No answer. My words floated away.

I walked through a kitchen that was too spotless, too perfect. A bowl of apples on the counter, so shiny green and unblemished they could have been plastic. No food stains on the counter or coffee grounds by the machine or dishes in the sink. Sterile.

"Mr. Dunn?" I called. "Are you here?"

Through a formal dining room. Another painting. Husband, wife, daughter. A family of three. My pulse was banging faster. Thinking of the boy with his glasses and little notebook and unruly hair crying out for a wet comb. A boy so desperate to escape that he spent his free time sitting at an airport watching planes soar off the tarmac. A boy who took refuge in books because there was nowhere else to find sanctuary. A boy forced to grow up in this house. Eating and walking and sleeping and living among these pictures.

I raised my voice. "Mr. Dunn? I'd like to talk to you."

This time there was an answer. "Who is that?"

His voice.

Now that it was starting I felt all the familiar feelings kick in.

"Who's here?" he called again. "Who are you?"

"My name's Nikki," I said. Coming closer. Following the voice.

I stepped around a door and saw him.

He was in his study, all dark wood and dim light. Physically, he wasn't so much older than the man in the photographs. I saw the same stern gray eyes, the cropped hair, the high forehead and sharp nose and bony neck, his face showing the reddened capillaries of a drinker. He had a glass in one hand and his phone in the other.

He stared at me. "Who are you and why are you in my house?"

"I can explain."

"I'm calling 9-1-1. Explain to the police."

"I want to talk to you about Mason," I said.

His face changed, from suspicion to understanding. "You must be one of his teachers, is that it? Is he misbehaving?" His voice sounded almost hopeful.

"*He's* not, no."

Understanding was replaced by hostility. "Oh, I see, the so-called bullying. Everyone teasing him, everyone else at fault. Let me guess—you're coming over with some misguided idea about your role in his life? A protector, is that it? Ready to preach about parental expectations in twenty-first-century education or some new-age jibber-jabber about nurturing and support? Do they really pay you enough to be working nights?"

I said, "Sometimes it's not about the money."

He set the phone down with a look of irritation. "Well, you might as well get on with it. What did he do this time?"

"You're not hearing me. *He* didn't do anything."

His eyes hardened. "So why are you here?"

"Why do you want him to be miserable?" I returned.

His knuckles tightened around his glass. "What did you just say to me?"

"It was a question. You heard it."

"I don't *want* him to be anything," Dunn finally said.

"Except invisible," I replied. Thinking again of the oil painting. A bush, where a boy used to stand. Transformed like some Ovidian myth.

Dunn's mouth twisted in disgust. "Oh, that's what he's gone and complained about? Not getting enough attention?" He took a slug off his drink and shook the glass at me. "You all coddle these kids so much. It's absurd. The boy has an allowance, toys, games, camps, classes, every comfort he could ever want—and he has the nerve to complain to his teacher about his horrible, lonely life?"

I sat down in an armchair uninvited. "Why do you hate your son so much?"

"I don't hate him. I ensure that he has everything he could possibly want."

"He doesn't!" I exclaimed. Feeling my pulse kicking up into a higher gear. "You think a bunch of toys and games add up to love? To warmth? After what he's been through?"

"After what *he's* been through?" Dunn snarled.

"You're his father. You're supposed to love your son—not buy him off like a cheap date."

"I won't tolerate much more of this," Dunn said. "I don't care if you're his teacher. None of this is your business. In fact, I think it's high time you left. And I'll be calling your principal tomorrow morning about this bizarre nocturnal visit. I give too much money to your school to have to put up with this kind of misguided, psychoanalytic guilt trip."

"It was an accident," I said. "It was tragic. Horrible. Every bad word in the book. But why blame your son?"

Dunn's eyes flared. "What do you know about any of that?"

"He told me," I said. "You think it doesn't tear him to pieces every single day?"

"*What* exactly did he tell you?"

"Everything," I said. "The intersection—the car running the red light. We can't control tragedies. But you still have a son. Why cripple him when he's just getting started?"

"*Because they'd be alive—if not for him!*"

I leaned forward, startled. "What are you talking about?"

Dunn's face shone in vicious triumph. "He didn't tell you that part, I see."

"What part?"

"The driver who ran the red light. That wasn't the other car."

"What?"

He sat back in his chair. "My son used to be quite the whiny little brat, you know. Always wanting attention, always sniveling for something. Never content. Never satisfied."

"What are you getting at?"

"That day, it seems the music my wife chose to play in the car wasn't good enough. He wanted *his* music. He demanded, and demanded, and demanded, until my wife, God rest her soul, finally turned around and said, '*Mason! Wait your turn!*'" Dunn's eyes burned. "Those were her last words. By the time she turned back, the light had changed and it was too late to stop. She ran the intersection, the truck hit them, and she and my daughter were killed instantly. While he sat in the back crying with a bloody nose."

"How do you know all this?"

"I was on speaker phone with them when they died." The muscles in his face twitched. "I heard everything. Even her last scream."

I had seen a lot of unpleasantness during the course of my life. But in this house of gloom I was filled with a special sense of horror.

I raised my eyes. "You blame a six-year-old boy for that? Because he wanted the *radio* station changed? You don't think he's suffered enough? Knowing what he must know?" I bit my lip, my eyes swelling with sudden tears. Wanting to go find the boy and put my arms around him and tell him that life wasn't always cold and aloof and sterile. That adults could offer cheer as well as poison.

Dunn said, "I'll provide for him. He won't go hungry or lack for any comfort. But I'll burn in hellfire before I forget that he took them from me."

I was aware that I was standing. "You've tortured him emotionally for years. Do you have any idea what kind of damage that causes? And not just emotionally. You've hit him—haven't you?"

"Wouldn't you like to know?" His lips tightened. Not denying it. "You're a teacher." His smile was a razor streak across his face. "I know all about mandated reporting laws. You think I'm going to pour my heart out to you? Now get out of my house."

"*You* said I was his teacher. I didn't."

Maybe he saw something in my eyes. Maybe it was just what I said.

His expression changed. More watchful now. "What do you mean, not his teacher?"

"I have a deal for you." I had made up my mind. The blood was singing in my head. "There's a boarding school up in the Bay Area. The Athenian School, in East Bay. Grades six through twelve. Send him there. You'll both be happier."

"How dare you come into my home and presume to suggest where I—"

"Not suggest. *Tell.* I'm telling you. This home doesn't deserve that boy."

My foster father, Darren. What he had done to me. Two years. Seventh and eighth grade. Two years I'd never shed.

I wouldn't let Mason be poisoned the way I had been.

"Give the okay and I leave right now," I told him. "He can stay at his aunt's in the meantime. Maybe that's better for both of you."

Dunn stood, too, his phone in his hand. "I'm calling the police. I've been far too kind to my son. Letting him run around unsupervised with strangers—whoever you are. Tonight, a new regimen will begin." His face twitched with anger. "My *son* has been spoiled for the last time."

"I should tell you something about how I work," I said. "I came in here to talk. To try to fix this."

Dunn pressed numbers on his keypad. "If you're here when they arrive, you'll be arrested for trespassing. I intend to find you and press charges regardless." He looked up at me. "What do you think about that?"

"I think I tried," I told him. Then I stepped to his left and hit him in the kidney.

The phone fell from his hands. He gasped and doubled over.

I kept circling him, only pausing to square my weight into the balls of my feet as I hit him again. The liver, this time. Bending my knees and twisting my torso into a driving left uppercut. Stepping around him, placing my feet. Twice more. In the stomach. Hard, savage blows with my full weight behind them.

He collapsed to the floor.

"You do a good job at inflicting invisible damage, don't you?" I said. "The kind of stuff that doesn't show unless someone looks close."

Putting him in good company with many of the worst abusers. People who seemed to delight not just in causing pain, but keeping it a raw secret from the outside world. From the people who might care enough to stop it.

I kicked him in the ribs. He coughed and wheezed and caterpillar-curled on the floor.

I kept talking, feeling the singing at full volume in my ears. "The kind of damage that makes life hell on earth—and no one even knows you're in pain."

I kicked him again, the reinforced toe of my motorcycle boot striking his shoulder. Then the small of his back. Staying away from his face. Someone might see him tomorrow and not have any idea of how much he was hurting. "The kind of invisible pain that people have to walk around with," I continued. "Pretending everything's fine when it's not." Two more kicks, one side of his body, then the other. He lay there gasping.

I let him. Forced myself to step back.

When he could talk again, he said, "I'm calling the police as soon as you leave. You'll do ten years for this. I'll be laughing in the witness stand during your whole trial."

I kicked his phone over to his hand. "Don't let me stop you."

He stared at me, looking for the trap. Tentatively clutching the phone. When I made no effort to move he dialed greedily. Finger about to press Talk.

"Child services," I told him, "has a twenty-four-hour hotline, county by county. Did you know that? You make your call. I'll make mine. You think you're miserable here? Wait until they drag you out of this nice big house, put your picture in the paper, and stick you in a smelly, dirty cell with ten other people while you wait to beg a judge for bail. I don't care how miserable you think you are. *Everything* can get worse."

His finger hovered over the screen.

"Maybe I'll go to prison for assault. You'll go for child abuse."

He looked at me, unsure.

I added, "Unless I'm wrong?"

He let go of the phone.

There was something new in his eyes. Defeat.

"One more thing." I squatted down.

He was gasping and wheezing. "What?"

"Until your son leaves for boarding school—which he will, as soon as the application goes through—you leave him alone. Don't go trying to win Parent of the Year and don't try to get even. Leave him alone. Don't poison him any more than you have." I rapped the floor next to his face with my Beretta. "Because I'll kill you next time."

I stood. "I'll see myself out."

His voice came after me. "You'd really kill me? You think I deserve to die?"

I stopped and looked back at the gaunt, twisted man on the floor.

"No. I don't. For what it's worth, I hope you drag yourself out of whatever hell you've locked yourself into. But I won't let you take that kid down with you. He gets to have a chance. He gets a future." Walking away, I said, "And you wouldn't be the first person in history to die without deserving it."

By the time I dropped Mason at his aunt's in Carmel, waited while he explained things to her, and got back to the Cypress, it was late in the night. If police had been at the inn earlier, there was no sign of them now. The toll-booth was deserted, its gate down. Which wasn't a problem. The gate was meant for cars. I just maneuvered my motorcycle to the edge of the driveway and around. Everything was quiet. Shut down. Which suited me. I was exhausted. I fell into bed, barely having the energy to set an alarm.

THURSDAY

20

The surfers call them *bluebird days*. A blue sky, blue so total it's more feeling than color, not a shred of cloud, the whole world alive and full of energy. The beach is crowded. Kids build elaborate sandcastles while dogs race after Frisbees, paws churning up little explosions of sand.

"Give it back, Nik!"

I laugh, bare feet dancing on warm sand, holding the toy truck out of reach.

"Nikki, don't tease your brother." My father sits on our red-and-white picnic blanket, one arm resting against my mother's smooth, bare leg.

"Fine." I toss the truck back to my brother, who throws himself onto the ground, *rev-revving* the plastic tires over the sand. I'm in one of those moods where I'm so happy that the only proper way to show it seems through petulance. "I'm famished," I announce. It's a word I learned recently and I've been using it constantly. "When's lunch?"

My mother looks up from her book and the sun catches her blond hair, spinning it into the most delicate wire. My mother is beautiful, everyone is always saying so, and I'm very proud of this. Secretly I hope it means that I'll grow up to be beautiful, too, even if I don't have her blond hair and my skin is naturally pale—I glance at my father, thinking resentfully of being stuck my whole life with his pale complexion—but I don't tell people this because it's vain, and also because I'm superstitious. I think growing up to be pretty is like a birthday wish. Admitting what you want means you might not get it.

"Soon. Go jump in the water first. Eating always feels better after a cold dip."

I run toward the waterline, the sand hardening. Sheets of white surf rock into the shore. I cast a look behind me to my family, framed by the high bluffs of Bolinas, and I get a happy shiver knowing that our little blue house is up there too, waiting for us.

The ocean seems strange. The water is sucking out, sucking away, so even as I run toward the sea it retreats. I run faster, but my feet seem slow, sticky. I can see lumps of slimy brown driftwood, and shells, and here and there my eyes take in white flashes that must be the bones of fish. Now the water is a strange pea color that I have never seen before, eerily calm, not a ripple. The ocean looks like a plane of flat green glass. Something building, forming, out on the horizon.

A wave. Impossibly big. The water towers up like a wall, building as it rushes toward me, arching higher, an immense, impossible wall of water.

I have to run.

I turn back to shore, but now my legs are covered in coils of seaweed. *Stuck.*

I kneel and tear with my nails, but the slick coils hold me as I move slower, sinking down. The beach is empty. Everyone gone. My family has disappeared. The wave is very close, a hurtling wall of water yawning above me, and I realize that it's too late to run, that everything is

too late.

I woke with a gasp. Soaked in sweat and breathing hard. I used to have the nightmares every night. Thankfully, they had become less frequent over the years. I was already getting out of bed despite the early hour. I knew that trying to return to sleep would be futile.

I turned the shower to its coldest, setting my teeth as the frigid water hit me in a hard spray. Bringing me back to the world.

I was in Monterey. Not Bolinas.

It wasn't the ocean I had to worry about.

And my parents hadn't just disappeared.

Thursday morning had washed away everything from the previous night as cleanly as a Zamboni sweeping over an ice rink. If police or ambulances had been there the night before, there was no trace now. No signs of kidnappings or gangsters or obnoxious tech bros. Just a beautiful morning in paradise. Outside my window, a maple ash spread patulous green branches, filtering sunshine into emerald.

It was early enough that draperies of fog still clung to the dewy ground, the sun just starting to burn mist off the ocean. I walked to the restaurant, where a breakfast buffet had been set up. I took a plate, poured coffee, and wandered over to the front desk. The sleepy night clerk had been replaced by a new woman. "How's Ben doing?" I asked. "I know him a bit."

The glaze of her professional smile flickered. "That was so horrible. No one understands it. They told us he has a concussion, but he'll be okay."

"Do they know who did it?"

"The police say it was an attempted robbery—whoever did it must have thought there was cash in the tollbooth. It's so scary what people will do." Her voice dropped as a guest passed. "Can you imagine?"

"Tell him Nikki said get well soon," I said, making a mental note to check in with him. Although I knew the four men would have come to the Cypress regardless, I felt responsible.

The man who called himself Mr. Z had hurt two people—just in the hour I had met him. I was starting to wonder how many others there might be.

The California DMV had something called a Request for Information Form. A service that allowed civilians to file VIN lookups. The problem was that doing so was only allowed in specific, strict circumstances and the process, like everything with the DMV, was anything but fast.

Charles Miller was different. He had someone at the DMV. For a few hundred dollars, the guy would give Charles everything he could find. In what was undeniably a point in favor of free market capitalism, he actually hurried.

I gave Charles the VIN. He told me to give him a few hours.

I still had some time before meeting Susan Johannessen. I left the Cypress and rode over to the Monterey Mercedes-Benz dealership. The showroom floor was scattered with sleek, shiny vehicles painted in lustrous colors. I found my way over to a G-Class. It was imposing, boxy and powerful, the kind of automotive species that would look right at home ferrying a rock star or state dignitary.

"Did you hear about the restaurant on the moon?"

I stared at the beanpole in a starched blue dress shirt who had ambled up to me. "What?"

"Great food, no atmosphere!" He grinned triumphantly. "I'm Jimmy. And you are . . . ?"

He stuck out his hand, so I had to shake it. "Nikki."

He gestured at the G-Class. "They're nice, aren't they? I always say, if you're gonna spend money, better on a car than at the bar! Thinking of getting one?"

I shrugged. "Never say never, right?"

"I wish my son had that attitude with his homework! He always says never! Well, if you got any questions, let me know. You can think of me as your new best friend . . . at least until you sign the papers!" He winked conspiratorially. In his fifties, with thinning hair, a fake tan, and bad teeth, he had the look of a B-team player, too anxious to make a good impression. From what I could see, he was one of the older guys working the floor. Maybe lapped by generation after generation of hungry, young go-getters who were promoted up the managerial chain or went on to different jobs while he stayed on the floor, working customers with his dad jokes.

I asked, "If I got one of these, how long could I keep the dealer plates?"

"State law says ninety days. We'd take care of registration so you'd get your permanent plates in the mail." He grinned again. "We believe in making life easy for our customers. How's that for a *craaaaazy* attitude?"

"What if I forgot to take the dealer plates off after ninety days?"

He looked puzzled. "Technically, you could get ticketed, if a cop happened to run the temporary registration. California's always been laid-back, but they've been cracking down more in the last few years. But like I said, we'd mail you the permanent plates." His smile was back. "You wouldn't have to do a thing except D-R-I-V-E!"

"Could I get a new set of dealer plates?"

Jimmy laughed and scratched his nose. "Not unless one of us was being very naughty and breaking the rules. Any temporary registration is reported to the DMV after each sale. But like I said—you wouldn't need to, so why worry? Hey, did you hear the rumor about butter?"

I felt like I was drowning. "I don't think so?"

"Well I'm not going to spread it!"

I thanked Jimmy, accepted his card, and left fast, before he could try another joke.

*   *   *

I got to Cannery Row at eleven thirty. I was habitually early when it came to client meetings. Not really politeness. More that when dealing with strangers, I liked being able to take a look around. Cannery Row was crowded. Everyone seemed hungry. Families laden with bags of saltwater taffy and fudge, people munching hot dogs and tacos, kids waving ice-cream cones, the restaurant bars lining the pier already filled with patrons starting in on their first draft pints and mimosas. To the right of the pier, I could see the Aquarium jutting over the water, a few colorful kayakers visible farther out.

I bought an iced coffee and newspaper and waited, reading the usual: how the Warriors would do, how bad wildfire season might get, police still investigating the U-Haul deaths, a popular Netflix show had just been renewed for a second season.

At ten to twelve, I got up to look for Susan. Given the urgency in her voice, I didn't expect her to be late. For all I knew, she'd been waiting all morning. I wondered about the woman I was about to meet. What it must be like—inheriting big money and the family to go with it, and trying so hard to free oneself of both.

My family had been taken from me. I'd spent most of my life trying to come to terms with the fact that I'd never have them back. Hard to imagine that there were people with the reverse problem. Having too much family was something I knew nothing about.

I had liked Susan, the single time we'd met. There had been something earnest about her. Something unfeigned. A quality missing in her three brothers. Maybe she hadn't forged her own way as much as she believed, but she was trying. That counted.

I checked my watch. Noon, exactly. My coffee was empty. I threw it away and kept walking the pier, scanning for Susan's face. Maybe she was finishing lunch.

Fifteen minutes passed. Then thirty. No Susan.

I went into a hotel, asked the concierge to use his phone, and dialed my voicemail. Four new messages. None from Susan and all from her brother. My client. Judging by the messages, Martin was becoming increasingly agitated that he couldn't reach me. No mention of his sister.

While I had the phone, I called Charles again. "Any word?" I asked.

He sounded perplexed. "He needs more time. There's something funny with the VIN. You're sure you copied it down right?"

"I'm sure. And it's urgent, Charles. Really urgent."

I put the phone down, went outside, and walked the pier again. Up and down, up and down again. No Susan.

I returned to the hotel and asked the concierge to borrow the phone once more. I got the phone plus a dirty look and dialed Susan's Hayes Valley gallery from the card I'd taken when I was there. "Is Susan in?"

Whoever picked up said, "I'm afraid not. She travels frequently. May I take a message?"

"That's okay." I hung up and tried Susan's cell phone. The call went straight to voicemail. I tried a second time, with the same result, and then dialed her brother.

This time Martin picked up immediately. "Who is this?"

"It's Nikki."

"Where have you been?" He sounded angry, as though I had stood him up on a date.

"Doing what you hired me to do. There were some complications."

"Where are you right now?" he demanded.

"Monterey."

"You haven't found him?"

"I'm working on it."

"There have been some changes," Martin told me.

I shifted the phone against my ear. "Changes?"

"Not over the phone," he said. "I need you to come back to San Francisco today. I need to see you."

I didn't bother to hide my annoyance. "I'm sort of in the middle of something."

"And I'm sort of paying you," he snapped. "I'm your client—I need to talk to you, and I need to do so today."

There was a different voice in my ear. "Excuse me!" The concierge was looking at me with something less than affection. "Are you a guest here?"

I covered the receiver with a hand. "Sorry. I'll be off in a second." I put the phone back to my mouth, conscious that the concierge was frowning openly, arms crossed. "I really need another day down here. One day. It's important."

"And it's important that I talk to you—today. I insist."

A little more than one hundred miles. Two hours up, two hours back.

I could meet with my client and then get back here while Charles worked on the VIN. "Okay," I agreed. "I'll meet you this afternoon." I left the hotel, ignoring the concierge's glare, and took one last look around for Susan. Nothing.

I think you'd try to save me without even thinking about it.

Coombs.

Barely thirty-six hours. That was how much time I had. To find him, and free him. And to find out more about the murky, dysfunctional family that had hired me. I rode north. Sand dunes blurred past on my left, the ocean visible behind the gentle rise and fall of their curves. I throttled up, increasing my speed and leaning into the wind.

21

When the driver of the U-Haul got the phone call, he felt sick to his stomach, even though he'd been expecting it. He was staying in a small, furnished room in a double-wide trailer. There were bunk beds in the room, but he was alone, so he napped on the lower and slept on the upper. A place he had stayed before from time to time, even though he had never paid rent or seen a utility bill. It had always just been a place to stay when he was doing a route. Now it felt more like a prison. He had stayed in those, too.

There was a lounge with a big television that he never turned off, no matter what time of day or night. When his phone rang he had been watching a rerun of a soccer game. The goalie dove, a gloved hand stretching out just enough to glance off the ball and change the trajectory from a certain goal, to nothing at all. As a boy, he had been passionate about one of the teams that was playing. Each victory had filled him with pride; a loss made him feel empty and defeated for days. As a teenager, he had gotten in vicious fights over his team, protecting its honor against anyone who dared say a bad word. He smiled to remember it. Little had he known what emotions like emptiness and defeat really felt like.

He listened to the voice on the phone tell him where to go. He smoked while he listened and didn't talk. He had been smoking a lot that week, even more than usual. The trailer was rank with cigarette smoke. The shades were drawn, and beer and tequila bottles were scattered among empty cartons of takeout food.

He had screwed up. Probably irredeemably. He knew that.

He smoked his cigarette until he felt the heat of the cherry on his fingers. Then he let the butt fall into a beer bottle. It extinguished with a little hiss. He got up and looked at his reflection in the bathroom mirror. His eyes were tired and puffy, his black hair unkempt. He looked a decade older than his twenty-five years. Through most of his life he had been a devoted gymgoer, proud of his muscles, putting in endless hours with free weights, but recently he had stopped caring, and his body looked pallid and unhealthy. He thought of those past days, the nightclubs, the endless money, the girls and parties and drugs. Everything seeming exciting, his success all but guaranteed, a rising star in the Organization. By thirty, he would transition into a management role, where the money would become serious and the day-to-day risk would lessen.

Dreams. Plans. All as stupid and pathetic as a little boy thinking that his team's victory meant anything for his own life.

He showered and put on jeans and a T-shirt. Combed his hair and took a last look around. There was a loaded Smith & Wesson semiautomatic under his pillow. He left it there. What was the point? On his way out, he stopped to tap powder out of a plastic bag. He finished the contents, two small lines, feeling the heroin connect pleasantly with his brain.

Why not?

He walked out, not bothering to turn off the lights or lock the door. He wouldn't finish the soccer game, but it was a rerun and he had seen it before. He knew what happened. His team lost.

The person on the phone had given him an unfamiliar address. The Organization had access to hundreds of places they used for different things, scattered everywhere, some out in the open, some hidden away. He got in a pickup, entered the address into his phone, and drove through miles of farmland before reaching a main road. He didn't mind the driving. He drove for a living. He'd spent untold thousands of hours behind the wheel. The heroin and straight lines of the road lulled him, made him feel like he was bumping pleasantly along a train track, comfortable and secure. He lit a cigarette and rolled his window down, letting his left arm drag out the side. The fresh air felt good against his skin.

His phone guided him away from the farmland and into an industrial neighborhood. Chimneys coughing out black smoke, eighteen-wheelers bumping along over uneven streets, harsh chemical smells, loading bays leading into wide, flat buildings. His ears were filled with the sounds of jack-hammers and beeping forklifts.

He parked the truck on the same block as the address he had been given and got out. A couple of rough-looking men walked past, their eyes challeng-ing him. He met their gaze, gave a hard stare back until they shrank away. He tried to use the moment to feel anything, adrenaline, fear, aggression. But there was nothing. He was empty.

The address was a warehouse with an olive-painted steel door to one side of a shuttered loading bay. There was a buzzer next to the door. He took a fi-nal look out at the street and buzzed. The door clicked open and then closed behind him.

For a moment, he thought he was alone. Then a big man stepped into the light and nodded at him. He lit a cigarette, but made no effort to speak as the big man patted him down. He had been patted down many times before. It didn't bother him any more than a handshake. The heroin buzzed in his head, adding strange little glimmers to his vision. The cigarette felt good and he took long, deep drags, barely feeling the strong hands pressing along his body.

He followed the big man into an immense space, maybe twenty meters by thirty. In the center of the room was a long wooden table, empty except for a half-full bottle of tequila, three small glasses, and a bolt-action hunting rifle. There were three chairs on the opposite side of the table, facing him. Three men sat in the chairs. A fourth man lay on the cement floor, close to where he stood. At first, he didn't know if the fourth man was alive, but he saw the chest rising and falling with labored breaths. It took him a few seconds to recognize his partner from the route. He had liked his partner well enough. They had spent hundreds of hours in small, enclosed spaces, cars and truck cabs and motel rooms. When you had spent that much time with someone you either liked them okay, or ended up killing them. In the past, he had done both. He knew the sound of his partner's snores, the smell of his breath, what he sounded like when he was with a woman, the names of his three children, his favorite foods.

Looking at his partner, he figured they must have used baseball bats or maybe pipes. Fists didn't do that kind of damage. He hoped, for the man's sake, that he'd die soon. Being alive didn't look worth it. He pushed the thought away. What he thought didn't matter. What he wanted didn't matter. It was the men at the table that mattered. While they wanted his partner to be alive, he would be alive. If they wanted him to be dead, that, too, would happen.

"It was good of you to come."

His eyes moved to the speaker. The middle of the three men. It was a face he recognized, even though they had never been in the same room before. He felt the dull, heroin-coated fear in his body kick up a sharp level. He wasn't supposed to be in a room with this man. They were on very different levels. Career-wise, he shouldn't have met the man speaking to him for another five years, at least.

He nodded but said nothing. He could feel the big guy who had opened the door standing close behind him, as though he might be foolish enough to try to run.

As if reading his mind, the speaker said, "Your partner did not come voluntarily. He tried to run. You made an intelligent decision. They told me that of the two of you, you were the more intelligent. Today's choices seem to bear that out, would you agree?"

He nodded again, aware that he was very thirsty. He wished he had stopped to buy a soda. Not doing so seemed stupid. Such a small thing, so easy to do, and now he had to stand here, so thirsty he would have happily lapped dirty bathwater off the concrete floor.

"How long have you worked for us?"

He tried to speak, but the words caught in his throat. He tried again, frightened of the impatient look that spread across his questioner's face. "Eight years. Since I was seventeen."

"You did a good job. Until this."

He remained silent.

"Some mistakes we could call bad luck, a learning curve. But not this. You both were incompetent, you made an error that cost me a great deal. Not just the loss of income, the bellyaches. That would have been excusable. You managed to attract the attention of American media, federal law enforcement. You created a big story. People are talking about us, asking questions."

"I'm sorry." He meant it. He was sorrier than he'd ever been about anything. "We tried to do everything right."

"Tell me what went wrong. Tell me in detail."

He spoke for a few minutes, explaining what had happened: the white car they had noticed, north of the border, driver plus a passenger with some kind of telephoto camera, his partner becoming agitated (here he omitted that both of them had been on methamphetamines and hadn't slept in two days), convinced the white car was photographing them, more agitation, arguments, finally a course of action carried out—and then realizing, too late for the occupants, that the white car had held only a couple of college kids and a bunch of movie-making equipment.

Then more arguing about whether they had been seen (he said yes, his partner insisted no), paranoia becoming panic as they heard his partner's rough description read over their police scanner—and finally the decision to ditch the truck by the Walmart and get away.

He still dreamed about the white car. Without the white car, everything would have been fine. They would have made their delivery, and he'd be on vacation with his girlfriend, down in some beachside resort, eating, drinking, screwing, getting high. The tiniest difference, and he'd be there instead of here.

A different trajectory. Such a small difference.

Unpleasant odors filled his nose. They were coming from his partner. He was making sounds. A hand twitched, grasping at something invisible. His moaning grew louder. Something sounded broken in his throat. A crushed windpipe, probably. He'd heard the sound before.

The man who had been asking him questions glanced at his partner with irritation. "Please," he said. "Tell him to be quiet. He is interrupting."

The man sitting on the speaker's right reached over and picked up the hunting rifle. It looked like a .30-30, what someone would use for deer. Without standing, the right-hand man worked the bolt, aimed, and fired a single shot into the twitching body. The sound was very loud in the enclosed space. He put the rifle back on the table. The smell grew worse but the noises stopped.

The man asking him questions seemed oblivious. "Do you know why we called you here?"

He nodded.

"Did you think about running?"

He shrugged. Glanced down at the still body. Blood was pooling, sluicing down a drain set into the floor. "What's the point?"

"Good boy. You understand."

The right-hand man leaned over and whispered something. The man in the center considered, then nodded. "He points out that you worked hard for us and did a good job for many years. He says you deserve an easy landing."

"Thank you." He spoke the words with genuine gratitude.

The man who had shot his partner stood up. He recognized this face, too, seeing the distinctive white scar against the grizzled forehead, the hatchet strapped to his thigh. Before transitioning into management, the man had been legendary in the Organization. The younger men were in awe of him; they whispered guesses at his body count. Despite everything, he could not help but feel a measure of pride that this person had spoken highly of his work. Now, the man poured a drink from the tequila bottle, walked over, and handed the small glass to him. He drank gratefully, feeling the alcohol burn his throat. It was getting hard to stand. He needed to use the bathroom. Everything seemed to move slower.

The man who had poured him the drink walked back to the table and picked up the rifle for a second time. He watched the rifle move up to him. It wasn't the first time he had looked down a gun barrel. In his work, not unheard of. But this time felt different.

The bolt clicked back with a sharp, precise clarity.

He could see the finger begin to tense against the trigger.

The man in the center was speaking again, sounding angrier. "The goddamn U.S. State Department even mentioned us. So much trouble, because you can't do your job." A fleshy hand suddenly pushed the rifle barrel down. "Why should you enjoy an easy landing? After the bellyache you've caused?"

The man in the center clenched his hand into a fist.

For the first time, he felt real panic, an electric fear that made the pleasant muddiness in his head crystalize into hard, sharp edges. It was impossible to just stand there. He started to spin around. He had counted steps as he habitually did. The door was eighteen walking paces behind him. Running, it would be half that. If he could make it through the door and outside, he could evade them. Get back over the border, into the mountains, find some small town to live in. He knew plenty of freelancers who did fake papers. A few owed him favors. He could live somewhere else, have a quiet life. A man with his talents could always find work.

His mind was working very quickly now. Not more than a half second had passed since he began to spin. He still held the empty tequila glass, which he intended to smash into the big man's eye. Violence came naturally to him. He wouldn't hesitate, least of all at this moment. The bolt action rifle would only get the chance to fire a single time before he reached the door. That gave him a chance.

As he turned there was the briefest glint, a kind of sparkle, a metallic thread that darted over his vision and was gone again. Briefer than blinking. He could have imagined it. As the sight connected to his brain and was analyzed for meaning, he realized what the glimmering line meant and tried to lurch down and away.

Too late.

The wire was around his neck. He jerked an elbow backward with desperate force, but the big man was expecting that and stepped with him neatly as a dance partner, staying directly behind him.

Time slowed even more. He heard a sound and realized it was his glass, shattering on the floor. He felt the wire jerk into his throat, sharp as a razor, and became aware of blood spilling down his neck as the garotte dug into his flesh. The room began to darken as the pain kicked in and he tried to scream through a throat that no longer worked. The big man was controlling him, now, holding him up as his legs gave way, and he slumped down, the weight from his body working treacherously against him. He felt the wire sawing through his neck even as it strangled him, and had the bizarre hope that he'd die before his whole head came off. He wanted to be buried in one piece.

As strength left his body and his knees gave way, his last, dispiriting thought was that if there was indeed a hell as he had been raised so strictly to believe, he would without a doubt go to the devil and burn eternally for the terrible things he had done in the brief handful of years that God had allotted him.

22

I'd never been in a Bentley before, much less a chauffeured one. Now, sitting behind the driver on soft, hand-stitched leather, the experience seemed almost anachronistic. As though I was in a Jane Austen novel, a world of rank and class, servants to carry up eggs and buttered toast in the morning and help you change out of your pajamas. A soundproof glass window divided the front from the back, and a wide, burled walnut center console separated the two rear bucket seats. Whatever Bentley used for their suspensions worked, and then some. As we cruised San Francisco's chipped and potholed streets, I felt like we were on a sleigh gliding over packed snow.

"Fancy hotel suites, fancy cars," I observed. "Careful—I'm starting to feel spoiled."

Martin Johannessen gave me a look that contained neither humor nor any of its distant cousins. "I can always pick you up on the bus next time." His narrow, greyhound face was pinched, and his hand tapped absently against his knee. We were driving south on Van Ness, without any obvious destination. I noticed that traffic seemed to give the Bentley a little extra room. Deference, or maybe prudence. No one wanted to get in a fender bender with a $300,000 vehicle.

"Have you heard from Susan recently?" I asked him.

He looked at me, surprised. "What does my sister have to do with any of this?"

"She wanted to talk to me. It sounded important. Did you talk to her yesterday or today?"

"No," Martin said, "which is far from abnormal. If I don't hear from her in a month or two, maybe I'll worry."

"Any idea where she'd be?"

Martin uncapped a green glass bottle of Perrier. "Probably one of the yoga or wellness retreats she always checks into after she gets into a huff. Maui, Malibu . . . they seem to always put them in such *comfortable* locations."

"What's she get into these huffs about?"

"My sister has always harbored resentment toward the family, even in the best of times." His annoyance was becoming suspicion. "Why these questions?"

"Just asking."

"I thought that's what the *client* is supposed to do. Asking questions."

"Ask away," I invited. "You're the one who wanted to see me."

"True enough." He stared out the window at the passing buildings. "Things have changed since we last spoke."

"Changed how?"

"Changed with regard to Coombs."

"How so?"

Martin said, "The man left town. I've realized that I'm throwing good money after bad. He's a mosquito—a tick, a bloodsucker. So now that he's buzzed away, let him go feed on someone else for a change." Martin's long, thin fingers turned the bottle cap in endless circles. "Life is too short—I have more important things to do than chasing after a cheap swindler in a nice suit."

"What about the blackmail? Aren't you still worried about that?"

"No," Martin said, "I'm not, actually. I believe I was wrong about that—misinformed. Coombs is no longer Mother's problem, and therefore he's not mine."

"You never asked me what I found out," I said.

"And what was that?"

"Apparently, you weren't the only one who had a problem with Coombs. Some men grabbed him out of his hotel. Down in Monterey."

"Men? Who? Which men?"

"I'm not sure. I'd never seen them before. They didn't seem nice."

"What did they want from him?"

"Money. How much, or why, I don't know."

Martin was openly curious as he said, "Grabbed him? What do you mean *grabbed*? Is that supposed to be a metaphor?"

I said, "They threw him into a suitcase and drove away. Not sure if that counts as metaphorical?"

"What?" Martin's surprise sounded real. "A *suitcase*? You can't just throw someone in a suitcase."

"Turns out you can. Turns out all you really need is a big enough suitcase."

"What are they going to do to him?"

"Nothing good." *I will watch while these two chain a fifty-pound cement block around each one of your ankles and toss you into Monterey Bay.*

"You're saying they'll hurt him?" Martin didn't sound particularly upset at the prospect.

"They will unless I can find him first. Which is what I was trying to do. When you dragged me back up here."

Martin sipped from his Perrier and fell silent, thinking. The big car had done a U-turn and was heading back up Van Ness. Aimless, as best as I could tell. Cruising and burning gas. Probably a lot of gas. I didn't think people who bought Bentleys worried about the price of unleaded. The car's sound insulation was as supreme as the shocks. Outside, the world was muted as a television set.

"This doesn't change anything," Martin finally said.

It was my turn to be surprised. "Doesn't it change everything?"

His voice sounded more assured by the second. As though he was sliding pieces into a puzzle frame and seeing the picture form. "If he upset those people—thugs, criminals, whoever they are—that's for him to work out. Certainly not my problem. What's that saying—the enemy of my enemy is my friend? I don't see the point of spending money or time trying to save a man who caused my family nothing but grief."

"Hurt," I explained, "sort of understates their plan for him. If you get my point."

He shrugged. "I don't care to know the details, frankly. If the man's greed and conniving and criminality led him into the lion's den, well, he'll have to find his way out."

"I got the sense that he hadn't wandered into the lion's den on his own."

Martin gave me a sharp look. "Meaning what, exactly? Did they mention anyone else?"

"Nothing like that." I asked the obvious question. "But why would Coombs be doing deals with a bunch of gangsters? He's a con man who goes after the upper crust. That doesn't seem his style."

Martin's face showed nothing except lingering peevishness. "Like I said . . . not really my problem. The man has spent his career cheating and deceiving people. If he finally flew too close to the sun, that's for him to work out on his own."

"What are you saying, Martin?"

"I'm saying that I no longer need your services."

"You're firing me?"

"Yes." The bottle cap rotated in his spindly fingers. "I'll pay any expenses you incurred, naturally, and the retainer is yours to keep. But I no longer need you—effective immediately."

"You called me up here just to fire me? You couldn't have done that by phone?"

"Your time did not go uncompensated." Martin looked me square in the face. "I no longer want or need you running around chasing this fellow. Are we clear?"

"Give me one more day. Just one more. To see what I can find."

"Impossible." Martin shook his head. "This meeting concludes our business. I suggest you move on to things worthier of your attention and forget all about Coombs."

"I've never liked giving up."

"You're not giving up. You're moving on. There's a difference."

"Not to me there isn't."

Martin blew out his breath in annoyance. "We aren't going to sit here quibbling over semantics. I'll be an excellent reference, in case that's what you're worried about."

"It isn't."

"Even better," he snapped. "But either way, you're no longer needed."

The conversation seemed over. "You can let me out here." Thinking of my poor credit card I added, "I'll send you my receipts."

"By all means." He tapped on the glass separating us from the front, and the big car slowed to the curb. I got out, ignoring two idlers who wolf-whistled as they saw me emerge from the majestic car.

"See you around, Martin," I said as the car pulled away.

Not having the support of a client was crippling. It wasn't just about the expense account. Law enforcement took a very dim view of anything that smelled of vigilantism. Brushing against police after having been fired from a case could mean losing the California PI license that had taken me all kinds of effort to get, and once stripped, the licenses were notoriously hard to gain back. Maybe worse consequences, if Martin got wind of my continued involvement and decided to throw his considerable influence around.

If I wanted to keep hunting for Coombs, I needed a new client. And if I wanted to find him, I had barely a day and a half to do so.

Susan Johannessen would have been perfect—but she had disappeared. And neither of her brothers seemed at all inclined to be helpful. I thought of William's blank, uncomprehending eyes, and Ron's hostile glare.

No, I wouldn't be working for any of the Johannessen siblings.

A client.

I realized who I needed to talk to.

23

The elder Mrs. Johannessen lived in a duplex apartment in a grand, prewar building in Russian Hill. A different doorman from my unsuccessful first visit watched me walk in.

"Can I help you?"

"Nikki Griffin, for Mrs. Johannessen."

His eyes stirred a bit at the name. The Johannessen name seemed to open doors—or close them. He walked back around the desk and clicked on his computer. "She's unavailable."

"When will she be available? I don't mind waiting."

"You're not on our calendar."

"Just dropping in."

"People don't 'drop in' here. Our residents value their privacy."

"It's important."

"Try *impossible*." He was already moving to the door, ushering me out.

I didn't budge. "Tell her it's about Coombs."

"What? Who?"

"Dr. Coombs. Two words. That's all."

He thrust the door open. "You need to leave now."

I still didn't move. "Fine. Don't. But then you better spend the rest of the day blowing dust off your résumé. You're going to need it. Probably by to-morrow in the a.m., if I had to guess."

"You can't threaten me," he said.

"*I* can't do anything to you," I said pointedly. "Don't worry about *me*."

His voice was almost apologetic. "I don't know who you are."

"One call," I said. "Two words. That's all I'm asking."

He considered, then nodded.

Thirty seconds later, I was in the elevator.

The duplex was incomparable to any apartment I'd ever seen, much less set foot in. A tall, slender man in a pinstriped suit who could not have been anything except a butler ushered me into a spacious foyer floored with pink-veined marble, all gilt-edged mirrors and crimson wallpaper.

"Boots off?" I asked.

He spread his hands politely. "Whatever you prefer."

"Then the boots stay on."

I followed him down a long hallway into a living room furnished with the same splendor. Ornate, handwoven carpets, grand marble fireplace, immense crystal chandelier, high walls of books bound in rich, dull leather. I took in some of the titles. This particular selection could have been drawn from Bloom's *The Western Canon*. Everything from the early Greeks to the Russian and European greats, Tolstoy and Dostoyevsky and Goethe and Mann and Maupassant and Stendhal and Flaubert, Samuel Johnson and Dryden and Pope onward.

To my right, a row of arched, leaded glass windows displayed the Bay, a swirl of fog curling over the Golden Gate. Framed oil paintings hung from the walls, intimidating men and women in Old World finery, dark clothes, dark backgrounds, expressionless set faces. I saw a signed painting, brightly colored nude figures dancing across a landscape. A Matisse. It didn't look like a copy. A brace of antique dueling pistols hung above the marble fireplace. I wondered if they'd ever been used. Some real or imagined slight, leading to words, and tempers, and inevitably blood.

"Nikki, yes?" said a sharp voice.

The speaker was a white-haired woman seated on a plush burgundy sofa. With the exquisite background, muted light, and her regal bearing, she looked like she could be sitting for a portrait herself. She stood, and I saw she was strikingly tall. Even bent with age she must have been five foot ten.

I crossed the room to her. "Mrs. Johannessen? Thanks for making the time."

"Don't thank me yet." She wore a flowing, formal dress, a light silk shawl around her shoulders. A weighty pair of sapphire earrings dangled from her ears, mirroring her ice blue eyes, and around her long neck was a matching silver and sapphire choker. Her hair, pure white and very fine, fell past her shoulders and her face, although wrinkled with age, was intelligent and astute. I couldn't see any resemblance to Martin. They had been cast from different molds. "A question," she continued. Her voice was cotton and steel, soft with something harder underneath.

"Yes?" I asked.

"Can you mix a martini?"

I looked at her, startled. "I think I like you already." Realizing that the foggy old lady I'd imagined was nonexistent. This woman was about as weak and foggy as Catherine the Great.

"You'll find the requisite materials on that bar cart across the room," she commented as she sat and picked up the book she had been reading. Chekhov. "As for liking you," she continued without looking up, "I'll reserve judgment until I see if I like my drink. Call me superficial if you wish. I've been called worse."

She turned a page.

The conversation seemed temporarily over.

I walked to the bar cart, an ornate walnut-and-brass model with large multispoked wheels the size of bicycle tires. There was ice in a silver bucket, a pair of silver tongs, a tray of garnishes, clusters of bottles, and several crystal decanters filled with amber liquid. I located a bottle of Beefeater gin and smiled, finding something refreshingly unpretentious in the twenty-dollar bottle. A choice that said the buyer knew what she liked and didn't give a damn about trendy. A pleasant change from the San Francisco bars boasting thirty kinds of local, botanical-infused this-and-that, and snooty bartenders who rolled their eyes if someone wasn't smart enough to order something utterly obscure.

My own taste in gin was a little like my taste in books. Contemporary could be great, but it was hard to beat the classics.

I eschewed the silver cocktail shaker and instead used a crystal beaker and long bartender's spoon. "Chekhov?" I asked while I stirred.

She looked up. "'Ward No. Six.' Are you familiar?"

I took two martini glasses, poured a big splash of vermouth into each, swirled, then dumped the vermouth. Maybe it was a hunch, but this woman seemed like she'd drink her martinis bone dry.

I said, *"Suffering leads man to perfection—something like that, right?"*

"And what do you think about that, Nikki? Must we suffer?"

"I don't think we must do anything." I continued stirring the gin, the cubes tinkling like wind chimes against the glass beaker. "But the man who thinks that—Dr. Ragin—becomes very good at seeing only what he wants. So good that he convinces himself the suffering and pain and injustice all around him aren't very real—and therefore aren't worth doing much about. Justification can be dangerous. Look where he ends up. Blinders don't always work out. So, I take the doctor's opinion with a grain of salt."

"I take mine with olives," she put in.

Instead of toothpicks there was a little stand, like a tiny umbrella stand, full of miniature silver rapiers. I took two of the little swords and skewered three olives with each.

She accepted the glass I handed her. "Made one for yourself?"

"Seemed rude to let you drink alone."

She didn't answer, but her blue eyes warmed with approval. She nodded at the armchair facing her. "Sit."

It wasn't a question. I sat.

She sipped her martini and nodded with satisfaction. "I've found, sadly, that mixing a good martini has become something of a lost art."

"Maybe you don't associate with the right people."

She laughed for the first time. "Maybe I don't." She ate an olive off the sword. "Now, what's this about Geoffrey—how are you mixed up with him?"

"I was hired by Martin," I said. "To follow him."

"You're a private detective?"

I nodded.

"Martin hired you to follow Geoffrey," she repeated. She would have made a fine poker player. Her eyes showed nothing. "How do I fit into this? And why show up at my doorstep unannounced?"

"Because announcing wasn't working too well," I answered. "I started to get the feeling that Martin was determined for us not to meet. Which made me curious."

"Well, what have you done to get my poor son in such a tizzy?"

Half against my will, I was liking the woman in front of me more and more. No tiptoeing around, no wasted words. Not doing that fake thing rich people did where they tried to make you feel that really, deep down, you were just like them.

And she liked gin.

"Your son got in a tizzy all by himself," I answered. "I've been trying to get him out of it. And best as I can tell, there's nothing poor about him. Must run in the family."

Her blue eyes were intent on mine. She didn't seem to take offense. "I expect he told you a word or two about our family? Our position in this city?"

I nodded.

"Good. And he told you about Geoffrey?"

I nodded again. "Sorry about how things worked out."

Her eyes flashed. "Why would you be? I ask for things I want. I recall asking you for a drink, not for your pity or condolences."

I was taken aback. "But he took so much from you."

"*Took?*"

I wasn't used to feeling off guard. "The money, the cars, the watches . . ."

"Let me correct the record," Mrs. Johannessen said. "Since my son seems to have neglected to do so. The relationship I had with Geoffrey was consensual in the most fundamental sense of the word. I went into it with open eyes, and my gifts to him were just that—gifts. If you're sitting there thinking the poor, old dotard was coerced or tricked, I strongly advise you to reconsider."

"I wasn't—"

She wasn't done. "And as you observed a moment ago about my son— unasked—there is nothing poor about me." She must have seen the doubt in my eyes because she went on. "You're a young and beautiful woman, Nikki."

I was having trouble keeping up. Not a feeling I was used to. "Thanks?"

"Don't thank me. It's not a compliment. It's a statement of fact. There's a difference. I have little interest in issuing compliments, especially these days. There isn't time. Facts, to me, are of much greater interest." She leaned forward, holding her drink in one hand. "Here's a fact. I used to look a lot closer to you than I do to myself, now. Which is natural, given that probably a half-century separates us in age. Stand up for a moment, will you?"

I put my drink down and stood.

She nodded toward several framed photographs on a mantel under the pair of dueling pistols. "Take a look over there. The second one from the right."

I walked over to the gelatin silver print, seeing a man and a woman, dressed formally and posing for the camera. The woman was taller than the man by at least several inches, and rather than trying to minimize this, she stood, shoulders straightened with an almost military posture, staring straight into the lens. She was beautiful, a full figure, skin creamy white, a classically proportioned face that a Renaissance painter would have begged to model. But the eyes, even in the faded black and white of the photograph, were the same, bright and bold and full of life.

I looked back toward the woman on the couch. "You were gorgeous."

"Come sit again."

I returned to the armchair as she continued speaking. "You reach a time in life when certain pleasures, once enjoyed easily, even thoughtlessly, become elusive. I'm a widow, but don't think for one moment that I buried any part of myself with my husband. You read, clearly. Are you familiar with *The Arabian Nights*?"

"Reasonably."

"With Sinbad?

I nodded.

"Now, he was a real character, a murderous, plundering adventurer of the first order—at least before those dreadful American cartoonists turned him into a castrated Mickey Mouse. Anyhow, on his fourth voyage Sinbad finds himself on the island of pepper-gatherers, where in short order he marries a noblewoman. She dies soon after, leaving him a widower. Are you familiar with what happens next?"

"Yes." As a girl I had loved *The Arabian Nights*, marveling at the casual brutality of the exotic world, the simultaneous cheapness and richness of life, and most of all Scheherazade, powerless and yet so much cleverer than the men around her, holding off her pending execution day by day through the power of her stories and imagination, nothing more.

I said, "They put him into the ground with her, according to their custom. Bury the living with the dead. He escaped, naturally, though I'm pretty sure he had to kill off a few innocents to manage it."

Mrs. Johannessen said, "You follow me, I assume?"

I did, and said so.

"I have every intention of enjoying life as long as I am able." She ate another olive off the little silver sword, then let it slide back into the glass. "And if you think that after my husband died I simply dried up and went into cold storage while waiting for the end, then you don't know me very well at all."

"I don't know you very well at all," I put in. "But I feel like I'm starting to."

"Have you had a chance to meet Geoffrey?"

"I have."

"And what did you think?"

I answered honestly. "I found him extremely impressive."

"It must have occurred to you that a charming, articulate, and handsome man in the prime of his life could probably have his choice of many beautiful women without turning his charms on the octogenarian crowd. I'm speaking factually, again."

I thought of Coombs's gaze, the magnetism of his eyes, his easy wit and confidence. That unmistakable feeling that life was a little warmer, a little more exciting, in his presence.

"It crossed my mind."

"I pride myself on being a realist," she said, sipping her drink. "It's an attitude that has taken me quite well through life. I find that if one is able to look clearly at who they are—willing to strip away the cheap, meaningless varnish of what others say to your face to gain favor—happiness becomes easier to grasp. So, what did you walk in here thinking? That you were going to talk to a senile old woman who thought that she'd ended up in this so-called mess thanks to the tenderness of her personality? Or perhaps her cooking skills? All, by the way, are nonexistent. I'm too old and too rich for charm, I'm acerbic to a fault, and I couldn't fry a lamb chop to save my life. But I know a few things. I'm eighty-one years old, Nikki, and I know who I am."

Her eyes caught and held mine. "Do you *really* think I believed he was in it for the pillow talk?"

"You make a good point," I acknowledged.

"I like to imagine that Geoffrey didn't despise the time we spent together, but that's my business, after all. I'm free to think what I wish. As is he, and as are you. What I do know is that he gave me a great deal of pleasure. And in return, I was happy to give him what I gave him." She set her drink down on a jade coaster. "Do you know what I'm worth?"

"I have a decent idea." I named a number that I'd come across in a *Time* profile of the family.

She nodded. "I don't mean to tromp into the boorish gardens of financial vulgarity. I bring up my wealth as a way of explaining that I could easily spend ten times what I gave Geoffrey, every year, should I live to be one hundred, which, by the way, I very much plan on doing. I do nothing for my money. It existed before me and it will exist after me. We have an office full of clever people who work industriously to ensure that our family's money grows each year. Some years less, some more, and other years it shoots up like a teenage boy. So why should I begrudge Geoffrey some baubles and pretty things?"

"But he left you. Didn't that sting?"

She finished her drink. "I knew he would leave eventually. Sticking around is not in that man's nature. If it was, I suspect he might be far less interesting. I enjoyed the time I spent with him. I enjoyed the conversation, his intelligence, his good taste, his spirit." She ate her last olive and tapped the edge of the miniature sword against the rim of the crystal glass with a sharp metallic sound. "And I consider myself richer, not poorer, for what I gave to get those things."

I finished off my martini, too. "May I say something honestly?"

"By all means."

"Martin gave me the impression that you were . . . showing your age a bit more." No wonder Martin had wanted to avoid this meeting. The mother was a hundred times stronger than the son.

"Parents, children, their relationships." She sighed. "So complicated. Tell me, Nikki, about your family."

I looked down at my glass. "I don't talk about my family. It's a thing of mine."

If she heard the change in my voice, she ignored it. "You're sitting in my living room, asking me probing, personal questions about my family, and you don't like to talk about your own?" she challenged. "*You* wanted to see *me*. Now *I'm* asking *you*."

She had a point.

"My parents are dead," I said. "They were murdered in our home when I was ten."

She didn't offer any of the horrified, sympathetic looks or, worse, hugs, that I was used to getting when I revealed this. A high school teacher of mine, once, had teared up and stroked my hair as though I was an Affenpinscher. All she asked was, "Who did it?"

"Two men. The younger one did some prison time and was eventually released."

"And the other one?"

"He lives quite close to here. His address is San Quentin. Specifically, the Adjustment Center. Located in Death Row."

"Adjustment Center? What is that?"

"For the worst of the worst. The ones so bad that the prison worries they'll hurt the serial killers out of plain boredom."

"They'll never release him, then?"

"Unfortunately not."

Her eyes didn't leave mine. "If they released him, what would you do?"

She had been honest with me. "I'd find him and kill him. I'd kill him exactly the way he killed them and I'd make absolutely sure he knew who was doing it."

Thanks to the autopsy photographs, I knew exactly which of the knife wounds were where. Like a ghoulish blueprint that I'd never forget, no matter how much I wanted to.

But I didn't want to. Just in case they ever freed Carson Peters.

"I don't know you very well at all," Mrs. Johannessen returned. "But I feel like I'm starting to."

We looked at each other. One of those long, understanding, uniquely female glances that convey more than most language. I was thinking that in a different world, the woman in front of me could have been one of my closest friends. I pushed the thought away. I was working. And I needed something that I couldn't ask her for.

Again, I thought of a poker game. "Your turn," I said.

"What do you want to know?"

"Tell me about your children."

She didn't shy away from the question. "My children, in different ways, have struggled to find purpose. Common enough with men and women of a certain standing. I've talked with peers enough to know it's a fairly general occurrence—this generational groping for meaning."

"Did you?"

She gave a thin smile. "I suppose I benefited from an unusually strong will."

"And your children didn't?"

She considered—whether the question or how much of it to answer, I couldn't tell. "William did." Her face shadowed. "Before his accident. He was such a strong and bright boy. My late husband always believed that he would be the one to take our family's helm. He had so much talent and drive."

"And the others?"

"Ronald, I suppose, always showed a preference for a more hedonistic existence. The type of boy who listens only when it suits him. As for my daughter, Susan, she certainly had willpower, but from a young age she was determined to forge her own way."

"And Martin?"

There was a flash of hesitation. "Perhaps Martin always felt in the shadow of his older brothers. He's eager to prove himself. In his mind, perhaps he thinks that my relationship with Geoffrey is an . . . embarrassment. A stain. A signal that he needs to step up and take control." She fell silent, her eyes clouded with thought.

"Have you talked to Susan recently?" I wanted to know.

Her eyes were still elsewhere. "My daughter and I don't have that kind of relationship. We've never been the kind to get manicures and mimosas every Sunday. Susan is independent, as I said. I admire that about her, even if it has created distance between us." Now she looked up. "Have you met my children? All of them?"

"Yes."

"What did you think?"

"I liked Susan, disliked Ron, think Martin is in over his head, and wasn't able to form an opinion on William."

"*In over his head*? What is that supposed to mean?"

She had bitten at the hook I'd dangled. I kept my voice casual. "Oh, just that he seemed a bit of a whiffle-waffler—hiring me, then calling me off just when things get interesting. I wondered why the change."

I could see her eyes brighten at the word *interesting* but she didn't take the opening I had left. Instead, she just said, "Enough about my family. How about you make us another round of those excellent martinis?"

It was a relief to do something as simple as making a drink. Olives didn't plan shenanigans and strategize against each other. They bobbed around and allowed themselves to be skewered. There was a gold-framed photograph hung above the bar cart. Four children, lined up in a row. Easy enough to figure out who was who. Martin and Susan looked to be high school age. Even in the picture I thought I could see Martin's petulant uncertainty, his eyes self-conscious, carriage a little too erect, as if trying to cast a longer shadow. Next to him stood Susan, pretty and smiling, one hand cocked on her hip. Ron slouched next to them, college-aged, handsome and arrogant and bored, a pair of sunglasses clipped to his open-neck shirt. The fourth face I didn't recognize, even though I knew it must be William, in his early twenties. He looked to be a natural leader, tall and blond and well built, looking directly into the camera with thoughtless confidence. Impossible to connect him to the hunched, muttering figure in the wheelchair I had met.

I walked the new drink over to Mrs. Johannessen and sat again.

"What exactly did my son hire you to do?" she wanted to know.

"He thought you were being taken advantage of—maybe worse. He was worried about blackmail."

"Blackmail? Whatever about? I should think I'm far too boring for anyone to want to blackmail."

Again, I thought of the poker game—revealing, bluffing, pushing the other to show more. "I have no idea. But he worried something was going on." I played my single ace carefully. "Which is hard not to agree with—given what happened to the poor guy, I mean."

"Poor guy?" she repeated quickly. "Who do you mean?"

"Coombs, of course."

This time she couldn't resist. "Happened?" Her voice remained casual, but her eyes were intent. "What do you mean, *happened*? What happened?"

"Last night. Coombs stepped on the wrong toes. Down in Monterey."

"How do you know such a thing?"

"I was there."

"What do you mean, *the wrong toes*?"

"I don't know exactly," I said. "But they belong to a very fat man with very delicate feet who absolutely shouldn't be stepped on. Coombs is with him now."

She leaned forward almost unconsciously. "Have they hurt Geoffrey?"

"No." Then I added, "Not yet."

"What do you mean, *not yet*?"

"He has until tomorrow night."

"Tomorrow night? To do what?"

"There's money involved. A negotiation. You could call him a hostage, at this point. I was hoping you could help me with that," I added.

"I know nothing about any money owed to any very fat men, or very thin men, or anyone else," she said dismissively. "But Geoffrey is being threatened?"

"*Threatened* is a very mild word."

"And what are you going to do about that?"

This was the moment. "Me? Nothing. Nothing I could do, even if I wanted to. Like I said, your son fired me about an hour ago. No longer my problem."

"Martin fired you? Why?"

Because you told him to? I wanted to ask. Instead I just said, "He wanted Coombs gone—and now he's gone. Although," I added, almost as an afterthought, "I don't know if your son fully understands how *gone* he'll be." However much the woman in front of me disdained outside meddling, I didn't know if she had considered the possibility of physical harm to Coombs himself.

She set down her drink and closed her hands over each other, as though her fingers had grown suddenly chilly. "What exactly do you do, Nikki?"

I tossed back more of my drink, feeling, along with the gin, sudden anger at the maddening opacity of this whole family. "You want to know what I do? I run a bookstore. That's what I do. Books. And when I'm not selling books, I try to do a little of what your crowd might call *philanthropy.* My own special brand of the stuff. Meaning that when I run into someone who has been treated badly, I don't turn my head away. Unlike the fellow in your book, I don't try to convince myself that suffering is okay, or necessary, or not that bad. You want to know what I do? I find the fellow who decided that rough was okay, and I give him the same taste of rough that he dished out. And I make sure to do it in a way that convinces him he should act like a goddamn kitten for the rest of his life." I leaned toward her. "That's what I do."

Her voice was more subdued when she spoke again. "What will they do to Geoffrey?"

"They'll kill him. Drowning is the plan, as of now, although they could always change their minds." I was being callous, maybe, but I had to be. I needed her to see what I saw. Maybe something else, too. Maybe I was tired of people pretending that little games and lessons didn't have consequences, didn't mean real things to real people. Tired of rich people using money to push pieces around a board and then getting up to go do something else.

She stood, showing no sign of having imbibed two strong cocktails. Once again, I was struck by her height, her presence, her command.

"Whatever my son was paying you, I'll triple it."

I stood, too. "To do what?"

Her face was once again hard and determined, her blue eyes icy. I felt her will pressing against me like a physical force. Like wind on a motorcycle. "I won't let these things you're talking about happen. I want you to find Geoffrey and free him."

"You're hiring me?"

In answer she rang a small silver bell. The butler appeared a moment later. "Go to my safe," she said. "I'll want ten thousand, cash, immediately." She turned back to me as the butler vanished. "For your expenses. Will that do, to start? Yes, I'm hiring you."

Five minutes later I was back in the elevator. A little buzzed from the gin, more than a little tired from the long day and the night before. And wiping away a small, victorious smile that had crept over my face.

I had my client.

FRIDAY

24

I woke up early Friday morning at my apartment in West Berkeley, questions running through my mind before my eyes opened. The last day I had to find Coombs. My last chance. Ethan was asleep next to me. He had come over last night as soon as I got home, cheerfully disregarding my warning that I would be exhausted, distracted, and just generally poor company.

I got up to shower, trying to be quiet, but I must have woken Ethan in the process. When I came back into the room, wrapped in a towel and brushing my teeth, he blinked groggily up at me. "Why so early?"

"Work." I spoke as clearly as I could manage with a mouth full of toothpaste. "There were unforeseen complications."

"I had a very specific dream when I was a boy," Ethan said. "That one day I might grow up and meet a sexy, mysterious girlfriend who was absolutely, infuriatingly, Guinness Record–level vague about *everything*. Little did I know that one day I'd actually find h—"

Still brushing my teeth, I bent down and flicked the tip of his ear. "Enough of this crazy talk."

"Speaking of crazy talk, how about what we talked about? Any thoughts?"

"Hang on. Two secs." I went into the bathroom, traded my toothbrush for a piece of floss, and came back, trying to dress, floss, and talk all at the same time. "Where were we?"

"Moving in together," he replied at once. "You've been thinking it over for about ten years now."

"If we were in a Victorian novel," I pointed out, "our families would disown us for living in sin."

"No," he corrected, "if we were in a Victorian novel, we'd have been married since we were fourteen and you'd be nursing your fifth child. But I happen to be dating a very contemporary-minded girl who considers marriage a four-letter word."

"All in due time! Don't you want something to look forward to?"

"Don't you think it would be kind of fun?" he returned. "Living together?"

"I'm not saying I don't want to. But what's the rush?"

He looked like he wanted to throw a pillow at me. "I mean, sorry to sound like my grandfather, but we're not in our early twenties, Nikki. We've been together over a year. It's a natural step."

A hard knocking on the door saved me from having to answer.

"Expecting company?" Ethan asked with a funny look.

"Stay there," I told him. "I'll go see."

Still holding my wet towel, I went into my closet and rummaged through my bottom drawer, where I kept my winter sweaters. Under the stacks of sweaters was an unloaded .40 caliber Walther PPQ. A longer barrel than my subcompact Beretta. I kept several full magazines wrapped in a woolen ski hat. I took one and clicked it into the empty pistol grip.

There was another series of loud knocks. Whoever was at the door didn't sound patient.

I chambered a round, draped my towel over the arm holding the gun, and went to check a little TV screen on my kitchen counter. Ordinarily, the screen showed a clear view of outside. Now it was dark. As though a finger was pressed against the camera lens.

I looked out the keyhole. Equally dark. Like someone was standing tight against it.

More knocks rattled the door.

"Who is it?" I called out, the towel draped over my left arm.

"Nikki Griffin? Open the door. It's the police."

Just because people said they were the police, it didn't make them the police. I stepped back from the door, flattened my back to the wall, pulled away a piece of curtain, and peered out a side window. Two men stood outside. One was in the uniform of the California Highway Patrol and the other was plainclothes. The uniform reassured me, but only up to a point. Uniforms could be acquired easily enough.

I cracked the door an inch, leaving the security lock chained.

"Badges," I said.

A few seconds passed and then a large, hairy hand wearing a rugged Shinola watch held a pair of badges up to the cracked door. One CHP, one San Francisco PD. They looked legitimate. None of the obvious markers of counterfeiting. Which, like the uniform, was not absolutely foolproof, but what was? I removed the chain and opened the door, finding myself face to face with two burly men in their forties. The badges had told me one of them was Jeffries and the other Clauson. I wondered who was who.

"I'm not going to offer you coffee," I said. "And no, you can't come in."

The guy in the plainclothes spoke. "We've had plenty of coffee this morning." He looked so much like a cop that he might as well have been in uniform. Cheap, sturdy dress shoes, slacks, black polo shirt, rumpled sports coat, buzz-cut hair. He gestured at the towel over my arm. "What you got there, the TV remote?"

"It's a remote I have a license for," I retorted. "What are you doing here?"

The one in the uniform drifted closer to the door. "Sure we can't come in?"

I blocked the door. "Extremely sure."

"You're not being very cooperative," he said.

"I'm not the one banging on your door. What do you want?" I asked again.

"We want to talk about Monterey."

"Monterey? What's in Monterey?" My voice was uninterested, but my mind was flashing. Had Mason's father gone to the police after all?

The uniform guy said, "You were just in Monterey. Right?"

I heard Ethan's voice, calling from the bedroom. "Everything okay, Nik?"

"Everything's fine! Be back in a few!" I looked back at the two cops. "Well, I *do* want coffee. Let's go up the street."

There was a taco truck I liked that did a morning route through the neighborhood. West Berkeley had enough construction going on these days that the truck did a brisk business with the work crews. I bought a breakfast burrito and a large coffee and then we walked across the street to a small park. Little kids played on a swing set while a group of young mothers in leggings did yoga in the grass.

I unpeeled foil from the burrito. "Which one of you is Jeffries and which one is Clauson?"

"Sergeant Jeffries," said the guy in uniform. He had a wide, freckled face and sandy hair. I saw his eyes wander to the yoga moms in their tight, high-waisted spandex.

"Detective Clauson," said the plainclothes guy. A sturdy brown mustache and crow's feet around his eyes made him look like a past-his-prime Tom Selleck.

"Were you in Monterey this week?" asked Jeffries.

"I stayed at the Cypress Inn. One night." He probably knew that. If he didn't, it would be his next question. There were worse things than appearing cooperative.

"Nice place, the Cypress," Clauson chipped in. "Pretty pricey, too. Special occasion?"

I took a bite of my burrito. "Not really."

"We heard there was an incident down there. An attempted robbery, one of the guards. I don't suppose that has anything to do with you showing up?"

I sipped coffee. "Are you asking me if I did that?"

"Chatting, that's all we're doing," said Jeffries.

"Well, I didn't. In case you're wondering."

Clauson had a notebook out and was writing something down while Jeffries continued the questions. "Can you account for your whereabouts from Wednesday night to Thursday night? Hour by hour, preferably?"

"If I need to, sure. Why?"

Jeffries' face was inscrutable. "Like I said, chatting."

Clauson raised his head from his notebook and I braced myself for the Mason questions to begin. He asked, "Are you familiar with the name Johannessen?"

Caught off guard, I paused before answering. "I was hired by a member of that family," I finally said.

"To do what?"

"You know I can't tell you that."

"A legal job?"

That annoyed me. "They wanted me to rob a bank. *Yes*, legal."

"Are you still working for them?" Jeffries asked.

"Why?"

"Because we're asking."

Clauson said, "Take us through Wednesday and Thursday. Where you were, who you were with. All the good stuff. Nice and specific."

"We don't get bored by details," Jeffries added. "Just in case you were wondering."

"I wasn't." I spent a few minutes answering the question, leaving out Mr. Z, Mason, and my interactions with Coombs, but keeping my locations as accurate as possible. The fact that I had been stopped by the Seaside police was a silver lining, I realized as Clauson scribbled away in his notebook. If they were suspicious of something, that was an ironclad alibi—and the Seaside cops, thank God, hadn't seen me with Mason. The cops didn't seem interested in the Cypress. This was something else.

By the time I finished, the taco truck had pulled away. The mothers were flowing through their poses. "What was in Monterey?" Jeffries wanted to know. "Why'd you go?"

I put my coffee down. "I'm done talking until you tell me what this is about."

The two of them glanced at each other.

Clauson asked, "Do you know Susan Johannessen?"

I stared at him, surprised. "We met once. At her gallery, Tuesday afternoon."

They traded another look.

"What?" I asked.

"Her car was found yesterday."

"Her car?"

Clauson said, "Parked at Monastery Beach, out on Highway 1. Are you familiar?"

"No."

Jeffries said, "The nickname is Mortuary Beach. It's been called the most dangerous beach in California. Looks like a total paradise—until you get in the water. Vicious undertow, all kinds of rip currents."

"It's not just swimmers," Clauson put in. "People wade in the surf, and next thing, they got a one-way ticket out to sea. People die like clockwork out at Monastery."

"Of course," said Jeffries, "it's not like drowning *has* to be accidental."

I didn't bother to hide my skepticism. "You think Susan killed herself?"

"It's possible, sure. We don't know. *Anything* is possible," Clauson said pointedly. "Some people die even though they don't plan on it."

"Or she's fine," I suggested. "Is that so crazy? People leave their cars at beaches all the time. Plenty of parking. Maybe she went backpacking."

"An optimist," said Clauson. "Good for you. That must be nice."

There was a burst of bright laughter from the kids playing. "Why did you ask if I knew Susan?" I wanted to know.

"That doesn't matter."

Police telling me something didn't matter meant that it probably did. "Her phone records," I realized. "You saw that she called me Wednesday evening." Once they had my number, they'd have my name. I would have been designated a person of interest. My credit card would have led them to the Cypress. Where they would have seen a call from my room back to Susan.

I've glimpsed this—this rot—this web.

Clauson was watching me closely. "You never saw her yesterday?"

I shook my head. "She wanted to talk to me. We had planned to meet in Monterey yesterday at noon. She never showed up."

"Was anything unusual going on in her life? Upset with anyone? Anyone upset with her?"

"I don't know her well enough to answer that. I met her once, for an hour."

Clauson put his notebook away and scratched his mustache. He handed me a card. "If you think of anything, let us know. The disappearance is under active investigation."

Something didn't make sense. The time line, I realized.

"Why all this urgency?" I asked. Maybe a deserted car at a beach didn't look great, but it wasn't the most damning thing in the world, either. This quick and intense of a response—digging through phone records, banging on my door—seemed extreme after just a day.

"We received a tip," said Jeffries. "Someone phoned in."

"Phoned in what?"

He kept his words vague. Not wanting to reveal specifics that might allow me to guess too much. "That she had been threatened. We tried to locate her. Then we put out an all-points bulletin when we couldn't find her at home or her gallery. A local sheriff saw her car at the beach and called it in."

Clauson said, "Call us if you learn anything. We need to find her."

I nodded and tossed my burrito wrapper and empty cup in the trash, where they landed on a crumpled pile of wrappers and napkins. We headed in different directions as though by mutual assent. I walked a block. Then I turned around and came back through the park. The two cops were gone. Everything else looked the same. Kids playing on monkey bars, yoga moms on their mats, squirrels and grass and sunshine.

Curious, I peered into the trash can where I had tossed my cup. The cup was gone, along with the wrapper. The other trash seemed untouched. They had wanted my DNA—to learn if I had been in Susan's car?

A missing person. A deserted car. A beach notorious for deadly currents.

Or a beach that could serve as a scapegoat. Seize a person, hide a body, move a car. All easy enough to do. Susan's car being at the beach didn't mean that she herself had left it there. Anyone could have taken her, then dropped the car there to be found. The cops had been holding back. A standard missing person case was one possibility. They thought they might be working a kidnapping. Or homicide. Maybe one involving me.

I had only until nightfall to find Coombs. That had seemed impossible enough.

Now I had to find Susan, too.

I wondered if the two of them might be in the same place.

With the same people.

25

A horn honked as I got back to my block. The sound came from an old blue Volvo parked on the quiet street. The Volvo needed a wash. Splats of mud streaked the balding tires and flaking paint. Through a dusty windshield I could see a man in the driver's seat.

I walked over. "Hey, Charles. Your phone stop working?"

"Haven't seen you in a while. Figured this was as good a time as any."

Charles Miller was a slight, forgettable man, bland eyes and smooth cheeks. His unimpressive appearance masked a ferocious determination. As an investigative journalist working for a Texas newspaper, he had been a Rottweiler in his pursuit of facts and truth. That inflexible instinct, and his refusal to defer to big money and big influence after he was told to back off a story, had gotten him sued, fired from his paper, divorced, and wiped out. Understandably embittered toward journalism, he had followed the finest American tradition and started over in California. Now, as a freelancer, he went after his investigations with similar intensity.

I got into his car, smelling cedar air freshener and wet dog. The radio was tuned to a sleepy blues station. "I'd invite you in for coffee but my boyfriend is probably still in bed," I explained.

Charles held up a stainless-steel thermos. "Got some right here." He gestured to a takeaway cup. "One for you, too."

"Thanks." I felt something lick my hand and realized that the wet dog smell was coming, indeed, from a wet dog. Two of them, actually. Golden retrievers, sprawled comfortably on the blanketed back seat. They wore bandanas, one red, one blue. The red-bandana dog looked at me with warm brown eyes and licked my hand again.

"Took them for a swim," Charles explained. "It was supposed to be a walk, but then they saw a duck."

"Ducks happen." I leaned back to pet their silky heads, still damp from the water. "What are their names?"

"The one you're scratching is Bernstein. Blue bandana is Woodward."

"I'm sure they're both great at digging things up."

He laughed. "A little too good, says my backyard."

I smiled. "They must get it from you. Things good?"

Charles nodded. "Kids visited last month. Took 'em to Disneyland."

"Glad to hear it," I said, meaning it. I knew that his wife, after divorcing him, had been awarded sole custody. He didn't see much of his children.

"I have good news and bad news," he said. "What do you want first?"

"I've always hated that question." I ruffled Bernstein's ears and he licked my hand.

"Fair enough. What do you know about VIN numbers?" Charles asked.

Of all the things I'd put thought into during my life, VINs were not high on the list. "Just that they're a unique code for each vehicle, I guess?"

He nodded. "Before 1981, there was no regulation. An auto company could slap down whatever they wanted. But on all vehicles since eighty-one, a VIN is a federally mandated seventeen-digit string containing all kinds of information. Each digit means something specific. You can learn all kinds of things. Country of origin, manufacturer, series, body style, engine size, even information on braking and suspension and what plant they were produced at, plus a unique identifier. That's what sixteen of the digits give you. But the ninth number in the sequence is a little different. That's what they call the check digit."

"Check digit," I repeated. I had never heard the term before.

"The check digit is the only one in the seventeen that doesn't have an inherent value. It's only there to validate the rest of the VIN sequence. They use a bunch of complex formulas and something called a transliteration table—A equals 1, B equals 2, etc.—basically to tell them if a VIN is real. You can run a check-digit validation and see if the calculated value equals the original. If it does, the VIN is kosher. If not, there might be a problem. If you like math and have an extra hour, I can tell you all about how to do it."

Neither of those was true, and I said so.

Charles smiled. "Anyway, that's what was confusing my DMV guy when he first ran the VIN you gave me. Something with the validation. But, just to make it more complicated, some of the European brands won't pass an American check-digit verification, and you're looking for a Mercedes, so he was trying to figure out what was going on."

"And?"

"You're looking for a stolen car," Charles said. "That VIN isn't going to get us anywhere. Whatever number you wrote down was put on at some point *after* it originally left the factory."

"That was the bad news?"

"Afraid so."

I didn't bother to hide my disappointment. "There's no way to figure out who owns the vehicle? No way to get an address or name?" My last link to Coombs. Disappearing like tissue paper held above a lit match. And by nightfall it would be too late.

"Not through the DMV," Charles said. "It's not in their system."

"Well, thanks for trying." Woodward, with the blue bandana, sighted a cat outside and barked sharply. The cat sensed the attention and watched us, inscrutable, as it licked its paw before continuing on its way. "How about the other things I asked about?"

"Right, the two names you gave me," Charles said. "Ron Johannessen did indeed get in some kind of trouble back at Princeton. There's nothing on his formal academic record, but I found a pretty hefty donation, made through a nonprofit controlled by the Johannessen family, that same year— his sophomore year in college."

"What kind of trouble?"

"Something happened with a female student. No idea about the specifics—nondisclosures were signed—but she withdrew from Princeton that same semester and transferred. It looks like they used a different shell company to make another payout to the girl's family that same year." I could tell Charles was interested. "Johannessen—that's the family with the pharmaceutical fortune, right? Better living through chemistry—and the more chemistry, the more profit?"

"Same family," I said. "And the other thing?"

"Dr. Geoffrey Coombs. He's a tricky one." Charles drank some coffee, lowered his window, and lit one of his foul-smelling cigarillos. "He's been a professional con man for almost half his life and is very adept at mixing the real and the fictional. All kinds of aliases pop up and he legally changed his name at least twice, according to court records. Hard to find anything solid on the guy. It's like he's made of water. Quite the journey, though, gotta give him that. He's not actually from the U.K.—he was born near Edmonton, Canada—and he never graduated from college, much less earned a graduate degree, although he does appear to have been at Oxford for at least several years studying psychology."

"Why didn't he graduate?"

"There was an affair with a prominent Oxford dean's wife. The dean returned home to find Coombs and his wife in flagrante delicto."

I nodded, unsurprised. That sounded like Coombs. "So he was expelled?"

"Not really," Charles said. He puffed bluish smoke out the window. "Actually, Coombs killed the fellow."

"What?" I stared at Charles. "Are you sure?" Nothing in the con man's elegant demeanor had suggested violence.

Or had it?

The professional way he had bound me. The ease with which he had handled a gun. Our night together. Out on the high bluffs, the ocean surging underneath. *I never said I was a romantic. Only you did.* The shadows on his face, as though taking off a mask.

"He was caught?" I asked. "What happened?"

"Tried and convicted of manslaughter. The man went from Oxford University to the Scrubs. A journey of fifty miles—plus a universe or two."

"The Scrubs?" I repeated. "What's that?"

"Nickname for Her Majesty's Prison—HM Prison Wormwood Scrubs, in West London. Gotta give it to them, the Brits sure can do names. The Scrubs is a Class B—the U.K. uses a four-tier prison system. Class A's are where they stick the absolute worst, but Class B's are no picnic. Not at all. The Scrubs was notorious for its poor conditions—rampant germs and disease, gang violence, abusive guards, you name it. They did a big investigation in the nineties, lawsuits and settlements and a warning to the prison that it better shape up or close down. The Scrubs is better, now, but your man Coombs would have been there for the worst of it."

Charles puffed more smoke. "A man who made it through the Scrubs would be able to make it through a lot. And the Scrubs would certainly leave a . . . distinct effect on anyone."

I tried to picture Coombs in that kind of squalor. No wonder he appreciated a good hotel.

"Anyway," Charles continued, "he served just over five years and then they kicked him out of the U.K. Gradually, over the next two decades, he fashioned his current identity. His cons seem to have gotten bolder and more complex as he gained experience, although usually they seem rooted around the common denominator of seduction. Wealthy widows and divorcees, family trusts, even an art museum convinced it had been dealing with a wealthy donor. By the time he reached the Johannessen lady, he'd been doing this kind of thing for the better part of twenty years. One could say he's at the peak of his career."

"Indeed." Susan Johannessen had told me that Coombs had been able to talk art like a professional collector. He seemed to be a man who studied for his roles. Meticulous. Prepared.

Charles flicked dead ash off the brown cigarillo. "I won't even begin to ask how you, and Coombs, and stolen cars, and the Johannessen family connect."

"I wish I knew." Thinking again that I had only the remainder of the day to find Coombs. Learning about his violent past didn't change that fact. It made me want to talk to him more than ever. More questions that I wanted answers to.

I thanked Charles and got out, lost in thought. A stolen vehicle. A stolen vehicle in a state with about 14.5 million registered vehicles and close to 200,000 auto thefts a year. And only a single day to do this. The odds hopelessly long even for a well-staffed police department—let alone one person. A needle in about ten acres of haystacks. Something that would be almost impossible for anyone to trace or track down.

Almost anyone.

I knew who I had to see.

26

Apparently, Buster was on some kind of health kick. When I found him, he was working out in a makeshift gym that had been set up in a relatively motorcycle-free corner of his Vallejo garage. Buster didn't go for ellipticals or rowing machines. His workout space was all bone-bare iron and concrete. He wore black jeans and his usual Timberland boots and was hammer-curling a pair of fifty-pound dumbbells. Under a sleeveless black undershirt, his massive, tattooed arms were glossy with sweat.

"If it isn't Nikki Griffin!" Buster gave me a broad smile, which, along with his six-foot-five frame, pirate's goatee, and ponytail, would have been ferocious enough to keep little children up at night. "How'd you know I needed some-one to spot me on the next set?"

"Intuition." I walked up close enough to reach out and pluck the lit cig-arette out of his mouth. "I'm not sure if you're supposed to smoke while lift-ing. Maybe your doctor forgot to mention it?"

"Listening to your doctor is the best way to tell you're getting old." He grunted, heaving the weights up in an alternating one-two pattern. "Why, you gonna tell on me?"

I dropped the cigarette and stepped on it. "We'll see."

"That means you need something." Buster put the weights down and pulled a new cigarette from a rumpled pack of Camels that lay on a big, chromed-out Indian motorcycle. The saddlebags were decorated with tasseled leather and the handlebars looked wide as a Boeing's wings. He stuck the cigarette in the same corner of his mouth that the first had resided in and lit it with a match, wiping sweat from his forehead as he took a deep drag.

I smiled. "Always so cynical. I could just have your health in mind." I gestured at the weights. "Glad you're getting your exercise in, at least."

Buster jetted smoke from his nostrils. The resemblance to a dragon was impossible to miss. "You get to be my age, and you'll be worrying about your delicate figure, too. Just you wait."

I had to laugh. The delicate figure in question was about 250 pounds. "You're really giving me something to look forward to."

"Aging, Nikki. It's the curse that handsome gentlemen like myself struggle with each and every day."

"Yeah, well, for the time being you're a very handsome gentleman, Buster, so enjoy it while you can."

He mopped more sweat off his face and jabbed his cigarette my way. "You *really* want something from me today. You're never this nice."

I gave him a bright smile. "I want to buy you lunch."

"Lunch?"

I waved stray smoke away from my head. "Don't worry, we can get salads. Not trying to spoil your delicate curves. Plus, I've always suspected you were secretly a quinoa guy."

He shook his head and lumbered past me, a very slight limp in one leg. "Quinoa. Sure. I know just the place."

I'd never seen someone stare a waiter in the face and—without any irony—order two separate orders of bacon cheeseburgers and fries along with two pints of beer for himself. Maybe I wasn't dining out with Buster enough. He had driven us to a nearby bar that looked like a low-rent knockoff of an Irish pub. None of the charm but all of the GUINNESS and JAMESON signs. Whoever had designed the place had forgotten windows. From the outside it looked like some German pillbox in an Alistair MacLean novel. Inside, the main source of illumination was a row of wide-screen TVs slung over the bar at different angles. There was no sign of a hostess so we sat ourselves at a booth. There were plenty to choose from. My half of our table was sticky with the remnants of a spilled drink. I tried to balance my elbows on a little paper placemat that seemed the only clean thing in sight.

This included our waiter. He was a lanky teenager with a diamond stud earring and a too-cool-to-be-here attitude. He looked down at Buster skeptically as he shoved a bread and butter plate onto our table. "Our kitchen makes big burgers. How 'bout I put in one order, and then you can order the second one if you're still hungry?"

Even seated, Buster didn't seem all that much shorter than the kid. He had thrown a black leather jacket over his undershirt, but the jacket only seemed to amplify his size. I watched as he pulled a serrated, four-inch folding knife from his pocket.

Buster flicked the knife open with his thumb and used the gleaming blade to spread butter on a piece of bread, his eyes never leaving our waiter. "How about you put in one burger, and then instead of the second one, I eat you?" he suggested, his mouth full of bread.

Our waiter turned the approximate color of our napkins.

"Two burgers for you, yes sir. Right away."

"Medium raw," added Buster. "With extra onions."

I ordered and the kid took off toward the kitchen like he was running the hundred-meter dash in the last meet of the season.

I looked fondly across the table at my friend. "Cannibalism. I always thought you'd find your way there eventually."

Buster stuffed more buttered bread in his mouth. "That skinny little prick should be so lucky."

Our waiter came back with our drinks: one beer for me, two for Buster. He set them down without a word and disappeared back toward the kitchen as fast as the first time.

Buster took a gulp of beer. Half of his first pint vanished.

"That's the beautiful thing about exercise," he observed. "The rest of the day, you get to do whatever you want."

I clinked my glass against his. "No heart attacks, please. I'm too busy to be bringing you flowers in the hospital."

"You do care, Nikki, you really do! I've always known it would slip out one day."

Our food came out with impressive alacrity. Buster sprayed hot sauce and ketchup under the buns and bit into the first of his two burgers, chewing with gusto. "Why don't you tell me why you're taking me to lunch?"

"I have a problem," I said.

He raised an eyebrow, still chewing. "Body to hide?"

It was a comment that would have been funny, except he was serious.

Buster had helped me hide bodies before. He'd probably hidden a few of his own, too. He'd do it again if asked.

"No," I said, then added, "not yet, anyway." I bit into my burger. It was delicious, the patty seared to a perfect medium rare, the bacon crispy against the melted Cheddar. "Right now, I have to find a vehicle."

Buster's first burger was already gone, along with both of his beers. He waved his empty glass at our waiter, who was cowering by the bar.

"A car. Okay, that's a start."

Buster was good at quite a few things. He was a great mechanic, an even better drinker, and, all jokes aside, as sturdy and reliable as a Swiss Army knife. If I had been asked to draw up a list of the five or six people I trusted most in the world, Buster would have made the cut. He also knew more about the stolen car business than anyone I had ever met. After all, he worked in it. Stolen cars were more his bread and butter than the stuff on our table.

He crunched through a pile of French fries like matchsticks but his eyes, now, were serious. "What do you have, what do you need?"

"A Mercedes G-Class. One of the big Jeep-y things that probably gets ten miles a gallon on a steep downhill."

He raised an eyebrow. "You're in the auto market?"

"I need a person. The car can get me to him. I hope."

Buster considered. "A G-Class should be a bit easier. There aren't that many floating around. You've seen it?"

"Yeah."

"How do you know it's hot?"

"I got someone at the DMV to run the VIN. It came back as stolen."

Buster accepted a third beer from our waiter. "Where was it?"

"Monterey."

He considered while working on his second burger. "Tough market, Central Coast, if you're looking for something. So much volume. Not nearly as bad as SoCal, though." He took another bite and kept thinking. "I know a couple Koreans down in San Jose who work Monterey. They deal with a lot of inventory. We can start there."

"When?"

He shrugged. "Tomorrow? Day after? I'm around."

"It's urgent. Like, today urgent. And," I felt I should add, "possibly dangerous."

"Dangerous, eh?" Buster dipped his folding knife into his untouched ice water and wiped the blade clean with his untouched napkin. He put the knife back in his pocket and looked at me, both his plates and row of pint glasses empty. "What are you waiting for, then? Check's all yours."

Like me, Buster was a motorcycle guy, but we took his car so we could talk on the way. One of his cars, anyway. I'd never seen him in the same car twice. Today's was a bright orange Z06 Corvette, low and mean and aggressive, the engine loud, leather racing seats molded firm against my back. I felt like I was in the cockpit of a fighter plane. We drove south on the 880, the San Francisco skyline visible across the Bay to our right. We passed the Oakland port and then a series of nondescript cities, Hayward, San Leandro, Fremont with its sprawling Tesla factory semi-visible on our left. The temperature grew hotter as we left the fog and cool air currents of the Bay behind.

Given his quick temper, Buster was a surprisingly laid-back driver. No aggression, no cursing, no weaving in and out of lanes for the best spot. With a cigarette in his mouth, a Miller tallboy "road soda" wedged between his thick thighs, ponytail and wraparound sunglasses, he was the picture of relaxed cool as he turned up the rock station on the radio and blew smoke out the side window.

"What's new? Still enjoying the single life?" I asked.

"I told you. Four divorces were enough. No one's putting a ring on this boy ever again." He held up a finger the size of a sausage. It was hard to imagine anyone fitting anything smaller than a Hula-Hoop around it. "How about you?" he wanted to know. "Probably breaking hearts right and left?"

"Actually, going steady," I admitted.

He glanced at me, surprise showing even through the mirrored sunglasses. "Not that Berkeley kid, still?"

"The very same."

"You can handle that? A civilian?" His tone was openly curious. "You got enough oxygen to breathe and all?"

I pushed away Coombs's face. "So far, no complaints."

"Does he know?"

This time I paused before answering. "A very, very approximate idea."

Buster said, "So, no."

I didn't say anything.

"And it works?"

"Yeah. It does. So far."

"If you say so." Buster's voice contained doubt but he didn't press me.

His questions had pushed Coombs back into my mind. His knowledge of me. The eyes that seemed to see me for who I really was. The challenge in his tone—as though daring me to show myself. The thrill of not knowing what would happen if I did.

The excitement.

I'd spent my whole life searching for dependability. Security. Control. And I'd found Ethan—been lucky to find him. I knew that. A partner who was compassionate and loyal and intelligent, the very definition of stable, tenure-track job and no secrets, and he accepted everything about me. I'd found someone good. And someone really good—for *me*.

Yet here I was searching for a bad man. Objectively bad, by any measure society had to judge. A cheat, a criminal, an outlaw. Not just a con artist, but apparently a convicted killer, a felon. A dangerous, murky chameleon, full of secrets and feints and uncertainties. A man whose presence in my life promised the very opposite of security and control and all the rest of the things I had tried so hard to get.

Why was all that uncertainty so damned exciting?

In San Jose we merged onto the 101, and then Buster took a cloverleaf exit that left us north of downtown. California wasn't all stunning coastlines and vistas. The state could be as ugly as anywhere else when it tried. Or when it didn't bother not trying. We drove through a charmless neighborhood, wide flat straight roads, all asphalt and endless strip malls. Fast-food and chain stores, gas stations and car washes and convenience marts, signs for auto parts and liquor specials. Aggressive colors trying to grab the eye, the hot sun pounding down. The ocean could have been as far away as Nebraska.

Thirty or fifty years ago the whole ugly mess had probably been shaded and fragrant with orange groves and lemon trees. The thought made me question progress.

"You know these guys pretty well?" I asked. We were driving south on 13th Street. Seen on a map, from above, we'd be roughly in between the 101 and 880 freeways that arched around us on either side.

Buster shrugged. "So-so. They do decent bodywork. We used to do business here and there."

"Used to?"

"One of them doesn't like me that much. Sort of a falling out."

"A falling out?"

The cigarette still in the corner of his mouth, Buster wriggled a toothpick between his teeth, one hand lightly on the wheel. "I think I beat up his cousin, a few years back. Apparently, these Koreans have great fucking memories. They're like elephants. I keep waiting for him to forget—and he just doesn't."

"Why did you beat up his cousin, Buster?"

He shrugged and tapped ash out his window. "I don't remember, honestly. My memory's a goddamn sieve. But I must have had a good reason. I think?" His cigarette butt vanished out the window. The toothpick followed. "Because in general, you know, I'm a total pacifist."

We pulled into a tiny used car shop circled by metal fencing, parked, and got out. A sign that hung off the fence advertised GREAT CARS LOW RATES. The great cars looked like they hadn't been washed in years. They sat jammed up against each other, claustrophobically close, like penned cattle. Four-digit prices were painted in neon green onto dusty windshields. Some were old enough to have stick antennae, the thin wires looking odd and old-fashioned. Like walking into a house and seeing a VCR.

A cinderblock garage squatted in the rear of the lot, a glass door opening to a phone booth of an office. Buster ignored it and circled around toward a pair of open bay doors in the back. We squeezed through rows of cars. There was a snap that made my head jerk. A man of Buster's bulk didn't squeeze so easily. He had snapped off a Honda's side mirror. He gave a what-can-you-do shrug and moved on.

As we reached the open bay, we were examined by a mechanic in blue overalls. Sure enough, he was Korean, late twenties and muscular, spiky black hair gelled so intensely it looked flash-frozen.

"What?" he said. No recognition in his words, but a little in his eyes.

Buster did the talking. "Mikey around?"

"He's busy."

Buster shook his head. "He's busy, you're busy, I'm busy. We're all fucking busy. I want to talk to Mikey. Got a question for him, drove all the way down here."

A name patch identified the mechanic as Eddie. "Hope you took the scenic route, at least." His voice was surly. "Get something out of the trip and all. We're closed for the day, Buster. Always a pleasure, great to see you, goodbye and good luck."

"If you're closed, open up," Buster said.

"Go bother someone else." Eddie started to turn away.

"I come in peace," Buster said.

Eddie turned back to see Buster removing his sunglasses and gazing down with a look that could almost have been paternal affection. "Peace for now, anyway."

27

We followed Eddie through the small garage. He walked casually but I could see the tension in his shoulder muscles. Two cars were up on lifts, metallic innards exposed. Korean hip-hop pounded from a speaker. I smelled oil, metal, laced with a burnt chemical edge I wasn't sure about. A few steps forward and I had the answer. A second Korean guy was using a welding torch on the fender of a red Saturn. The odor of burnt metal became stronger. He looked up at us, and his expression changed as he recognized Buster.

He turned the torch off and got up. "Why are you here?"

Buster had lit yet another cigarette, flying in the face of every HIGHLY FLAMMABLE warning I'd ever heard of. I looked around nervously for nearby oil puddles.

"Hey, Mikey," he said. "Got five minutes?"

"What do you want?" Mikey asked again.

"Trying to track down a G-Class. Would mean the world to me if you could help." Buster's voice was cheerful. I wondered if he noticed a third mechanic who had drifted behind us. I hadn't seen him when we came in. He looked like a bodybuilder and held a monkey wrench.

"Can't help you," Mikey said. "Maybe call next time. Save you a trip down."

"That's what I told him," said Eddie.

"Yeah, but you haven't really tried," said Buster.

Eddie stared. "Tried what?"

"You know—helping us."

Eddie said something in Korean and Mikey answered in fast words. It was obvious they were brothers. From a distance I could have mistaken them for twins. When Eddie spoke again, he sounded angrier. "If you wanted my help, maybe you shouldn't have messed up Dave, asshole."

Buster gave me a helpless look. "See? What did I tell you? Great memories."

I didn't answer. I found myself wishing that Mikey wasn't still holding his welding torch. I heard a grinding noise and glanced behind us. The third mechanic had hit a switch and the bay doors were clanking down, the chain drive rumbling in the ceiling.

"Look," Buster said. "I'm sorry, honestly. It was a big misunderstanding, not really sure what happened—"

"You broke his jaw, dude!" Eddie exploded. "That's what happened! He was drinking through sippy cups for two months! And now you walk in here with your girlfriend asking for a goddamn favor?"

He was interrupted by Buster's booming laugh. We all stared at Buster like he had cracked up. "Girlfriend?" he finally managed. He pointed at me. "Have you seen *her*?" His finger flipped around to his own chest. "And *me*? Girlfriend, right. And the goddamn Pope calls me on my birthday." He was still chuckling.

No one else seemed to see the humor.

Eddie's voice was low and dangerous as a rattlesnake. "How about we break *both* your jaws and send you back up to North Bay to eat applesauce? Would that help you?"

Buster stopped smiling.

I was remembering that under all his jocularity he had an awful temper. He scratched his jaw like he was at a loss, then shrugged and folded his sunglasses into a back pocket. "You're not being nice."

All four men in the garage looked like they didn't see the point of talking more. The big guy behind us had moved closer, hefting the monkey wrench. Mikey and Eddie were spreading out, flanking us. I'd never been attacked by a guy with a welding torch before. My mind filled with unpleasant technical questions. Questions like how long it would take to relight, and how close skin could safely get to the nozzle. I knew aluminum melted at about twelve hundred degrees Fahrenheit. Gold, about two thousand degrees. Steel, closer to three thousand degrees.

I wondered how hot the welding torch got.

The triangle tightened. Faces resolute, eyes angry. The look of three men committing to an action, preparing for violence. The garage practically stunk of testosterone.

"Guys," I interjected. "Can I say something, please?"

Everyone stared at me. I took the silence as an invitation to continue. "First of all, this is my fault. Buster is doing me a favor."

Mikey asked, "If you're not his girlfriend, who are you?"

"You could say we're old friends. And I'm sorry about Dave, really—we both are. Whatever happened, whoever's fault."

"I don't know who you are—" started Eddie.

"I'll explain." It was useful having an expense account. Especially in cash. I took a rubber-banded packet of hundred-dollar bills that equaled $2,500 out of my purse and tossed them to Eddie, ignoring Buster's disappointed look. "Call that medical expenses, reimbursement, whatever. That's for Dave, whether you help us or not."

He held the money, uncertain.

I wasn't done. I produced a packet of bills identical to the first. This one I held on to. "For your time," I said. "Like I said, we drove down here, but I know you're busy. I want to buy an hour of your time. For twenty-five hundred dollars. To see if I can learn anything about this car I'm looking for. If I can, great. If not, the money's yours to keep—as long as you put in a good faith effort."

Eddie's eyes shifted from me to the money. Then back again.

He pulled a phone from his pocket and touched the screen. The loud music went quiet. In the silence, everyone seemed to relax a little.

Mikey set the welding torch down. "Tell me everything you know about this Mercedes."

There had been plenty of times in my life when I'd gotten better value out of $5,000, but the money I'd spent—rather, what Mrs. Johannessen had spent—wasn't wasted, either. After almost an hour of nonstop phone calls and text messages, they reached a wholesale auction place down in Salinas that made Eddie reach for a pen. I was starting to glimpse how connected the auto theft network was. Everyone doing business with everyone else, constant communication, ceaseless interaction. Hundreds of roving groups out on the streets and probably hundreds more garages all over the state, repainting, chopping up for parts, maybe putting them back on the road. A thriving, humming hive devoted to the stealing and reselling of cars.

Eddie made another two calls in quick succession, then handed us a yellow Post-It Note. On the little square of paper there was a Salinas address. There was also a name.

Leo.

Five minutes later we were back in Buster's Corvette on the 101, heading south. Almost three o'clock. The big eight-cylinder engine rumbled under us. The pavement streaked by.

"That was productive," Buster commented, lighting yet another Camel. He exhaled, looking wistful. "Should've said you had five grand to play with, though. Those two shitheads didn't deserve it half as much as I do."

"You weren't kidding about them not liking you."

"Great men are always polarizing, Nikki," he sighed. "It's the curse of greatness, all through history. JFK, MLK, me . . . We can't be universally loved."

"I'm glad you're keeping such good company."

Buster tossed his empty road soda on the floor behind him and cracked a second Miller tallboy that he pulled from under his seat. "You should spend more time with me. See how much fun we have?"

Salinas was an hour south. As we left South San Jose behind, the landscape rose and seemed to stretch, relax, rolling brown hills replacing the endless asphalt of Silicon Valley. The Mamas & the Papas came on the radio and I fell quiet, listening, thinking of my parents as I always did. One of their favorite bands. I wondered what my parents would be like today. If they would have changed, or moved, or grown apart. I hoped not. I liked to imagine them still in Bolinas, in the same little blue house where I had been raised, evening strolls along the beach, teasing each other while doing dishes. Still being alive.

I was curious about something. "I thought new cars were impossible to steal—especially the nice ones?"

Buster drummed the beat on the steering wheel with a big hand. "No such thing as impossible to steal. If it has wheels we can steal it. Hell—if they ever make flying cars we'll steal them, too. A nice model like the G-Class is actually easier for us to find because not as many people have the skill set to jack 'em. You have to be an expert and there aren't that many experts. If you were looking for a 1990 Honda there'd be two million idiots running around with a screwdriver who could've done it."

"What do people even do with stolen cars these days?" It was an area I knew little about. "Hasn't technology made it impossible to move them?"

"Far from it." He smiled and adjusted his visor to block the sun as the road twisted. "You got the chop shops, same as always. Cut stuff into parts, resell pretty much anywhere you want. Shipping international is bigger than ever, too. Tons of countries charge import taxes and tariffs that would make loan sharks drool. Who wants to pay that? Easy enough to fill a couple of shipping containers and sail them out of Oakland or Long Beach—off they go to Asia or South America or wherever. People line up to buy everything we send. And retagging has gotten huge."

"Retagging? License plates, you mean?"

He shook his head. "VINs. The cops call it *VIN cloning*. Swap out the VIN on the hot car with one belonging to a legal registered vehicle, have someone resell it online. By the time they find out, it's someone else's problem." He took a gulp of beer and wiped his mouth. "You got a stolen car, you can make money off it. Trust me."

As we approached Gilroy the landscape became agricultural, hills steeper, cattle grazing, freeway narrowing to two lanes. My parents had brought us down once for the Gilroy Garlic Festival and I could still remember the pungent taste of my garlic ice cream cone.

"Don't worry," said Buster. "I'm not a nosy man. I won't ask. Let's just enjoy this little road trip together and appreciate each other's company."

I leaned back, stretching my legs comfortably against the dash. "Ask what?"

"Well, I suppose if I *was* nosy, which I'm not, I might wonder who drives this Mercedes you're looking for, and why the frugal, sensible Nikki Griffin is throwing five grand at a couple of chop shop dummies who talk better and more honest when they're hanging upside down being tickled."

"Guess we got lucky," I said.

"Lucky?"

"That you're not the nosy type."

"Right."

We drove a few more miles.

"Fine," I said.

Buster scratched his jaw and looked over. "Fine?"

"Fine, as in what do you want to know? Keeping in mind that I can't use anything but hypotheticals and would hope that even hypothetically you would not ever say a word about any of this. To anyone."

Buster was, after all, putting himself in a fair bit of danger to do me a sizable favor. More than sizable. I owed him a bit of an explanation.

"Hypothetically," Buster said, "I should be able to handle that."

"Okay. Then let's say I'm tracking down a con man. And let's say I was hired to do this by the adult son of a very prominent San Francisco family, because he thought his elderly mother was being blackmailed by said con man. Furthermore, let's say that this guy was recently kidnapped by a couple of Central Coast gangsters who plan to throw him into Monterey Bay tonight if they don't get what they want."

"They want money?"

"How'd you know?"

Buster grinned. "Everyone does."

I acknowledged this point with a nod.

"What about the blackmail?" Buster asked. "The son was wrong about that?"

"Not entirely." Talking through everything aloud, to someone else, was helping. "I just think the son heard *part* of a conversation and, since he hated this guy anyway, assumed the worst—wanted to assume the worst. But I don't think the mother—who, by the way, makes flint look soft—was being blackmailed by the guy I'm after. I think she was asking for his help. With something else. Because she wanted me out of the picture, until I told her the con man had been kidnapped, and now"—as I spoke I was realizing—"it's not *just* that she has a soft spot for the fellow and doesn't want him hurt. She needs *someone* down there as her proxy, and until the guy is free . . ."

"That someone is you," Buster finished.

"Exactly."

He thought this over. "So who's actually blackmailing the family? The fine upstanding Central Coast gents?"

"Right." Mr. Z looking me over, eyes appraising. *You're still pretty . . . Come find us if you ever need a job.* "At first I just thought they were a particularly nasty bunch of pimps, but there's more going on with them."

"They're the ones with the G-wagon. Who you're trying to find."

"Right."

We drove another mile or two.

"You gotta watch it with some of these guys," Buster observed. "Everyone thinks all the dangerous people live in the big cities, but the groups who control trucking routes through the state, they got all kinds of things going on. Drugs, girls, gambling, protection, hits for hire, you name it. Stolen cars are the *nice* part of their business. I've bumped into them here and there. I keep my distance when I can."

"You telling me to be careful? That's a first." My voice was half-teasing.

Buster's was not. "Crazy as that sounds, what I'm hearing, yeah. I am. Hypothetically, of course."

"Duly noted."

He asked the obvious question. "How the hell did the rattlesnakes you're looking for get involved with some blue-blooded, ball-and-gown SF types? Where in all hell is *that* connection?"

"I have no idea," I admitted. "But I'm starting to think I really have to find out."

After Gilroy, the 101 started to ease west, as if searching for the ocean with biological instinct. We drove on another ten miles in silence, gentle hills swelling up from the ground, white cloud puffs drifting through blue sky. The land untightened. Steinbeck country, here. It felt good to be free of the clogged, urgent arteries of the Bay Area. Good to have air and space and land. Salinas Valley wasn't far from Monterey, maybe twenty miles inland, but it seemed a different universe from the ocean-side boutiques and hillside mansions I had been around the day before. Now we were in a vast, agricultural flatland, thousands of acres of artichokes and lettuce and tomatoes and strawberries, a staggering wealth of produce that reached every corner of the nation.

Buster drove us east, away from downtown Salinas, turning the Corvette onto a dirt road. Infinite rows of crops spread in all directions, planted with the geometric precision of a chessboard. The Corvette wasn't built for dirt, but Buster didn't seem to care a bit. We jounced along, throwing up a brown dust cloud behind us. I could see groups of migrant pickers scattered among the vast fields and wondered what they were picking. The laborers were tiny against the landscape. It seemed impossible that humans could harvest so much produce by hand.

"We're going the right way?" I asked.

"Shortcuts," Buster said.

In another minute he turned off the dirt onto a paved, curving two-lane road that eventually widened and straightened. Urban life returned quickly. Traffic lights and suicide lanes, low-rent buildings, cheap motels and dingy gas stations and liquor stores. Nothing looked expensive. Nothing looked new. None of the big Holiday Inns or shiny, twenty-pump Chevron stations that cropped up around the freeway exits. We were far enough from the 101 that the people running these secondary franchises had to be happy with whatever spill-off traffic they could get. Crumbs. We passed a roadside produce stand selling fruit and vegetables out of cardboard boxes. The dusty guy working the stand watched the Corvette pass, expressionless, stolid under his straw hat.

I watched the road go by.

Thinking about cars, and the people who took them.

28

The wholesale car lot covered what must have been several full acres of asphalt. Endless rows of newly washed cars were lined up with the same precision as the crop fields we had driven through. There was a series of low, flat buildings, like squashed hangars, on the far side of the lot. Buster pointed the Corvette toward the buildings. Heat waves shimmered off the blacktop. Rows of cars slid by in dizzying numbers.

"The guys who work these things are geniuses," he commented.

"How so?"

"At putting cheap lipstick on old pigs." He gestured at the rows of gleaming vehicles. "Half of these are probably two hundred miles away from falling apart, but they look like they're ready for the Daytona. Take any piece of junk in the whole damn world, hammer out the dents, paint the dings, give it a buff and polish, sand down the curb rash, throw some nice new oil into a crap engine, kill the Check Engine light if it blinks, whatever they gotta do. Just get them looking good enough to sell."

"How many of these do you think were stolen?"

Buster laughed. "How many stars in the night sky?"

I was curious. "Who buys at these places?"

He parked near the first of the buildings and finished the last of his beer. This one he tossed out the window. The empty can landed with a small *clank* on the hot pavement. "You need a wholesale dealer's license. Which isn't hard to get. Then they go out and resell 'em for whatever they can, anywhere they can. A volume business. Barely any profit margin. Just keep the stuff pumping in and going out. Volume. That's all that matters."

We parked and got out. Cars were everywhere. Sure enough, they looked beautiful, windshields spotless, paint gleaming, tires a crisp, clean black. I wondered what they were like on the inside. Maybe fine. Maybe rotting away. Like people, not safe to trust appearances.

Workers darted here and there. Everyone seemed in a rush. Contrary to the motionless rows of cars and still, sedate landscape, there was a shifty, hustler energy in the air. I thought of flies buzzing around spoiled fruit. Buster stopped a short guy in a yellow Hawaiian shirt who was bustling around with a clipboard.

"We're looking for Leo."

"Good luck with that. I'm busy."

The guy was already walking away.

He stopped as he realized Buster was now holding his clipboard.

"Think you dropped this," said Buster.

"Hey, give that back!"

Hawaiian Shirt flushed and reached. Buster raised the clipboard slightly higher.

Buster was six foot five. The man in front of him must have been five foot six. He would have needed a stepladder to get his clipboard. Realizing that he looked foolish trying, he gave up. "Leo's back that way." He nodded toward the buildings. "Give that back, okay? C'mon, I need it. I got work to do."

"Show us where Leo is." It wasn't a question.

We followed Hawaiian Shirt as he trotted into the middle hangar. I found myself walking quickly to stay apace. He took short steps but a lot of them. Low margin, high volume. Like the used car business. Inside, the hangar floor was poured concrete. High ceilings lined with fluorescent lights. The front space was set up as a commercial car wash. Sweepers, brushes, a motorized track built into the floor. A line of cars waited their turn. At the other end, a handful of men vacuumed and dried and rubbed stray marks off tires and hoods. A substantial operation. Our new friend ignored the commotion as he led us past the car wash into a warren of offices and drywall partitions and narrow corridors. The concrete here was painted white, like the walls and ceiling. Everything had a temporary, on-the-fly feel, a military base in the middle of a desert. As though tomorrow they could all be somewhere else.

Our conscripted guide opened a door and called out to a man who was barking into a cell phone. "Leo. Someone looking for you."

Hawaiian Shirt snatched his clipboard back, gave Buster a dirty look, and hastened away.

The man on his cell phone said something, hung up, and turned to us.

Leo, from what I understood, auctioned off stolen cars, and he looked like a man who did exactly that. His slicked-back hair was the color of unwashed fox fur. Small, shrewd eyes looked like a pair of adding machines set into flesh and blood, and he was smiling with all the whimsy of an alligator. His three-quarter-length leather jacket was the color of an old penny and he sported a diamond pinky ring that could have been bigger, but could have been smaller, too.

He looked us over, taking in my chest and Buster's size. "Help ya?"

"Mikey and Eddie in San Jose sent us down," Buster said. "About the G-Class."

"Oh, yeah, Buster, right?" Leo stuck out a hand that vanished into Buster's paw. Then he looked at me. "Hey, sweetheart, how ya doin'?" He wasn't looking into my eyes and didn't even try to shake my hand. That was okay. I'd seen cleaner hands. I didn't bother with an answer.

"Lady Luck is smiling down upon you," Leo said. "I think we can find what you're here for, and we might even be able to do it before the next moon landing. Follow me, ladies and gents, follow me, right this way." He didn't bother to look back to see if we were.

We followed Leo farther back into the disorienting maze of hallways. He took a right, then a left, then another left until we reached a door that led into a room set up as an office. There was a cheap couch at one end and a cheap desk at the other. The desk held a boxy old PC that looked like it should have great-grandchildren by now. A closed door led to what must have been a bathroom or closet.

Leo walked over to a side table that held a bottle of Four Roses Bourbon and poured into two glasses. If he was worried about not having an ice machine, I wasn't seeing it. The glasses looked like they could have used a spin through the car wash out front. He handed one to Buster and took one for himself, then grinned at me, showing gold-capped teeth. "Sorry, doll, I forgot the margarita mix." He chuckled as though he'd said something funny.

I didn't say anything. Buster looked like he was about to say something, but I caught his eye. We were here to get something. No need to let pride get in the way. If Leo got us a lead on the G-Class, he could make all the margarita jokes in the world, and worse.

The door opened. A younger guy walked in. His jeans were smeared with paint and his hands were smudged with grease.

"Devin's gonna help us track the bitch down," Leo explained. His eyes found me again. "No offense, sweetheart. My mom used to wash my mouth out with soap but I guess it didn't stick."

"Maybe she didn't use enough soap," I suggested.

Leo's face froze in a grin. "Maybe not."

The door opened again and a giant walked in. Like a sitcom, where someone new jumps in every minute. Except no one here had said anything funny. The car auction business seemed to be a constant blur of people coming and going. I took an evaluative look at the newest addition. He had a big, dull face and big hands that were also smudged with grease. Suddenly, Buster was only the second-biggest guy in the room. The new man must have weighed three hundred pounds and he had at least an inch of height on Buster. Big, but soft in the middle. He looked like he'd played linebacker for a good college team and then spent the next five years hitting dollar wing nights. The little room was feeling smaller and smaller.

"Big Brad's gonna help, too," Leo said. "He's a whiz at this stuff. Speaking of which, I gotta take a leak." He stepped into what turned out to be the bathroom. I glimpsed a slice of toilet seat and sink before the door shut.

Buster looked up at Big Brad. "So, you're a whiz at this stuff?"

Big Brad looked down at Buster. "That's what the man said."

I heard water and pipes running and then Leo was back. As he closed the bathroom door behind him I saw the same slice of seat and sink. He checked his wristwatch, a square gold face and alligator strap. "I'll be right back. I got a guy callin' me back about this any second. I'm gonna try to get you a name and maybe an address, too, if we get lucky." He gestured at the couch. "Make yourselves comfortable. Hell, take your shoes off, as long as your socks are clean. Be back in five, ladies and gents. Don't have too much fun without me." He winked at me. "Especially you, sweetheart. I wouldn't want to miss any kinda fun *you're* having."

He stepped out and closed the door.

"He keeps up that shit and *I'm* gonna wash his mouth with soap, whether you want me to or not," Buster grumbled. He helped himself to another drink. Between the beers at lunch, the road sodas, and the bourbon he must have had at least five or six through the afternoon. He seemed about as tipsy as if he'd been drinking chamomile tea. This time he poured a bourbon for me, too. A liberal pour, which seemed to be the only kind Buster knew.

Buster and I sat on the couch. Devin sat at the desk and clicked away at the computer. No one spoke much. Big Brad sat next to Devin on a stool that shuddered under his weight. He reached into a pocket and took out, improbably, a Game Boy. As if he had never left the '90s, he started pressing buttons with both thumbs, the console lost between enormous, grease-stained hands.

Buster yawned, lit a cigarette, and scratched his nose.

Big Brad looked up from the Game Boy. "You're getting ash on the carpet."

"Lucky it's a shit carpet." Buster flicked more ash.

Big Brad's eyes followed the ash as it drifted down but he said nothing more as he went back to his game.

Devin's phone rang. He picked up and listened, then nodded and said, "We can wait." He hung up and looked our way. "Another couple minutes. Hang tight."

Buster smoked. Big Brad loomed like a lighthouse. Devin fiddled with the computer.

I got a strange feeling.

There was an analogue clock on the wall. Another minute ticked past.

I tried to decide where the strange feeling was coming from.

Buster finished his cigarette and stubbed it out on the side table. "How much longer we gonna be here?" he wanted to know. "We didn't bring our sleeping bags." He waved his glass. "And the bourbon's going fast." He sounded annoyed. Buster sounding annoyed was a useful sort of gauge. Like a barometer signifying that a storm was on the horizon. Not something to panic about, no need to drop everything right then and there, but maybe time to move the sails a bit, head in a different direction.

Devin looked up. "Sorry," he said. "Almost there. Leo's gonna call any second. We have a lot of inventory to sort through."

"Good," said Buster. "I haven't felt this cooped up since my San Quentin days."

I looked around again. The two men, plain walls, bathroom door, desk, computer.

I realized why I had the strange feeling.

I spilled half my drink on Buster's leg.

"Hey, watch it!" he exclaimed. Then he saw my eyes.

That was enough. His face changed the smallest bit. We were on the same wavelength.

Several things happened at almost the same time.

I stood. Devin's cell phone chimed as I reached my feet. A single, bright beep. He looked at the screen, then over to us. "Good to go." The smallest trace of puzzlement beginning to form as he spoke. Seeing me standing. In motion.

By that time I had taken three fast steps and kicked the bathroom door open. A hard push-kick, throwing my hips into it, my full weight behind my outstretched right leg. The sole of my boot crashed into the door, leg and door meeting at a perfect perpendicular angle. The cheap latch broke and the door flew backward. There was a pained grunt and a man holding a gun staggered from where the door had bounced off his forehead. Dazed, he tried to get the gun up. Not enough time. I was too close. I got my left hand on his right wrist, angling the gun barrel away toward the floor. He might have been stronger than me but I was pushing down and he was pushing up. Less than a second later any debatable differences in deltoid and triceps capabilities stopped mattering as I put my right hand around the back of his neck, pulled him close, and drove my knee into his groin three vicious times.

My ears registered confused noises and moving bodies in the office behind me. *Bangs* and *crashes* and *thuds*. General mayhem.

The guy's fingers had loosened with the first knee and opened somewhere between the second and third. The gun clattered to the ground as I let go of his neck, took a half step back, straightened the fingers of my right hand, and drove my hand into his throat just below his Adam's apple. He groaned and collapsed to his knees, both hands clutching his throat and, in that process, unintentionally bringing his unguarded face to foot level just as I swept my left foot around in a short, tight roundhouse kick that slammed my lower shin into his right temple.

He sprawled forward prone, arms flung akimbo. Out. Gone. Over. Looking like he might think about moving sometime next year. By the next moon landing, as Leo might have said.

There were thudding and crunching and smashing noises from behind me.

I picked up his gun, checking the magazine and chamber as I straightened. Some back part of my mind computing the salient facts—Ruger .22, semiautomatic, safety off, full magazine, round chambered—and stepped back into the room in time to see Buster removing a sawed-off shotgun from Devin's unconscious hands. Devin was unconscious because Buster seemed to have launched his head into the boxy old PC.

Buster brought the shotgun up toward Big Brad.

A fraction of a second too late.

Big Brad got a hand on the barrel and wrenched it away. He grabbed Buster by the throat as the shotgun fell to the floor.

Whatever the dollar wing nights had done to Big Brad's stomach, they had yet to adversely affect his grip. Buster looked like he'd been seized by a robotic claw. His hands scrabbled at Big Brad's wrists. The two of them looked like a pair of grizzly bears locked in combat, straining and grunting with effort. Buster lunged forward and Big Brad crashed into the wall. He pushed hard off it and sent both of them over the desk onto the ground. Big Brad, with the momentum of his rush, landed on top. A superior position. He straddled Buster, raising a huge fist, just as I broke the Four Roses bottle over his head.

Bourbon and glass splashed as he slumped forward. Somehow still moving.

Buster found his feet and brought what was left of the PC down over him.

Big Brad stopped moving.

Breathing, but not much else. He looked like he'd sleep longer than my guy in the bathroom.

Buster looked down sadly at the shattered whiskey bottle, rubbing his throat. "You couldn't have hit him with a table?"

"I'm so very sorry." I was going through Devin's pockets. He had a new iPhone. One of the big, fancy models with multiple camera lenses and facial scanning.

"Why'd they wait?" asked Buster. "Why not jump us as soon as we walked in?"

I had been thinking about that. "They couldn't—they're not in charge. Neither is Leo. A chain of command. They're all the way at the bottom. They were waiting for someone else to give the okay. A shot-caller, probably off site. Someone higher up. Maybe that guy was waiting for someone else, too. All the way up the ladder."

"Who?"

"Let's find out."

Buster cradled Devin's chin and placed his big thumbs over Devin's eyelids as I held the phone to its owner's face. The screen unlocked and Buster let Devin spill back down. I opened the Messages app. The most recent text chain was with Leo. One unread message. I opened it.

Tell me when it's done.

I found a little yellow emoji of a thumbs-up and sent it.

Almost instantly I saw the blinking dots indicating a message being typed. I pictured Leo in his office, anxiously checking his phone, maybe ten times a minute, waiting for news. No one liked to be left in the dark.

The phone beeped.

Hillman will be ☺

Leo was eager to see how things had gone. He must have been typing fast and walking faster. He opened the door and stepped into the room less than a minute after he sent the text. By the time he had taken in the scene, he had plenty of time to think about the sawed-off shotgun Buster was pointing at his chest.

Buster had been getting steadily more upset ever since San Jose. His face, sinister even during his sunniest moments, now conveyed a powerful ill will.

"You're going to start talking and stop moving," Buster told Leo.

Leo blanched, his adding machine eyes working overtime. Devin was holding his head, moaning in pain. Big Brad was still out cold. Through the bathroom door I had kicked open, a motionless outflung hand and arm were visible on the floor.

Leo's alligator smile was gone, replaced by a nervous grimace. "I can explain."

"Good," I said. "You should."

"We didn't have a choice. It was nothing personal. Honest."

"Who said you didn't have a choice? Hillman?"

Leo's eyes worked around the room.

"I really can't tell you that."

Then he spun and dove for the door.

He barely got his hand on the knob before Buster stopped him from leaving.

A few minutes later, when we were back in the Corvette with the wholesale car lot behind us, Buster would apologize for his fraying temper. His contrition, though genuine, didn't mean much for Leo's health. Buster had dropped the shotgun, seized Leo by the shoulders, and put his head through the door. The door was cheap painted plywood, but it was still a door. There had been a terrific *cracking* sound. I needed only to look at the door, now with a ragged head-size hole, to realize that Leo wouldn't be saying much for a few days.

"Buster," I had said, exasperated. "We wanted to talk to him. You knew this."

Buster had shaken his head in frustration. "I know, I know! I'm doing better with my anger management skills, I really am. Everyone at work agrees."

Leo's iPhone had been an older model than Devin's. Thumbprint instead of facial scan. Once his phone had been opened, I had changed the Auto-Lock setting to Never. Then I had found Hillman's number and messaged:

All set. They had something you'll want to see.

Now, back in the Corvette, Leo's phone chimed with a new message.

Come by the office. I'm there now.

Which was a problem.

I had no idea which office he was talking about. Or where. Leo clearly would have known but I couldn't ask him. Meaning I couldn't ask Hillman, either.

With a mental crossing of my fingers, I went to the phone's Contacts and pulled up Hillman. We were in luck. There was a phone number and, sure enough, an address: 319 Strawberry Drive, Salinas, CA 93906. I opened Maps on Leo's phone and typed in the address.

Maps said we were twenty-three minutes away. The way Buster was driving, I figured it was under twenty.

"How'd you know?" Buster wondered as aging blacktop fled before the Corvette's orange prow. "That something was wrong?"

I watched the little blue dot—us—move smoothly along on the screen toward Hillman. "The whole thing felt off. Too many people were coming in, everyone so accommodating. You saw how busy everyone was, running around like ants with a million things to do. Why be so helpful? They didn't know us. And then the bathroom."

Buster looked puzzled. "The bathroom?"

"Those guys were slobs—why were they so careful to keep the bathroom door closed? Leo said he was taking a leak, but when he walked in, the seat was down, and it still was when he walked out. He wanted to give the guy in there some kind of *here-we-go* notice."

Buster laughed. "I think I got divorced at least once for not putting the seat down. You're giving me terrible flashbacks to married life." Lighting a Camel, he observed, "They weren't very good at what they were supposed to be doing. Killing us, I mean. Total amateur hour."

"True," I agreed, "but I bet they would have been great at fixing your engine."

"What's that supposed to mean?"

"You see the grease all over their hands? Their clothes? Their line of work isn't violence—it's cars. It makes sense that auto thieves would work in groups of three, right? One to drive their car, another to drive the car they steal, and a third as a lookout. The three of them were probably a crew Leo recruited last-minute. Maybe they moonlight as mechanics and happened to be nearby. Remember, he barely had an hour to set this up—from when Mikey and Eddie called from San Jose, to when we arrived in Salinas."

Buster's face darkened ominously. "I'm going to go back up to San Jose and stick that goddamn blowtorch up both their—"

"I doubt they were in on it. I think they were actually trying to help," I interjected hastily. Privately I thought there was a decent chance that the brothers had not hated the idea of sending Buster into hot water, but I kept the thought to myself. I didn't want to rile him up. If he thought he had been sent into an ambush, at some point in the near future Mikey and Eddie wouldn't be much more than spots on the floor.

"So why go after us?" Buster wondered.

I had been thinking about that, too. "It was something about that vehicle. The Mercedes belongs to someone important. Anyone looking for it was a red flag. Us calling around must have tripped some kind of wire, sent some kind of signal. Something that sent reverberations and ripples out through the stolen car world—until the signal reached the wrong person."

"You mean the right person." Buster smiled like a tiger shark.

"True," I agreed. "For us, the right person. Whoever Hillman is, when he found out we were looking for the Mercedes, he must have either told Leo to stop us, or, more likely, gone one step up the chain of command and gotten the instructions. Same thing, either way. We need Hillman to keep going up the ladder."

Hillman had seemed eager to meet us.

I was feeling equally eager to meet him.

29

Strawberry Drive was a lonely, two-lane road cutting through huge flat expanses of crop fields. It seemed forlorn, a road that didn't appear to have any real interest in getting anywhere, flat and straight and dusty and unhurried. We passed a large green tractor plodding along the roadside, slow as a beetle. The driver turned to squint down at the low-slung orange rocket passing him, offering a slow wave with his trucker hat. As the road's name suggested, we were surrounded by what looked like strawberry fields. No berries visible, just rows of leafy, green plants stretching endlessly to the horizon. A hot, arid afternoon. Buster worked the windshield wipers, erasing a layer of brown dust that had accumulated like snow. I saw a low, vague shape ahead of us and wondered if it was a heat mirage. As we approached, the shape came into focus: a pair of black buzzards, dipping their beaks into a red mess of roadkill.

They eyed us without fear as we drew abreast; then, in the side mirror, I could see them behind us, beaks dipping and rising, rhythmic as oil pumping jacks.

We almost missed the address. Number 319 was a featureless gravel driveway marked only by a slender numbered post. The driveway curved away, hiding from view. Power lines stretched overhead. A row of perched black crows stared down at us.

We turned in. The crows watched us.

When imagining Hillman's headquarters, I hadn't known what to picture— maybe some innocuous building in a bland office park. What we found was very different. Hillman's office consisted of two mobile trailers spaced about thirty feet apart. The trailer farther from us had a jacked-up, tinted-out Ford F-150 parked in front. A dozen moving trucks were flocked off to one side like tired farm animals, painted with the colors and names of the big companies, U-Haul and Penske and Ryder. Some looked dustier than others. None looked new.

"Wait in the car, okay?" I asked Buster.

"Not a chance." Buster didn't look pleased. "Whoever's in there just tried to kill us."

"And we're going to find out why."

I told him what I was thinking.

"We don't even know how many people he's with. And how will I know when to come in?" Buster wanted to know.

"Easy. Listen for the gunshot," I said. "Then give it a couple of minutes."

I stepped out of the car into the hot sun. I could hear nothing except the whine of insects. Gravel dusted my boots as my feet crunched against the stones. A crow cawed, then another. The area in front of the trailer was set up as a crude outdoor gym. Dumbbells, a bench press, a heavy bag dangling from a tubular stand-alone frame. No sign of any people.

The trailer door was unlocked. I opened it and walked down a short hallway, seeing a door ajar at the opposite end.

I knocked on the door. "Hillman?"

"Who's that?"

I stepped into the small room and saw Hillman for the first time. He had a shock of red hair and a flat, unfriendly face. I figured him to be about thirty. He sat at a desk covered with a phone and stacks of papers. His feet were up on the desk. He wore jeans and pointed cowboy boots and a black shirt that showed a triangle of hairy chest and a tangle of gold chains.

He scowled. "Who the hell are you?"

"Leo sent me."

"Leo sent you," he repeated. His voice was quick and abrasive and there was something jittery in his manner. "Why?"

"Because he couldn't make it."

"What?" Hillman took a closer look at me. "Is this some kind of joke?"

"I'm not sure what you mean by joke."

"Him sending you over here." His eyes moved over my body and he suddenly grinned. "Like, are you gonna get in a star-spangled bikini and sing 'Happy Birthday, Mr. President'?"

"I really don't see that happening."

"Too bad. Bet you'd look great in a bikini." He rubbed his nose. "So why are you here, exactly?" When he scratched his nose, I could see a tattoo across the back of his right hand. A fanged snake coiled around a five-pointed star.

I was already wondering if he'd been doing coke, but Hillman put the question to rest by swinging his feet to the floor, revealing a pocket mirror covered by a pile of white powder. He used a razor blade to parse out two lines, then bent to the mirror with a rolled-up bill held to his nose. He sat up, sniffed, and held the bill to me. "Want one?"

"No, thanks."

"Your loss. I get the best stuff. Straight over the border, totally uncut. Great shit." He squinted at me. "Where's Leo? What happened?"

"Something unexpected came up. Very last-minute."

"You could give that lazy pansy a winning Megabucks ticket and he'd bitch about having to drive to the bank to cash it in." Hillman shook his head in disgust. "He give you a message or something?"

"Sort of."

"Sort of?" Hillman looked irritated as he licked his thumb, rubbed it in the coke, and jammed it against the inside of his bottom lip. "Did he, or didn't he? Or do I have to go drive over there and slap it outa him?" He wiped his nose. "Or outa *you*? I'm not as nice as I look, you know."

"Don't worry," I reassured him. "Neither am I."

His grin was back. "You sure I don't get to see you in a bikini? Come over here and sit down. My lap's got an empty parking spot with your name on it. You want a drink or something?" He gestured to a bottle of Tito's vodka on his desk. "Come on, let's do a couple of lines and have a drink. We can party for a bit and wait for Leo. Better yet, maybe that loser won't show up at all. Never been at a party that dweeb wouldn't make worse."

"What was it about the Mercedes?" I asked. "Why go after the people looking for it?"

"What do you know about any of that?" Hillman said. He looked suspicious for the first time. "That's big-picture shit. Nothing to do with your cute little ass."

"It's got everything to do with me. I was the one looking for it."

His eyes narrowed and his hand moved, but I was expecting that and my Beretta was already out. "Don't," I told him.

The warning didn't register. Maybe he was still expecting bikinis and birthday cakes. His hand kept moving.

Although it was too fast for the eye to see, the bullet from my gun shattered the coke mirror, gouged across the desk, spun off, and lodged into the back wall. Hillman cried out in pain and surprise as he was speckled with broken glass and white powder. "Jesus!" he yelped. "What the hell was that?"

"Right now, I just want to talk," I said. "But you tried to have me killed. So for the record, I reserve the right to change my mind about the talking part."

Hillman shook his head, eying the scant remains of his cocaine. "Goddamn Leo. I never should have trusted him to do anything important." He looked up to me. "What do you want?"

"I want to learn why you wanted me dead. And your hands on the desk," I added, "or you'll get the worst manicure of your life."

"Who says anyone wanted you dead?" He scratched his nose and looked around jumpily. "Maybe you're being paranoid."

"A roomful of men with guns made that kind of obvious."

Hillman folded his hands on his desk. "You don't know who you're messing with, do you?" He answered his own question. "You wouldn't be, if you did."

"Five points for the tautology, but it doesn't answer my question."

He blinked. "Astrology?"

"Forget it. Who I'm messing with is exactly what I'm trying to find out."

He wiped a drop of blood from his chin, where a bit of glass must have nicked him. "That tells me you're soft-headed or flat-out nuts. The guys I work for won't just kill you." He stared up at me. I could see a smidgeon of white powder caked against the inside of his nostril. "You get that, right?" he continued. "There're worse things than dead. Way worse. They'll run you up and down the circuit like a goddamn rodeo pony. By the time they're through with you, you'll be selling three-dollar blow jobs in Kansas City at fifty percent off and thanking every poor bastard who comes along to sign up."

I said, "There's an image."

"I'm being fucking serious!" Hillman exploded. "These guys are into everything and they run this area! They got a hand in every pie in the whole damn bakeshop. You're crazy to be going anywhere near them."

"Keep talking. What's with all the moving trucks outside? Your friends in the moving business, too? Is that one of the pies?"

He paused a fractional moment and then spat on the floor. "None of your concern."

I raised my gun for emphasis. "You don't get to say that right now."

"I don't?" Hillman's eyes had changed. There was something new in them. His posture was different, too. More confident. More confrontational. Bolder. His hands drifted off the surface of the desk.

He wasn't afraid anymore.

The floor creaked behind me.

I realized why Hillman was no longer afraid.

There were two men behind me.

They had snuck up through the doorway. Maybe they had been in the second trailer. I kept my gun on Hillman as I turned my head. Two burly men, big and mean and mad, dripping menace like cheap cologne. Each had the same tattoo as Hillman's.

One of them spoke up. "What do you want us to do with her?"

Hillman looked happier now. He leaned back in his chair and smirked. "Oh, I'm gonna think of all kinds of things—"

His smirk faded.

He stopped speaking.

The two men who had snuck up on me each craned his neck. As if sensing something behind him. The one on the right craning right, the one on the left craning left.

Smiles dripped off their faces like candle wax.

Each wondering about the massive hand draped over his shoulder.

Hillman was looking not at the hands but at the face above the hands. A face towering almost a half foot above his two guys. A smiling, ferocious face, eyes blazing with animosity. A face promising all kinds of imminent harm.

Buster's hands lifted as he seized each of the men by his outside ear. His face contorted with effort as in a trio of concussive motions he slammed their heads together three times. Dense, dull sounds. Like an ax splitting hardwood.

Both men went down.

I was watching Hillman.

Predictably, he went for whatever was in his drawer once again.

I shot the phone on his desk. It exploded in a shower of plastic fragments. Hillman was a bit unluckier, this time. A two-inch shard of plastic embedded itself into his cheek. He screamed in pain as Buster grabbed him.

"Now," I said, "we're going to approach this from a different angle."

30

"Personally, I think you look better upside down," I observed. "Almost dashing. But maybe that's just me. What do you think, Buster?"

"I think he looks ugly as a broken teakettle."

"Sorry," I said to Hillman. "Hung jury, here."

Hillman didn't find it funny. Even swinging from side to side and upside down, he managed to spit at me.

The gesture earned him a tremendous slap from Buster that sent him groaning and spinning back and forth. The tubular frame he hung off creaked as he swung. The heavy bag had been about 150 pounds. We had replaced it with Hillman, who was closer to two hundred, but hopefully the frame could handle the extra weight. So far it was holding up. His wrists were taped behind his back and the top of his head swung a few inches above the gravel. His two friends were still in the office, taped in tandem, head to toe. We had used a whole roll of packing tape. They wouldn't free themselves anytime soon.

"You're both dead!" Hillman screamed. His eyes bugged up at us. "Do you understand me?"

"I've had four ex-wives tell me that," said Buster as he stuck a Camel in his mouth. "Yet here I stand." He lit the cigarette. "And my ex-wives were a hell of a lot scarier than you."

"He's not kidding," I said. "I met one of them. She was terrifying."

Hillman glared at Buster. "If you let me go, I won't tell them what happened. I swear. You can get away. It's not too late."

"Who's *them*?" I asked.

Hillman's eyes were still on Buster, his voice now almost plaintive. "I mean it. I'll say it was a break-in, some local kids or some shit. My guys will keep quiet."

"Talk to her," said Buster. "She's calling the shots. And you're lucky she is, and not me, because I'm hungry and pissed off and don't really feel like talking to you at all. If it was up to me, I'd run that truck over you a few times, get you nice and two-dimensional, and then go try to find a good steak somewhere in this hick town while your nearest and dearest spent the day looking for a pancake-shaped coffin."

Hillman looked to me. "What do you want?"

"I told you. I want to know why you wanted us dead."

"Go to hell," he said.

"I saw your tattoo. Who is Mr. Z? Do you know him?"

His face tightened. "You're asking dangerous questions."

"So you do?"

"I don't know what you're talking about."

"Sure about that?"

"As a goddamn heart attack." The plaintive note had left his voice. His face looked like a soldier digging into a trench.

I crossed my arms and looked down at him. "You need to understand something. I believe in proportional response."

"One of the many differences between us," Buster put in with a grin. "It's the Y chromosome, I bet you anything." He had taken Devin's sawed-off shotgun and was tapping it against the palm of his hand. It was a twelve-gauge, double-barreled, shorn to about eighteen inches of barrel. To see him, Buster could have been a poster board for the virtues of unrestrained confession. If I had been Hillman I would have started at my great-great-grandfather's sins and gone down the family line from there.

But Hillman was tough, or stupid, or both. He kept quiet.

"What I mean," I continued, "is that I don't hurt people unless they hurt someone helpless or try to hurt me first. And I don't escalate—not unless someone else does first. Think of it as a poker game. I don't raise, ever. But I *always* match."

Hillman didn't look like he was following. "Poker. Sure, whatever."

"I've always stuck to that," I told him. "Proportionality. Not to sound pretentious, but it's sort of my career philosophy."

"Not mine," Buster said. "My career philosophy is more set the bastards on fire, burn it all down, and piss on the goddamn ashes."

Hillman didn't look impressed. "What is this, good cop bad cop?"

"If we were cops, you'd be a lot safer right now," I said. "What I'm trying to tell you is that normally, I wouldn't want to do anything disproportionate to what you'd done. And even though you're honestly a bit of a creep and a bit more of an asshole, I haven't personally seen you be violent or abusive. Which counts for something."

"Great. Then your poker rules or whatever should say to let me go."

"On the other hand, you did try to have us killed. Proportionality kind of goes out the window when it comes to attempted murder."

"See?" Buster smiled. "Deep down, she's the bad cop, too."

Hillman started to say something. I shook my head. "Hold on a second. This is the important part. Because I do my best to behave proportionally, I would like to avoid things becoming unpleasant. But like I said, you *did* try to kill us, and I feel like that gives me a certain latitude." He was still on the verge of saying something, so I held up a finger. "Almost done. By latitude, I mean a freedom to act without feeling too guilty. Anyway," I finished, "you were trying to tell me something?"

Hillman glared up at me. "Women," he said. "They always love to talk."

I stepped behind him, kneeled down, and broke his left pinkie.

Fingers were easy enough to break. Sideways was easiest. Very little force was needed. Fingers were easier than toes, which, being shorter, were harder to grip, or arms and legs, with far bigger bones. I'd always found it was more mental than physical. A ten-year-old could break a finger, strength-wise. It was more about being clinical, not getting squeamish. Maybe everyone had their own way of doing things, their own little tricks. Whenever I had to break a finger, my trick was that I closed my eyes just before, and pretended I was snapping a small, dry branch. That always helped. It was no good picturing the actual bone cracking under the skin, not unless you were someone who took pleasure in the act, and then the whole twig thing probably didn't apply. Certain people probably snapped twigs wishing they were fingers. I was glad I wasn't one of those people. I'd break fingers if needed, but it was never my favorite part.

Hillman screamed for a minute, but settled down eventually.

"You were saying?" I prompted.

He called me a series of foul names. He seemed to be working his way through the alphabet. He had reached the C's when I broke his other pinkie.

There was more screaming and swearing, more jerking and flopping around. The chain rattled and the metal frame creaked.

"The ring fingers will be worse," I warned. "Sometimes it takes me two or three tries. They take longer to heal, too. More trouble all around."

"You goddamn b—" he snarled.

"Here we go." I took his left ring finger in my hands. "Ready?"

The finger started to bend.

"Wait! Wait! Please!" he begged. "I'll talk!"

I paused, my hands still on his finger. "Yeah?" His crooked pinkies were swelling terribly.

"I'll tell you! No more fingers!"

"I'd say do another two or three to be safe," advised Buster, lighting another cigarette. He looked more relaxed, as though bashing the bodyguards' heads together had let off some steam.

"No!" yelped Hillman. "I'll talk!"

I stepped around to his front and looked down at him. "The Mercedes. What was it?"

His words were slow and reluctant, but he talked as promised. "I didn't want you dead. I was following orders. That particular vehicle belongs to a VIP in our Organization. When they heard that someone was looking for it, that was all they needed. These guys don't take chances even in the best of times, and lately they've been spooked. Definitely *not* the best of times, right now."

"What spooked them?"

"Business took a hit recently. A lot of unwanted attention. Everyone's been running on fumes trying to get things moving smoothly again."

"Why drive a stolen car if you're spooked?"

I'd never seen someone shrug upside down, but Hillman managed it. "We get more cars than the dealerships. Drive something for a couple of months, swap it out, drive something else. We all do it. Call it a perk of the job. Another month or two and that Mercedes will be on its way to China or Brazil."

"That's why the ninety-day dealer plates work," I realized. "By the time they expire, you get a new vehicle with new tags."

Buster said, "They probably have a dozen guys at a dozen different dealerships hooking them up."

I asked, "Who told you to kill us?"

Hillman blanched. "You don't want to know. Honest."

"I do," I said. "Honest. Was it Mr. Z? Did it go that far up the chain?"

"Can you take me to a doctor?" he begged. "My fingers are really starting to hurt."

"Not quite yet."

"I'm just a guy doing a job," Hillman said, sounding plaintive again. "I don't know any Mr. Z, I told you!"

"You sure? He looks like an evil John Belushi. He's hard to forget."

"I don't know him!"

I changed direction. "If your bosses were holding someone hostage, where would they take them? Where would they keep them?"

Hillman's face squeezed in pain. "I don't know. They have dozens of sites all over. Maybe more. Maybe hundreds."

"Like where?"

"What is wrong with you?" Hillman shouted. "You're chasing people you should be running away from!"

"What spooked them?" I asked again. "You said something spooked them. What happened?"

"I don't know," he said. "Something went wrong—that's all I know."

"Wrong with what?"

He paused, squinting up at us. "Logistics."

I pointed over at the moving trucks. Something tugged at my mind. "What are those trucks for? Drugs? Weapons? What do you put in them? Where do they go?"

"We—" Hillman stopped himself and looked up at us, his eyes crafty. "You're never gonna let me go, are you?"

"That depends on you."

"You can't," he said. "I get it. And even if you did, my boss would think I talked, and that's a hundred times worse."

Buster was trimming a hangnail with his folding knife. "That's a very negative attitude. Try to focus on the bright side. You're still alive and swinging."

"You can't let me go," Hillman repeated. He spasmed, as though he was about to be sick. Too much stress, too much coke, maybe. I hoped he wouldn't have a heart attack. "I should have realized that right off," he said, convulsing once more.

"Relax," Buster told him. "You're not dead yet."

Hillman's right hand whipped around. Somehow, he was holding a small pistol. The barrel was lined up with Buster's chest. I managed to kick his arm as a *crack* split the day's quiet.

Buster gave a low grunt and staggered backward.

There was a rush of unsettled wings as the row of crows above us flapped into the air.

Hillman had managed to hold onto the gun. He twisted to turn it on me, eyes wild and triumphant, as I stepped forward and kicked him in the face.

He dropped the pistol and hung motionless, limp arms scraping the ground.

I was angry at Hillman. I kicked him again. Then I ran to Buster. He was sitting on the ground, wincing, face two shades paler. "That tricky son of a bitch," he said.

"Where?" I asked.

"The arm."

I looked at the wound. The gun had been a small-caliber .22. The bullet appeared to have gone clean through the meaty part of his upper left arm, missing the biceps muscles. Blood pulsed out of the small hole.

"Hang on," I said. I ran into the trailer's bathroom, washed my hands thoroughly, and emerged with a roll of paper towels, more tape, and Hillman's vodka, which Buster eyed greedily.

"Easy," I said, as he took a swig. "Save some for your arm."

I spent a few minutes doing crude first aid, pressing and taping layers of paper towels against his arm. Blood soaked quickly through the first layers. I added more towels, pressing steadily, until the flow of blood stopped.

The startled crows had returned to the power line.

They watched us in silence.

"Goddamn Houdini over there." Buster swore and took a long pull off the vodka bottle. "I thought we tied him up."

I saw a glint of metal in the gravel near Hillman's dangling arms. "He had that razor blade he was doing coke with," I realized. "He must have palmed it before we grabbed him. And a gun in his boot."

One of Hillman's hands was bleeding, drops spilling onto the gravel. While we'd been talking he must have been hacking away at the tape and his fingers, all in one. No wonder he'd looked unwell.

"I'll drive you to a hospital," I told Buster.

He didn't look happy. "No way. Not when things are getting interesting."

"Nonnegotiable. You need stitches."

"What about him?" Buster's face showed exactly what he wanted to do about Hillman.

I followed his gaze to Hillman, who was groaning and rubbing his head. "Leave him here. His two friends will get free eventually."

Buster didn't look delighted but he shrugged in acquiescence. "More than the sneaky bastard deserves, but sure, him staying alive can be my good deed for the year." Even with one arm I noticed that Buster had managed to light up a Camel. Between that and the vodka, he didn't seem entirely miserable.

"I'll be back soon," I said.

"Where are you going?"

I was watching the pair of trailers and the group of moving trucks. "Looking for answers."

31

I hadn't been in the second trailer yet so I started there. It reminded me of a college dorm. Several makeshift bedrooms full of bunk beds, a rec room with a TV and PlayStation, stacks of games and movies, an old refrigerator full of beer and soda. The trailer was rank with stale cigarette smoke. I pictured bored people killing time. Waiting, resting. Ready to get back on the move. Maybe a stopover for whoever drove the moving trucks parked outside.

Or the kind of place where Coombs could have been.

Except he wasn't.

I walked back to Hillman's trailer. The two guys we had taped were in the hallway where we had left them, wriggling like fish and mumbling through the tape over their mouths. I ignored them and went back to search Hillman's office. The office had nothing obviously useful that might lead to Coombs. Which didn't shock me. Hillman didn't work in the kind of business where writing things down and keeping careful records was beneficial to health or freedom. No telling when police might show up, waving a warrant. Or a rival organization, without one.

Lately they've been spooked.

Meaning even less chance he would have left a trail. No bags full of drugs or weapons, no secret compartments stuffed full of incriminating evidence. A corner of his desk held a stack of folders showing logistics routes. Like a trucking operation. Maps squiggled with red lines, following freeways up through California from the border before spreading out into a writing red

Gorgon's head of tendrils through the southwest and beyond. There were regional maps, too. Smaller roads, smaller scale. More red squiggles, along with blue dots, here and there, over towns and cities, like a scattergram. I held onto the sheaf of maps and kept looking. A television in the corner, a stack of magazines, all porn and sports, a man's jacket with nothing in the pockets.

I did find a duffel bag under his desk. Full of cash. Banded stacks of hundreds. Maybe a hundred thousand dollars. I took the bag, unsatisfied.

Nothing that could lead me to Coombs.

No mention of Susan Johannessen.

Nothing telling me what to do next.

And the sun getting lower in the sky.

I looked around again. The TV, I realized, was sitting on a black fireproof safe. Just a cube of black metal. Locked. I didn't see keys anywhere in the office and we had already looked through Hillman's pockets before we tied him up. But they had to be somewhere. If someone had a safe, they wanted to be able to open it. But no keys in any of the obvious spots—his pockets, the jacket, the desk. So where?

I thought of something and walked outside to the F-150. Jacked up artificially high on studded tires, windows tinted almost opaque, a row of menacing spotlights on the roll bar. A real cowboy truck, proclaiming itself ready to take on any job, anywhere, anytime.

The keys were in the ignition.

A carabiner holding five different keys. One for the truck, another for a motorcycle, two more brass keys that I guessed were for the trailers and wherever Hillman lived, and a fifth, a silver key that was smaller than the others.

The silver key opened the safe.

Nothing exciting. A dozen more vehicle keys hung on hooks, each with a remote locking fob. For the moving trucks. I grabbed a few at random and went back out to open the trucks. They were all clean and empty, both cabs and backs. Identical to any rental fleet anywhere. The only other items in the safe were a stack of DVDs, each in a plastic case. Maybe twenty or thirty of them. I flipped through the DVDs. They all seemed to all be '80s action movies, Willis, Stallone, Schwarzenegger.

Action movies didn't belong in a locked safe. I took the whole stack back into the first trailer. The rec room. I turned on the TV and popped a *Die Hard* disc into the PlayStation. I heard it boot up, start spinning and whirring. A menu appeared onscreen.

I hit Play.

I was watching porn. Low-budget amateur porn. Bad lighting, cheap set, no HD, shot from above by a single camera. No cuts or pans or sweeps. Just a motionless downward angle showing a man and a much younger woman, gasping and groaning as they rutted on a cheap-looking flowered bedspread. There was a small time stamp in the upper corner of the screen: 6-2-19.

I pulled out the DVD and put in *Rocky*.

Same thing. Same downward camera angle, same bad lighting, same amateur quality. Only the room and people were different. This time there were three people. An older man and two young women. Very young. I looked closer. The two of them looked like they could be in their teens. The man seemed to be having a great time. The women acted along half-heartedly, tossing their hair and moaning extravagantly. This time stamp showed 1-16-18.

I tried three more DVDs. All similar variations of the first two, the same amateur camera, poor lighting, unedited production.

The tapes didn't feel like porn. Too much of a mismatch in pleasure. And too much physical discrepancy. The women were young and attractive but the men were neither. Not just older. They weren't in great shape, flabby buttocks, sagging stomachs, their movements lacking even a modicum of grace or sexiness, showing no awareness of the camera. Even with the advent of free streaming, they didn't appear to be the type that anyone would want to watch.

There was something here. Just not Coombs.

Where was he?

I swept the DVDs into the duffel bag with the money and hauled everything outside. "Hospital time," I told Buster.

Hillman seemed to have woken up a bit. Still hanging upside down, between his face and fingers he was looking the worse for wear. "Can I come?" he mumbled. "I think you broke my jaw." It sounded like, *Ahh ffink yuh bruk mah jah.*

"Go call an ambulance."

He started to say something but was interrupted by a crow's caw. Then another.

I looked up at the row of black birds, comfortably settled on the power line.

Another crow cawed.

Buster and I looked at each other. Then we heard the engine. A moment later, tires against gravel. The engine was louder now. The crows watched with interest.

"Oh, shit," said Hillman. "Now you've done it." It sounded like, *Aahhh, shhhii, nuh yuhv dunneht.*

"Come on," I said to Buster. We scrambled behind Hillman's F-150 as a vehicle came into view.

A black Mercedes G-Class.

I looked at the duffel bag of cash that sat next to Hillman in the driveway. Neatly packed and zipped up. Not under lock and key, even though there had been room in the safe. As though waiting for someone to pick it up. A routine. A regular, appointed time. Like a Friday afternoon. End of the week, get the books clear, count things up, collect the week's earnings, gear up for next week.

The Mercedes rolled up the driveway and stopped, engine running. I could see a driver and a passenger. Impossible to tell if anyone was in the back.

The driver's door opened.

A man got out and looked around, confused.

He was someone I recognized. Big, powerful build, jeans, combat boots, small shark eyes set into a rough face. One of the bodyguards from the Cypress. Not the one with the hatchet, but the other. He took in Hillman, hanging upside down next to the duffel bag, and without a word reached into the vehicle. I could hear Hillman mumbling something unintelligible.

When the bodyguard turned back he was holding an assault rifle. A 30-round banana clip jutted out like a wasp's stinger. He started to bring the rifle up in our general direction as Buster kneeled, sighted the stubby sawed-off as best he could, and fired the first barrel.

From a sufficiently short distance, and from a target's point of view, shotguns were the absolute worst. Not even a machine gun was so destructive. The bodyguard staggered back as if struck in the chest by a giant fist, the rifle falling to the ground.

Buster stood and stepped forward, the sawed-off looking like a pistol in his huge hand, and fired the second barrel one-handed before the bodyguard could even fall.

Most of the man's head disappeared. There were metallic *pings* as stray buckshot peppered the Mercedes.

I saw a flurry of motion from within. The passenger frantically scrambling over the console to the driver's seat.

I ran for the open door.

Whoever was inside was panicking. If he hadn't been, his first action would have been to get the door shut and locked, and then go for the driver's seat.

He saw me coming. Changed his mind. His hand scrabbled at the door. A second mistake.

Now he was trying and failing at two different, contradictory actions.

I got my hand on the door handle just as he tried to pull it shut from inside. I was on my feet and had leverage. The passenger wasn't, and didn't. No contest.

My other hand held my stun gun.

I leaned in, jammed the twin pincers into the soft flesh of his hand, and pressed the switch. He screamed in pain and stopped trying to do anything. I got a hand on his collar and jerked him out of the Mercedes and down into the gravel.

I leaned in and pressed the engine button. The engine died.

I looked down at the passenger.

"Hi, Albert," I said. "It's good to see you again."

32

Albert didn't look like it was good to see me again.

He had a seventy-five-thousand-volt excuse. Hillman's vodka was really coming in handy. I tilted some into his mouth. The accountant choked and sputtered, vodka dribbling down his chin. He was wearing another one of his boxy, dated suits. This one was herringbone beige with a pistachio green tie squashed into a button-down collar. He looked like he should have retired to Miami by 1970 at the absolute latest.

"Let's not give him the whole bottle," suggested Buster. "Save some for the people who actually appreciate a drink."

Albert looked up at us, bewildered and frightened. "Who are you?"

The afternoon was getting later. I didn't have time to waste. "You're going to take me to Coombs. That's all you need to care about."

"He has nothing to do with me. I only handle numbers, that's my only role." He blinked owlishly through his glasses, noticing Hillman, then growing paler as he saw his bodyguard lying in a growing pool of blood. High above in the sky several black shapes circled, much higher than the crows flew. Buzzards. They knew what was down here.

"I don't want trouble," Albert said. He licked his lips, eyes darting. "Please."

"You're going to take us to Coombs," I said. "Or we'll tape you right next to Hillman, here."

Hillman moaned something unintelligible. One of the buzzards swooped lower, still circling. The sun was declining and the huge bird wheeled in stark silhouette against the darkening sky.

Buster nodded up at it. "I hear that if you're alive, they go for the eyes first."

Albert looked up at the circling bird. He looked at Buster, then Hillman, then his bodyguard, and finally back to me.

He started to say something.

I cut him off. "Save it. We're going to talk in the car."

Before we left, we took Hillman down, re-taped his hands, and carried him inside the trailer to join his friends on the floor. He was on the ladder, too. Just like Leo had been. One rung up, but still not calling the shots. Not making the big decisions. Tempting as it was, I didn't want to leave him dangling for the buzzards.

I also didn't want him warning anyone we were on our way.

Albert and I climbed into the Mercedes. Buster followed in the Corvette. As I closed my door I could hear the crows, agitated by all the commotion. Their cawing sounded urgent and displeased, as if they knew that things in the world were bad, and maybe getting worse.

We stopped just before the entrance to an urgent care clinic that we found back the way we'd come. "You going to be okay?" I asked Buster.

"Could Elvis sell records?" He had his usual pirate grin, but his eyes showed concern. "I'm not worried about *me*. Let me come with you. This is a scratch. My cat's done worse."

I squeezed his good shoulder. "Go get stitched up. I'll be fine." I could see blood soaking through the makeshift bandage on his arm.

"You sure?"

"I'll call you soon," I promised.

"Okay, but I don't like it," he grumbled. "Not at all. Can't you wait until I'm out?"

I shook my head. "No time. I'll be okay," I reassured him.

He looked past me to Albert. "If you drag her into hot water, I'll boil you alive."

"That's not fair! She's dragging *me* into hot water," Albert protested.

Buster didn't bother to answer. Just gunned the Corvette in the direction of the parking lot. I watched the fierce, loud car with affection. Maybe the doctors would call the police when they saw the gunshot, but even if they did I wasn't very worried. Buster had been shot before. He had his just-cleaning-my-gun story down pat.

I turned to Albert. "Let's go find Coombs before it's too late."

From the clinic we got back on a main road. The Mercedes rode high up, giving us a commanding presence. I tried to relax, deep, slow breaths, expelling the stale adrenaline from the afternoon. The human body wasn't designed to operate at a continuous *go-go-go*. A Dylan song came on the radio.

"Please don't do this," said Albert. His hands were trembling on the wheel.

I didn't answer. The song had opened up a memory. My mother sitting next to me at the breakfast table, strumming an acoustic guitar. That was all. All I could remember. I must have been three or four. I wondered if the rest of the memory was there, somewhere, or gone forever. I turned the moment around in my mind, hungering for more. Had she been singing to me? She had been smiling. Happy. I was sure of that much.

Albert's voice wormed into my mind. "Don't do this. For your own sake."

I put the memory away. It was mine. I wouldn't let this man get near it.

"It's not too late to change your mind," he urged. "You don't know these people."

"Everyone seems to be telling me that."

"It's no joke." His voice was strained and fearful. "You'll get us both killed. Forget about Coombs. He is a dead man—but you don't have to be. Is it money you want? I can give you money. I can give you a lot."

"What does Mr. Z do, exactly?" I asked.

Albert shook his head quickly. "It doesn't matter."

"Pull over." My voice was sharp. He heard my tone and eased the Mercedes onto the shoulder. Traffic flashed by. I held the stun gun up. "You need to do a better job of answering my questions."

There was a small amount of defiance in his voice. "You can't kill me. Only I can take you to Coombs. You know this is true."

I pressed the switch on the stun gun and it came to life, the blue arc of electricity crackling between the scorpion-stinger points. "In case you forgot, there's a whole lot of room between dead and feeling like a daisy."

The stun gun was two inches from his cheek. The electricity crackled and spat.

He flinched away. "Please!"

"You're right," I acknowledged. "I can't kill you. In fact, I don't even want to. But hurt you? That can happen all day long. Tell me about Mr. Z."

Albert swallowed, sweat beading his forehead. "He leads an Organization that is involved in various illicit activities."

"Don't get too specific. My God."

He answered in little snippets, his sentences shorn of human subjects, as though afraid he was being recorded. "Guns go south over the border. Narcotics come up, north."

"That's all?"

"Some loans are made within the community, some used goods are resold, some businesses receive protection against threats."

Loan-sharking. Fencing. Extortion.

"Keep driving. What else? How about the women?"

He cast a nervous glance my way as he picked up speed again. "Women?"

"Come on." I turned the radio off. "Your *Organization* is involved in sex trafficking. What do you have, brothels? Massage parlors? Where?"

Albert swallowed again. "This is part of the business, yes. There's a network of places throughout the state."

I remembered the wriggling, Gorgon's head of red lines, radiating across the map of the southwestern U.S. and beyond. The scattergram of blue dots.

They'll run you up and down the circuit like a goddamn rodeo pony.

"Just in state?" I prodded.

"And possibly elsewhere," he added with reluctance.

We had turned off the main road and were driving through more agriculture, vineyards and artichokes and lettuce, high, parched hills rising in the distance. Impossible to ever guess that a twenty-mile drive would bring us to the Pacific's shores. I thought of the first explorers crossing the vast continent, struggling over mountains, sunburned, frozen, bug-bit, malnourished, beaten down by a thousand hardships. Reaching this point, could they have suspected that the end to their journey was so close?

The sun had declined to just above the hills and the sky had purpled. The suspension of the Mercedes wasn't tuned to make us feel the road, alive and exciting underneath. It was a hovercraft. A confident, Bavarian, fist-in-velvet message that the dangerous excitement of the world could be mastered, tamed, held at bay.

"Why did you guys really take Coombs?" I asked.

Albert's knuckles were tight on the wheel. "I don't know. They never involve me in those decisions."

"You're an accountant."

"Exactly!" he exclaimed as if I had just exonerated him. "I'm an accountant. That is all I know."

"You're the accountant, and there was money involved. A lot of money. Of course you know about Coombs."

I was getting used to Albert's squirming, slippery style. Deny, deny, deny, then admit the minimum and deny again. I felt like a prosecutor grilling a subpoenaed witness.

"Why grab Coombs?" I asked again.

"We were negotiating with him. He was an intermediary. Mr. Z lost patience."

I laughed. "You're good at telling me things you know I already know. If you remember, I was in the room when he said that. How about a little insider's perspective?"

Albert sighed helplessly as though I had asked him to recite *The Iliad* from memory. "Coombs represented a client who had . . . business with our Organization."

"Business?"

"We had discovered him in a compromising position."

"Blackmail." I thought of the DVDs. Amateur porn that felt a little too amateur. The older, out-of-shape men and the teenage-looking girls.

Albert gave a philosophical shrug. "Whatever you wish to call it. They wanted the matter to go away and our people wished to capitalize on the situation. Creating a buyer and seller, the fundamentals of any economic system. Simple. But these people we were dealing with are in one ecosystem, and Mr. Z is in another. Coombs was the bridge between us."

"So why burn the bridge?" I had a pretty good idea of the answers to some of my questions, but I wanted to keep him talking, get him comfortable. The more he talked, the likelier that he'd slip up and give me something real.

"Mr. Z grew impatient," Albert replied. "He decided they were stonewalling. But if he had Coombs, then a strict deadline could be set. Specific consequences could be communicated."

We had driven away from the fields and were in a commercial stretch, all big box stores and gas stations and fast food. No more farmland, here. Just asphalt and ugly buildings and loud billboards full of 800 numbers for cheap liposuction and ambulance-chasers.

Steinbeck country. I wondered what Steinbeck would have thought.

I asked the question that mattered. "Who was the client Coombs was representing?"

Albert took his eyes off the road long enough to look at me. "That, I do not know."

I let the stun gun brush his arm and he flinched.

"Sure?"

"I swear. All I know is that there was a lot of money at stake."

"How much?"

"Millions," he said.

"How many millions?"

"An eight-figure sum." He braked hard as a yellow light turned red. "The exact amount was being negotiated, but it was close to ten million."

"And Coombs is still alive?"

"As far as I know."

The light turned green and Albert turned left. "It's still not too late to turn around. I have some money saved, that I can give you. Walk away from all this. Go free. Take my advice."

"No, thanks."

"You really don't care about money?" He sounded incredulous. We had passed through the commercial district, now. Buildings were farther apart. More space, fewer cars, no pedestrians.

"It's not that," I said. "I care about some things more."

"What about your safety? Your life? Do you value those things?"

I think you'd try to save me without even thinking about it.

"I intend to stay healthy," I said. "And if you're lucky, and you listen, maybe you can, too."

"Impossible."

"I disagree," I said. "It's very possible. But only if I know what to expect. So why don't you tell me all about where we're going and who's there, and then I'll tell you what we're going to do when we arrive."

33

I was looking at a motel.

Two stories, faded blue paint, outdoor stairwells, built in the classic mid-century motor court design. A three-sided rectangle, a wing on each side reaching out like a hungry embrace around a front courtyard. Parking spaces slotted along each wing so people could drive their cars right up to the rooms. Almost all of the parking spots were empty except for a cluster of moving trucks along the right-hand wing. No people in sight anywhere. A neon sign proclaimed NO VACANCY in tired red. Surprising. This motel seemed like it should have a sign saying NOTHING BUT VACANCIES.

"What is this place?" I wondered.

He sounded glum. "It's where Coombs is staying."

In front of us was a gated, empty swimming pool aproned by concrete. Next to it was an ancient charcoal grill, planted in the concrete like a dead tree stump. No kids running around, no families unpacking their cars. As lifeless as the surface of the moon. I could see nothing through the motel's windows except drawn blinds. A dusty, unappealing place. Out of the way, unfriendly, suggesting the very opposite of comforts from the long road.

We parked in front of the empty pool next to a big black SUV and a pair of white, windowless cargo vans. The accountant was nervous. Sweat, quivers, all the obvious signs that something was amiss. Signaling distress as obviously as a flare shot off a lifeboat.

"You need to pull yourself together," I said.

He slammed a hand against the dashboard. "This was a mistake! I told you it was. Why didn't you listen?"

"Come on. Let's go."

Anger dusted into pleas. "You're sure? We can still drive away. Please."

I opened my door. "You talk too much."

It was almost dusk, the air cooling as the sun retreated behind the hills. We walked toward the lobby entrance. The barbecue grill by the pool was orange with rust. It was impossible to see the gaping rectangle of the water-less pool and not think of an unfilled grave. The bottom was covered by a scuzz of dead leaves. It was hard to imagine that kids had ever splashed and played and laughed there.

As we approached the front doors a man emerged to intercept us. Maybe twenty-five, he wore brand-new white sneakers and a red Adidas tracksuit that did a bad job of hiding the gun in his waistband. The familiar snake-and-star tattoo on his hand.

"We're here to pick up our guest," Albert said. "His time's up."

Adidas stared at him, working a bulge in his lip that must have been chewing tobacco. "No one told us anything."

To my relief, Albert's voice sounded authoritative. "You know what you need to know, when you need to know it."

"Sorry." Adidas looked chastened. Clearly there was a hierarchy. Maybe the accountant wasn't in direct charge of Adidas, but he occupied a higher rung. "Follow me." He spat a brown stream into the dead soil of a planter and shifted the bulge in his lip to the other side of his mouth.

He made a big show of holding the door for me. Then I felt his hand cupping my butt in an appreciative squeeze. I ignored him and followed Albert inside.

The lobby looked like any motel lobby. Yet it felt off. I realized why after a moment. There was something artificial about it. I thought of props, facades, like walking on the deserted stage set of a performance that had closed years before. Everything that was supposed to be in a motel was there. A check-in counter with a real live clerk and a little silver bell, coffee urn and stack of cups, TV tuned to a football game, potted ferns, armchairs, coffee tables cov-ered with magazines. But lifeless. No trace of hospitality. Nothing to suggest that normal people checked in and ate and slept and showered and checked out.

A facsimile of a motel lobby. Fake.

Spooky.

I wondered if the silver bell would even *ding* if I pushed it. The magazines on the tables were years old, covered in dust. The clerk watched us. He didn't look like any motel clerk I'd ever seen. A brawny, dead-eyed man who looked like he'd sooner give up his right arm than smile. He watched us without a word.

Fake.

"Where is he?" Albert asked Adidas.

"He's staying in 107." Adidas took a cup from the stack by the coffee urn and spat another stream of brown liquid, working the bulge in his lip. The coffee urn was empty and dust-covered, its unplugged cord dangling from the wall. He opened a second door and led us into the ground level corridor. Fluorescent lights lit up peeling walls and scuffed carpets patterned with twining flowers. We passed an alcove with an ice machine and vending machine. The vending machine was unplugged, its racks empty. The ice machine didn't hum. Like an abandoned set, I thought again. Decrepit.

Room 107 was halfway down the corridor. Adidas spat into his cup and used a key card. The door opened to reveal an ordinary motel room. Blinds drawn, bed and desk and nightstand and bathroom. Everything correct.

Yet off.

The blinds, I saw, were sealed with electrical tape. The desk was bare of lamps or pens or glasses. The bed and bed frame looked normal enough except, like the desk, they were bolted to the floor. And except for the chain that ran from the bed frame, across the flowery comforter, to a metal cuff, which encircled a bare ankle.

Coombs lay on the bed.

Adidas stormed over, eager to show how on top of things he was. "Get up, asshole," he yelled. "You have company."

Coombs, unshaven and unwashed, looked a far cry from the suave, elegant man I had last seen. There were bags under his eyes and bruises across his face. He wore only a dirty white V-neck and boxer shorts.

"Get up!" Adidas shouted again. He grabbed Coombs's shoulder and jerked him up. "Move it!"

Coombs climbed to his feet. I saw his face change fractionally as he saw me. Perplexed, questioning. And then a moment later, understanding.

He shifted anxious eyes to Albert, as though my presence was the least important thing in the world. "What's happening?" he asked.

Albert said, "Your time is up. Two days."

Coombs licked his lips. "I want to stay here."

I couldn't help but admire his delivery. Thinking of our dinner, the way he had started to walk away—as though sitting, or not sitting, was all the same. Now the man had been beaten, frightened, maybe worse, but already he was reading the room, looking for the minute cues that told him how to act and what to say. Understanding that a man in his position, as miserable as he was, would be desperate *not* to leave.

Adidas smacked Coombs across the face with the back of his free hand. "No one cares what you want, asshole."

Coombs addressed Albert, his voice rising. "The money is on the verge of going through! You got what you wanted!"

"Too late," replied the accountant. "We have lost all patience, I'm afraid."

A show. The two of them. Performing.

There was a metallic clinking as Adidas unlocked the bracelet around Coombs's ankle. He threw a pair of gray sweatpants and flip-flops toward him.

"Get dressed. Hurry."

I glanced at Albert. His face was clammy.

A few more minutes. That was all I needed. A few more minutes for him to avoid having a complete breakdown. A few more minutes of good luck. Just a few.

Then we were free.

Coombs pulled on the sweatpants.

Almost there.

Adidas spat into his cup. "Good to go?"

Albert nodded. "Let's go." He opened the door and stepped into the corridor. The three of us behind him.

Something strange happened.

Albert's hands flew to his throat.

Blood spouted through his fingers as I heard the air explode, split by supersonic force. Albert had already fallen to his knees. He clawed at his throat and fell sideways. Another bullet cracked into the doorframe, sending splinters flying. The hallway was a kill zone. I pushed Coombs back into the room as a third bullet split the wall where his head had been. Adidas stared in confusion, his tobacco cup still in his hand, too surprised to even remember his gun. He looked from us to the accountant's body as I stepped back into the room. As the door swung shut, I saw him running down the hallway in the opposite direction of the gunshots. There were two more shots as I pulled the door closed and heard it latch.

Coombs and I alone in the room. The two of us.

"We have to get out of here." I ran over to the window and stripped away the taped blinds. I stopped. Instead of a glass window was a thick sheet of plywood, nailed into the wall. The nails holding it looked like lawn darts.

"We have to break it," I said.

Coombs gestured hopelessly around the room. "Everything's bolted down. I've spent the last two days thinking about getting out of this room. It's a prison cell. The only way out is the door."

"There has to be a way."

I looked around, thinking.

There was a small click from the door.

The click of a lock unlatching.

Usually an innocuous sound. This time, deadly.

I lunged for the deadbolt. Too late.

The door opened.

Once again, I saw Mr. Z walk into a room. On one side of him was the hard-eyed motel clerk. The machine pistol he held made him look even less clerkish. Mr. Z's remaining bodyguard, the one with the scarred brow and hatchet, was on the other side.

He was holding a hunting rifle.

34

"Albert . . . such a weak and disloyal man," Mr. Z said. "So disappointing." He had pulled a Snickers bar from his pocket and was eating it in quick bites. "Such a betrayal." I could see the butt of some big cowboy gun sticking out of his wide jeans.

"You didn't have to shoot him," I said. "I forced him to help us. He didn't want to. He didn't have a choice."

Mr. Z waved the candy bar at me. "He chose to betray me. Always, there is a choice."

"To die in a blaze of glory? Is that really more honorable?"

Mr. Z shrugged. "He died anyway. Why not do it honorably? Albert was one of my most valued employees. It will be difficult to replace him, extremely difficult." He let the empty candy wrapper fall to the floor. "But not impossible."

Coombs said, "The money is ready. Put me in front of a computer and I can have it transferred in less than five minutes."

Mr. Z looked bored. "Or I'll send them your head, and then they can send me my money." He jabbed a fat finger toward me. "I recognize you. You were there—in Monterey. You're not a whore? Who are you?"

"The problem about blackmail," I said, "is that eventually you end up catching a tiger by the tail. Just a question of when. How many rich and powerful men can you videotape before one of them decides to do something about it?"

"So you have learned a little about part of my business," Mr. Z said. "But you're wrong—these men are reasonable—or they become reasonable. They are not tigers. They understand that a few pennies from their pockets are worth infinitely less than the consequences of exposure. No one wishes his life to be destroyed."

"The dead women found in the U-Haul—it's been all over the news," I said. "That was you."

Mr. Z said, "No one wanted that to happen."

"Who was driving? I'd like to meet him."

Mr. Z exchanged a grin with the bodyguard holding the hunting rifle. "That will be impossible, I'm afraid. They are no longer in this world."

"And neither are the six women they killed. What are you going to do about that?"

"Do?" He opened a bag of Skittles and chewed a handful. "Why do anything? There are many more where they came from."

"The case made national headlines, it's all over the news. There's too much public outrage. They won't let it go."

The fat man didn't look convinced. "The women who died, they were not Americans. They were penniless, foreign, here without papers, no friends. An unfortunate combination, if you desire fairness, but that is how the world is." He ate more Skittles. "They don't have families to hire expensive lawyers or go on television to cry for justice. And so much news, every day, so much going on. People have short memories. No, I don't think there will be more trouble for us."

"Let us go," Coombs said again. "We can all get what we want."

Mr. Z shook his head. "Life doesn't work like that. People want different things. We cannot all get what we want. For example, imagine what I want, after all this bellyache?" He gestured to his bodyguard. "Show them what I mean."

The bodyguard raised the hunting rifle and sighted through its scope. A .30-30 bolt action. He was maybe ten feet away and the rifle was rock-steady. He could have hit me with his eyes closed. I could have been a hundred feet away and that would have been equally true.

Coombs stepped forward. Standing between me and the rifle.

"Don't do this," he said. "Please."

I hadn't expected that. "Get out of the way," I told him, slipping a hand into my handbag while he blocked me from view.

Mr. Z laughed. "You've always been so slippery, such a greasy little weasel, so concerned with saving your own skin. And yet now, at the very end, you decide to become a hero? For what—for *her*?"

Coombs said, "Let her go. She's done nothing to you. I got her into this."

If anything, his words seemed to make the fat man angrier. "*Nothing*? Look at this mess, these problems I have! All because of the two of you! In fact, why should she get an easy landing, after all this bellyache she caused?"

He exchanged a look with the bodyguard, who nodded and set down his rifle. He took something out of a holster strapped to his thigh. The hatchet.

The fat man said, "Teach her a lesson. Nice and slow."

Coombs didn't move. "You'll have to kill me first," he said. "Maybe I have cared a bit too much about my own skin, all these years." Under the forced insouciance his voice was dry. "Never too late to turn over a new leaf, I suppose."

"Keep him alive," Mr. Z said. "But you can teach him how to behave."

The bodyguard stepped toward us. Eyes blank, white scar running down his temple, right hand cocked back. The steel blade was like a dividing horizon line. Life on one side, death on the other.

"This isn't fair," I said, now standing next to Coombs. "It's not a fair fight."

The fat man laughed. "What do you Americans say? *Life* isn't fair. Start with their hands," he instructed. He was grinning. Enjoying himself. He had taken another candy bar out of his pocket. Like he was at the movies.

The bodyguard drew his arm back.

At its apex, the blade paused for the slightest moment.

The hatchet came down in a wicked swing as Coombs threw his hands up instinctively.

I shot the bodyguard through my handbag. I'd practiced at much greater distances. Three or four feet was nothing. The bullet and muzzle flash tore a ragged hole through the bag's fabric and, seemingly simultaneously, through his forehead.

I shifted my aim a few inches and shot the fake clerk three times in the chest.

Mr. Z dropped his chocolate, stunned. He was faster than his weight suggested. He lunged out the door as I sent two more bullets after him.

I stepped cautiously into the hallway and then ducked back as bullets cracked down the corridor. There was movement in the interior stairwell by the lobby entrance. I ran, seeing a spotty trail of blood along the ugly flowered carpet. Heavy footsteps clanged up the bare metal of the stairwell.

I started up the stairs, then flattened myself against the wall as another bullet ricocheted off the staircase. The footsteps resumed. I followed the ponderous *thuds* to the second floor. Mr. Z was lumbering away from me. Toward the end of the hallway. An exit sign marking the outside stairwell.

I held my Beretta with both hands, sighted carefully, and pulled the trigger in a smooth, clean motion. His body jolted. His gun dropped from his hands as he staggered.

I shot him again and he fell.

Coombs had caught up to me. Together we approached the wounded man. He was making a pained, gurgling sound. Something wrong with his lungs, as though there was fluid filling them. He looked up at us as we approached and moved his lips like he was trying to speak. I couldn't think of anything to say so I just shot him twice more and he became one of the approximately hundred people in the world who had died in that particular minute.

Coombs stared at me as though seeing something new. "Violence seems to come rather naturally to you."

I regarded him. Wondering how the harsh overhead light fell across my face. What lines and shadows it might reveal. Wondering whether I, too, looked like I had shed a mask.

"I never said I considered violence the option of last recourse," I reminded him. "Only you did." I bent and found Mr. Z's key card in his back pocket. "Now let's see who's staying here."

35

We picked the closest room to us: 211. It seemed as good a place as any to start.

I swiped the keycard. A light blinked green.

The door clicked open.

Room 211 looked identical to Coombs's room. The same bare, bolted desk, blinds sealed with electrical tape, the same flowered bedspread and musty motel smell.

Room 211 was occupied.

A very young woman sat in a chair, watching us with dull eyes. The television was turned to some sitcom. *Young woman* was stretching it. She looked like she was sixteen or seventeen, her body girlishly thin, not yet filled out. Her black hair was long and straight and her dilated pupils were black pools. She wore pink sweatpants and a sleeveless top showing matchstick arms. I wondered what they had her on. Maybe a sedative. Maybe some antidepressant. Maybe just one of the countless opiates that was strangling the country at a rate of about seventy thousand deaths a year. Some pharmaceutical cocktail designed to make a person comfortable, plus a little extra. Compliant. Obedient. Untroublesome.

Unlike Coombs, there was no metal bracelet on her ankle. Hard to consider this girl a flight risk.

She spoke in heavily accented English, her voice sluggish. "Who are you?"

"We're going to help you," I said. "Everything else, I'll explain later. But for now, we have to leave this place as soon as we can."

.   .   .

We went down the hallway door by door, first sweeping the second floor, then going down to the first. In total we found seven women. All about the same age. All radiating that gluey, pharmaceutical compliance. We helped them pack their scant possessions as fast as we could. I didn't know when more of Mr. Z's people might show up.

The women obeyed robotically, barely asking questions, moving without urgency. As if only vaguely aware of what was happening.

Ultimately, they'd need housing, and maybe immigration lawyers to help reunite them with their families, plus a dozen other things, but for now I only wanted to get them away from the motel as fast as we could. I had Hillman's duffel bag. Maybe a hundred thousand dollars. More than ten thousand each. That would be a good start. But first, somewhere safe. Somewhere they could get medical attention, and food, and rest, while time flushed out whatever was in their systems. Somewhere safe. There was a shelter I had worked with once in Monterey. It seemed the best solution for the moment.

When we got outside it was dark and chilly, the sky shrouded with clouds. One of the two white vans had been driven about a hundred feet from its original location and was now parked crookedly in the middle of the motel lot, engine on, idling. I walked up cautiously. Adidas slumped in the driver's seat. He wasn't breathing and the top of his tracksuit was soaked in blood. He must have taken a bullet in the hallway.

I spent a few minutes wiping away any traces of my presence I could think of: door handles, the inside of the Mercedes. There didn't seem to be a working security camera system. I could see why. Like Hillman avoiding notes and documents. Cameras created evidence. Evidence could be seized.

We all crammed into the remaining van. I drove. Coombs sat next to me. I glanced one last time at the blue motel. Feeling like I should see a huge pyrotechnic burst, fire licking up its roof, walls crumbling, burning hard and fierce and bright until there was nothing but ash.

Coombs seemed to have read my mind. "Feels like it should go up in bloody flames, doesn't it?" he said as we pulled away.

"It should."

Instead, the blue motel simply receded into the background and disappeared from view.

At the shelter I went inside with the girls. Coombs offered to come with us, but I told him it wasn't necessary. "I suppose a strange man barging in isn't ideal," he said, understanding.

I tossed him the keys to the van. "Go find a razor. And a pair of real pants. This will take a while."

I spent an hour getting the women situated, relieved there were enough beds at the shelter for all of them. I didn't want to split them up. I explained the situation to the on-duty staff, giving them some of Hillman's cash for any incidental expenses for the next few days. More would follow soon, I promised. There would be a lot to do. Authorities to file reports with. Long-term housing. Legal aid. But for now, most important, they were safe.

I borrowed the phone and after a flurry of transfers and holds managed to reach an on-duty nurse at the urgent care center where I had left Buster. "Sorry," he said, "he can't come to the phone—"

The nurse was interrupted by Buster's voice, in the background, announcing in the most definite terms that he would indeed come to the phone, immediately, and anyone trying to stop him or suggest otherwise might find themselves learning to fly.

"Nikki?"

"How you feeling?" I asked.

"Right as rain. You okay?"

It felt good hearing his familiar growl. "I'm fine," I said.

"You need me?" he offered. "I'll leave without even changing out of this cute little hospital gown they got me in. I've always wanted to show off my legs."

I pictured Buster barreling down the sidewalk in a skimpy hospital gown. "I'll see those sexy calves of yours another time. Just making sure you're good."

"You liar," Buster said. "Why don't you admit the real reason you called?"

"And what might that be?"

"Admit it, Nikki Griffin. You missed the sweet sugar of my voice."

"Tell whoever's in charge of your morphine that they should ease up. It's making you loopy."

I hung up. A smile on my face.

When Coombs returned in new clothes, hair combed, with a fresh shave, he looked restored, newly vital. He was, after all, a man who made his living on appearances. We drove a short distance north to a beachside hotel I knew.

The hotel sold little bundles of firewood at the front desk. Five dollars for guests, ten otherwise. We paid ten. We had picked up a pizza and a six-pack and carried the food and firewood onto the beach, taking off our shoes as we reached the sand.

The beach glowed with small fires. Music drifted, faint, a guitar playing slow reggae. My mother had started taking guitar lessons a few years before her death, joking that, the way my brother and I ate, she'd have to go and become a rock star to feed the family. *Rockmom!* Brandon had screamed. The nickname had stuck.

I arranged sticks and crumpled newspaper and struck a match. Flames flared, caressing the wood even as they chewed into it, tender and duplicitous, the way fire was. "I didn't think I'd ever see this bloody ocean again," Coombs said with great feeling. "Except the bottom." He stretched out on the beach, not bothering to disguise his pleasure as he squeezed handfuls of sand between his fingers.

I offered him a slice of pizza. "Hungry?"

"Hungry?" He devoured the slice in several huge bites, then sat back. "I've eaten at some really first-rate restaurants, you know. Alain Ducasse at the Dorchester. Collonges-au-Mont-d'Or and L'Ambroisie in France, Enoteca Pinchiorri in Florence. And yet this lukewarm sausage and mushroom pizza is perhaps the most exquisite thing I've ever had."

I cracked a can of beer and handed it to him.

Opened one for myself.

For a few minutes we didn't say much. Just ate pizza and drank beer in comfortable silence. The fire crackled and the ocean swirled and foamed against the sand. I could hear the guitar, languorous, bouncy notes drifting down the beach.

"How're you feeling?" I asked.

Coombs wiped his mouth. "I'll live. A couple of days of rude mistreatment, but nothing I haven't faced before."

I thought of Wormwood Scrubs but said nothing. Wondering, for the thousandth time, who exactly the man sitting next to me really was.

Instead I said, "You made quite the impression on Mrs. Johannessen."

His smile was fond. "So you've met her. Marie is a firecracker, isn't she?"

"You tell me."

He wriggled his toes in the loose sand. "We get along."

"Unlike you and the rest of her family."

"I doubt they had the kindest words. But what do *you* think?"

"Of what?"

"Of me." His eyes, warm with firelight, held mine. "That interests me more."

"I don't know. Every time I form an opinion, something comes along to change it."

"Maybe you should trust your instincts, then." He opened a second beer, placing his empty can carefully in the sand.

"Says the man who devoted his life to deception."

He didn't argue. "I'm a firm believer in identifying one's talents early, working hard, and letting that take you as far as possible."

"And what's your talent?"

"You know. You just said so. Deception. I present myself in a certain light, tailored to what someone wants to see. And then I allow them to form their own assumptions." He sipped his beer. "Same as you, I would imagine."

"You don't have to use that to con people, though. I don't."

He nodded. "True enough. I suppose I've always had a taste for the finer things. You happen to learn where I grew up?"

"Edmonton, Canada."

"Northeast of there, actually, by enough to matter. Wandering River. A tiny little town, a hamlet, technically—not much of anything. For a boy with dreams and imagination, it seemed awfully far from anywhere. I had no wish to spend my life breaking my back in hard labor for a lumber company or oil conglomerate."

I opened a second can of beer for myself. "And that excuses you?"

He picked up a handful of sand, opened his fingers, watched the grains fall. "Context, my dear. I offer context, not excuses. I could have lived my whole life without ever getting south of Edmonton. From up there, you know, Toronto seems like Miami Beach. I've worked in subzero weather on chainsaw crews for four bucks an hour. Can you blame me for realizing there's a world of nice things out there and wanting my share?"

"*Your* share? Or what belongs to others?"

His eyes were penetrating. "You've never struck me as puritanical."

"I have morals," I said. "Maybe different than some, but I have them. And they don't blow over in a strong wind."

"I haven't exactly gotten off scot-free." He gazed out at the ocean. "Never get mixed up with old money or gangsters. If I ever write my memoirs, that would make a good first chapter. They're both so damn prideful and unforgiving."

"You seem to have done pretty well for yourself," I observed.

"For a boy from northern Canada who was never fated to leave his postal code? Sure, I suppose." He shrugged. "At least I avoided the oil fields and lumber yards."

"But you didn't avoid everything," I said.

Coombs used a piece of driftwood to prod the coals glowing on the sand. A flurry of orange sparks swarmed up like ants, floated downwind. "What are you getting at?"

"That Oxford dean. You killed him—why?"

He placed the driftwood on the fire, his face expressionless. "Forks in the road," he mused. "Funny to think about what could have been." He picked up another handful of sand and squeezed, the grains trickling away. "I went off to Oxford on scholarship, knowing it was the chance of a lifetime. Ten lifetimes, with a background like mine. I threw myself into my studies. Was there wealth, privilege, class, the likes of which I'd never dreamt of? Of course—all around me. And I can't deny I felt enchanted, intoxicated, by these glimpses at a more exciting world. But I still believed that diligence and merit would net me those things for myself. I had my wits, after all. And I'd managed to reach the right place to exercise them."

"Until you decided that murder would get you there quicker?"

"Do you really think I'd embark on some kind of cold-blooded *Double Indemnity* scheme for a quick payday?" His eyes might have been disappointed.

"You tell me."

Coombs tilted his beer to his mouth, then rested the can in the sand next to the first. "Very well. It began with a simple affair. As so many unfortunate things do. She was a married woman, twenty years older. I didn't think any of that should matter. She said she was unhappy, and I was a starry-eyed young buck with the whole world in front of him. We both went into things willingly enough—more than willingly, I should say."

"So why kill her husband? He found out?"

"The night it happened he had been out at some reception—he felt unwell, I learned later, and came home early. When he found us, he seized a fireplace poker and charged me."

"And?"

Coombs smiled without humor. "You think I brained him with it? I didn't. Nothing nearly so dramatic. I grabbed it to keep from having my head knocked in. And then the next thing I knew he was having some kind of heart attack. He collapsed, hit his head on the way down, and died on his bedroom floor. His grieving wife decided she loved her husband considerably more in death than in life—and the authorities decided that a respected Oxford dean deserved vengeance against a troublesome Canadian hick. I had the bad luck to draw a particularly hard-hearted magistrate, and so off I went—"

"To Wormwood Scrubs," I finished.

Coombs nodded, his eyes distant with memory. "And what I saw there convinced me that the world was a damn sight more dog-eat-dog than I'd realized. How did Hobbes put it—nasty, brutish, short? That summed up life at Wormwood Scrubs."

I was quiet. Thinking about parallels. Coombs had drawn a bad card. I had drawn a few myself. The two men who took my family; later, my foster father, Darren. And we had both learned how unpleasant life could be.

"By the time I got out," he continued, "I was a bit less trusting in Boy Scout ideals. I was a convict, too, of course, so no more school, no more studies. I couldn't have gotten hired to slap sandwiches together." His eyes locked with mine. "Broke, alone, and only my own wits to carry me through life—and not much trust in other people to help me get there."

"Susan Johannessen disappeared," I told him. "Do you know anything about that?"

"She's missing? Since when?"

His surprise seemed genuine, although I knew I probably couldn't tell if it wasn't. Not with this man. "Not long," I said. "She was driving down to meet me—she wanted to tell me something about her brother. They found her car in the parking lot of a state beach. Police are asking around. Did Mr. Z say anything?"

"About her? Not a thing." Coombs frowned. "That family is a snake pit of jealousy and rivalries. Little scores always being tallied and settled, new feuds and alliances blowing up like summer squalls. Marie holds it all in check, as best she can, and Susan—well, from what I understand, Susan grew increasingly disgusted with the whole mess. You want my opinion? Even odds that she bought a plane ticket to somewhere far away. She'll turn up."

"Let's talk about her brother."

He didn't hesitate. "Ron was being blackmailed. That started all this. He had been in the habit of frequenting a particular San Francisco establishment that Mr. Z's Organization ran."

"What was particular about it?"

"It caters to men who prefer women slightly underage. Like those poor girls in the motel. Not pedophiles, per se, but deep-pocketed men who are willing to pay enormous premiums for what I suppose is the illicitness of the act." He had picked up another piece of driftwood and ran it through the sand, sketching invisible lines. "For men like that it's not only sexual. They already have so much money, so much power. It's transgression. A way of sneering in the face of society, stating they can take what they want, rules be damned."

I thought of the girls in the blue motel and my stomach turned.

Coombs said, "If the news had broken it would have been devastating for the family. The threat put them in an intolerable position; something had to be done. The blackmailers were asking for a lot, but that wasn't the sticking point. Marie worried—not without cause—that if she paid, it could become a leaching without end, on and on, forever. She asked me to travel down to meet them and finalize the negotiations."

"You agreed to put yourself in harm's way for a man like Ron?"

Coombs chuckled. "Don't get me wrong, Nikki, I've never been much for community service. My fee was to have been ten percent. Almost a million dollars—for what I thought would be a few days' work." His smile faded. "Although had I known who that bloody fool of a playboy had gotten wrapped up with, I would sooner have jumped in a shark tank."

"Did Mr. Z's people blackmail everyone? What kind of business model is that?"

Coombs shook his head. "Not everyone. They *taped* all their customers, but I believe they only selected a small percentage of men who were deemed VIP for blackmail. The men who could afford the most, and had the most to lose."

"Do you know where this place is? In San Francisco?"

"Why?"

"To shut it down, of course. And that *is* your community service."

Coombs tore a scrap off the pizza box and wrote on it. "Here you are."

I put the piece of cardboard in my pocket. I'd give it to the police, along with the route maps and files from Hillman's office.

The fire had crouched into orange embers. The guitar had fallen silent. I looked at the man next to me, feeling that same flick of danger and excitement, like being near a wild animal. He turned his head, his eyes unreadable. Looked at me with that same obsidian sphinx smile. I tried to guess what he might do. What he was thinking. We watched each other for a long moment, our faces barely a foot apart. Maybe he read my hesitation, or maybe just spoke in accordance with his own private thoughts, but he simply said, "I suppose we should be getting on with things. Can I offer you a lift?"

The moment, whatever it had been, passed like a cloud across the moon. "You don't have a car," I reminded him.

Coombs looked at me, a real smile now, teasing the corners of his mouth. A smile suggesting fun and play and possibility and all kinds of excitement.

"Have you forgotten you're talking to a man who likes to take flight?"

"Where'd you learn to fly?"

The engine was very loud, even taxiing, but his answer came clearly through my headphones as we turned onto the short runway. "I grew up in rural Canada. Very few people, very large distances. Everyone uses puddle-jumpers and seaplanes. I could fly almost before I could drive." He did a last check of the controls, the plane pausing as though an animal about to leap, the propeller a vague blur through the cockpit glass.

"If you ever care to learn, I'd be delighted to teach you." He throttled up and the little plane raced down the runway, eager for the sky, the engine noise now deafening. The pavement and lights streaked beneath us.

"I think I'll stick to two wheels."

"The offer stands. In case you change your mind." He worked the controls and we were suddenly buoyant, the lights of Monterey falling away beneath us. "So, where's next for you?"

"Back to work. My bookstore. Nothing exciting. You?"

"I believe I rather deserve a vacation." Still ascending, he banked steeply north, the ocean to our left as we followed the coast. "Are you sure I can't convince you to spend a week dallying at Le Meurice?"

"Le Meurice?"

He sounded disappointed. "Clearly you don't care about fine Parisian hotels."

A bump of turbulence jolted the plane. "Thanks, but take-out Chinese food and the TCM channel is how I plan to celebrate. I'll let you handle five-star Paris."

"Old movies and take-out noodles. How devastatingly mundane," Coombs said. "I'm starting to think you really *do* need me."

"How about you?" I shot back. "Off to find the next wealthy widow to pay the bills?"

He tweaked the yoke. "Believe it or not, I might take a hiatus from the widows."

We had stopped ascending and leveled out, flying under the clouds. I could see the glitter of lights below us, the homes set into the hills and valleys of the coastline. During the day it would have been a breathtaking flight.

"Do you ever get bothered by what you do to people?" I asked.

"Do you ever get bothered by what *you* do to people?" he returned.

"The people I hurt deserve it."

He glanced at me. "Is that your only answer?"

I watched the lights underneath us. "It bothers me. Sometimes. Even when they deserve it." We hit a bank of low clouds and for a few seconds everything disappeared in a blizzard of whiteness.

The clouds whipped away. The night was clear again.

"When I was younger, hungrier, I was less discriminating," Coombs acknowledged. "To put it in the forestry jargon of my boyhood, I sometimes engaged in clear-cutting. Now, it's more selective trimming. I take what people can afford to lose. Would many call that dishonest or evil? Of course." He twitched the nose of the plane as another spot of turbulence rocked us. "They won't build monuments when I die. No flags will fly at half-mast. If you're after actual honesty, Nikki, that's the best I can give you."

I thought about his answer. "I understand."

And I did. Plenty of people would say I deserved prison or worse for the things I'd done. The man sitting next to me wasn't like most in the world. But neither was I. And we all had to live with the things we did.

"You think we'll see each other again?" I asked.

"Kindred spirits can't keep apart."

"Are we kindred spirits?"

Coombs smiled. "The two of us are different from every other person here."

I smiled, too. He knew me.

And that would always be exciting.

And after all, up here, alone in the cold and lonely night, thousands of feet above the ground, sitting next to each other in this little airplane with nothing but the wind-whipped clouds and star-pricked sky for company, it was hard to disagree.

SATURDAY

36

The doorman must have been expecting me.

He waved me through with barely a word.

The elevator rose, smooth and silent as a switchblade.

The butler was waiting for me at the landing when I stepped out. This time he ushered me into a dining room with inlaid parquet floors like a ballroom. Crystal chandeliers, wood-paneled walls, heavy framed paintings. Lavish, anachronistic. As if the room had chained itself to a fallen century, resistive or uninterested in the passage of time.

I seemed to have interrupted a family dinner. Mrs. Johannessen sat at the head of the long table, her three sons scattered down its length. Martin sat closest to his mother, hands folded primly around his napkin, lines of stress showing on his narrow face, the only one wearing a coat and tie. Ron slouched in shirtsleeves rolled up to his elbows, drink in hand. William drooped in his wheelchair like a wilted flower.

The table looked ready for a state dinner. Candles flickered in pewter candlesticks. Crystal goblets and polished steak knives and a magnificent flower display, all blood-red roses and scarlet tulips. A silver platter held an enormous cut of prime rib. The meat, in its drippings, was cooked so rare as to appear almost raw. Blood from the beef had seeped into a dark surrounding pool.

Mrs. Johannessen looked to be the only one still eating. Ron looked like he was seething with boredom, desperate to be anywhere but here. Martin seemed frustrated, his thin lips set in a petulant line. William's head tilted as though his neck was rubberized.

Mrs. Johannessen looked up as I was shown in. "Nikki," she said. "As you can see, we're in the middle of supper. Have you eaten? I'd be happy to have them fix you a plate."

"No, thanks," I said. "I don't think I'll stay long. Don't want to interrupt the whole family meal. Almost the whole family," I amended. "Where's Susan?"

If I was fishing, I got nothing. She merely said, "My daughter could not be here tonight, as is frequently the case."

Martin was on his feet, clenching his napkin. "What are *you* doing here?"

"Martin, sit," his mother instructed. "I asked her to come."

Martin sat obediently but his eyes were furious. "How did you . . . ?"

I didn't feel like doing a whole song and dance, so I simply said, "You fired me. She hired me."

His eyes shot to his mother. "But *you* made me get rid of—"

"Merely a change of heart." His mother used an ivory-handled steak knife to slice a piece of red meat. "There was something that needed to be done. Once we met, Nikki struck me as someone uniquely capable of carrying that out." She forked the bite of meat into her mouth and chewed without hurry. "*Did* you do as I asked, Nikki? Don't leave us standing on the razor's edge, now."

I nodded. "It's taken care of. And he's free."

Martin flushed. "You don't mean Coo—"

"*Coo, coo.*" All of us turned to William as he opened his mouth with a smacking sound. "*Coo, coo, coo,*" he said again. His voice was high, as though imitating a bird. There was drool on his chin as he drooped into silence once again.

Ron took a slug of his drink and turned to his mother. "Okay, Christ, the woman did whatever garbage-hauling you wanted her to do. Can you please get her out of here, now, so we can actually talk?"

"Patience, Ronald," Mrs. Johannessen said. "You lacked it even as a child." She turned from her middle son to me, not sounding the slightest bit perturbed by the interruptions. "Where is he?"

"I'd check Paris," I said. "I think he said something about a vacation."

"And the people who were holding him?"

"I wouldn't worry about them. They won't bother you."

She took that in as she poured herself more red wine from a cut-glass decanter. "Thank you, Nikki. You did excellent work, finding Geoffrey. Send me any invoices for fees and expenses you incurred, and know that you have my heartfelt gratitude."

She turned away.

I was dismissed.

I said, "I'd have thought you'd be more curious about the rest of it."

"Rest of it?" She looked up again. "Rest of what?"

"You know—why Coombs was down there in the first place."

Her blue eyes showed nothing, but I had her attention.

"I don't follow."

"Your family was being blackmailed," I said. "I'm sure you're fond of Coombs, but we both know why you really needed me to go down there. And it wasn't for *his* well-being."

She cut into a roasted potato, her voice now very cold. "I'm not sure that I care for these insinuations. My thoughts, I believe, are mine alone, as are my motivations. I don't see the point of you haphazardly guessing at matters that are not at all your concern."

"See?" Ron said to me. "That's her polite way of telling you good night."

I looked at him. "I'm curious—what happened, back in the Princeton days? What did you do to that poor girl your family had to buy off?"

He flushed. "What did you say to me?"

"I asked what happened at Princeton," I repeated. "I've been wondering."

"This is too much." He knocked back the new whiskey he had just poured and stood. "I don't have the patience to sit here listening to some chick who looks like an extra in *Sons of Anarchy* cracking this cheap innuendo about me." He stepped around the table, hands balled into fists. "That's *my* polite way of saying good night. You're not needed or wanted. And I'm about two seconds away from carrying you out of here myself." He took another step toward me, as if planning to sling me over his shoulder like a load of laundry.

Punching Ron in the nose felt good. Even better than I would have imagined. Which was saying something.

He grunted and fell back against the table, blood pouring from his nose.

"You had that coming," I told him.

Mrs. Johannessen and Martin made shocked noises. William's head flew up to the source of the noise and he started bellowing like a cow, a loud, pained, unpleasant bovine sound. Mrs. Johannessen stood, towering over me, eyes dangerous. "How dare you!"

Martin snickered as though he was kind of liking the newest turn of events. Suddenly I could see the twelve-year-old boy he'd once been, petty and malicious in a mosquito sort of way. Ron's voice was muffled and nasal as he pinched a napkin to the bridge of his nose. "After they lock you up for assault, I'm going to destroy you in civil court."

"I shall call security?" The butler had arrived, summoned by the commotion. He hurriedly righted a tipped candle before it burned into the linen, then stared at Ron, who was wheezing painfully, now back in a chair. Splotches of bright red showed on the white cloth napkin.

I ignored them and addressed only Mrs. Johannessen. "Should he call security? Or would you like to talk to me first?"

She was still staring at me, her eyes fierce and wild as a falcon's. Then she gave the smallest movement of her head. "Why don't you and I talk in the parlor, Nikki." She called over my shoulder, "Ronald, darling, put some ice on your nose, ice always helps."

She sat on the same couch as last time.

I sat across from her in the same armchair.

No drinks, this time. No back-and-forth, no feeling each other out. I knew who she was, more or less. She probably felt the same about me.

I got to the point before she could even ask. "If what your son did was publicly exposed, you knew that would destroy your family name. You didn't trust that the blackmailers would go away on their own, either—not that I blame you. Why would they? They knew they had snagged a golden goose. But your son couldn't manage the negotiations on his own, and I doubt your lawyers would have dared—not once they realized who was on the other end, and how far outside of the law this would take them. You needed someone with a foot on each side of the line. So you enlisted Coombs, thinking he'd be a perfect intermediary between your world and theirs. You knew he'd been in prison, that he'd spent time around violent criminals, knew the streets. And you trusted him—especially because he had a stake in things. His ten percent commission. Self-interest. You figured he could negotiate."

She folded her hands on her lap. "And what if that's true?"

I kept going. "Only you didn't realize how dangerous these people were, and you failed to appreciate that Coombs was the wrong sort to deal with them. He's not a violent guy. He lives by his wits. And just in this particular situation, with these particular people, he was out of his league."

Mrs. Johannessen considered what I had said. Then she spoke. "My son, bless his heart, made a mistake. It was very foolish of him. He knows that."

I was tired of tiptoes and whispers. Tired of good manners and perfect breeding. Tired of using polite words and gentle sentences to smooth and pave the things people did.

"He paid to sleep with underage teens. I don't know if *foolish* is the right word."

She looked at me and once again I could feel the force of her will, pressing against me like a hard, onrushing wind. Our eyes met and I felt myself in a physical contest, taut, clashing, straining, like two blades locked against each other.

Then she relaxed and the tautness slipped away.

"I'm hardly going to excuse my son's actions," she answered. "Equally, I won't apologize for protecting my family—my *children*. My family will always come first, Nikki. I'm surprised I have to even remind you of that truth."

"You don't. I understand."

For a moment we were both quiet.

"What do you actually want?" she asked. "Maybe I should have asked you that at the beginning."

"Don't feel too bad. I would have given a different answer then."

"What do you mean?"

"I know more now. What I want has changed."

"What, then?" Her long fingers unfolded, refolded. "Tell me, and maybe I'll give it to you."

"You think you can just buy your way out of this?"

"I don't know," she replied evenly. "Can I?"

I held her gaze. "I want the amount of money you were being blackmailed for—the same amount you would have paid. Let's round up to a nice round number. Ten million even."

Her face relaxed, a little, but there was something new in her expression, a look that was both more understanding and also, deeper, a note of gentle contempt, as though she now saw something she hadn't at first recognized. "Greedy," she said. "Somehow I misjudged you, Nikki."

"But you'd give it to me, just the same?"

"To stay quiet and go away?" She thought for several seconds, then came to a decision. "Very well. It's yours. Assuming what you said is true and these people will not bother my family anymore, we have an agreement."

"Good." I named several charities and nonprofits. Legal aid firms, domestic shelters, women's rights groups. The Monterey shelter was one of the names. "We can divide it up between those places," I said. "I might think of a few others, too."

Her voice was mild. "As you wish."

"I can't help but get the sense I disappointed you."

"There's always a moment," Mrs. Johannessen observed, "when you realize what someone's price is. To me, the most interesting part of meeting someone is *before* that moment. Because a price is just a number. It's people that are interesting to me—not numbers. Maybe part of me didn't want to learn your price, Nikki, even though I'm very glad I did."

I said nothing.

"No matter." Her voice grew brisk as she stood. "You do what you like with the money. It's no concern of mine. As for me, I intend to have dessert."

"I wasn't done. Not quite."

She looked down at me. "But I am, Nikki. I am quite done. I admire your tenacity, but I can be pushed only so far by anyone, and you've reached that point. I'll trust you to provide us with the necessary banking details for these places. We'll wire the money tomorrow."

She walked into the dining room.

I followed.

Not much had changed in the ten minutes we'd been gone. Ron had a fresh napkin pressed to his nose. That was the only difference I could see. He and Martin were in furious conversation, their voices low and urgent. William lolled in his wheelchair.

Ron looked up. "I think you broke my nose." There was hatred in his voice.

I gave him a big smile. "Finally, we agree on something."

Mrs. Johannessen said, "Nikki and I have settled this matter to my satisfaction." She motioned to the butler. "We'll take coffee now, and you can show Ms. Griffin out. And I suppose we had better call a physician to come look at Ronald's poor nose. Get him some Tylenol, in the meantime, too."

I didn't move. "You didn't give me a chance to finish. There's something else I want."

She barely looked at me. "I should think you've asked for—and gotten—quite enough."

"I want your son to turn himself in."

"*What?*"

Mrs. Johannessen pressed her hand against the table hard enough to rattle the glassware as everyone in the room stared at me. I had her attention now. That was for sure.

"They're going to find out anyway," I said. "The whole business—the brothel, the girls, the recordings—it's all about to come crashing down. You can get ahead of things, if you want. The money I asked for—announce you're making a major donation, set up a foundation. And come clean about what he did. Your family name can probably get through this if you set an example. I'm sure if you step forward first, voluntarily, prosecutors will offer a good deal—and there'll be plenty of other headlines, I bet. Or, skulk in the shadows, deny, conceal, bloviate, threaten—and between the courts and the press, your family will be torn to pieces."

"Nikki, this is outrageous." Mrs. Johannessen looked as close to shocked as I could imagine her ever looking. "That would ruin us."

"Take the chance. It's the right thing to do."

"Come clean about *what*, exactly?" Martin said.

I had no idea how much Martin knew or didn't know, and didn't care. "Your brother. He decided to dip below the age of consent."

Ron threw his napkin down, his eyes glinting with anger. There was dried blood crusted under his nose. "I've never done such a thing in my life."

"Not you."

I pointed a finger.

"Your other brother. William."

Everyone except William stared at me. His head lolled like he had fallen asleep. I wasn't done. "And I'm only the *third* person in this room to know that." My finger stayed on William. "He knows, of course." My finger moved. "And so does his mother."

"Have you lost your mind?" Mrs. Johannessen asked. "Even if all of these crazy allegations are true, how could William do *anything*?"

I said, "Play dumb all you want. He's on a videotape with a teenager. It's time stamped. That was before his accident, of course. Then, after the blackmail began, William had the bad luck to be on the wrong end of that hit-and-run. Someone decided a smart move would be for him to play possum, pretend brain damage, until you all figured out how much trouble he was in. Like that mob boss, Vincent Gigante—people don't like to convict crazy." I addressed William directly. "You knew there was a chance the whole thing would leak. If worse came to worst and you did end up in a courtroom, no jury would ever convict you. Not babbling and drooling in a wheelchair."

William's eyes showed no comprehension, so I kept going. "The best part? Once things were settled you could suddenly get better. That's the thing with brain injuries. No one *really* understands them. And hinting to anyone poking around that it was *Ron* was a nice touch—because he does seem the type, doesn't he, especially with the Princeton thing in his background?"

Ron's teeth were clenched. "Are you implying that I'm some sort of sacrificial lamb?"

"Not at all." Seeing his furious bewilderment, I felt almost sorry for him. "That's what was so clever. Just disinformation. Muddying the waters to confuse anyone looking at your family. The only way anyone could find out about William was the same thing that definitively absolved you—the actual tape."

Very calmly, Mrs. Johannessen asked, "Which tape might that be, Nikki?"

I held up a DVD case. *Predator*, from 1987. Hillman, or someone else, had possessed a sense of irony. "Like I said. Come clean. I'll give you the weekend. This goes to the police on Monday."

No one said anything.

Then Mrs. Johannessen said, "You can't do that." Again, I felt the power of her will pressing against me like tangible weight. "This is a family matter and will be handled as such. My son has been confined to a wheelchair since his injury."

"This is absurd," Ron put in. "Will's a goddamn vegetable—look at the poor bastard."

"He's not bad," I said, "although personally, I think the coo-cooing and rhyming was overdoing it a bit. Less is more—just my two cents."

"Give that to me."

A new voice. William's nurse. He had stepped into the room, muscles bulky under aquamarine scrubs.

"You're supposed to at least act like a nurse," I said as he walked toward me.

He was closer. "Of course I'm a nurse."

"Nights plus days, now? Hope you're getting overtime."

He spread his hands as though trying to defuse an argument. "I'm substituting. The regular guy is out sick. That's all." The nurse got closer.

Then he grabbed my wrist just as William startled all of us by bursting out of his wheelchair, seizing the DVD from me, and bolting from the room.

The nurse was even stronger than he looked. He had an iron grip on my wrist. I kneed him in the groin, felt him falter, and, in an insult to fair fights all over the world, I jabbed my free thumb into his eye and twisted hard. He shouted in pain, fingers loosening, as I threw his arm off and got past him.

My boots pounded against the parquet floor. I saw the open front door of the apartment.

The elevator door closing.

Going up.

There was an adjoining stairwell. I sprinted up the stairs, taking them two at a time, legs pumping, breath burning, grateful that Mrs. Johannessen lived toward the top.

The final flight of stairs ended at a plain, unpainted door. I pushed it open and found myself on the building's exposed roof. Wind howled. San Francisco glittered below. Tatters of clouds swept across a bare wedge of moon. The Bay Bridge and Golden Gate were strings of light strewn across inkpot blackness.

William was standing across the roof from me. A row of blue emergency lights marking the roof's edge cast an eerie cobalt pallor over him, and his face looked beaked and dangerous. He watched me warily as he cracked the DVD into jagged pieces that disappeared over the edge.

"You're not thinking," I told him. "You think that's the only copy? Breaking DVDs all night won't solve your problems."

"How did you know?" he asked. His voice was cracked and deep. I thought of frozen pipes, rusted and unused, water gradually starting to resume its flow.

"Little things. Your exaggerations. And your so-called nurse. He said you'd been a lion before the accident—why would he have known anything about you until afterwards? But I didn't know for sure until down there. Just now. When I told your mother I was going to *turn in her son.*" The statement, deliberately harsh, abrupt, spoken to shock. "Not *Ron* but *son*. You weren't prepared for that—you couldn't help but look at me, same as everyone else in the room." I added, "Jumping out of the wheelchair, though—that did surprise me." I shrugged. "I guess if you can fake a brain injury, why not your legs, too?"

A river of emotions was flowing across his face, anger and hope and cunning and desperation, so fluid that I could barely tell one from the next. "Please," he said. "There has to be some way we can work this out. Don't let this ruin me. Don't you care about all the good I've done in the world? My contributions? My philanthropy? And I've suffered—the accident, my health. I've been punished enough."

"Come on downstairs, William. Let's not stay up here all night."

"I can give you money," he said. "Whatever you want. Anything at all."

"No, thanks."

"There *has* to be something. I can't change your mind?"

"No. You really can't."

He considered this.

Then he nodded, resolute, grim, like a prisoner being walked to an execution.

"Very well. Let's go, then."

I had turned and was walking back toward the stairwell when I heard his steps behind me, following. A little too fast. Too hurried. I lunged sideways, spinning around and throwing my arm up as I saw the ascending flash of silver, and then there was a gash in the leather of my jacket sleeve as William turned the ivory-handled steak knife and reset his feet for another try.

I stepped toward him, not away, surprising him, the opposite of what someone with a knife expected, and got my left hand low on his right forearm, just above the wrist, and the other high up on his right biceps, under the shoulder, my right elbow pressing under his chin, rotating us, hunching in behind my forward shoulder so that the flailing blows from his free hand were nothing more than an annoyance.

Then I drove my shoulder hard against him, feeling his feet take an involuntary step back, off-balance, and as I felt his foot lift I twisted my right elbow up several inches into his chin, a sharp, short, precise motion that clipped him perfectly on the point of the jaw.

He grunted and wobbled. His hand loosened and the knife fell.

I picked up the knife.

He retreated back across the roof.

I stepped after him.

He reached the edge.

The edge of the roof was bordered by a waist-high stone parapet, like a miniature castle wall. Beyond that, a sheer drop to the asphalt twenty floors below. It had started to rain, a cold, mean drizzle that slashed almost sideways, driven by the wind.

I took another step forward.

"Are you going to kill me?" William asked.

I put the knife in my pocket. "Don't be so dramatic."

He licked his lips, eyes darting. "I'll jump," he said. "I will."

"I think suicide might be overreacting."

"They'll lock me up. I can't survive prison."

"They don't put people like you in the kinds of prisons you can't survive. Besides, think how many good lawyers you must have."

"My family's name will be ruined."

"The world will move on. You'll be a story for a few weeks. Then something else bad will happen, and people will pay attention to that, instead. Now come downstairs, will you?"

"I can't," he said miserably. "I should just jump." His hair was bedraggled, his shirt untucked and soaked.

I was tired. It had been a long day. A long week. I didn't feel like standing on a roof in the rain all night doing free counseling. I didn't want to be anywhere near this man. I didn't want to be anywhere near this family. I wanted to leave all their schemes and machinations and gloomy opulence behind. I wanted to leave San Francisco behind. I wanted to cross the bridge and go home. Back to the East Bay. Ethan, Jess, my brother. My bookstore. Everything I had.

"I don't think you should jump," I said. "But then again, I've always been a big believer in free will. You decide."

I walked back to the stairwell, leaving him poised and uncertain at the roof's edge.

With one last thing to do.

One last person to see.

37

The apartment above Susan Johannessen's Hayes Valley gallery looked deserted. Shades drawn, dark, no sign of life. I had to ring the buzzer for at least a minute before I heard anything on the other side of the door. I kept ringing. Buzzers were easy. Just push them. Not like knocking on a hard door all night. No need to hurt the knuckles.

When I finally heard movement I called, "Susan, open up. It's Nikki. I can hear you."

There was no answer.

I waited.

When I was tired of waiting I started buzzing again. "Susan, it's Nikki. Don't make me stand here in the rain all night."

More silence. Then the clicking of a lock or latch.

The door opened, just an inch. The voice that spoke was timid and frightened. "Who is that?"

"You owe me a coffee," I said. "I've come to cash in."

Her apartment was furnished with plenty of taste and plenty of money. Scandinavian appliances, Italian fixtures, modernist furniture. The colors were monochrome, all grays and blacks and whites. Paintings hung off the walls, colorless, abstract works, along with a series of photographs taken at such extreme close range it was impossible to tell anything about the larger scenes depicted.

"How did you know I was here?" Susan wondered. She was wearing comfortable clothing, no makeup, square graphite glasses over her nervous brown eyes.

"We'll get there," I said. "But I was serious about that coffee. Black works fine for me."

While Susan went into the kitchen I looked around. Not much to see besides the art on the walls. Not many possessions. Not a primary residence. A pair of curtained French doors led to a covered balcony. I opened the doors and stepped outside. The rain was falling harder and the air smelled sweet and clean and new. I looked down onto Grove Street, seeing cars passing on pavement shiny with rainwater, brake lights glimmering off the puddles.

"Here you go."

Susan had come up behind me. I turned, accepting the mug of coffee she handed me, and took an appreciative sip. "Thanks."

She shivered. "Would you mind if we talked inside? I'm getting over a terrible cold."

I did mind, a little. The fresh air had felt good. I was tired of being inside. But without a word I followed her to the kitchen table.

"I was reported missing," she said after a moment. "Did you know that?"

"I knew they couldn't find you. Not sure if that's the same thing."

"I called the police this evening," she admitted. "I told them I was okay—that I had fallen quite ill but was feeling much better."

"Tell them whatever you want. Not my business." I sipped coffee. "Since you mention it, how did you explain your car being left at the beach? Lapse of memory?"

"My car?" Her eyes showed surprise and she paused, as though asking herself something. Then she said, "A friend had borrowed it. I own several. A misunderstanding."

"Like I said. Tell them whatever you want."

"How did you know I was here?" she asked again. Her face was wan, anxious lines showing around her brown eyes. "How could you possibly have known that?"

"Don't give me the credit. *You* told me."

Now she looked astonished. "What?"

"When we first met. You said you were so busy you were practically living at work. It got me thinking—someone with plenty of money, an apartment above your gallery—why wouldn't you want to own the place, be able to relax, invite an artist up for a private conversation, have somewhere to sleep after working late? Instead of having some stranger live above you. I'm sure your family has a hundred different trusts and LLCs to buy up property. No wonder the police didn't know about this one. They couldn't possibly have—not right away."

She looked more worried. "Police? They contacted you?"

I helped myself to more coffee. "Of course they did. You made sure of that. I was one of the last people you called. Leaving your car in a place sure to arouse suspicion."

"You didn't wonder if I had drowned? Or thrown myself into the sea?"

"Not really. The timing was too much of a coincidence. The location, too. Not just any old beach, but the deadliest beach in the whole damn state. If anything, I thought you'd been kidnapped by the same people I was looking for."

"Why *didn't* you think that?" Under the worry blanketing her voice, I could detect a trace of her mother's sharpness in the questions, but her face was a study in simple curiosity, as though asking me about some abstract subject—calculus or geography—that had no bearing on Susan herself.

"One, because *someone* had phoned in a tip. That was you, I realized. Who else would have—that day?" I snowplowed over the protest rising on her face. "Mostly, though, I just doubted they would have been so stupid. Those guys were looking to dodge attention. They'd been in the headlines even before all this, and they hated it. Taking a con man, a criminal, is one thing. Kidnap a wealthy heiress with a famous last name, and you have the FBI involved, all kinds of scary federal statutes kicking in, reporters, the whole state poking around. Bad for business. Could they have been dumb enough, even so? Sure. Except your car was there."

Susan looked confused by this. "My car? What does that have to do with anything?"

"The people I was after dealt with stolen cars. If they had done anything to you, they would never have left your car sitting at a public beach that's patrolled probably twice an hour. It would have vanished into some scrapyard or chop shop. They wouldn't have left it to arouse suspicion."

She seemed to want to ask something more, but stopped herself and changed direction. "You didn't answer my first question. How you knew I'd be *here*. I could have been anywhere in the entire world."

"Could you have? I'm guessing you never tried to go missing before," I said. "Not as easy as it looks, is it? Where do you go? As soon as you have the police looking for you, no more credit cards or banks, no passports or cell phones. Can't stay at home, of course, that's the first place they check—same with friends and family—but you have to go *somewhere*. So where? Hotels won't take cash without a credit card and ID. Forget airports. Can't rent a car. Can't even buy a train ticket without photo ID anymore. Not even a Greyhound. Running, hiding, these are tricky things to pull off." I thought of Coombs. "Same as anything else. You need practice to get good."

She seemed not to notice the strangeness or irony of her asking me the same questions I should have been asking her. "But why would I try to hide? Are you trying to say I did something wrong?"

I said, "In my experience, if you've done something wrong, sometimes you want people to be worried about you. Basic deflection. Act like a victim."

I ticked off points on my fingers. "Something I said when we first talked made you nervous. You decided you needed to see me—to find out what I knew. Only after we talked on the phone, the second time, you realized I wasn't barking up whatever tree *you* were worried about. But you had made everything sound too urgent when you called me—and you knew it. You couldn't just not show up without making me wonder why. I would have tried to find you, been suspicious. So you decided to disappear for a bit instead. Lay low until you could learn what was going on."

Not to mention pointing the police my way, I could have added. The anonymous tip, probably mentioning my name specifically, surely made to slow me down.

Susan flinched as though I was holding hot metal to her skin. "You have no idea how frightened I've been, Nikki. Living in this—this blur, this fog, of fear, panic. Not knowing who I could trust. I had learned about the terrible things my brother had done. He's been so cruel to me, my whole life. I didn't even know if I was safe."

"Too late for that," I told her. "About two days ago, I would have loved to have that conversation. You could have told me everything. You didn't."

After her first sip, Susan's coffee had remained untouched. She stirred a silver teaspoon in little circles in her mug as she said, "But that was my brother. Nothing to do with me."

"Which brother?"

She paused, as if looking for a trap, and then said, "Ron, of course."

"Ron? Really?"

Uncertainty crept again into her voice. "Of course. Who else would it be? Martin has his flaws, but something like this? Impossible."

"You're very good," I told Susan.

"Good?"

"Good. You. You know what I mean."

Her hands, spread on the table, trembled. "Nikki, what are you getting at?"

"See?" I pointed at one of her hands. Like a pinned butterfly, it quivered more. "All of that. The whole thing. You're a natural."

"Natural *what*? What are you getting at?"

I remembered something and took William's steak knife from my pocket. "Before I forget. For your mother. She'll want the full set back, I'm sure." I placed the knife on the table between us, noticing the smallest bit of leather from my jacket, still caught on the blade's serrations.

Susan eyed the ivory-handled knife. "You've been to see my mother?"

Rather than answer her question, I said, "I couldn't figure out *why* you were so worried, though. You hadn't done anything. How could something I'd said scare you so much?"

"And?" she murmured. "What did you conclude?"

"I realized the answer had to be in our conversations—and we'd only had two, after all. I must have said *something*. Whatever it was, it was there, in my memory, waiting to be noticed. Which just made it a matter of thinking things through."

Susan's hands still trembled. "I don't feel very well," she said in the same soft voice. "I think I should go to bed and rest."

"You can rest in a minute. I have a question of my own. For you."

She watched me in silence but made no effort to speak.

"When you hit William with the car, were you trying to kill him? Or just scare him?"

"*What?*" Now she was shocked. Her face flushed and she drew herself up in her seat. "Are you mad? How dare you accuse me of—"

"There was something too neat about it," I interrupted. There had been the smallest bit of *something* in her eyes at my question. Like the speck of leather on the knife blade. Almost invisible, but there.

"I walked up and down that block," I told her. "He happened to be hit in the *one* spot without any cameras. Hard to pull off a hit-and-run, these days. Especially in a city. Too many people, too many cameras. Takes careful planning, unless you're the hope-and-pray type. Which you're most definitely not."

I pushed my empty coffee cup aside. "When I came by the gallery, you didn't even want to give me five minutes of your time—until I happened to mention William and the accident. Then you had all the time in the world to chat. At first you thought Martin had hired me to look into the hit-and-run, since the police weren't getting anywhere. That's what scared you, and that's why you agreed to talk—to find out how much I knew, and decide if you had to throw me off."

"But why . . . ?"

"That, Susan, is what I want to know. *Why?*"

"How can I tell you something I don't—"

I interrupted her a second time. "I can't make up my mind about you. The good-little-girl-mean-older-brother thing threw me for a bit, but you're a whole lot less innocent than you let on. You've got some dirt under your nails, no doubt. On the other hand, my compass spins a bit different than most. Can't blame you for not knowing that. I don't know if running your brother over with a car bothers me as much as it would some people. He sort of deserved it. But I do want to know *why.*"

Her face was in her hands and her shoulders shuddered as though she was weeping inaudibly. Her voice was muffled by her hands as she repeated, "How can I tell you something I don't know the an—"

"One chance. No sob stories. Or I go to the police with everything. At the very least, that will cause scrutiny you really don't want."

For a moment more she rocked and trembled.

"I will," I said. "I mean it."

Her shoulders stopped shaking and she moved her hands, wiping her cheeks and looking up at me through fogged lenses and glistening eyes. "Please. Let me be."

"No. Talk."

Susan sat for another moment, head bowed as though in prayer.

Then she said, "Maybe you think you know my family a bit, Nikki, but you don't really know us—none of us. Sometimes I think *we* barely know each other."

Her voice was different, now. No quaver. Her hands were still. She stood, and I followed her into the dimly lit living room. She walked gracefully, feet silently padding over the hardwood floor.

"My brothers, you see—each of them, in his own vainglorious way, thinks he is the only one capable of leading our family after Mother passes.

They're so pathetic—the bickering, the squabbling, as though we were all still little children, quarreling over the last bit of Christmas pie. I've never been able to stand it."

She turned away from the window to face me, the translucent curtained doors behind her, her skin pale as lemon pith. "Put yourself in my shoes, Nikki. To learn that your celebrated eldest brother, the toast of the family, the firstborn, has been engaging in such tawdry and disgusting behavior. Worse—*risky* behavior. And then he goes and manages to get caught—*hooked*—in a manner that could destroy all of us. Our entire family. Do you know what that's like? For me? Being shackled, for life, to such dangerous irresponsibility?"

Her eyes, now clear and dry, held mine, and in her gaze, I realized that she was truly her mother's daughter—maybe even a purer form, something more distilled.

"My mother is the strongest person I know," Susan said. "The strongest person I've ever met. But her weakness has *always* been her three sons. She knows it, deep down. She's admitted as much, to me, even though she can never come out and *say* so. My mother couldn't—wouldn't—do what truly had to be done. If a weed is overgrowing a garden, you don't blame the garden or cut the flowers—you yank it out by the roots. Why would anyone *possibly* think I'd simply stand by and watch as my brother threw away a centuries-old legacy, all for his weak-willed pursuit of pleasure?"

Susan stepped closer to me. No trace, now, of the nervous, frightened woman who had cried at her kitchen table. I was seeing someone else now. "My mother was willing to do anything in the world—except the one thing that truly needed to be done."

"You don't care about what he did," I said. "You care about your family. Your name. That's all any of you care about. That's all you've *ever* cared about—all of you."

"Martin is weak," Susan said. "Ron is nothing more than a hedonistic drunk. And William—William is the worst of all. None of them are fit to lead our family."

"That's what you want," I said. Realizing. "That's what you've always wanted—all you've ever wanted."

"*Not* wanted. I never wanted any of this," she retorted. "*Needed*. A duty, Nikki, a responsibility. Because there's no one else. My mother is in her eighties. There's no one else but me. And I *will always* do what it takes."

She held my eyes as she took a breath. "Go to the police if you want, with whatever story you want to give them. I've admitted nothing."

"You don't have to worry about that," I told Susan. I wondered if she had known or guessed that William had been faking his mental state. I didn't care. It didn't matter—not here. "Whatever you did to your brother," I continued, "I won't be talking about it."

Despite what I'd told her earlier she seemed taken aback to hear this.

"Why not?"

"Like I said. My compass spins a bit differently. North, for most people, isn't always quite north for me. If you'd gone after anyone innocent it would be different. But here? All this? The best punishment I can imagine is letting you work things out with your family—for the rest of your lives. Goodbye, Susan."

I let myself out. The seat of the Aprilia soaked my jeans as I started the motorcycle, feeling the engine thrum and rumble against my thighs. The rain was pounding down now, hard, cleansing, streaming down the visor of my helmet, against my jacket, pelting my legs, but I didn't mind. I rode up Market Street, late-night revelers mixed with clusters of homeless on the sidewalks, merriment and despondency jammed thoughtlessly together, voices, cars, high empty office towers, each with blanketed bodies in their doorways, the bison groan of a street sweeper, carnival bright lights leaping off hotels and bars and marquees. I rode back over the bridge to Berkeley and went to bed.

SUNDAY

38

Sunday afternoon brought a blizzard of news that tore through the city. The scion of one of San Francisco's most prominent families, stepping forward out of the blue to "come clean" via a popular weekend show. His admissions were met with widespread disgust and condemnation, but there was also some quieter talk of his having "done the right thing" and "taking it on the chin." The family issued a statement: a foundation was being set up, enormous donations being made, steps being taken, soul-searching being done. All media requests were referred to a crisis management firm with a reputation for being the best in the city. There was talk that the DA's office was hurriedly preparing its own news conference for Monday morning, a joint statement with several state and national law enforcement agencies to announce a sweeping set of linked investigations that might well carry outside of California. By Sunday night the story had broken into cable news and was being picked up all over the country.

That was what people told me, anyway. I never watched the news.

Ethan and I had agreed to meet at the bookstore on Sunday evening. I'd come from a heated yoga session and felt good, my muscles warm and relaxed. About a year ago I'd started supplementing the sparring I had done since the age of fourteen with a few hours of yoga each week. Right hooks and crow pose. There were stranger combinations.

Before going inside, I went next door to the former noodle place. My brother had beaten me there and was conversing with the landlord, who stepped outside to let us talk.

"So, what do you think?" I asked.

"Looks okay, I guess." Brandon was trying to act nonchalant but was too excited. He gave up completely after a few seconds. "It's perfect, Nik! It's amazing!" He hugged me and tried to waltz me around the space, pointing out different places where he envisioned this or that going. "And I think my big sister is even cooler than I gave her credit for."

"I'm very cool," I said, laughing as I broke free. "Even if it took a damn restaurant to finally get you to admit that."

He was walking around, inspecting everything. "You think this can really work?"

"That depends on you," I said. "Can you make it work?"

Brandon nodded, his green eyes dancing with excitement. "Yes. I'm positive."

"Lots of responsibility," I said. "From one small business owner to another. Different from punching a clock. Different kind of pressure and it's all on you."

He understood what I meant. "I feel great, Nik. I go to meetings, I'm feeling sharp, clean—I got this. Honest."

"Then you better get to work," I told him. "What's it gonna be? Seafood? Burgers?"

"So many options. Ethan keeps telling me to open a steakhouse. But I'm leaning more casual."

"I'm sure Ethan will forgive you if you crush his dreams of getting on-the-house filet mignon five nights a week." I glanced at my watch. "You want to join us for dinner?"

"I would," Brandon said, "but I have plans."

"Not the—"

"Yup! The hot doctor." He laughed, seeing my dubious expression. "What can I say? We hit it off." He gave me a second, longer hug. "Thanks, Nik. Seriously. For everything."

"I'll see you soon, okay? We can sign the lease next week."

His voice stopped me at the door. "What do you think Mom and Dad would think?"

I turned back to my younger brother. "Of what?"

"Us. This." His gesture took in the empty noodle shop, the adjacent bookstore, the two of us. "Everything. If they could see the whole thing, the whole trail, and see where we ended up."

I blinked moisture out of my eyes. Talked over the swelling lump in my throat. "I think they'd be pretty happy with us."

"Yeah," Brandon agreed. "I think they'd be pretty happy, too."

I said good night to my brother and walked next door.

The BRIMSTONE MAGPIE was crowded, despite the evening hour. Customers read in armchairs and browsed the shelves. All the tactile delight of holding and touching books. The bookstore was fragrant with the smells of roasted coffee beans and bound pages.

I greeted Jess and then stepped away to make a quick call.

He picked up on the second ring. "Hello?"

"Hey there, sidekick," I said.

"Nikki?" Mason sounded excited. "Where are you?"

"Back in Berkeley. You okay?"

"Yeah, I am. My aunt talked to my dad. I'm going to stay with her for a while."

"I got another adventure for you," I said. "Not as exciting, but important."

His voice quickened. "What is it?"

"The Athenian School, up here, where I am. It's a boarding school. If you want, I can send you an application."

"Really?" His voice fled from excited to worried. "Do you think my father would allow it?"

"I'm pretty sure he will. I can ask if they'll make an exception and let you start midway through the year. If you want." I had done a substantial favor for one of the deans there, years ago. Given the nature of the favor, I had a feeling she'd be receptive to Mason's plight.

"Really? You would? Thank you thank you thank you tha—"

I cut him off with a laugh. "Don't thank me. This is totally selfish, I promise. I need a really trusty sidekick up here and don't have time to train someone new."

Mason said, "You can always count on me."

We said goodbye and I put the phone down. At the register, Jess was ringing up a young woman with a stack of used paperbacks, short stories,

Ann Beattie, Amy Hempel, Dawn Powell. "English major?" I asked her. She smiled and nodded. A threatened species. It was good to know they were still out there.

Jess raised an eyebrow my way. "Going into the admissions business?"

"I think I found us an intern."

"Thank God. He can start in the mailroom. Speaking of which." She handed me an envelope with my name on the front. "Someone slid this under the door. It was here when I arrived this morning."

The white envelope bore an elegant red wax seal. No stamp. No return address. Inside was a postcard. A watercolor picture of a Parisian café, glamorous and chic, champagne in an ice bucket stand, fashionably dressed patrons milling in the background. A scene painted to make you wonder if you were in the right place if you were anywhere but there. Elegant, bold cursive filled the inside of the card.

To a Kindred Spirit:

I fear the Old World won't be the same without you. If you ever find yourself needing a break from takeout and TCM, come find me— once again. Regardless, I have a feeling we'll run into each other, sooner or later, and I've learned to always trust a hunch.

In the meantime, I remain,

Faithfully yours,
GTC

I looked from the postcard back to the bookstore, seeing Ethan, sitting comfortably on a beanbag, paperback in one hand, Bartleby the cat purring on his lap.

I read the card once more. Looked back and forth again.

I walked over to my boyfriend.

"Hey, there. What are you reading?"

He flipped the cover up to show me the title. *The Sorrows of Young Werther.*

"Goethe? God. You're such a romantic."

"You knew that already." He was smiling as he stood to kiss me. The gray cat scrambled off his lap, paused to consider the next move, and then took over the beanbag with a drowsy finality that stated he didn't intend to move again anytime soon.

"What's that?" Ethan asked.

I looked down and realized I was still holding the postcard.

"Oh, just something from an old friend."

"Looks fancy! You're not about to break my heart and run off to Paris with some dashing, mysterious gentleman, are you?" Ethan teased, seeing the café scene as I turned the writing inward.

"I don't think so." I smiled as I slid the postcard into my pocket. "I guess one got away."

Ethan returned my smile. "Lucky for me." He checked his watch, a basic Seiko on a battered leather strap. "We have a couple of hours before the movie. How's Chinese food sound?"

"For *The Maltese Falcon*? I feel like we should be doing chops and potatoes."

"Yeah, well, try finding a good chophouse in Berkeley, at least until your brother takes my advice and opens one. Maybe we can get our hands on a bottle of scotch and a soda syphon, at least. I've always wanted to sneak hard liquor into a movie theater." He winked at me with a sincere attempt at roguishness. "Not sure if you're aware, but you are dating a true outlaw. I'll stop at nothing."

I smiled. "Scotch, sure. Just no ice picks, please."

Ethan gave me a knowing look. "That kind of week?"

I didn't share much about my work. But we'd been together almost a year. I had grown comfortable talking. A little. He had grown comfortable hearing a little, too. So far, it was working.

I nodded. "That kind of week. Yeah."

"Very well," he agreed. "An ice pick–free evening it shall be."

I looked at him standing there, blue eyes, tobacco-wheat beard coming in across his jaw, jeans skinny enough that I knew I'd make fun of them at some point that evening, wearing his favorite corduroy jacket that he'd found in some Marin thrift shop, rumpled paperback held like it was an extension of his hand.

I spoke without having planned to speak. "Okay, fine. Let's."

"Chinese food? When have I ever said no?"

"That's not what I mean. We can try it. Moving in. If you still want."

He was surprised. "I was letting it rest. I hadn't been asking. Seriously."

"I know. But we can see how it goes."

"You want to? Like *actually* want to?"

I nodded. "I do. But I need my space. I'm telling you that up front."

"There's something I've been meaning to tell you, too," he said.

"Oh, yeah?"

He took a breath as though preparing for confession. "I'm a bit of a hoarder. I've got every copy of the *Farmer's Almanac* going back to 1818. And you should see my rock garden."

"Come on, seriously."

"Also, have you considered pet ferrets? I think we should try them. They eat socks and pee everywhere, sure, but they're very cuddly."

"Jesus. I'm serious, Ethan! And in the morning, I get to shower first. Non-negotiable."

"The shower," he said. "Glad you brought that up. That's where my model NASCAR collection can go. We'll have to sponge each other with buckets and loofahs over the kitchen sink once a week instead."

"I'm going to change my mind. And my closet—"

"—would be *perfect* for my old soccer trophies. There're a lot of them. I was really good in sixth grade, you know. Midfield. You'll have to be careful where you step. Some of them are really pointy—"

I had thought I was done punching people for a while, but it turned out I had one left in me. I popped a nice left straight into his chin. Pulling back my hand at the last second, knuckles brushing the stubbly softness of his beard.

"Careful," I warned. "You're dating a very dangerous woman, you know."

"Especially when she's hungry." He kissed me. "Come on. Let's get dinner, you dangerous woman, you."

We walked along Telegraph Avenue into the soft dusk of evening. A few brittle leaves danced along in the breeze of a passing bus, spinning up above the street before settling into stillness once again. I heard the *cling-cling* of a bicyclist's bell, the reflector catching streetlight luminescence and sparking the radiance back in ruby fragments.

I turned my head for a last look at the bookstore. Seen from outside, it was a tempting destination, cozy, warmly lit, the stacks of books beckoning. Recently, we had found a painter who had etched a black magpie onto the glass storefront, and the name, BRIMSTONE MAGPIE, in ornate Victorian lettering above the bird. The kind of place that urged a passerby to pause, maybe step inside to see what they might find. A place where someone could leave behind the noise and splinters of the day and step anywhere at all. Infinite worlds, familiar and foreign, rows and rows of possibility and promise. Ethan followed my glance back to the store and his hand tightened in mine. Hand in hand, we walked down the street.

ACKNOWLEDGMENTS

When Victoria Skurnick first agreed to represent me, I knew at once that I had found an incredible agent—but I soon realized that I had also made a great new friend. I cannot thank her enough for all she has done and continues to do on my behalf. Many thanks also to Jim Levine and everyone at LGR Literary Agency for their wide-ranging support, and to Alice Lawson at The Gersh Agency for her deftness in navigating the film/television world.

This book wouldn't exist without the belief, enthusiasm, and editorial wizardry of my brilliant editors, Amy Einhorn and Christine Kopprasch. I'm very grateful for their willingness to read and reread to get this book to where it is, and having the chance to work with them once again has been a pleasure.

So many people at Flatiron Books have put their energy and expertise into this series. I want to especially thank Marlena Bittner, Nancy Trypuc, Katherine Turro, Chris Smith, Conor Mintzer, Sam Zukergood, Keith Hayes, and Kelly Gatesman. Thanks also to the amazing marketing, sales, and foreign rights teams at Flatiron as well as Matie Argiropoulos and everyone at Macmillan Audio. I am grateful to the editors around the world who have supported the series, especially the incredible group at Simon & Schuster U.K. Special thanks also to January LaVoy for (literally) giving a voice to my writing, and to Crystal Patriarche and everyone at BookSparks.

Catherine Plato cheerfully tolerated all the wild vacillations in mood that inevitably accompany writing and revision—as did my cat, with perhaps even greater equanimity. I am indebted as always to my parents, Alan and

Barbara, and my brother, Daniel, for their unquantifiable support throughout both my life and the writing of this book. Tim Colla allowed me to shamelessly test the limits of friendship with his willingness to read and discuss this book from its nascency, and whenever I found myself stuck or uncertain our conversations proved invaluable. These acknowledgments would also be incomplete if I did not mention the Albatross Pub in Berkeley, a de facto office where so many of these pages were written over a pint and bowl of dollar popcorn.

They say one can't be a writer without being a reader, and I want to note two libraries that have been formative in my life: the British Council Library in Jerusalem (sadly since closed) and the Canaan Town Library in New Hampshire (thankfully going strong). Finally, many thanks to the bookstores, libraries, bloggers, reviewers, authors, and most of all readers who took the time to read and support this book.

ABOUT THE AUTHOR

S. A. Lelchuk holds a master's degree from Dartmouth College and lives in Berkeley, California. Lelchuk's first novel, *Save Me from Dangerous Men*, was a *Kirkus Reviews* Best Mysteries and Thrillers of the Year, a *Booklist* Year's Best Debut Crime Novels, and one of *USA Today*'s Best Books of the Year.